THE
YOUNG FOLKS'
LIBRARY

YOUNG FOLKS' LIBRARY

*SELECTIONS FROM THE CHOICEST LITERATURE OF ALL
LANDS: FOLK-LORE, FAIRY TALES, FABLES, LEGENDS,
NATURAL HISTORY, WONDERS OF EARTH, SEA
AND SKY, ANIMAL STORIES, SEA TALES,
BRAVE DEEDS, EXPLORATIONS, STORIES
OF SCHOOL AND COLLEGE LIFE,
BIOGRAPHY, HISTORY, PATRI-
OTIC ELOQUENCE, POETRY*

THIRD EDITION

REVISED IN CONFERENCE BY

THOMAS BAILEY ALDRICH, EDITOR-IN-CHIEF,
PRESIDENT WILLIAM JEWETT TUCKER,
HAMILTON WRIGHT MABIE, HENRY
VAN DYKE, NATHAN HASKELL DOLE

TWENTY VOLUMES   RICHLY ILLUSTRATED

BOSTON
HALL AND LOCKE COMPANY
PUBLISHERS

Stanhope Press

F. H. GILSON COMPANY
BOSTON, U. S. A.

EDITORIAL BOARD

LIST OF VOLUMES

THERE HE CALLED HIS WIFE AND SHOWED ME TO HER.

Young Folks' Library in Twenty Volumes
Thomas Bailey Aldrich, Editor=in=Chief

TALES OF FANTASY

EDITED BY
TUDOR JENKS

VOLUME IV

BOSTON
HALL AND LOCKE COMPANY
PUBLISHERS

Stanhope Press
F. H. GILSON COMPANY
BOSTON, U. S. A.

CONTENTS

x Contents

LIST OF COLORED ILLUSTRATIONS

AND ONE HUNDRED AND THIRTY-FIVE BLACK AND WHITE
PICTURES IN THE TEXT.

THE MAGIC OF IMAGINATION

BY

TUDOR JENKS.

———

SINCE fathers and mothers, sisters and brothers, have lived on this big ball, the earth, that goes spinning around the sun, they have found that they have two worlds to enjoy. One is real, the other is make-believe; one has been given us ready-made, though in such shape that we can change it in some respects, the other we have made for ourselves, and we are continually adding to it.

The real world of earth and water is stubborn, and resists our efforts. It requires us to use axes and crowbars, if we wish to take it apart, and nails, cords, and glue must be used to put it together again in new shapes. The other world — the world of make-believe — is created by magic, the magic of imagination. If you know the magic words, the poor goose-girl becomes a princess, or the despised youngest son wins a throne.

The first stories were probably all true; they were hunters' tales of fights with wild animals, or warriors' songs of victory over men. But a time came when these stories were changed in being repeated, when additions were made to them, or two or three stories were rolled into one. Then arose the class of minstrels, of poets, of bards, of jesters — in short, of good story-tellers who made a business of repeating or inventing the tales and ballads of their times. These men handed down the treasures of their memory to one another, and so began the world of make-believe, in which men, women, and children have ever since found delight.

Books and printed pages are only another form of memory; they enable us to recall at will what others wish us to know or to think. To-day each great people has its store-house of literature, a treasury open to every child who can read. Whatever is worth remembering is put into words and preserved for all time.

But literature is more like a museum than like a treasury. In a treasury you would expect only what was unusually valuable, precious, or rare; but in the museum is kept whatever is interesting, whether it be a king's crown or a wasps' nest, a great diamond or a child's toy. And so in literature we find recorded a nation's beliefs and prophecies, its history, amusements, and even its jokes and absurdities. Some poems or stories make us sad, others merry; some men teach us to be noble, others remind us not to take ourselves too seriously.

You will find no locked gate to keep you out of this world of make-believe, but you must learn to understand its language and its thoughts, or you will not be admitted to its loveliest regions. You may know its people — its high-minded, brave and loyal men, its noble, tender, charming women, its bright and lovable boys and girls, but you must first make yourself fit company for them.

Unhappily, the unreal world has its darker portions, its undesirable inhabitants. If you stray among these, you may become like them, and thus render yourself unfit for better company.

To choose rightly the young traveller needs guidance. If his own taste is true and good, he will not make a wrong choice among the places and peoples of the land of books; but he will be likely to go astray, and thereby waste time and effort. If wise, he will welcome every aid to right choosing, as none of us have too many hours to spend among the delightful pleasures of Literary Land. This land has been explored and mapped; and there is no excuse for plunging into it blindly, taking every road that seems to begin pleasantly, without inquiring whence it leads and whither it runs.

Each volume of the YOUNG FOLKS' LIBRARY is a guide-book. Each gives glimpses of a separate region worth a mental visit, and enables you to decide whether you will profit by a journey or a sojourn therein. No guide-book can show all the delightful views, or tell all the interesting features of a new land; but by skilful selection it makes the traveller acquainted with a place or a people, and leaves him to judge intelligently of its claims upon his time and thought.

Literature has its pleasure grounds as well as its academies and galleries. Creative power at work is imagination; creative power at play is fantasy.

This fourth volume of the LIBRARY contains stories of fantasy. The authors of them have said what they chose, not being bound by any rules except those of good taste and good sense. Mere unmeaning nonsense is not what is meant by fantasy. Fantasy must have some purpose, some idea to guide it, or it would not differ from lunacy.

Thackeray's " The Rose and the Ring," for instance, though unreal, impossible, and full of whimsical oddi- ties, is far from being nonsense. It is a consistent, carefully planned story, with an ingenious plot, well- drawn characters, and humorous or exciting incidents throughout. The magic rose and marvellous ring do not prevent our finding Rosalba a lovable heroine, or Giglio an admirable hero. The story is only a " Let us pretend." The author and the reader understand beforehand that the events of the story need not be real, or even probable. It is as if one child said to another, " Let's play I am a giant," and then both *acted* as if there were a giant in the game. There

will be no objection to this game so long as the giant
acts like a giant.

"Baron Munchausen" takes us into another world —
a world of made-up stories. If they were meant to
be believed, they would be atrocious lies; but it is
no harm to read them when they do not pretend to
be true. We ask only that they shall not be impossible to pretend.

To make this plainer, let us suppose that a little
boy has an old Noah's Ark, and that he decides to
chop up the animals into bits, and then to put the
pieces together in new ways. If he takes a dozen
wooden legs and glues them into a rosette, he has
made an absurd thing. It may be decorative, or it
may be ugly, or amusing; but it is mere nonsense.
If, however, he puts together a new animal, — say,
with an elephant's head, a beaver's tail, ostrich's legs,
and a camel's body, — then he has made something
fantastic. Though there is no such creature, yet we
can pretend there might be, and we can imagine how
it might act.

So in Mark Lemon's story, "The Enchanted Doll,"
we can believe it possible while we read it, and thus
we find it interesting. "The Caliph Turned Stork"
and "The Mad Tailor" are true tales of fantasy for
the same reason.

Some grown-up persons see little value in stories
of fantasy. They think children waste time in read-

ing them when they might be reading truths. But it must be remembered that even in fanciful tales, the element of truth is by far the greater. A good fanciful story must be true to life, true in feeling, true in moral, true in its workmanship, or it is worthless. Who would say that there was no value in Æsop's Fables because they contain no facts? The truth is in the lessons taught; and the same principle applies to fairy tales and fanciful stories, as well as to all fiction.

In "Prince Prigio" and in "A Christmas Fantasy," the moral is plainly set forth, but the stories are worth more than the mere teaching they carry. Prince Prigio shows us how unpleasant a prig may be, but he also takes us into a queer, creepy land of mysteries; the little heroine who entraps the Jack-in-the-box, is much easier for us to understand than is the fisherman of the Arabian Nights, who hauls ashore the jar of preserved genie sealed by the trade-mark of King Solomon. We all have seen a Jack-in-the-box, but who would know a genie by sight?

"Peter Schlemihl" is a story of remarkable fascination, yet the moral of it has never been plain to me. Certainly none of us is likely to sell his shadow. Perhaps the author's idea was to make the reader feel how easily one might lose a life's happiness by becoming something not quite human, and so to teach the great worth of human sympathy — without which all else is valueless.

Possibly we have treated all these stories too seriously. It should be repeated here that they belong to the play-ground of literature, and mainly are written "just for fun." But there is the fun of good sense and good taste, as well as the "fun," so-called, of ill-natured joking, or of utter folly; and it has seemed to me that the stories of fantasy — such as make up this volume — are often undervalued.

Above all things, see that you keep a kindly, loving spirit toward others; and in this disposition there must mingle true humor. Humor is the salt of the soul, and prevents corruption; but the saving humor is the humor of kindness — such as you will learn from the authors whose playfulness never makes us despise or scorn others.

Tudor Jenks

TALES OF FANTASY

GULLIVER IN LILLIPUT

BY JONATHAN SWIFT, D.D.

E set sail from Bristol, May 4, 1699, and our voyage at first was very prosperous.

On the 5th of November, which was the beginning of summer in those parts, the seamen spied a rock within half a cable's length of the ship; but the wind was so strong that we were driven directly upon it, and immediately split.

Six of the crew, of whom I was one, having let down the boat into the sea, made a shift to get clear of the ship and rock. We trusted ourselves to the mercy of the waves, and in about half an hour the boat was overset by a sudden gust from the north. What became of my companions in the boat, as well as of those who escaped on the rock, I cannot tell; but conclude they were all lost. For my own part, I swam as fortune directed me, and was pushed forward by wind and tide. I was almost exhausted. But when able to struggle no longer, I found myself within my depth; and by this time the storm was much abated. The declivity was so small, that I

1

walked near a mile before I got to the shore; the time
I conjectured was about eight o'clock in the evening. I
then advanced nearly half a mile, but could not discover
any sign of houses or inhabitants. I was extremely
tired, and with that, and the heat of the weather, and
about half a pint of brandy that I drank as I left the
ship, I found myself much inclined to sleep. I lay
down on the grass, which was very short and soft,
where I slept sounder than ever I remember to have
done in my life, and as I reckoned, about nine hours;
for when I waked, it was just daylight. I attempted
to rise, but was not able to stir; for as I happened to
lie on my back, I found my arms and legs were strongly
fastened on each side to the ground; and my hair,
which was long and thick, tied down in the same manner. I likewise felt several slender ligatures across my
body from my armpits to my thighs. I heard a confused noise about me; but in the posture I lay, could
see nothing except the sky. In a little time I felt something alive moving on my left leg, which advancing
gently forward over my breast, came almost up to my
chin; then bending my eyes downward as much as I
could, I perceived it to be a human creature not six

inches h i g h,
with a bow and
arrow in his
hands, and a
quiver   at   his
back.   In the
mean time, I
felt at least forty more of the same kind (as I conjectured) following the first. I was in the utmost aston-

ishment, and roared so loud, that they all ran back in a fright; and some of them, as I was afterwards told, were hurt with the falls they got by leaping from my sides upon the ground. However, they soon returned, and one of them, who ventured so far as to get a full sight of my face, lifting up his hands and eyes by way of admiration, cried out in a shrill but distinct voice, *Hekihah degul:* the others repeated the same words several times, but I then knew not what they meant.

I lay all this while, as the reader may believe, in great uneasiness; at length, struggling to get loose, I had the fortune to break the strings, and wrench out the pegs that fastened my left arm to the ground; for, by lifting it up to my face I discovered the methods they had taken to bind me, and at the same time with a violent pull, which gave me excessive pain, I a little loosened the strings that tied down my hair on the left side, so that I was just able to turn my head about two inches. But the creatures ran off a second time, before I could seize them; whereupon there was a great shout in a very shrill accent, and after it ceased I heard one of them cry aloud, *Tolgo phonac;* when in an instant I felt above a hundred arrows discharged on my left hand, which pricked me like so many needles. When this shower of arrows was over, I fell a groaning with grief and pain, then striving again to get loose, they discharged another volley larger than the first, and some of them attempted with spears to stick me in the sides; but by good luck I had on a buff jerkin, which they could not pierce. I thought it the most prudent method to lie still, and my design was to continue so till night, when,

my left hand being already loose, I could easily free
myself : and as for the inhabitants, I had reason to believe I might be a match for the greatest army they
could bring against me, if they were all of the same
size with him that I saw.   But fortune disposed otherwise of me.   When the people observed that I was
quiet, they discharged no more arrows ; but by the
noise I heard, I knew their numbers increased ; and
about four yards from me, over against my right ear,
I heard a knocking for above an hour, like that of a
people at work ; when turning my head that way, as
well as the pegs and strings would permit me, I saw a
stage erected about a foot and a half from the ground,
capable of holding four of the inhabitants, with two or
three ladders to mount it ; from whence one of them,
who seemed to be a person of quality, made me a long
speech, whereof I understood not one syllable.   But I
should have mentioned, that before the principal person
began his oration, he cried out three times, *Langro de-*
hul san ; whereupon immediately about fifty of the inhabitants came and cut the strings that fastened the
left side of my head, which gave me the liberty of turning it to the right, and of observing the person and
gesture of him that was to speak.   He appeared to be
of a middle age, and taller than any of the other three
who attended him, whereof one was a page that held up
his train, and seemed to be somewhat longer than my
middle finger : the other two stood one on each side to
support him.   He acted every part of an orator, and I
could observe many periods of threatenings, and others
of promises, pity, and kindness.   I answered in a few
words, but in the most submissive manner, lifting up

my left hand and both my eyes to the sun, as calling him for a witness; and being almost famished with hunger, having not eaten a morsel for some hours before I left the ship, I found the demands of nature so strong upon me that I could not forbear showing my impatience by putting my finger frequently to my mouth, to signify that I wanted food. The *hurgo* (for so they called a great lord, as I afterwards learnt) understood me very well. He descended from the stage, and commanded that several ladders should be applied to my sides, on which above a hundred of the inhabitants mounted, and walked towards my mouth, laden with baskets full of meat, which had been provided and sent thither by the king's orders, upon the first intelligence he received of me. I observed there was the flesh of several animals, but could not distinguish them by the taste. There were shoulders, legs, and loins, shaped like those of mutton, and very well dressed, but smaller than the wings of a lark. I ate them by two or three at a mouthful, and took three loaves at a time, about the bigness of musket-bullets. They supplied me as fast as they could, showing a thousand marks of wonder and astonishment at my bulk and appetite. I then made another sign that I wanted drink. They found by my eating that a small quantity would not suffice me: and slung up with great dexterity, one of their largest hogsheads, then rolled it towards my hand, and beat out the top; I drank it off at a draught, which I might well do, for it did not hold half a pint, and tasted like a small wine of Burgundy, but more delicious. A second hogshead I drank in the same manner, and make signs for more; but they had none to give me. When I had performed these wonders, they shouted for joy, and danced upon my breast, repeating several times, as they did at first, *Hekinah degul.* They made me a sign that I should throw down the two hogsheads, but first warning the people below to stand out of the way, crying aloud, *Borach Mevolah;* and when they saw the vessels in the air, there was a universal shout of *Hekinah degul.* I confess I was often tempted while they were passing backwards and forwards on my body, to seize forty or fifty of the first that came in my reach, and dash them against the ground. But the remembrance of what I had felt, which probably might not be the worst they could do, soon drove out these imaginations. Besides, I now considered myself as bound by the laws of hospitality to a people who had treated me with so much expense and munificence. However, I could not sufficiently wonder at the intrepidity of these diminutive mortals, who durst venture to mount and walk upon my body, while one of my hands was at liberty, without trembling at the very sight of so prodigious a creature as I must appear to them. After some time, when they observed that I made no more demands for meat, there appeared before me a person of high rank from his imperial majesty. His excellency having mounted on the small of my right leg, advanced forwards up to my face, with about a dozen of his retinue; and producing his credentials under the signet royal, spoke about ten minutes without any signs of anger, but with a kind of determined resolution; often pointing forwards, which, as I afterwards found, was towards the capital city about half a mile distant; whither it was agreed by his

majesty in council that I must be conveyed. I made a
sign with my hand that was loose, putting it to the
other, and then to my own body, to signify that I desired my liberty. It appeared that he understood me
well enough, for he shook his head by way of disappro-
bation, and held his hand in a posture to show that I
must be carried as a prisoner. However, he made other
signs to let me understand, that I should have meat
and drink enough, and very good treatment. Whereupon I once more thought of attempting to break my
bonds; but again, when I felt the smart of the arrows
upon my face and hands, which were all in blisters, and
many of the darts still sticking in them, and observing
likewise that the number of my enemies increased, I
gave tokens to let them know that they might do with
me what they pleased. Upon this, the *hurgo* and his
train withdrew, with much civility and cheerful countenances. Soon after I heard a general shout, with
frequent repetition of the words *Peplom selam*, and I
felt great numbers of people on my left side relaxing
the cords to such a degree, that I was able to turn upon
my right side. But before this, they had daubed my
face and both my hands with a sort of ointment, very
pleasant to the smell, which in a few minutes removed
all the smarts of their arrows. These circumstances,
added to the refreshment I had received by their victuals
and drink, which were very nourishing, disposed me to
sleep.

It seems, that upon the first moment I was discovered sleeping on the ground, after my landing, the
emperor had early notice of it by an express; and
determined in council that I should be tied in the man-

ner I have related (which was done in the night while
I slept); that plenty of meat and drink should be sent
me, and a machine prepared to carry me to the capital
city.

These people are most excellent mathematicians, and
arrived to a great perfection in mechanics by the countenance and encouragement of the emperor, who is a
renowned patron of learning. This prince has several
machines fixed on wheels, for the carriage of trees and
other great weights. He often builds his largest men-
of-war, whereof some are nine feet long, in the woods
where the timber grows, and has them carried on these
engines three or four hundred yards to the sea. Five
hundred carpenters and engineers were immediately
set at work to prepare the greatest engine they had.
It was a frame of wood raised three inches from the
ground, about seven feet long, and four wide, and moving upon twenty-two wheels. The shout I heard was
upon the arrival of this engine, which it seems set out
in four hours after my landing. It was brought parallel to me as I lay. But the principal difficulty was to
raise and place me in this vehicle. Eighty poles, each
of one foot high, were erected for this purpose, and
very strong cords, of the bigness of packthread, were
fastened by hooks to many bandages, which the workmen had girt round my neck, my hands, my body, and
my legs. Nine hundred of the strongest men were
employed to draw up these cords, by many pulleys
fastened on the poles, and thus, in less than three
hours, I was raised and slung into the engine, and there
tied fast. All this I was told; for, while the opera-
tion was performing, I lay in a profound sleep, by the

force of soporiferous medicine infused into my liquor.
Fifteen hundred of the emperor's largest horses, each
about four inches and a half high, were employed to
draw me towards the metropolis, which as I said, was
half a mile distant.

About four hours after we began our journey, I was
awaked by a very ridiculous accident; for the carriage
being stopped awhile, to adjust something that was out
of order, two or three of the young natives had the
curiosity to see how I looked when I was asleep; they
climbed up into the engine, and advancing very softly
to my face, one of them, an officer in the guards, put
the sharp end of his halfpike a good way up into my
left nostril, which tickled my nose like a straw, and
made me sneeze violently; whereupon they stole off
unperceived, and it was three weeks before I knew the
cause of my waking so suddenly. We made a long
march the remaining part of the day, and rested at
night with
five hundred
guards on
each side me,
half with
torches, and

half with bows and arrows, ready to shoot me if I
should offer to stir. The next morning at sunrise we
continued our march, and arrived within two hundred
yards of the city gates about noon. The emperor and
all his court came out to meet us; but his great officers
would by no means suffer his majesty to endanger
his person by mounting on my body.

At the place where the carriage stopped, there stood

an ancient temple, esteemed to be the largest in the whole kingdom ; which having been polluted some years before by an unnatural murder, was, according to the zeal of those people, looked upon as profane, and therefore had been applied to common use, and all the ornaments and furniture carried away. In this edifice it was determined I should lodge. On each side of the gate was a small window, not above six inches from the ground ; into that on the left side, the king's smith conveyed four score and eleven chains, like those that hang to a lady's watch in Europe, and almost as large, which were locked to my left leg with six-and-thirty padlocks. Over against this temple, on the other side of the great highway, at twenty feet distance, there was a turret at least five feet high. Here the emperor ascended, with many principal lords of his court, to have an opportunity of viewing me, as I was told, for I could not see them. It was reckoned that above a hundred thousand inhabitants came out of the town upon the same errand ; and in spite of my guards, I believe there could not have been fewer than ten thousand, at several times, who mounted my body by the help of ladders. But a proclamation was soon issued, to forbid it upon pain of death. When the workmen found it was impossible for me to break loose, they cut all the strings that bound me ; whereupon I rose up with as melancholy a disposition as ever I had in my life. But the noise and astonishment of the people at seeing me rise and walk, are not to be expressed.

When I found myself on my feet, I looked about me, and must confess I never beheld a more entertaining prospect. The country around appeared like a continued garden, and the inclosed fields, which were generally forty feet square, resembled so many beds of flowers. These fields were intermingled with woods, and the tallest trees, as I could judge, appeared to be seven feet high. I viewed the town on my left hand, which looked like the painted scene of a city in a theatre.

The emperor was already descended from the tower, and advancing on horseback towards me, which had liked to have cost him dear : for the beast, though very well trained, yet wholly unused to such a sight, which appeared as if a mountain moved before him, reared up on his hinder feet ; but the prince, who is an excellent horseman, kept his seat till his attendants ran in, and held the bridle, while his majesty had time to dismount. When he alighted he surveyed me round with great admiration ; but kept beyond the length of my chain. He ordered his cooks and butlers to give me victuals and drink, which they pushed forward in a sort of vehicle upon wheels, till I could reach them. I took these vehicles, and soon emptied them all; twenty of them were filled with meat, and ten with liquor ; each of the former afforded me two or three good mouthfuls ; and I emptied the liquor of the ten vessels, which was contained in earthen vials, into one vehicle, drinking it off at a draught ; and so I did with the rest. The empress, and young princes of the blood of both sexes, attended by many ladies, sat at some distance in their chairs ; but upon the accident that happened to the emperor's horse, they alighted and came near his person, which I am now going to describe. He is taller by almost the breadth of my nail, than any of his court; which alone is enough to strike an awe into the beholders. His features are strong and masculine, with an Austrian lip and arched nose, his complexion olive, his countenance erect, his body and limbs well proportioned, all his motions graceful, and his deportment majestic. He was then past his prime, being twenty-eight years and three-quarters old, of which he had reigned about seven in great felicity, and generally victorious. For the better convenience of beholding him, I lay on my side, so that my face was parallel to his and stood but three yards off: however, I have had him since many times in my hand, and therefore cannot be deceived in the description. His dress was very plain and simple, and the fashion of it between the Asiatic and the European: but he had on his head a light helmet of gold, adorned with jewels and a plume on the crest. He held his sword drawn in his hand to defend himself, if I should happen to break loose; it was almost three inches long; the hilt and scabbard were gold enriched with diamonds. His voice was shrill, but very clear and articulate; and I could distinctly hear it when I stood up. The ladies and the courtiers were all most magnificently clad; so that the spot they stood upon seemed to resemble a petticoat

spread on the ground, embroidered with figures of gold
and silver. His imperial majesty spoke often to me,
and I returned answers; but neither of us could understand a syllable. There were several of his priests
and lawyers present (as I conjectured by their habits),
who were commanded to address themselves to me;
and I spoke to them in as many languages as I had
the least smattering of, which were High and Low
Dutch, Latin, French, Spanish, Italian, and Lingua
Franca, but all to no purpose. After about two hours
the court retired, and I was left with a strong guard,
to prevent the impertinence and probably the malice
of the rabble, who were very impatient to crowd about
me as near as they durst; and some of them had the
impudence to shoot their arrows at me as I sat on the
ground by the door of my house, whereof one very
narrowly missed my left eye. But the colonel ordered
six of the ringleaders to be seized, and thought no
punishment so proper as to deliver them bound into
my hands; which some of his soldiers accordingly did,
pushing them forward with the but-ends of their pikes
into my reach. I took them all into my right hand,
put five of them into my coat-pocket, and as to the
sixth, I made a countenance as if I would eat him
alive. The poor man squalled terribly, and the colonel
and his officers were in much pain, especially when
they saw me take out my penknife; but I soon put
them out of fear; for, looking mildly and immediately
cutting the strings he was bound with, I set him gently
on the ground and away he ran. I treated the rest in
the same manner, taking them one by one out of my
pocket; and I observed both the soldiers and people

were highly delighted at this mark of my clemency, which was represented very much to my advantage at court. . . .

GULLIVER CAPTURES THE ENEMIES' SHIPS.

The empire of Blefuscu is an island situated to the northeast of Lilliput, from which it is parted only by a channel eight hundred yards wide. I had not yet seen it, and receiving notice of an intended invasion, I avoided appearing on that side of the coast, for fear of being discovered by some of the enemy's ships, who had received no intelligence of me; all intercourse between the empires having been strictly forbidden during the war, upon pain of death, and an embargo laid by our Emperor upon all vessels whatsoever. I communicated to his Majesty a project I had formed, of seizing the enemy's whole fleet: which, as our scouts assured us lay at anchor in the harbor, ready to sail with the first fair wind. I consulted the most experienced seamen upon the depth of the channel, which they had often plumbed; who told me that in the middle at high water it was seventy *glumgluffs* deep, which is about six feet of European measure; and the rest of it fifty *glumgluffs* at most. I walked towards the northeast coast, over against Blefuscu; where, lying down behind a hillock, I took out my small perspective glass, and viewed the enemy's fleet at anchor, consisting of about fifty men-of-war, and a great number of transports: I then came back to my house, and gave orders (for which I had a warrant) for a great quantity of the strongest cable and bars of iron. The cable was about as thick as packthread, and the bars of the length and size of a knitting-needle. I trebled the cable to make it stronger, and for the same reason I twisted three of the iron bars together, bending the extremities into a hook. Having thus fixed fifty hooks to as many cables, I went back to the northeast coast, and taking off my coat, shoes, and stockings, walked into the sea, in my leather jerkin, about half an hour before high-water. I waded through with what haste I could, and swam in the middle about thirty yards, till I felt ground. I arrived at the fleet in less than half an hour. The enemy was so frightened when they saw me, that they leaped out of the ships, and swam to shore, where there could not be fewer than thirty thousand souls. I then took my tackling, and fastening a hook to the hole at the prow of each, I tied all the cords together at the end. While I was thus employed, the enemy discharged several thousand arrows, many of which stuck in my hands and face; and, besides the excessive smart, gave me much disturbance in my work. My greatest apprehension was for my eyes, which I should have infallibly lost, if I had not suddenly thought of an expedient. I kept, among other little necessaries, a pair of spectacles in a private pocket; these I took out and fastened as strongly as I could upon my nose, and thus armed, went on boldly with my work, in spite of the enemy's arrows, many of which struck against the glasses of my spectacles, but without any effect. I had now fastened all the hooks, and taking the knot in my hand, began to pull; but not a ship would stir, for they were all held too fast by their anchors, so that the boldest part of my enterprise remained.   I therefore let go the cord, and leaving the hooks fixed to the ships, I resolutely cut with my knife the cables that fastened the anchors, receiving about two hundred shots in my face and hands; then I took up the knotted end of the cables, to which my hooks were tied, and with great ease drew fifty of the enemy's largest men-of-war after me.

The Blefuscudians, who had not the least notion of what I intended, were at first confounded with astonishment.   They had seen me cut the cables, and thought my design was only to let the ships run adrift, or fall foul of each other; but when they perceived the whole fleet moving in order, and saw me pulling at the end, they set up such a scream of grief and despair as it is almost impossible to describe. When I had got out of danger, I stopped awhile to pick out the arrows that stuck in my face; and rubbed on some of the same ointment that was given me on my arrival, as I have formerly mentioned.   I then took off my spectacles, and waiting about an hour, till the tide was a little fallen, I waded through the middle with my cargo, and arrived safe in the port of Lilliput.

The Emperor and his whole court stood on the shore, expecting the issue of this great adventure.   They saw the ships move forward in a large half-moon, but could not discern me, who was up to my breast in water. When I advanced to the middle of the channel, they were yet more in pain, because I was under water to my neck.   The Emperor concluded me to be drowned, and that the enemy's fleet was approaching in a hostile manner: but he was soon eased of his fears; for the channel growing shallower every step I made, I came in a short time within hearing, and holding up the end of the cable by which the fleet was fastened, I cried in a loud voice, "Long live the most puissant king of Lilliput!" The prince received me at my landing with all possible encomiums, and created me a *nardac* upon the spot, which is the highest title of honor among them. . . .

Although I intend to leave the description of this empire to a particular treatise, yet, in the mean time, I am content to gratify the curious reader with some general ideas. As the common size of the natives is somewhat under six inches high, so there is an exact proportion in all other animals, as well as plants and trees; for instance, the tallest horses and oxen are between four and five inches in height, the sheep an inch and a half, more or less; their geese about the bigness of a sparrow, and so the several gradations downwards, till you come to the smallest, which, to my sight, were almost invisible; but nature has adapted the eyes of the Lilliputians to all objects proper for their view; they see with great exactness, but at no great distance. And to show the sharpness of their sight towards objects that are near, I have been much pleased with observing a cook pulling a lark, which was not so large as a common fly; and a young girl threading an invisible needle with invisible silk. Their tallest trees are about seven feet high: I mean some of those in the great royal park, the tops whereof I could but just reach with my fist clinched. The other vegetables are in the same proportion; but this I leave to the reader's imagination. . . .

And here it may, perhaps, divert the curious reader, to give some account of my domestics, and my manner of living in this country, during a residence of nine months and thirteen days. Having a head mechanically turned, and being likewise forced by necessity, I had made for myself a table and chair convenient enough, out of the largest trees in the royal park. Two hundred seamstresses were employed to make me shirts, and linen for my bed and table, all of the strongest and coarsest kind they could get; which, however, they were forced to quilt together in several folds, for the thickest was some degrees finer than lawn. Their linen is usually three inches wide, and three feet make a piece. The seamstresses took my measure as I lay on the ground, one standing at my neck, and another at my midleg, with a strong cord extended, that each held by the end, while a third measured the length of the cord with the rule of an inch long. Then they measured my right thumb, and desired no more; for by a mathematical computation, that twice round the thumb is once round the wrist, and so on to the neck and waist, and by the help of my old shirt, which I displayed on the ground before them for a pattern, they fitted me exactly. Three hundred tailors were employed in the same manner to make me clothes; but they had another contrivance for taking my measure. I kneeled down and they raised a ladder from the ground to my neck; upon this ladder one of them mounted, and let fall a plumb-line from my collar to the floor, which just answered the length of my coat; but my waist and arms I measured myself. When my clothes were finished, which was done in my house (for the largest of theirs would not have been able to hold them), they looked like the patch-work made by the ladies in England, only that mine were all of a color.

I had three hundred cooks to dress my victuals, in little convenient huts built about my house, where they and their families lived, and prepared me two dishes apiece. I took up twenty waiters in my hand, and placed them on the table: a hundred more attended below on the ground, some with dishes of meat, and some with barrels of wine and other liquors slung on their shoulders: all which the waiters above drew up, as I wanted, in a very ingenious manner by certain cords, as we draw the bucket up a well in Europe. A dish of their meat was a good mouthful, and a barrel of their liquor a reasonable draught. Their mutton yields to ours, but their beef is excellent. I have had a sirloin so large that I have been forced to make three bites of it; but this is rare. My servants were astonished to see me eat it, bones and all, as in our country we do the leg of a lark. Their geese and turkeys I usually ate at a mouthful, and I confess they far exceed ours. Of their smaller fowl I could take up twenty or thirty at the end of my knife.

One day His Imperial Majesty, being informed of my
way of living, desired "that he and his royal consort,
with the young princes of the blood of both sexes,
might have the happiness," as he was pleased to call it
"of dining with me." They
came accordingly, and I placed
them in chairs of state, upon
my table, just over against
me, with their guards about
them. Flimnap, the lord
high treasurer, attended
there likewise with his white
staff; and I observed he
often looked on me with
a sour countenance, which I would not seem to
regard, but ate more than usual in honor of my dear
country, as well as to fill the court with admiration.
I have private reasons to believe, that this visit from
his majesty gave Flimnap an opportunity of doing me
ill offices to his Majesty. That minister had always
been my secret enemy, though he outwardly caressed
me more than was usual to the moroseness of his
nature. He represented to the emperor "the low condition of the treasury; that he was forced to take up
money at a great discount; that exchequer bills would
not circulate under nine per cent. below par; that I
had cost his majesty above a million and a half of
sprugs (their greatest gold coin, about the bigness of a
spangle); and, upon the whole, that it would be advis-
able in the emperor to take the first fair occasion of
dismissing me."

"They came accordingly, and I placed Them in Chairs of State, upon My Table."

GULLIVER IN BROBDINGNAG

By JONATHAN SWIFT, D.D.

N the 16th day of June, 1703, a boy on the topmast discovered land. On the 17th, we came in full view of a great island or continent (for we knew not whether); on the south side whereof was a small neck of land jutting out into the sea, and a creek too shallow to hold a ship of above one hundred tons. We cast anchor within a league of this creek, and our captain sent a dozen of his men well armed, in the long-boat, with vessels for water, if any could be found. I desired his leave to go with them, that I might see the country, and make what discoveries I could. When we came to land, we saw no river, or spring, nor any sign of inhabitants. Our men therefore wandered on the shore to find out some fresh water near the sea, and I walked alone about a mile on the other side, where I observed the country all barren and rocky. I now began to be weary, and seeing nothing to entertain my curiosity, I returned gently down towards the creek; and the sea being full in my view, I saw our men already got into the boat, and rowing for life to the ship. I was going to holla after them, although it had been to little purpose, when I observed a huge creature walking after them in the sea, as fast as he could: he waded not much deeper than his knees, and took prodigious strides: but our men had the start of him half a league, and, the sea thereabouts being full of sharp-pointed rocks, the monster was not able to overtake the boat. This I was afterwards told, for I durst not stay to see the issue of the adventure; but ran as fast as I could the way I first went, and then climbed up a steep hill, which gave me some prospect of the country. I found it fully cultivated; but that which first surprised me was the length of the grass, which in those grounds, that seemed to be kept for hay, was about twenty feet high.

I fell into a high road, for so I took it to be, though it served to the inhabitants only as a footpath, through a field of barley. Here I walked on for some time, but could see little on either side, it being near harvest and the corn rising at least forty feet. I was an hour walking to the end of this field, which was fenced in with a hedge of at least one hundred and twenty feet high, and the trees so lofty that I could make no computation of their altitude. There was a stile to pass from this field into the next. It had four steps, and a stone to cross over when you came to the uppermost. It was impossible for me to climb this stile, because every step was six feet high, and the upper stone about twenty. I was endeavoring to find some gap in the hedge, when I discovered one of the inhabitants in the next field, advancing towards the stile, of the same size with him whom I saw in the sea pursuing our boat. He appeared as tall as an ordinary spire steeple, and took about ten yards at every stride, as near as I could guess. I was struck with the utmost fear and astonishment, and ran to hide myself in the corn, whence I saw him at the top of the stile looking back into the next field on the right hand, and heard him call in

a voice many degrees louder than a speaking-trumpet;
but the noise was so high in the air, that at first I certainly thought it was thunder. Whereupon seven
monsters like himself, came towards him, with reaping-
hooks in their hands, each hook about the largeness
of six scythes. These people were not so well clad as
the first, whose servants or laborers they seemed to be;
for, upon some words he spoke, they went to reap the
corn in the field where I lay. I kept from them at as
great a distance as I could, but was forced to move with
extreme difficulty, for the stalks of the corn were sometimes not above a foot distant, so that I could hardly
squeeze my body betwixt them. However, I made
a shift to go forward, till I came to a part of the field
where the corn had been laid by the rain and wind.
Here it was impossible for me to advance a step; for
the stalks were so interwoven that I could not creep
through, and the beards of the fallen ears so strong
and pointed, that they pierced through my clothes into
my flesh. At the same time I heard the reapers not
above a hundred yards behind me. Being quite dis-
spirited with toil, I lay down between two ridges, and
heartily wished I might there end my days. I bemoaned
my desolate widow and fatherless children, lamenting
my own folly and wilfulness in attempting a second
voyage. In this terrible agitation of mind, I could not
forbear thinking of Lilliput, whose inhabitants looked
upon me as the greatest prodigy that ever appeared in
the world; where I was able to draw an imperial fleet
in my hand, and perform those other actions, which
will be recorded forever in the chronicles of that
empire, while posterity shall hardly believe them,

although attested by millions. I reflected what a mortification it must prove to me to appear as inconsiderable in this nation, as one single Lilliputian would be among us. But this I conceived was to be the least of my misfortunes; for, as human creatures are observed to be more savage and cruel in proportion to their bulk, what could I expect but to be a morsel in the mouth of the first of these enormous barbarians that should happen to seize me? Undoubtedly philosophers are in the right, when they tell us nothing is great or little otherwise than by comparison. It might have pleased fortune to have let the Lilliputians find some nation where the people were as diminutive with respect to them, as they were to me. And who knows but that even this prodigious race of mortals might be equally overmatched in some distant part of the world, whereof we have yet made no discovery.

Scared and confounded as I was I could not forbear going on with these reflections, when one of the reapers approaching within ten yards of the ridge where I lay, made me apprehend that with the next step I should be squashed to death under his foot, or cut in two with his reaping-hook. And therefore, when he was again about to move, I screamed as loud as fear could make me; whereupon the huge creature trod short, and looking round about under him for some time, at last espied me as I lay on the ground. He considered a while, with the caution of one who endeavors to lay hold on a small dangerous animal in such a manner that it shall not be able either to scratch or bite him, as I myself have sometimes done with a weasel in England. At length he ventured to take me behind, by the middle, between his fore-finger and thumb, and brought me within three yards of his eyes, that he might behold my shape more perfectly. I guessed his meaning, and my good fortune gave me so much presence of mind, that I resolved not to struggle in the least as he held me in the air above sixty feet from the ground, although he grievously pinched my sides, for fear I should slip through his fingers. All I ventured was to raise my eyes towards the sun, and place my hands together in a supplicating posture, and to speak some words in a humble, melancholy tone, suitable to the condition I then was in: for I apprehended every moment that he would dash me against the ground, as we usually do any little hateful animal which we have a mind to destroy. He appeared pleased, however, with my voice and gestures, and began to look upon me as a curiosity, much wondering to hear me pronounce articulate words, although he could not understand them. In the mean time I was not able to forbear groaning and shedding tears, and turning my head towards my sides; letting him know, as well as I could how cruelly I was hurt by the pressure of his thumb and finger. He seemed to apprehend my meaning; for, lifting up the lappet of his coat, he put me gently into it, and immediately ran along with me to his master, who was a substantial farmer, and the same person I had seen in the field.

The farmer having received such an account of me as his servant could give him, took a piece of a small straw, about the size of a walking-staff, and therewith lifted up the lappets of my coat; which it seems he thought to be some kind of covering that nature had given me. He blew my hair aside to take a better view of my face. He called his hinds about him, and asked them, as I afterwards learned, "Whether they had ever seen in the fields any little creature that resembled me?" He then placed me softly on the ground upon all fours, but I got immediately up, and walked slowly backward and forward, to let those people see that I had no intent to run away. They all sat in a circle about me, the better to observe my motions. I pulled off my hat, and made a low bow towards the farmer. I fell on my knees, and lifted up my hands and eyes, and spoke several words as loud as I could; I took a purse of gold out of my pocket, and humbly presented it to him. He received it on the palm of his hand, then applied it close to his eye to see what it was, and afterwards turned it several times with a point of a pin (which he took out of his sleeve), but could make nothing of it. Whereupon I made a sign that he should place his hand on the ground. I then took the purse, and opening it, poured all the gold into his palm. There were six Spanish pieces of four pistoles each, besides twenty or thirty smaller coins. I saw him wet the tip of his little finger upon his tongue, and take up one of my largest pieces, and then another; but he seemed to be wholly ignorant of what they were. He made me a sign to put them again into my purse, and the purse again into my pocket, which, after offering it to him several times, I thought it best to do.

The farmer, by this time, was convinced I must be a rational creature. He spoke often to me; but the sound of his voice pierced my ears like that of a water-mill, though his words were articulate enough. I answered as loud as I could in several languages, and he often laid his ear within two yards of me: but all in vain, for we were wholly unintelligible to each other. He then sent his servants to their work, and taking his handkerchief out of his pocket, he doubled it and spread it on his left hand, which he placed flat on the ground with the palm upward, making me a sign to step into it, as I could easily do, for it was not above a foot in thickness. I thought it my part to obey, and, for fear of falling, laid myself at full length upon the handkerchief, with the remainder of which he lapped me up to the head for farther security, and in this manner carried me home to his house. There he called his wife, and showed me to her; but she screamed and ran back, as women in England do at the sight of a toad or a spider. However, when she had awhile seen my behavior, and how well I observed the signs her husband made, she was soon reconciled, and by degrees grew extremely tender of me.

It was about twelve at noon, and a servant brought in dinner. It was only one substantial dish of meat (fit for the plain condition of a husbandman), in a dish of about four-and-twenty feet diameter. The company were the farmer and his wife, three children, and an old grandmother. When they were sat down, the farmer placed me at some distance from him on the table, which was thirty feet high from the floor. I was in a terrible fright, and kept as far as I could from the edge, for fear of falling. The wife minced a bit of meat, then crumbled some bread on a trencher, and placed it before me. I made her a low bow, took out my knife and fork, and fell to eat, which gave them exceeding delight. The mistress sent her maid for a small dram cup, which held about two gallons, and filled it with drink; I took up the vessel with much difficulty in both hands, and in a most respectful manner drank to her ladyship's health, expressing the words as loud as I could in English, which made the company laugh so heartily, that I was almost deafened with the noise. This liquor tasted like cider, and was not unpleasant. Then the master made me a sign to come to his trencher side; but as I walked on the table, being in great surprise all the time, as the indulgent reader will easily conceive and excuse, I happened to stumble against a crust, and fell flat on my face, but received no hurt. I got up immediately, and observing the good people to be in much concern, I took my hat (which I held under my arm out of good manners), and waving it over my head, made three huzzas, to show I had got no mischief by my fall. But advancing forward towards my master (as I shall henceforth call him), his youngest son, who sat next to him, an arch boy of about ten years old, took me up by the legs, and held me so high in the air, that I trembled in every limb; but his father snatched me from him, and at the same time gave him such a box on the left ear, as

would have felled a European troop of horse to the
earth, ordering him to be taken from the table. But
being afraid this boy might owe me a spite, and well
remembering how mischievous all children among us
naturally are to sparrows, rabbits, young kittens, and
puppy dogs, I fell on my knees, and pointing to the
boy made my master to understand, as well as I could,
that I desired that his son might be pardoned. The
father complied, and the lad took his seat again, whereupon I went to him and kissed his hand, which my
master took, and made him stroke me gently with it.

In the midst of dinner, my mistress's favorite cat
leaped into her lap. I heard a noise behind me like

that of a dozen stocking-weav-
ers at work; and turning my
head, I found it proceeded
from the purring of that animal, who seemed to be three
times larger than an ox, as I
computed by the view of her head, and one of her
paws, while her mistress was feeding and stroking her.
The fierceness of this creature's countenance altogether
discomposed me; though I stood at the farther end
of the table, above fifty feet off; and though my mistress held her fast, for fear she might give a spring
and seize me in her talons. But it happened there was
no danger, for the cat took not the least notice of me,
when my master placed me within three yards of her.
And as I have been always told, and found true by
experience in my travels, that flying or discovering fear
before a fierce animal, is a certain way to make it
pursue or attack you, so I resolved, in this dangerous

juncture, to show no manner of concern. I walked
with intrepidity five or six times before the very
head of the cat, and came within half a yard of her;
whereupon she drew herself back, as if she were more
afraid of me: I had less apprehension concerning the
dogs, whereof three or four came into the room, as
is usual in farmers' houses; one of which was a mastiff, equal in bulk to four elephants, and a grey-
hound, somewhat taller than the mastiff, but not so
large. . . .

My mistress had a daughter of nine years old, a
child of towardly parts for her age, very dexterous at
her needle, and skilful in dressing her baby. Her
mother and she contrived to fit up the baby's cradle for
me against night: the cradle was put into a small
drawer of a cabinet, and the drawer placed upon a
hanging shelf for fear of the rats. This was my bed
all the time I staid with those people, though made
more convenient by degrees, as I began to learn their
language and make my wants known. This young
girl was so handy, that she made me seven shirts, and
some other linen, of as fine cloth as could be got, which
indeed was coarser than sackcloth; and these she con-
stantly washed for me with her own hands. She was
likewise my schoolmistress, to teach me the language:
when I pointed to any thing, she told me the name of
it in her own tongue, so that in a few days I was able
to call for whatever I had a mind to. She was very
good-natured, and not above forty feet high, being little
of her age. She gave me the name of *Grildrig*, which
the family took up, and afterwards the whole kingdom.
The word imports what the Latins call *homunculus*, the

Italians *homunceletino,* and the English *mannikin.* To her I chiefly owe my preservation in that country; we never parted while I was there; I called her my *Glumdalclitch,* or little nurse; and should be guilty of great ingratitude, if I omitted this honorable mention of her care and affection towards me, which I heartily wish it lay in my power to requite as she deserves, instead of being the innocent, but unhappy instrument of her disgrace, as I have too much reason to fear.

It now began to be known and talked of in the neighborhood, that my master had found a strange animal in the field, about the bigness of a *splacnuck,* but exactly shaped in every part like a human creature; which it likewise imitated in all its actions; seemed to speak in a little language of its own, had already learned several words of theirs, went erect upon two legs, was tame and gentle, would come when it was called, do whatever it was bid, had the finest limbs in the world, and a complexion fairer than a nobleman's daughter of three years old. Another farmer who lived hard by, and was a particular friend of my master, came on a visit on purpose to inquire into the truth of this story. I was immediately produced and placed upon a table, where I walked as I was commanded, drew my hanger, put it up again, made my reverence to my master's guest, asked him in his own language how he did, and told him *he was welcome,* just as my little nurse had instructed me. This man, who was old and dim-sighted, put on his spectacles to behold me better; at which I could not forbear laughing very heartily, for his eyes appeared like the full moon shining into a chamber at two windows. Our

people, who discovered the cause of my mirth, bore me
company in laughing, at which the old fellow was fool
enough to be angry and out of countenance. He had
the character of a great miser; and, to my misfortune,
he well deserved it, by the cursed advice he gave my
master, to show me as a sight upon a market-day in
the next town, which was half an hour's riding, about
two-and-twenty miles, from our house.   I guessed there
was some mischief contriving, when I observed my
master and his friend whispering long together, and
sometimes pointing at me.   But the next morning, my
little nurse told me the whole matter, which she had
picked out from her mother.   The poor girl fell
a-weeping with shame and grief.   She apprehended some
mischief would happen to me from rude vulgar folks,
who might squeeze me to death, or break one of my
limbs by taking me in their hands. She had also
observed how modest I was by nature, how nicely I
regarded my honor, and what an indignity I should
conceive it, to be exposed for money as a public spectacle, to the meanest of the people. She said her
parents had promised that Grildrig should be hers;
but now she found they meant to serve her as they did
last year, when they pretended to give her a lamb, and
yet, as soon as it was fat, sold it to a butcher. For
my own part, I may truly affirm that I was less concerned than my nurse. I had a strong hope, which
never left me, that I should one day recover my
liberty: and as to the ignominy of being carried about
for a monster, I considered myself to be a perfect
stranger in the country, and that such a misfortune
could never be charged upon me as a reproach if ever

I should return to England ; since the king of Great Britain himself, in my condition, must have undergone the same distress. . . .

My master, finding how profitable I was likely to be, resolved to carry me to the most considerable cities of the kingdom. Having therefore provided himself with all things necessary for a long journey, and settled his affairs at home, he took leave of his wife, and on the 17th of August, 1703, about two months after my arrival, we set out for the metropolis, situate near the middle of that empire, and about three thousand miles distance from our house.

My master's design was to show me in all the towns by the way, and to step out of the road, for fifty or a hundred miles, to any village or person of quality's house, where he might expect custom. We made easy journeys, of not above seven or eight score miles a day : for Glumdalclitch, on purpose to spare me, complained she was tired with the trotting of the horse. She often took me out of my box, at my desire, to give me air, and show me the country, but always held me fast by a leading-string. We passed over five or six rivers, many degrees broader and deeper than the Ganges : and there was hardly a rivulet so small as the Thames at London Bridge. We were ten weeks on our journey, and I was shown in eighteen large towns, besides many villages and private families.

On the 26th day of October we arrived at the metropolis, called in their language *Lorbrulgrud*, or Pride of the Universe. My master took a lodging in the principal street of the city, not far from the royal palace, and put out bills in the usual form, containing

an exact description of my person and parts. He hired
a large room between three and four hundred feet wide.
He provided a table sixty feet in diameter, upon which
I was to act my part, and palisadoed it round three
feet from the edge, and as many high, to prevent my
falling over. I was shown ten times a day, to the
wonder and satisfaction of all people. I could now
speak the language tolerably well, and perfectly understood every word that was spoken to me. Besides,
I had learnt their alphabet, and could make a shift to
explain a sentence, here and there: for Glumdalclitch
had been my instructor while we were at home, and
at leisure hours during our journey.

The frequent labors I underwent every day, made,
in a few weeks, a very considerable change in my
health; the more my master got by me, the more
insatiable he grew. I had quite lost my appetite, and
was almost reduced to a skeleton. The farmer observed it, and concluding I must soon die, resolved to
make as good a hand of me as he could. While he
was thus reasoning and resolving with himself, a
sardral, or gentleman-usher, came from court, commanding my master to carry me immediately thither,
for the diversion of the queen and her ladies. Some
of the latter had already been to see me, and reported
strange things of my beauty, behavior, and good sense.
Her majesty, and those who attended her, were beyond
measure delighted with my demeanor. I fell on my
knees, and this gracious princess held out her little
finger towards me, after I was set on the table, which
I embraced in both my arms, and put the tip of it with
the utmost respect to my lips. She made me some

general questions about my country and my travels, which I answered as distinctly, and in as few words as I could. She asked, "whether I could be content to live at court?" I bowed down to the board of the table, and humbly answered, "that I was my master's slave; but if I were at my own disposal, I should be proud to devote my life to her majesty's service." She then asked my master, "whether he was willing to sell me at a good price?" He, who apprehended that I could not live a month, was ready enough to part with me, and demanded a thousand pieces of gold, which were ordered him on the spot, each piece being about the bigness of eight hundred moidores, but allowing for the proportion of all things between that country and Europe, and the high price of gold among them, was hardly so great a sum as a thousand guineas would be in England. I then said to the queen, "since I was now her majesty's most humble creature and vassal, I must beg the favor that Glumdalclitch, who had always tended me with so much care and kindness, and understood to do it so well, might be admitted into the service, and continue to be my nurse and instructor."

Her majesty agreed to my petition, and easily got the farmer's consent, who was glad enough to have his daughter preferred at court, and the poor girl herself was not able to hide her joy. My late master withdrew, bidding me farewell, and saying he had left me in a good service: to which I replied not a word, only making him a slight bow.

The queen observed my coldness: and, when the farmer was gone out of the apartment, asked me the reason. I made bold to tell her majesty "that I owed no other obligation to my late master, than his not dashing out the brains of a poor harmless creature, found by chance in his fields; which obligation was amply recompensed by the gain he had made in showing me through half the kingdom, and the price he had now sold me for. That the life I had since led, was laborious enough to kill an animal of ten times my strength. That my health was much impaired by the continual drudgery of entertaining the rabble every hour of the day; and that, if my master had not thought my life in danger, her majesty would not have got so cheap a bargain. But as I was out of all fear of being ill treated, under the protection of so great and good an empress, the ornament of nature, the darling of the world, the delight of her subjects, the phœnix of the creation; so, I hoped my late master's apprehensions would appear to be groundless; for I already found my spirits revive, by the influence of her most august presence."

This was the sum of my speech, delivered with great improprieties and hesitation. The latter part was altogether framed in the style peculiar to that people, whereof I learned some phrases from Glumdalclitch, while she was carrying me into court.

The queen, making great allowance for my defectiveness in speaking, was surprised at so much wit and good sense in so diminutive an animal. She took me in her own hand, and carried me to the king, who was then retired to his cabinet. His majesty, a prince of much gravity, and austere countenance, not well observing my shape at first view, asked the queen after

HIS MAJESTY SENT FOR THREE GREAT SCHOLARS

a cold manner, "how long it was since she grew fond
of a *splacnuck?*" for such it seems he took me to be,
as I lay in her majesty's right hand.   But the princess,
who has an infinite deal of wit and
humor, set me gently on my feet upon
the scrutoire, and commanded me
to give his majesty an account
of myself, which I did in a very
few words : and Glumdalclitch, who
attended at the cabinet door, being
admitted, confirmed all that had
passed from my arrival at her
father's house.

The king, although he be as
learned a person as any in his dominions, and had been educated in
the study of philosophy, and par-
ticularly mathematics ; yet when he observed my shape
exactly, and saw me walk erect, before I began to
speak, conceived I might be a piece of clock-work
(which is in that country arrived to a very great perfection) contrived by some ingenious artist.   But when
he heard my voice, and found what I delivered to be
regular and rational, he could not conceal his astonishment.   He was by no means satisfied with the relation
I gave him of the manner I came into his kingdom, but
thought it a story concerted between Glumdalclitch and
her father, who had taught me a set of words to make
me sell at a better price.   Upon this imagination, he
put several other questions to me, and still received
rational answers : no otherwise defective, than by a
foreign accent, and an imperfect knowledge in the lan-

guage, with some rustic phrases which I had learned at the farmer's house, and did not suit the polite style of a court.

His majesty sent for three great scholars, who were then in weekly waiting, according to the custom in that country. These gentlemen, after they had awhile examined my shape with much nicety, were of different opinions concerning me. They all agreed that I could not be produced according to the regular laws of nature, because I was not framed with a capacity of preserving my life, either by swiftness, or climbing of trees, or digging holes in the earth. They observed by my teeth, which they viewed with great exactness, that I was a carnivorous animal; yet most quadrupeds being an over-match for me, and field mice, with some others, too nimble, they could not imagine how I should be able to support myself, unless I fed upon snails and other insects, which they offered, by many learned arguments, to evince that I could not possibly do. After much debate, they concluded unanimously, that I was only *relplum scalcath*, which is, interpreted literally, *lusus naturæ;* a determination exactly agreeable to the modern philosophy of Europe, whose professors, disdaining the old evasion of occult causes, whereby the followers of Aristotle endeavored in vain to disguise their ignorance, have invented this wonderful solution of all difficulties, to the unspeakable advancement of human knowledge. . . .

Nothing angered and mortified me so much as the queen's dwarf; who being of the lowest stature that was ever in that country (for he was not full thirty feet high), became so insolent at seeing a creature so much beneath him, that he would affect to swagger and look big as he passed by me in the queen's ante-chamber, while I was standing on some table talking with the lords or ladies of the court, and he seldom failed of a smart word or two upon my littleness; against which I could only revenge myself by calling him brother, challenging him to wrestle, and such repartees as are usually in the mouths of court pages. One day at dinner, this malicious little cub was so nettled with something I had said to him, that raising himself upon the frame of her majesty's chair, he took me up by the middle, as I was sitting down not thinking any harm, and let me drop into  a large silver bowl of cream, and then ran away as fast as he could. I fell over head and ears, and, if I had not been a good swimmer, it might have gone very hard with me; for Glumdalclitch in that instant happened to be at the other end of the room, and the queen was in such a fright, that she wanted presence of mind to assist me. But my little nurse ran to my relief, and took me out, after I had swallowed above a quart of cream. I was put to bed: however, I received no other damage than the loss of a suit of clothes, which was utterly spoiled. The dwarf was soundly whipped, and as a further punishment, forced to drink up the bowl of cream into which he had thrown me; neither was he ever restored to favor; for soon after the queen bestowed him on a lady of high quality, so that I saw him no more, to my very great satisfaction: for I could not tell to what extremity such a malicious urchin might have carried his resentment.

I was frequently rallied by the queen on account of my fearfulness; and she used to ask me whether the people of my country were as great cowards as myself? The occasion was this: the kingdom is much pestered with flies in summer; and these odious insects, each of them as big as a Dunstable lark, hardly gave me any rest while I sat at dinner, with their continual humming and buzzing about my ears. I had much ado to defend myself against these detestable animals, and could not forbear starting when they came on my face. It was the common practice of the dwarf, to catch a number of these insects in his hand, as school-boys do among us, and let them out suddenly under my nose, on purpose to frighten me, and divert the queen. My remedy was to cut them in pieces with my knife, as they flew in the air, wherein my dexterity was much admired.

I remember, one morning, when Glumdalclitch had set me in a box upon a window, as she usually did in fair days, to give me air (for I durst not venture to let the box be hung on a nail out of the window, as we do with cages in England), after I had lifted up one of

my sashes, and sat down at my table to eat a piece of
sweet cake for my breakfast, above twenty wasps,
allured by the smell, came flying into the room humming louder than the drones of as many bag-
pipes. Some of them seized my
cake, and carried it piece-meal
away; others flew about my head
and face, confounding me with the
noise, and putting me in the utmost
terror of their stings. However, I
had the courage to rise and draw
my hanger, and attack them in the
air. I despatched four of them, but
the rest got away, and I presently
shut my window. These insects were as large as par-
tridges; I took out their stings, found them an inch
and a half long, and as sharp as needles. I carefully
preserved them all; and having since shown them,
with some other curiosities, in several parts of Europe,
upon my return to England I gave three of them to
Gresham College, and kept the fourth for myself.

A CHRISTMAS FANTASY, WITH A MORAL

By THOMAS BAILEY ALDRICH.

HER name was Mildred Wentworth, and she lived on the slope of Beacon Hill, in one of those old-fashioned swell-front houses which have the inestimable privilege of looking upon Boston Common. It was Christmas afternoon, and she had gone up to the blue room, on the fourth floor, in order to make a careful inspection in solitude of the various gifts that had been left in her slender stocking and at her bedside the previous night.

Mildred was in some respects a very old child for her age, which she described as being "half past seven," and had a habit of spending hours alone in the large front chamber occupied by herself and the governess. This day the governess had gone to keep Christmas with her own family in South Boston, and it so chanced that Mildred had been left to dispose of her time as she pleased during the entire afternoon. She was well content to have the opportunity, for fortune had treated her magnificently, and it was deep satisfaction, after

the excitement of the morning, to sit in the middle of
that spacious room, with its three windows overlooking
the pearl-crusted trees in the Common, and examine
her treasures without any chance of interruption.

The looms of Cashmere and the workshops of Germany, the patient Chinaman and the irresponsible
polar bear, had alike contributed to those treasures.
Among other articles was a small square box, covered
with mottled paper and having an outlandish, mysterious aspect, as if it belonged to a magician. When
you loosened the catch of this box, possibly supposing
it to contain bonbons of a superior quality, there
sprang forth a terrible little monster, with a drifting
white beard like a snow-storm, round emerald-green
eyes, and a pessimistic expression of countenance
generally, as though he had been reading Tolstoï or
Schopenhauer.

This abrupt personage, whose family name was
Heliogabalus, was known for simplicity's sake as
Jumping Jack; and though the explanation of the
matter is beset with difficulties, it is not to be concealed that he held a higher place in the esteem of
Miss Wentworth than any of her other possessions,
not excluding a tall wax doll with a pallid complexion
and a profusion of blonde hair. Titania was not more
in love with Nick Bottom the weaver than Mildred
with Jumping Jack. It was surely not his personal
beauty that won her, for he had none; it was not his
intellect, for intellect does not take up its abode in a
forehead of such singular construction as that of Jumping Jack. But whatever the secret charm was, it
worked. On a more realistic stage than this we see

analogous cases every day.　Perhaps Oberon still exercises his fairy craft in our material world, and scatters at will upon the eyelids of mortals the magic distillation of that "little Western flower" which

> "Will make or man or woman madly dote
> Upon the next live creature that it sees."

For an hour or so Mildred amused herself sufficiently by shutting Heliogabalus up in the box and letting him spring out again; then she grew weary of the diversion, and finally began to lose patience with her elastic companion because he was unable to crowd himself into the box and undo the latch with his own fingers.　This was extremely unreasonable; but so was Mildred made.

"How tedious you are!" she cried, at last.　"You dull little old man, I don't see how I ever came to like you.　I don't like you any more, with your glass eyes, and your silly pink mouth always open and never saying the least thing. What do you mean, sir, by standing and staring at me in that tiresome way? You look enough like Dobbs the butcher to be his brother, or to be Dobbs himself.　I wonder you don't up and say, 'Steaks or chops, mum?'　Dear me! I wish you really had some life in you, and could move about, and talk with me, and make yourself agreeable.　Do be alive!"

Mildred gave a little laugh at her own absurdity, and then, being an imaginative creature, came presently to regard the idea as not altogether absurd, and, finally, as not absurd at all.　If a bough that has been frozen to death all winter can put forth blossoms in the spring, why might not an inanimate object, which already possessed many of the surface attributes of humanity, and possibly some of the internal mechanism, add to itself the crowning gift of speech ? In view of the daily phenomena of existence, would that be so very astonishing ? Of course the problem took a simpler shape than this in Mildred's unsophisticated thought.

She folded her hands in her lap, and, rocking to and fro, reflected how pleasant it would be if Jumping Jack, or her doll, could come to life, like the marble lady in the play, and do some of the talking. What wonderful stories Jumping Jack would have to tell, for example. He must have had no end of remarkable adventures before he lost his mind. Probably the very latest intelligence from Lilliput was in his possession, and perhaps he was even now vainly trying to deliver himself of it. His fixed, open mouth hinted as much. The Land of the Pygmies, in the heart of Darkest Africa — just then widely discussed in the newspapers — was of course familiar ground to him. How interesting it would be to learn, at first hand, of the manners and customs of those little folk. Doubtless he had been a great traveller in foreign parts ; the label, in German text, on the bottom of his box showed that he had recently come from Munich. Munich ! What magic there was in the very word ! As Mildred rocked to and fro, her active little brain weaving the most grotesque fancies, a drowsiness stole over her. She was crooning to herself fainter and fainter, and every instant drifting nearer to the shadowy reefs on the western coast of Nowhere, when she heard a soft, inexplicable rustling sound close at her side. Mildred lifted her head quickly, just in time to behold Heliogabalus describe a graceful curve in the air and land lightly in the midst of her best Dresden china teaset.

"Ho, ho!" he cried, in a voice preternaturally gruff for an individual not above five inches in height. "Ho, ho!" And he immediately began to throw Mildred's cups and saucers and plates all about the apartment.

"Oh, you horrid, wicked little man!" cried Mildred, starting to her feet. "Stop it!"

"Oh, you cross little girl!" returned the dwarf, with his family leer. "You surprise me!" And another plate crashed against the blue-flowered wall-paper.

"Stop it!" she repeated; and then to herself, "It's a mercy I waked up just when I did!"

"Patience, my child; I'm coming there shortly, to smooth your hair and kiss you."

"Do!" screamed Mildred, stooping to pick up a large Japanese crystal which lay absorbing the wintry sunlight at her feet.

When Heliogabalus saw that, he retired to the farther side of his tenement, peeping cautiously over the top and around the corner, and disappearing altogether whenever Mildred threatened to throw the crystal at him. Now Miss Wentworth was naturally a courageous girl, and when she perceived that the pygmy was afraid of her she resolved to make an example of him. He was such a small affair that it really did not seem worth while to treat him with much ceremony. He had startled her at first, his manners had been so very violent; but now that her pulse had gone down she regarded him with calm curiosity, and wondered what he would do next.

"Listen," he said presently, in a queer, deferential

way, as he partly emerged from his hiding-place; "I came to request the hand of mademoiselle yonder," and, nodding his head in the direction of Blondella, the doll, he retreated bashfully.

"Her?" cried Mildred, aghast.

"*You* are very nice, but I can't marry out of my own set, you know," observed Heliogabalus, invisible behind his breastwork. This shyness was mere dissimulation, as his subsequent behavior proved.

"Who would have thought it!" murmured Mildred to herself; and as she glanced suspiciously at Blondella, sitting bolt upright between the windows, with her back against the mopboard, Mildred fancied that she could almost detect a faint roseate hue stealing into the waxen cheek. "Who would have thought it!" And then, addressing Jumping Jack, she cried, "Come here directly; you audacious person!" and she stamped her foot in a manner that would have discouraged most suitors.

But Heliogabalus, who had now seated himself on the lid of his box and showed no trace of his late diffidence, smiled superciliously as he twisted off a bit of wire that protruded from the heel of one of his boots.

This effrontery increased Miss Wentworth's indignation, and likewise rather embarrassed her. Perhaps he was not afraid of her after all. In which case he was worth nothing as an example.

"I will brush you off, and tread on you," she observed tentatively, as if she were addressing an insect.

"Oh, indeed," he rejoined derisively, crossing his legs.

"I will!" cried Mildred, making an impulsive dash at him.

Though taken at a disadvantage the manikin eluded her with surprising ease. His agility was such as to render it impossible to determine whether he was an old young man or a very young old man. Mildred eyed him doubtfully for a moment, and then gave chase. Away went the quaint little figure, now darting under the brass bedstead, now dodging around the legs of the table, and now slipping between the feet of his pursuer at the instant she was on the point of laying hand on him. Owing doubtless to some peculiarity of his articulation, each movement of his limbs was accompanied by a rustling wiry sound like the faint reverberation of a banjo-string somewhere in the distance.

Heliogabalus may have been a person with no great conversational gift, but his gymnastic acquirements were of the first order.

Mildred not only could not catch him, but she could not restrain the manikin from meanwhile doing all kinds of desultory mischief; for in the midst of his course he would pause to overturn her tin kitchen, or shy a plate across the room, or give a vicious twitch to the lovely golden hair of Blondella, in spite of — perhaps in consequence of — his recent tender advances. It was plain that in eluding Mildred he was prompted by caprice rather than by fear.

"If things go on in this way," she reflected, "I sha'n't have anything left. If I could only get the dreadful little creature into a corner! There goes my tureen! What *shall* I do?"

To quit the room, even for a moment, in order to call for assistance at the head of the staircase, where, moreover, her voice was not likely to reach any one, was to leave everything at the mercy of that small demon. Mildred was out of breath with running, and ready to burst into tears with exasperation, when a different mode of procedure suggested itself to her. She would make believe that she was no longer angry, and possibly she could accomplish by cunning what she had failed to compass by violence. She would consent — at least seem to consent — to let him marry Blondella, though he had lately given no signs of a very fervid attachment. Beyond this Mildred had no definite scheme, when the story of the Fisherman and the Evil Afrite flashed upon her memory from the pages of the "Arabian Nights." Her dilemma was exactly that of the unlucky fisherman, and her line of action should be the same, with such modification as the exigencies might demand. As in his case, too, there was no time to be lost. An expression of ineffable benevolence and serenity instantly overspread the features of Miss Wentworth. She leaned against the wardrobe, and regarded Jumping Jack with a look of gentle reproach.

"I thought you were going to be interesting," she remarked softly.

"Ain't I interesting?" asked the goblin, with a touch of pardonable sensitiveness.

"No," said Mildred candidly, "you are not. Perhaps you try to be. That's something, to be sure, though it's not everything. Oh, *I* don't want to touch you," she went on, with an indifferent toss of her curls. "How old are you?"

"Ever so old and ever so young."

"Truly? How very odd to be both at once! Can you read?"

"Never tried."

"I'm afraid your parents didn't bring you up very well," reflected Mildred.

"I speak all languages. The little folk of every age and every country understand me."

"You're a great traveller, then."

"I should say so!"

"You don't seem to carry much baggage about with you. I suppose you belong some-where, and keep your clothes there. I really should like to know where you came from, if it's all the same to you."

"Out of that box, my dove," replied Jumping Jack, having become affable in his turn.

"Never!" exclaimed Mildred, with a delightful air of incredulity.

"I hope I may die," declared Heliogabalus, laying one hand on the left breast of his mainspring.

"I don't believe it," said Mildred confidently.

"Ho, ho!"

"You are too tall, and too wide, and too — fluffy. I don't mean to hurt your feelings, but you *are* fluffy. And I just want you to stop that ho-hoing. No; I don't believe it."

"You don't, don't you? Behold!" And placing both hands on the floor, Heliogabalus described a circle in the air, and neatly landed himself in the box.

He was no sooner in than Mildred clapped down the lid, and seated herself upon it victoriously. In the suddenness of her movement she had necessarily neglected to fasten the catch; but that was a detail that could be attended to later. Meanwhile she was mistress of the situation and could dictate terms. One thing was resolved : Jumping Jack was never to jump again. To-morrow he should be thrown into the Charles at the foot of Mount Vernon Street, in order that the tide might carry him out to sea. What would she not have given if she could have sealed him up with that talismanic Seal of Solomon which held the cruel marid so securely in his brazen casket? Of course it was not in Mildred's blood to resist the temptation to tease her captive a little.

"Now, Mr. Jack, I guess I've got you where you belong. If you are not an old man this very minute, you will be when you get out. You wanted to carry off my Blondella, did you? The idea! I hope you're quite comfortable."

"Let me out!" growled Heliogabalus in his deepest bass.

"I couldn't think of it, dear. You are one of those little boys that shouldn't be *either* seen or heard; and I don't want you to speak again, for I'm sitting on your head, and your voice goes right through me. So you will please remember not to speak unless you are spoken to." And Mildred broke into the merriest laugh imaginable, recollecting how many times she herself had been extinguished by the same instructions.

But Mildred's triumph was premature, for the little man in the box was as strong as a giant in a dime museum; and now that he had fully recovered his breath, he began pushing in a most systematic manner with his head and shoulders, and Mildred, to her great consternation, found herself being slowly lifted up on the lid of the box, do what she might. In a minute or two more she must inevitably fall off, and Jumping Jack would have her! And what mercy could she expect at his hands, after her treatment of him! She was lost! Mildred stretched out her arms in despair, gave a shriek, and opened her eyes, which had been all the while as tightly shut as a couple of morning-glories at sundown.

She was sitting on a rug in the middle of the room. Though the window-panes were still flushed with the memory of the winter sunset, the iridescent lights had faded out in the Japanese crystal at her feet. She was not anywhere near the little imp. There he was over by the fireplace, staring at nothing in his usual sense-less fashion. Not a piece of crockery had been broken, not a chair upset, and Blondella, the too fascinating Blondella, had not had a single tress disarranged.

Mildred drew a long breath of relief. What had

happened? Had she been dreaming? She was unable to answer the question; but as she abstractedly shook out the creases in the folds of her skirt, she remarked to herself that she did not care, on the whole, to have any of her things come to life, certainly not Jumping Jack. Just then the splintering of an icicle on the window-ledge outside sent a faint whiteness into her cheeks, and caused her to throw a quick, apprehensive glance toward the fireplace. After an instant's hesitation, Mildred, unconsciously dragging Blondella by the hair, stole softly from the room, where the spectres of the twilight were beginning to gather rather menacingly, and went down-stairs to join the family and relate her strange adventure.

The analysis of Miss Wentworth's dream — if it were a dream, for later on she declared it was not, and hurriedly gave Heliogabalus to an unpleasant small boy who lived next door — the analysis of her dream, I repeat, shows strong traces of a moral. Indeed, the residuum is purely of that stringent quality. Heliogabalus must be accepted as the symbol of an ill-considered desire realized. The earnestness with which Miss Wentworth invoked the phantasm and the misery that came of it are a common experience. Painfully to attain possession of what we do not want, and then painfully to waste our days in attempting to rid ourselves of it, seems to be a part of our discipline here below. I know a great many excellent persons who are spending the latter moiety of life in the endeavor to get their particular Jumping Jack snugly back into its box again.

THE KNIGHT AND HIS STORY

(From Undine.)

By THE BARON DE LA MOTTE FOUQUÉ.

NCE — it may be some hundreds of years ago — there lived a good old Fisherman, who, on a fine summer's evening, was sitting before the door mending his nets. He dwelt in a land of exceeding beauty. The green slope upon which he had built his hut, stretched far out into a great lake; and it seemed either that the cape, enamored of the glassy blue waters, had pressed forward into their bosom, or that the lake had lovingly folded in its arms the blooming promontory, with her waving grass and flowers, and the refreshing shade of her tall trees. Each bade the other welcome, and increased its own beauty by so doing. This lovely nook was scarcely ever visited by mankind, except by the Fisherman and his family. For behind the promontory lay a very wild forest, which, besides being gloomy and pathless, had too bad a name as the resort of wondrous spirits and goblins, to be crossed by any one who could help it. Yet the pious old Fisherman went through it without being molested, whenever he walked to a large city beyond the forest, to dispose of the costly fish that he caught in the lake. For him, indeed, there was little danger, even in that forest; for his thoughts were almost all thoughts of devotion, and his custom was to carol forth to Heaven a loud and heartfelt hymn, on first setting foot within the treacherous shades.

As he sat this evening most peacefully over his nets, he was startled in an unwonted manner by a rustling sound in the forest, like that of a man and horse; and the noise came nearer and nearer. The dreams he had had in many a stormy night of the spirits of the forest started up before his mind, particularly the image of a gigantic, long snow-white man, who kept nodding his head mysteriously. Nay, as he raised his eyes and looked into the forest, he could fancy he saw, through the thick screen of leaves, the nodding creature advance toward him. But he soon composed himself, recollecting that even in the heart of the woods nothing had ever befallen him; much less here, in the open air, could the bad spirits have power to touch him. He moreover repeated a text from the Bible aloud and earnestly, which quite restored his courage, and he almost laughed to see how his fancy had misled him. The white nodding man suddenly resolved himself into a little brook he knew of old, which gushed bubbling out of the wood, and emptied itself into the lake. And the rustling had been caused by a horseman in gorgeous attire, who now came forward toward the hut from beneath the trees.

He wore a scarlet mantle over his purple, gold-embroidered jerkin; a plume of red and purple feathers waved over his gold-colored barret-cap; and from his golden belt hung a glittering jewelled sword. The

white courser which carried him was of lighter make
than the generality of chargers, and trod so airily, that
the enamelled turf seemed scarcely to bend under him.
The aged Fisherman could not quite shake off his
uneasiness, although he told himself that so noble a
guest could bring him no harm, and accordingly doffed
his hat courteously, and interrupted his work when he
approached.

The Knight reined in his horse, and asked whether
they could both obtain one night's shelter.

"As to your horse, good sir," answered the Fisherman, "I have no better stable to offer him than the
shady meadow, and no provender but the grass which
grows upon it. But you shall yourself be heartily
welcome to my poor house, and to the best of my
supper and night lodging."

The stranger seemed quite content; he dismounted,
and they helped each other to take off the horse's girth
and saddle, after which the Knight let him graze on
the flowery pasture, saying to his host, "Even if I had
found you less kind and hospitable, my good old man,
you must have borne with me till to-morrow; for I see
we are shut in by a wide lake, and Heaven forbid that
I should cross the haunted forest again at nightfall!"

"We will not say much about that," replied the
Fisherman; and he led his guest into the cottage.

There, close by the hearth, from whence a scanty fire
shed its glimmering light over the clean little room, sat
the Fisherman's old wife. When their noble guest came
in, she rose to give him a kind welcome, but immediately resumed her place of honor, without offering it
to him; and the Fisherman said with a smile: "Do not

take it amiss, young sir, if she does not give up to you
the most comfortable place; it is the custom among us
poor people, that it should always belong to the oldest."

"Why, husband!" said his wife quietly, "what are
you thinking of?   Our guest is surely a Christian gentleman, and how could it come into his kind young
heart to turn old people out of their places? Sit down,
my young lord," added she, turning to the Knight;
"there stands a very comfortable chair for you; only
remember it must not be too roughly handled, for one
leg is not so steady as it has been." The Knight drew
the chair carefully forward, seated himself sociably, and
soon felt quite at home in this little household, and as
if he had just returned to it from a far journey.

The three friends began to converse openly and familiarly together. First the Knight asked a few questions
about the forest, but the old man would not say much
of that; least of all, said he, was it fitting to talk of
such things at nightfall; but, on household concerns,
and their own way of life, the old folks talked readily;
and were pleased when the Knight told them of his
travels, and that he had a castle near the source of the
Danube, and that his name was Lord Huldbrand of
Ringstetten. In the middle of their discourse, the
stranger often observed a noise outside the small window, as if some one were dashing water against it. The
old man knit his brows and looked grave whenever this
occurred; at last, when a great splash of water came
full against the panes, and some found its way into the
room, he could bear it no longer, but started up, crying,
"Undine! will you never leave off these childish tricks,
—when we have a stranger gentleman in the house

too ! "   This produced silence outside, all but a sound
of suppressed giggling, and the Fisherman said as he
came back : " My honored guest, you must put up with
this, and perhaps with many another piece of mischief ;
but she means no harm.   It is our adopted child Undine ;
there is no breaking her of her childish ways, though
she is eighteen years old now.   But as I told you she
is as good a child as ever lived, at bottom."

" Ay, so you may say ! " rejoined his wife, shaking
her head.   " When you come home from fishing, or
from a journey, her playful nonsense may be pleasant
enough.   But, to be keeping her out of mischief all
day long, as I must do, and never get a word of sense
from her, nor a bit of help and comfort in my old age,
is enough to weary the patience of a saint."

" Well, well," said the good man, " you feel toward
Undine as I do toward the lake.   Though its waves
are apt enough to burst my banks and my nets, yet I
love them for all that, and so do you love our pretty
wench, with all her plaguy tricks.   Don't you ? "

" Why, one cannot be really angry with her, to be
sure," said the dame smiling.

Here the door flew open, and a beautiful fair creature tripped in, and said, playfully : " Well, father, you
made game of me ; where is your guest ? "   The next
moment she perceived the Knight, and stood fixed in
mute admiration ; while Huldbrand gazed upon her
lovely form, and tried to impress her image on his
mind, thinking that he must avail himself of her
amazement to do so, and that in a moment she would
shrink away in a fit of bashfulness.   But it proved
otherwise.   After looking at him a good while, she

came up to him familiarly, knelt down beside him, and
playing with a golden medal that hung from his rich
chain, she said : " So, thou kind, thou beautiful guest !
hast thou found us out in our poor hut at last ? Why
didst thou roam the world so many years without
coming near us ? Art come through the wild forest,
my handsome friend ? " The old woman allowed him
no time to answer. She desired
her to get up instantly, like
a modest girl, and to
set about her work.
But Undine, without
replying, fetched a
footstool and put it
close to Huldbrand's
chair, sat down
there with her
spinning, and said
cheerfully, — " I
will sit and work
here." The old
man behaved as
parents are apt to
do with spoilt chil-
dren. He pretended not
to see Undine's waywardness, and was beginning to
talk of something else ; but she would not let him.
She said, " I asked our visitor where he came from,
and he has not answered me yet."

" From the forest I came, you beautiful sprite,"
answered Huldbrand ; and she continued : —

" Then you must tell me how you came there, and

what wonderful adventures you had in it, for I know that nobody can escape without some."

Huldbrand could not help shuddering on being reminded of his adventures, and involuntarily glanced at the window, half expecting to see one of the strange beings he had encountered in the forest grinning at him through it; but nothing was to be seen except the deep black night, which had now closed in. He recollected himself, and was just beginning his narrative, when the old man interposed : "Not just now, Sir Knight ; this is no time for such tales."

But Undine jumped up passionately, put her beautiful arms akimbo, and standing before the Fisherman, exclaimed : "What! may not he tell his story; father — may not he? But I will have it; he must. He shall indeed!" And she stamped angrily with her pretty feet, but it was all done in so comical and graceful a manner, that Huldbrand thought her still more bewitching in her wrath, than in her playful mood.

Not so the old man ; his long-restrained anger burst out uncontrolled. He scolded Undine smartly for her disobedience, and unmannerly conduct to the stranger, his wife chiming in.

Undine then said : "Very well, if you will be quarrelsome, and not let me have my own way, you may sleep alone in your smoky old hut!" and she shot through the door like an arrow, and rushed into the dark night.

Huldbrand and the Fisherman sprang from their seats, and tried to catch the angry maiden; but before they could reach the house door, Undine had vanished far into the thick shades, and not a sound of her light footsteps was to be heard, by which to track her course. Huldbrand looked doubtfully at his host; he almost thought that the whole fair vision which had so suddenly plunged into the night, must be a continuation of the phantom play which had whirled around him in his passage through the forest. But the old man mumbled through his teeth: "It is not the first time she has served us so. And here are we, left in our anxiety with a sleepless night before us; for who can tell what harm may befall her, all alone out-of-doors till daybreak?"

"Then let us be after her, good father, for God's sake!" cried Huldbrand, eagerly.

The old man replied, "Where would be the use? It were a sin to let you set off alone in pursuit of the foolish girl, and my old legs would never overtake such a Will-o'-the-wisp — even if we could guess which way she is gone."

"At least, let us call her, and beg her to come back," said Huldbrand; and he began calling after her in most moving tones: "Undine! O Undine, do return!"

The old man shook his head, and said that all the shouting in the world would do no good with such a wilful little thing. But yet he could not himself help calling out from time to time in the darkness: "Undine! ah, sweet Undine! I entreat thee, come back this once."

The Fisherman's words proved true. Nothing was to be seen or heard of Undine; and as her foster-father would by no means suffer Huldbrand to pursue her, they had nothing for it but to go in again. They found the fire on the hearth nearly burnt out, and the dame, who did not take to heart Undine's flight and danger so much as her husband, was gone to bed. The old man blew the coals, laid on dry wood, and by the light of the reviving flames he found a flagon of wine, which he put between himself and his guest. "You are uneasy about that silly wench, Sir Knight," said he, "and we had better kill part of the night chatting and drinking, than toss about in our beds, trying to sleep in vain. Had not we?"

Huldbrand agreed; the Fisherman made him sit in his wife's empty arm-chair, and they both drank and talked together, as a couple of worthy friends should do. Whenever, indeed, there was the least stir outside the window, or even sometimes without any, one of them would look up and say, "There she comes." Then they would keep silence for a few moments, and as nothing came, resume their conversation, with a shake of the head and a sigh.

But as neither could think of much besides Undine, the best means they could devise for beguiling the time was, that the Fisherman should relate, and the Knight listen to, the history of her first coming to the cottage. He began as follows: —

"One day, some fifteen years ago, I was carrying my fish through that dreary wood to the town. My wife stayed at home, as usual; and at that time she had a good and pretty reason for it; — the Lord had bestowed upon us (old as we already were) a lovely babe. It was a girl; and so anxious were we to do our best for the little treasure, that we began to talk of leaving our beautiful home, in order to give our darling a good education among other human beings. With us poor folks, wishing is one thing, and doing is quite another, Sir Knight; but what then? we can only try our best. Well then, as I plodded on, I turned over the scheme in my head. I was loth to leave our own dear nook, and it made me shudder to think, in the din and brawls of the town, So it is here we shall soon live, or in some place nearly as bad! Yet I never murmured against our good God, but rather thanked Him in secret for His last blessing; nor can I say that I met with any thing extraordinary in the forest, either coming or going; indeed nothing to frighten me has ever crossed my path. The Lord was ever with me in the awful shades."

Here he uncovered his bald head, and sat for a time in silent prayer; then putting his cap on again, he continued: "On this side of the wood it was, — on this side, that the sad news met me. My wife came toward me with eyes streaming like two fountains; she was in deep mourning. 'Oh, good Heaven!' I called out, 'where is our dear child? Tell me?'

"'Gone, dear husband,' she replied; and we went into our cottage together, weeping silently. I looked for the little corpse, and then first heard how it had happened. My wife had been sitting on the shore with the child, and playing with it, all peace and happiness; when the babe all at once leaned over, as if she saw something most beautiful in the water; there she sat smiling, sweet angel! and stretching out her little hands; but the next moment she darted suddenly out of her arms, and down into the smooth waters. I made much search for the poor little corpse; but in vain; not a trace of her could I find.

"When evening was come, we childless parents were

sitting together in the hut, silent; neither of us had a mind to speak, even if the tears had let us. We were looking idly into the fire. Just then something made a noise at the door. It opened, and a beautiful little maid, of three or four years old, stood there gaily dressed, and smiling in our faces. We were struck dumb with surprise, and at first hardly knew if she were a little human being, or only an empty shadow. But I soon saw that her golden hair and gay clothes were dripping wet, and it struck me the little fairy must have been in the water, and distressed for help. 'Wife,' said I, 'our dear child had no friend to save her; shall we not do for others what would have made our remaining days so happy, if any one had done it for us?' We undressed the child, put her to bed, and gave her a warm drink, while she never said a word, but kept smiling at us with her sky-blue eyes.

"The next morning we found that she had done herself no harm; and I asked her who were her parents, and what had brought her here; but she gave me a strange, confused answer. I am sure she must have been born far away, for these fifteen years have we kept her, without ever finding out where she came from; and besides, she is apt to let drop such marvellous things in her talk, that you might think she had lived in the moon. She will speak of golden castles, of crystal roofs, and I can't tell what besides. The only thing she has told us clearly, is, that as she was sailing on the lake with her mother, she fell into the water, and when she recovered her senses found herself lying under these trees, in safety and comfort, upon our pretty shore.

"So now we had a serious, anxious charge thrown upon us. To keep and bring up the foundling, instead of our poor drowned child, — that was soon resolved upon; but who should tell us if she had yet been baptized or no? She knew not how to answer the question. That she was one of God's creatures, made for His glory and service, that much she knew; and anything that would glorify and please Him, she was willing to have done. So my wife and I said to each other: 'If she has never been baptized, there is no doubt it should be done; and if she has, better do too much than too little, in a matter of such consequence.' We therefore began to seek a good name for the child. Dorothea seemed to us the best; for I had once heard that meant God's gift; and she had indeed been sent us by Him as a special blessing, to comfort us in our misery. But she would not hear of that name. She said Undine was what her parents used to call her, and Undine she would still be. That, I thought, sounded like a heathen name, and occurred in no Calendar; and I took counsel with a priest in the town about it. He also objected to the name Undine; and at my earnest request, came home with me, through the dark forest, in order to baptize her. The little creature stood before us, looking so gay and charming in her holiday clothes, that the priest's heart warmed toward her; and what with coaxing and wilfulness, she got the better of him, so that he clean forgot all the objections he had thought of to the name Undine. She was therefore so christened, and behaved particularly well and decently during the sacred rite, wild and unruly as she had always been

before.   For, what my wife said just now was too
true — we have indeed found her the wildest little
fairy ! If I were to tell you all " —

Here the Knight interrupted the Fisherman, to call
his attention to a sound of roaring waters, which he
had noticed already in the pauses of the old man's
speech, and which now rose in fury as it rushed past
the windows.   They both ran to the door.   By the
light of the newly risen moon, they saw the brook
which gushed out of the forest breaking wildly over its
banks, and whirling along stones and branches in its
eddying course.   A storm, as if awakened by the up-
roar, burst from the heavy clouds that were chasing
each other across the moon ; the lake howled under
the wings of the wind ; the trees on the shore groaned
from top to bottom, and bowed themselves over the
rushing waters.   " Undine ! for God's sake, Undine ! "
cried the Knight, and the old man.   No answer was to
be heard ; and, heedless now of any danger to themselves, they ran off in different directions, calling her
in frantic anxiety.

The longer Huldbrand wandered in vain pursuit of
Undine, the more bewildered he became.   The idea
that she might be a mere spirit of the woods, sometimes returned upon him with double force ; nay, amid
the howling of waves and storm, the groaning of trees,
and the wild commotion of the once-peaceful spot, he
might have fancied the whole promontory, its hut and
its inhabitants, to be a delusion of magic, but that he
still heard in the distance the Fisherman's piteous cries
of " Undine ! " and the old housewife's loud prayers
and hymns, above the whistling of the blast.

At last he found himself on the margin of the over-flowing stream, and saw it by the moonlight rushing violently along, close to the edge of the mysterious forest, so as to make an island of the peninsula on which he stood. "Gracious Heaven!" thought he, "Undine may have ventured a step or two into that awful forest, — perhaps in her pretty waywardness, just because I would not tell her my story — and the swollen stream has cut her off, and left her weeping alone among the spectres!" A cry of terror escaped him, and he clambered down the bank by means of some stones and fallen trees, hoping to wade or swim across the flood, and seek the fugitive beyond it. Fearful and unearthly visions did indeed float before him, like those he had met with in the morning, beneath these groaning, tossing branches. Especially he was haunted by the appearance of a tall white man, whom he remembered but too well, grinning and nodding at him from the opposite bank; however, the thought of these grim monsters did but urge him onward as he recollected Undine, now perhaps in deadly fear among them, and alone.

He had laid hold of a stout pine branch, and leaning on it, was standing in the eddy, though scarcely able to stem it, but he stepped boldly forward — when a sweet voice exclaimed close behind him: "Trust him not — trust not! The old fellow is tricksy — the stream!"

Well he knew those silver tones: the moon was just disappearing behind a cloud, and he stood amid the deepening shades, made dizzy as the water shot by him with the speed of an arrow. Yet he would not desist. "And if thou art not truly there, if thou flittest before

me an empty shadow, I care not to live; I will melt
into air like thee, my beloved Undine!" This he cried
aloud, and strode further into the flood.

"Look round then,—look round, fair youth!" he
heard just behind him, and looking round, he beheld
by the returning moonbeams, on a fair island left by
the flood, under some thickly interlaced branches,
Undine all smiles and loveliness, nestling in the flowery
grass. How much more joyfully than before did the
young man use his pine staff to cross the waters! A
few strides brought him through the flood that had
parted them; and he found himself at her side, on the
nook of soft grass, securely sheltered under the shade
of the old trees. Undine half arose, and twined her
arms round his neck in the green arbor, making him
sit down by her on the turf. "Here you shall tell me
all, my own friend," said she in a low whisper; "the
cross old folks cannot overhear us. And our pretty
bower of leaves is well worth their wretched hut."

"This is heaven!" cried Huldbrand, as he clasped
in his arms the beautiful flatterer.

Meantime the old man had reached the banks of the
stream, and he called out: "So, Sir Knight, when I
had made you welcome, as one honest man should
another, here are you making love to my adopted
child,— to say nothing of your leaving me to seek her,
alone and terrified, all night."

"I have but this moment found her, old man!"
cried the Knight in reply.

"Well, I am glad of that," said the Fisherman;
"now then bring her back to me at once."

But Undine would not hear of it. She had rather

she said, go quite away into the wild woods with the handsome stranger, than return to the hut, where she had never had her own way, and which the Knight must sooner or later leave. Embracing Huldbrand, she sang with peculiar charm and grace : —

> " From misty cave the mountain wave
> Leapt out and sought the main !
> The Ocean's foam she made her home,
> And ne'er returned again."

The old man wept bitterly as she sang, but this did not seem to move her. She continued to caress her lover, till at length he said: " Undine, the poor old man's grief goes to my heart, if not to yours. Let us go back to him."

Astonished, she raised her large blue eyes toward him, and after a pause answered slowly and reluctantly : " To please you, I will : whatever you like pleases me too. But the old man yonder must first promise me that he will let you tell me all you saw in the forest, and the rest we shall see about."

" Only come back, — do come ! " cried the Fisherman, and not another word could he say. At the same moment he stretched his arms over the stream toward her, and nodded his head by way of giving her the desired promise; and as his white hair fell over his face, it gave him a strange look, and reminded Huldbrand involuntarily of the nodding white man in the woods. Determined, however, that nothing should stop him, the young Knight took the fair damsel in his arms, and carried her through the short space of foaming flood, which divided the island from the main-land.

The old man fell upon Undine's neck, and rejoiced, and kissed her in the fulness of his heart; his aged wife also came up, and welcomed their recovered child most warmly. All reproaches were forgotten; the more so, as Undine seemed to have left her sauciness behind, and overwhelmed her foster parents with kind words and caresses.

When these transports of joy had subsided, and they began to look about them, the rosy dawn was just shedding its glow over the lake, the storm had ceased, and the birds were singing merrily on the wet branches. As Undine insisted upon hearing the story of the Knight's adventure, both the old folks cheerfully indulged her. Breakfast was set out under the trees between the cottage and the lake, and they sat down before it with glad hearts, Undine placing herself resolutely on the grass at the Knight's feet. Huldbrand began his narrative as follows.

"About eight days ago, I rode into the imperial city beyond this forest. A grand tournament and tilting was held there, and I spared neither lance nor steed. As I stood still a moment to rest myself, in a pause of the noble game, and had just given my helmet in charge to a squire, my eye fell upon a most beautiful woman, who stood, richly adorned, in one of the galleries, looking on. I inquired her name, and found that this charming lady was Bertalda, the adopted daughter of one of the principal lords in the neighborhood. I observed that her eye was upon me too, and as is the way with us young knights, I had not been slack before, but I now fought more bravely still. That evening I was Bertalda's partner in the dance,

and so I was again every evening during the joust-
ing."

Here a sudden pain in his left hand, which hung
beside him, checked the Knight in his tale, and he
looked at his hand. Undine's pearly teeth had bitten
one of his fingers sharply, and she looked very black
at him. But the next moment that look changed into
an expression of tender sadness, and she whispered
low: "So you are faithless too!" Then she hid her
face in her hands, and the Knight proceeded with his
tale, although staggered and perplexed.

"That Bertalda is a high-spirited, extraordinary maid.
On the second day she charmed me far less than the
first, and on the third, less still. But I remained with
her, because she was more gracious to me than to any
other knight, and so it fell out that I asked her in jest
for one of her gloves. ' You shall have it,' said she, ' if
you will visit the haunted forest alone, and bring me an
account of it.' It was not that I cared much for her
glove, but the words had been spoken, and a knight that
loves his fame does not wait to be twice urged to such
a feat."

"I thought she had loved you," interrupted Undine.

"It looked like it," he replied.

"Well," cried the maiden, laughing, "she must be a
fool indeed! To drive *him* away whom she loves!
and into a haunted forest besides! The forest and its
mysteries might have waited long enough, for me."

"I set out yesterday morning," continued the Knight,
smiling kindly at Undine. "The stems of the trees
looked so bright in the morning sunshine, as it played
upon the green turf, and the leaves whispered together
so pleasantly, that I could not but laugh at those who

imagined any evil to lurk in such a beautiful place. I
shall very soon have ridden through it and back again,
thought I, pushing on cheerily, and before I was aware
of it, I found myself in the depths of its leafy shades,
and the plains behind me far out of sight. It then
occurred to me that I was likely enough to lose my
way in this wilderness of trees, and that this might be
the only real danger to which the traveller was here
exposed. So I halted, and took notice of the course of
the sun; it was now high in the heavens.

" On looking up, I saw something black among the
boughs of a tall oak. I took it for a bear, and seized
my rifle; but it addressed me in a human voice, most
hoarse and grating, saying: 'If I did not break off
the twigs up here, what should we do to-night for
fuel to roast you with, Sir Simpleton?' And he gnashed
his teeth, and rattled the boughs, so as to startle my
horse, which ran away with me before I could make
out what kind of a devil it was.

" You should not mention *his* name," said the Fisherman, crossing himself; his wife silently did the same,
while Undine turned her beaming eyes upon her lover,
and said, —

" He is safe now ; it is well they did not really roast
him. Go on, pretty youth."

He continued : " My terrified horse had almost dashed
me against many a trunk and branch; he was running
down with fright and heat, and yet there was no stopping him. At length he rushed madly toward the brink
of a stony precipice ; but here, as it seemed to me, a tall
white man threw himself across the plunging animal's
path, and made him start back, and stop. I then re-

covered the control of him, and found that, instead of a
white man, my preserver was no other than a bright
silvery brook, which gushed down from a hill beside
me, checking and
crossing my horse
in his course."

"Thanks, dear
brook!" cried
Undine, clapping
her hands. But
the old man
shook his
head, and
seemed lost
in thought.

"Scarcely
had I settled
myself in the
saddle, and
got firm hold
of my reins
again," pro-
ceeded Huld-
brand, "when
an extraordi-
nary little
man sprang
up beside me, wizen and hideous beyond measure; he
was of a yellow-brown hue, and his nose almost as big
as the whole of his body. He grinned at me in the
most fulsome way with his wide mouth bowing and
scraping every moment. As I could not abide these

antics, I thanked him abruptly, pulled my still-trembling horse another way, and thought I would seek some other adventure, or perhaps go home; for during my wild gallop the sun had passed his meridian, and was now declining westward. But the little imp sprang round like lightning, and stood in front of my horse again.

"'Make way!' cried I impatiently, 'the animal is unruly, and may run over you.'

"'Oh,' snarled the imp, with a laugh more disgusting than before, 'first give me a piece of coin for having caught your horse so nicely; but for me, you and your pretty beast would be lying in the pit down yonder: whew!'

"'Only have done with your grimaces,' said I, 'and take your money along with you, though it is all a lie: look there, it was that honest brook that saved me, not you — you pitiful wretch!' So saying, I dropped a gold coin into his comical cap, which he held out toward me like a beggar.

"I trotted on, but he still followed, screaming, and, with inconceivable rapidity, whisked up to my side. I put my horse into a gallop; he kept pace with me, though with much difficulty, and twisted his body into various frightful and ridiculous attitudes, crying at each step as he held up the money: 'Bad coin! bad gold! bad gold! bad coin!' And this he shrieked in such a ghastly tone, that you would have expected him to drop down dead after each cry.

"At last I stopped, much vexed, and asked, 'What do you want, with your shrieks? Take another gold coin; take two if you will, only let me alone.'

" He began his odious smirking again, and snarled, ' It's not gold, it's not gold that I want, young gentleman ; I have rather more of that than I can use : you shall see.'

" All at once the surface of the ground became transparent ; it looked like a smooth globe of green glass, and within it I saw a crowd of goblins at play with silver and gold. Tumbling about, head over heels they pelted each other in sport, making a toy of the precious metals, and powdering their faces with gold-dust. My ugly companion stood half above, half below the surface ; he made the others reach up to him quantities of gold, and showed it me laughing, and then flung it into the fathomless depths beneath. He displayed the piece of gold I had given him to the goblins below, who held their sides with laughing, and hissed at me in scorn. At length all their bony fingers pointed at me together ; and louder and louder, closer and closer, wilder and wilder grew the turmoil, as it rose toward me, till not my horse only, but I myself was terrified ; I put spurs into him, and cannot tell how long I may have scoured the forest this time.

" When at last I halted, the shades of evening had closed in. Through the branches I saw a white footpath gleaming, and hoped it must be a road out of the forest to the town. I resolved to work my way thither ; but lo ! an indistinct, dead-white face, with ever-changing features, peeped at me through the leaves ; I tried to avoid it, but wherever I went, there it was. Provoked, I attempted to push my horse against it ; then it splashed us both over with white foam, and we turned away, blinded for the moment. So it drove us, step by step, further and further from the footpath, and indeed never letting us go on undisturbed but in one direction. While we kept to this, it was close upon our heels, but did not thwart us. Having looked round once or twice, I observed that the white foaming head was placed on a gigantic body, equally white. I sometimes doubted my first impression, and thought it merely a water-fall, but I never could satisfy myself that it was so. Wearily did my horse and I precede this active white pursuer, who often nodded at us, as if saying, ' That's right! that's right! ' and it ended by our issuing from the wood here, where I rejoiced to see your lawn, the lake, and this cottage, and where the long white man vanished."

" Thank Heaven, he is gone," said the old man, and he then proceeded to consider how his guest could best return to his friends in the city. Upon this, Undine was heard to laugh in a whisper.

Huldbrand observed it, and said : " I thought you had wished me to stay ; and now you seem pleased when we talk of my going ? "

" Because," replied Undine, " you cannot get away. Only try to cross the swollen brook, in a boat, on horse-back, or on foot. Or rather, do not try, for you would be dashed to pieces by the branches and stones that it hurls along. And as to the lake, I know how that is : father never ventures across it in his boat."

Huldbrand laughed, and got up to see whether she had spoken true ; the old man went with him, and the maiden tripped along playfully · by their side. They found she had told them no worse than the truth and the Knight resigned himself to staying in the island, as it might now be called, till the floods had subsided. As they returned homeward, he whispered in his pretty companion's ear, — "Well, my little Undine! are you angry at my staying?"

"Ah," said she sullenly, "never mind. If I had not bitten you, who knows what might have come out in your story of Bertalda?"

THE MERCHANT AND THE GENIE

(FROM THE ARABIAN NIGHTS.)

THERE was formerly, sire, a merchant, who was possessed of great wealth, in land, merchandise, and ready money. Having one day an affair of great importance to settle at a considerable distance from home, he mounted his horse, and with only a sort of cloak-bag behind him, in which he had put a few biscuits and dates, he began his journey. He arrived without any accident at the place of his destination; and having finished his business, set out on his return.

On the fourth day of his journey, he felt himself so incommoded by the heat of the sun, that he turned out of his road, in order to rest under some trees, by which there was a fountain. He alighted, and tying his horse to a branch of the tree, sat down on the bank to eat some biscuits and dates from his little store. When he had satisfied his hunger, he amused himself with throwing about the stones of the fruit with considerable velocity. When he had finished his frugal repast, he washed his hands, his face, and his feet, and repeated a prayer, like a good Mussulman.

He was still on his knees, when he saw a genie, white with age, and of an enormous stature, advancing toward him, with a scimitar in his hand. As soon as he was close to him, he said in a most terrible tone:

THE MERCHANT AND THE GENIE.

" Get up, that I may kill thee with this scimitar, as thou hast caused the death of my son." He accompanied these words with a dreadful yell. The merchant, alarmed by the horrible figure of this giant, as well as the words he heard, replied in trembling accents : " How can I have slain him? I do not know him, nor have I ever seen him." " Didst thou not," replied the giant, " on thine arrival here, sit down, and take some dates from thy wallet ; and after eating them, didst thou not throw the stones about on all sides ? " " This is all true," replied the merchant ; " I do not deny it." " Well, then," said the other, " I tell thee thou hast killed my son ; for while thou wast throwing about the stones, my son passed by ; one of them struck him in the eye, and caused his death, and thus thou hast slain my son." " Ah, sire, forgive me," cried the merchant. " I have neither forgiveness nor mercy," added the giant ; " and is it not just that he who has inflicted death should suffer it ? " " I grant this ; yet surely I have not done so : and even if I have, I have done so, innocently, and therefore I entreat you to pardon me, and suffer me to live." " No, no," cried the genie, still persisting in his resolution, " I must destroy thee, as thou hast done my son." At these words, he took the merchant in his arms, and having thrown him with his face on the ground, he lifted up his sabre, in order to strike off his head. . . .

When the merchant, sire, perceived that the genie was about to execute his purpose, he cried aloud : " One word more, I entreat you ; have the goodness to grant me a little delay ; give me only one year to go and take leave of my dear wife and children, and I promise to return to this spot, and submit myself entirely to your pleasure." "Take Allah to witness of the promise thou hast made me," said the other. "Again I swear," replied he, "and you may rely on my oath." On this the genie left him near the fountain, and immediately disappeared.

The merchant, on his reaching home, related faithfully all that had happened to him. On hearing the

sad news, his wife uttered the most lamentable groans, tearing her hair and beating her breast; and his children made the house resound with their grief; while the father, overcome by affection, mingled his tears with theirs. The year quickly passed away. The good merchant having settled his affairs, paid his just debts, given alms to the poor, and made provision to the best of his ability for his wife and family, tore himself away amid the most frantic expressions of grief; and mindful of his oath, arrived at the destined spot on the very day he had promised. While he was waiting for the arrival of the genie, there suddenly appeared an old man leading a hind, who, after a respectful salutation, inquired what brought him to that desert place. The merchant satisfied the old man's curiosity, and related his adventure, on which he expressed a wish to witness his interview with the genie. He had scarcely finished his speech when another old man, accompanied with two black dogs, came in sight, and having heard the tale of the merchant, determined also to remain to see the event.

Soon they perceived, toward the plain, a thick vapor or smoke, like a column of dust raised by the wind. This vapor approached them, and then suddenly disappearing, they saw the genie, who, without noticing them, went toward the merchant, with his scimitar in his hand; and taking him by the arm, "Get up," said he, "that I may kill thee, as thou hast slain my son." Both the merchant and the two old men, struck with terror, began to weep and fill the air with their lamentations. When the old man who conducted the hind saw the genie lay hold of the merchant, and about to murder him without mercy, he threw himself at the monster's feet, and, kissing them, said, "Lord Genie, I humbly entreat you to suspend your rage, and hear my history, and that of the hind, which you see; and if you find it more wonderful and surprising than the adventure of this merchant, whose life you wish to take, may I not hope that you will at least grant me one-half part of the blood of this unfortunate man?" After meditating some time, the genie answered, "Well, then, I agree to it."

THE FIRST OLD MAN AND THE HIND

(FROM THE ARABIAN NIGHTS.)

THE hind, whom you, Lord Genie, see here, is my wife. I married her when she was twelve years old, and we lived together thirty years, without having any children. At the end of that time I adopted into my family a son, whom a slave had borne. This act of mine excited against the mother and her child the hatred and jealousy of my wife. She availed herself, during my absence on a journey, of her knowledge of magic, to change the slave and my adopted son into a cow and a calf, and sent them to my farm to be fed and taken care of by the steward.

Immediately, on my return, I inquired after my child and his mother. "Your slave is dead," said she, "and it is now more than two months since I have beheld your son; nor do I know what is become of him." I was sensibly affected at the death of the slave; but as my son had only disappeared, I flattered myself that he would soon be found. Eight months, however, passed, and he did not return; nor could I learn any tidings of him. In order to celebrate the festival of the great Bairam, which was approaching, I ordered my bailiff to bring me the fattest cow I possessed, for a sacrifice. He obeyed my commands. Having bound the cow, I was about to make the sacrifice, when at the

very instant she lowed most sorrowfully, and the tears
even fell from her eyes. This seemed to me so extraordinary, that I could not but feel compassion for her,
and was unable to give the fatal blow. I therefore
ordered her to be taken away, and another brought.

My wife, who was present, seemed very angry at my
compassion, and opposed my order.

I then said to my steward, "Make the sacrifice yourself; the lamentations and tears of the animal have
overcome me."

The steward was less compassionate, and sacrificed
her. On taking off the skin we found hardly anything
but bones, though she appeared very fat. "Take her
away," said I to the steward, truly chagrined, "and if
you have another very fat calf, bring it in her place."
He returned with a remarkably fine calf, who, as soon
as he perceived me, made so great an effort to come to
me, that he broke his cord. He lay down
at my feet, with his head on
the ground, as if he endeavored to excite my compassion,
and to entreat me not to
have the cruelty to take away
his life.

"Wife," answered I, "I
will not sacrifice this calf, I
wish to favor him: do not
you, therefore, oppose it."
She, however, did not agree
to my proposal; and continued to demand his sacrifice
so obstinately, that I was compelled to yield. I bound
the calf, and took the fatal knife to bury it in his

throat, when he turned his eyes, filled with tears, so persuasively upon me, that I had no power to execute my intention. The knife fell from my hand, and I told my wife I was determined to have another calf. She tried every means to induce me to alter my mind; I continued firm, however, in my resolution, in spite of all she could say; promising, for the sake of appeasing her, to sacrifice this calf at the feast of Bairam on the following year.

The next morning my steward desired to speak with me in private. He informed me that his daughter, who had some knowledge of magic, wished to speak with me. On being admitted to my presence, she informed me that, during my absence, my wife had turned the slave and my son into a cow and calf, that I had already sacrificed the cow, but that she could restore my son to life, if I would give him to her for her husband, and allow her to visit my wife with the punishment her cruelty had deserved. To these proposals I gave my consent.

The damsel then took a vessel full of water, and pronouncing over it some words I did not understand, she threw the water over the calf, and he instantly regained his own form.

"My son! my son!" I exclaimed, and embraced him with transport; "this damsel has destroyed the horrible charm with which you were surrounded. I am sure your gratitude will induce you to marry her, as I have already promised for you." He joyfully consented; but before they were united the damsel changed my wife into this hind, which you see here.

Since this, my son has become a widower, and is now

travelling. Many years have passed since I have heard anything of him; I have, therefore, now set out with a view to gain some information; and as I did not like to trust my wife to the care of any one during my search, I thought proper to carry her along with me. This is the history of myself and this hind; can anything be more wonderful? "I agree with you," said the genie, "and in consequence, I grant to you a half of the blood of this merchant."

As soon as the first old man had finished, the second, who led the two black dogs, made the same request to the genie for a half of the merchant's blood, on the condition that his tale exceeded in interest the one that had been just related. On the genie signifying his assent, the old man began.

THE SECOND OLD MAN AND THE TWO BLACK DOGS

(From The Arabian Nights.)

GREAT Prince of the genies, you must know that these two black dogs, which you see here, and myself are three brothers. Our father, when he died, left us one thousand sequins each. With this sum we all embarked in business as merchants. My two brothers determined to travel, that they might trade in foreign parts. They were both unfortunate, and returned at the end of two years in a state of abject poverty, having lost their all. I had in the meanwhile prospered, and I gladly received them, and gave them one thousand sequins each, and again set them up as merchants. My brothers frequently proposed to me that I should make a voyage with them for the purpose of traffic. Knowing their former want of success, I refused to join them, until at the end of five years I at length yielded to their repeated solicitations. On consulting on the merchandise to be bought for the voyage, I discovered that nothing remained of the thousand sequins I had given to each. I did not reproach them; on the contrary, as my capital was increased to six thousand sequins, I gave them each one thousand sequins, and kept a like sum myself, and concealed the other three thousand in a corner of my house, in order that if our voyage proved unsuccessful, we might be able to console our-

selves and begin our former profession.   We purchased
our goods, embarked in a vessel, which we ourselves
freighted, and set sail with a favorable wind.   After
sailing about a month, we arrived, without any accident, at a port, where we landed, and had a most
advantageous sale for our merchandise.   I, in particular, sold mine so well, that I gained ten for one.

About the time that we were ready to embark on our
return, I accidentally met on the seashore a female of
great beauty, but very poorly dressed.   She accosted
me by kissing my hand, and entreated me most earnestly to permit her to be my wife.   I started many
difficulties to such a plan; but at length she said so
much to persuade me that I ought not to regard her
poverty, and that I should be well satisfied with her
conduct, I was quite overcome.   I directly procured
proper dresses for her, and after marrying her in due
form, she embarked with me, and we set sail.

During our voyage, I found my wife possessed of so
many good qualities, that I loved her every day more
and more.   In the mean time my two brothers, who
had not traded so advantageously as myself, and who
were jealous of my prosperity, began to feel exceedingly envious.   They even went so far as to conspire
against my life; for one night, while my wife and I
were asleep, they threw us into the sea.   I had hardly,
however, fallen into the water, before my wife took me
up and transported me into an island.   As soon as it
was day she thus addressed me: " You must know that
I am a fairy, and being upon the shore when you were
about to sail, I wished to try the goodness of your heart,
and for this purpose I presented myself before you

in the disguise you saw. You acted most generously, and I am therefore delighted in finding an occasion of showing my gratitude, and I trust, my husband, that in saving your life, I have not ill rewarded the good you have done me, but I am enraged against your brothers, nor shall I be satisfied till I have taken their lives."

I listened with astonishment to the discourse of the fairy, and thanked her, as well as I was able, for the great obligation she had conferred on me. "But, madam," said I to her, "I must entreat you to pardon my brothers." I related to her what I had done for each of them, but my account only increased her anger. "I must instantly fly after these ungrateful wretches," cried she, "and bring them to a just punishment; I will sink their vessel, and precipitate them to the bottom of the sea." "No, beautiful lady," replied I, "for heaven's sake, moderate your indignation, and do not execute so dreadful an intention; remember they are still my brothers, and that we are bound to return good for evil."

No sooner had I pronounced these words, than I was transported in an instant from the island, where we

were, to the top of my own house. I descended, opened the doors, and dug up the three thousand sequins which I had hidden. I afterward repaired to my shop, opened it, and received the congratulations of the merchants in the neighborhood on my arrival. When I returned home, I perceived these two black dogs, which came toward me with a submissive air. I could not imagine what this meant, but the fairy, who soon appeared, satisfied my curiosity. "My dear husband," said she, "be not surprised at seeing these two dogs in your house; they are your brothers." My blood ran cold on hearing this, and I inquired by what power they had been transformed into that state. "It is I," replied the fairy, "who have done it, and I have sunk their ship; for the loss of the merchandise it contained, I shall recompense you. As to your brothers, I have condemned them to remain under this form for ten years, as a punishment for their perfidy." Then informing me where I might hear of her, she disappeared.

The ten years are now completed, and I am travelling in search of her. This, O Lord Genie, is my history; does it not appear to you of a most extraordinary nature? "Yes," replied the genie, "I confess it is most wonderful, and therefore I grant you the other half of this merchant's blood," and having said this, the genie disappeared, to the great joy of the merchant and of the two old men.

The merchant did not omit to bestow many thanks upon his liberators, who, bidding him adieu, proceeded on their travels. He remounted his horse, and returned home to his wife and children, and spent the remainder of his days with them in tranquillity.

SINDBAD THE SAILOR AND THE ROCS

(FROM THE ARABIAN NIGHTS.)

THAT I might have a ship at my own command, I remained till one was built. When the ship was ready I went on board with my goods; but not having enough to load her, I agreed to take with me several merchants with their merchandise.

We sailed with the first fair wind, and after a long navigation, the first place we touched at was a desert island, where we found the egg of a roc, equal in size to that I formerly mentioned. There was a young roc in it, just ready to be hatched, and its beak had begun to break the egg.

The merchants who landed with me broke the egg with hatchets, and making a hole in it, pulled out the young roc piece-meal, and roasted it. I had in vain entreated them not to meddle with the egg.

Scarcely had they finished their repast, when there appeared in the air, at a considerable distance, two great clouds. The captain of my ship, knowing by experience what they meant, said they were the male and female parents of the roc, and pressed us to re-embark with all speed, to prevent the misfortune which he saw would otherwise befall us.

The two rocs approached with a frightful noise, which they redoubled when they saw the egg broken, and their

young one gone. They flew back in the direction they
had come, and disappeared for some time, while we
made all the sail we could to endeavor to prevent that
which unhappily befell us.

They soon returned, and we observed that each of
them carried between its talons an enormous rock.
When they came directly over my ship, they hovered,
and one of them let go his rock; but by the dexterity
of the steersman it missed us and fell into the sea.
The other so exactly hit the middle of the ship as to
split it into pieces. The mariners and passengers were
all crushed to death or fell into the sea. I myself was
of the number of the latter; but, as I came up again,
I fortunately caught hold of a piece of the wreck, and
swimming, sometimes with one hand and sometimes
with the other, but always holding fast the plank, the
wind and the tide favoring me, I came to an island, and
got safely ashore.

I sat down upon the grass, to recover myself from my
fatigue, after which I went into the island to explore it.
It seemed to be a delicious garden. I found trees everywhere, some of them bearing green and others ripe
fruits, and streams of fresh pure water. I ate the
fruits, which I found excellent; and drank of the water
which was very light and good.

When I was a little advanced into the island, I saw
an old man, who appeared very weak and infirm. He
was sitting on the bank of a stream, and at first I took
him to be one who had been shipwrecked like myself.
I went toward him and saluted him, but he only
slightly bowed his head. I asked him why he sat so
still; but instead of answering me, he made a sign for

me to take him upon my back, and carry him over the brook.

I believed him really to stand in need of my assistance, took him upon my back, and having carried him over, bade him get down, and for that end stooped, that he might get off with ease; but instead of doing so (which I laugh at every time I think of it), the old man, who to me appeared quite decrepit, threw his legs nimbly about my neck. He sat astride upon my shoulders, and held my throat so tight that I thought he would have strangled me, and I fainted away.

Notwithstanding my fainting, the ill-natured old fellow still kept his seat upon my neck. When I had recovered my breath, he thrust one of his feet against my side, and struck me so rudely with the other that he forced me to rise up, against my will. Having arisen, he made me carry him under the trees, and forced me now and then to stop, that he might gather and eat fruit. He never left his seat all day; and when I lay down to rest at night, he laid himself down with me, holding still fast about my neck. Every morning he pinched me to make me awake, and afterward obliged me to get up and walk, and spurred me with his feet.

One day I found several dry calabashes that had fallen from a tree. I took a large one, and after cleaning it, pressed into it some juice of grapes, which abounded in the island; having filled the calabash, I put it by in a convenient place, and going thither again some days after, I tasted it, and found the wine so good, that it gave me new vigor, and so exhilarated my spirits, that I began to sing and dance as I carried my burden.

The old man, perceiving the effect which this had

"WHEN THEY CAME DIRECTLY OVER MY SHIP, THEY HOVERED,
AND ONE OF THEM LET GO HIS ROCK."

upon me, and that I carried him with more ease than before, made me a sign to give him some of it. I handed him the calabash, and the liquor pleasing his palate, he drank it off. There being a considerable quantity of it, he soon began to sing, and to move about from side to side in his seat upon

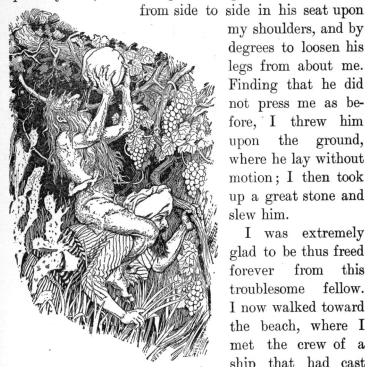

my shoulders, and by degrees to loosen his legs from about me. Finding that he did not press me as before, I threw him upon the ground, where he lay without motion; I then took up a great stone and slew him.

I was extremely glad to be thus freed forever from this troublesome fellow. I now walked toward the beach, where I met the crew of a ship that had cast anchor, to take in water; they were surprised to see me, but more so at hearing the particulars of my adventures. "You fell," said they, "into the hands of the old man of the sea, and are the first who ever escaped strangling by his malicious embraces. He never quitted those he had once made himself master of, till he had destroyed them, and he has made this island notorious by the number of men he has slain." They carried me with them to the captain, who received me with great kindness. He put out again to sea, and after some days' sail, we arrived at the harbor of a great city, the houses of which overhung the sea.

One of the merchants who had taken me into his friendship invited me to go along with him. He gave me a large sack, and having recommended me to some people of the town, who used to gather cocoa-nuts, desired them to take me with them. "Go," said he, "follow them, and act as you see them do; but do not separate from them, otherwise you may endanger your life." Having thus spoken, he gave me provisions for the journey, and I went with them.

We came to a thick forest of cocoa trees, very lofty, with trunks so smooth that it was not possible to climb to the branches that bore the fruit. When we entered the forest we saw a great number of apes of several sizes, who fled as soon as they perceived us, and climbed to the tops of the trees with amazing swift-ness.

The merchants with whom I was, gathered stones and threw them at the apes on the trees. I did the same; and the apes, out of revenge, threw cocoa-nuts at us so fast, and with such gestures, as sufficiently testified their anger and resentment. We gathered up the cocoa-nuts, and from time to time threw stones to provoke the apes; so that by this stratagem we filled our bags with cocoa-nuts. I thus gradually collected as many cocoa-nuts as produced me a considerable sum.

Having laden our vessel with cocoa-nuts, we set sail,

and passed by the islands where pepper grows in great plenty. From thence we went to the Isle of Comari, where the best species of wood of aloes grows. I exchanged my cocoa in those two islands for pepper and wood of aloes, and went with other merchants a-pearl-fishing. I hired divers, who brought me up some that were very large and pure. I embarked in a vessel that happily arrived at Bussorah; from thence I returned to Bagdad, where I realized vast sums from my pepper, wood of aloes, and pearls. I gave the tenth of my gains in alms, as I had done upon my return from my other voyages, and rested from my fatigues.

THE CALIPH TURNED STORK

By WILLIAM HAUFF.

GHASID, the Caliph of Bagdad, leaned
back one sunny afternoon upon the
cushions of his divan, feeling comfortably content with all the world. He
had dozed somewhat, for the day was a
sultry one; and, seemingly, this little nap
had pleasantly refreshed him. Between
the whiffs from a long rosewood pipe, he sipped the
coffee poured out for him at intervals by a slave, ever
and again stroking his beard in sign of relishment.
Clearly the Caliph was in a right good humor. A time
like this was always the best in which to obtain an
audience of him — now, when he was so mild, so
thoroughly amiable. And that was why at this hour
the Grand Vizier Mansor usually paid his daily visit
to the Caliph. On this particular afternoon, too, he
had come to his royal master; contrary to custom,
however, his face wore a gravely thoughtful look.
The Caliph, as he slightly changed the position of the
pipe between his lips, said: "Well, Grand Vizier, how
is it that you are looking so grave to-day?" The
Grand Vizier, crossing both arms over his chest, bowed
low to his lord, as he answered: "I know not, Your
Majesty, whether I look grave or not; but below there,

96

in the courtyard, is a pedlar, whose wares are so temptingly beautiful, that forsooth it vexed me to have no spare money wherewith to buy some of them."

Then the Caliph, who had long been wishful to give his minister a pleasure, sent down a slave to bring the pedlar up into the royal presence. The servant soon came back, accompanied by the pedlar, who was a short, thick-set little man, with a face the color of mahogany, and with clothes that hung in tatters about him. He carried a pack upon his back; in this were divers wares — pearls, rings, richly-mounted pistols, jewelled combs and goblets. Both the Caliph and the Grand Vizier looked through and examined everything, and finally His Majesty bought some handsome pistols for himself and the Vizier, while for the latter's wife he purchased a comb.

As the pedlar was about to shut up his box again, the Caliph noticed in it a little drawer, which led him to ask whether in that, too, there was anything for sale. The pedlar pulled open the drawer, showing a box that contained some dark-colored powder, and a parchment on which was a strange writing that neither the Caliph nor Mansor could decipher. "These two things," he said, "a merchant once gave to me; he found them in Mecca, in the streets there. I know not what may be their worth; but you shall have them both for a small sum, as to me they are useless."

The Caliph, being glad to gain any ancient manuscripts for his library, even though quite unable to read them himself, bought both box and parchment of the pedlar, and then let him go. Yet he was very anxious to learn the meaning of this writing; and he asked the Grand Vizier whether he knew of any one who could make it plain to him.

"My gracious lord and master," answered the latter, "nigh to the great mosque there lives one Selim the Sage by name; all tongues and languages are known to him — let him be brought, for perhaps he can read and explain these mysterious characters to us."

The learned Selim was summoned to the palace without delay.

"Selim," said the Caliph, "Selim, by report you are a very learned man; look now at this old manuscript and see if you can read what is written there. If you are able to understand it, I will present you with a new and costly robe to wear; but if you fail to read it aright, the penalty is twelve boxes on the ear and five-and-twenty stripes upon the soles of your feet, for having thus falsely earned the title of Selim the Sage."

Selim made a low bow to the Caliph, and said: "Let it be done even as thou wilt, my lord." Then for a long time he gazed closely and earnestly at the writing, exclaiming on a sudden, "This is Latin, my Lord, Latin, or may my head suffer for it!"

"Tell us, then, what it means, if it be Latin," was the answer.

So Selim began to translate as follows : " O mortal, that hast found this, give praise to Allah for his merciful kindness unto thee.   Whoever takes a pinch of this powder, and, putting it to his nostrils, exclaims *Mutabor*, the same can change himself at will into any sort of animal, and can also understand the language of every beast.   If desirous to regain human shape, he must turn twice towards the east pronouncing the same word, *Mutabor*.   But have a care lest while thou art transformed a laugh escape thee, for in such case the magic word will vanish utterly from thy memory; and thou wilt be ever doomed to remain a beast ! "

When Selim the Sage had finished reading the writing on the parchment, the Caliph's delight seemed to know no bounds.   He made him swear never to tell others of this secret; and, having presented him with a beautiful garment, he dismissed him from the palace. Then, in a low tone to the Grand Vizier, he said: " That is, in sooth, driving a good bargain, Mansor; I shall not rest until I am changed into a beast.   You must come here at early morning to-morrow, and we will walk out together across the meadows, and give this wonderful powder a trial — this powder that will enable us to hear all that is spoken in the air or in the water, among the woods or in the fields."

Early next day, before ever the Caliph had finished his morning meal, the Grand Vizier arrived at the palace, ready to accompany the monarch in the walk that they had planned to take.   The Caliph put the box of magic powder in his girdle; and, after having dismissed his suite, both he and Mansor started together upon their way.   First they passed through the luxurious gardens and grounds of the palace, making there a vain search for some living beast or bird which should help them to test the success of their experiment. At length the Vizier proposed that they should go on for some distance to a certain pond, where, as he had noticed, animals and birds often came, more especially storks, that by their ludicrous gravity and noisy chatter had frequently led him to watch their habits.

To this the Caliph entirely agreed, so they both walked together towards the pond. On reaching its edge they saw a stork pacing earnestly up and down, hunting for frogs and splashing the water about with its bill. Just at that moment they noticed against the sky another stork, flying towards them.

"I will wager my beard, Your Majesty," said the Grand Vizier, "that these two long-legged fellows will hold a pretty confab together. How would it be, supposing we turned ourselves into storks and listened to what they said?"

"Good; we will do it," answered the Caliph; "but first let us just think about how we are to change ourselves back into human beings again. Oh! I have it! Make a bow three times towards the east and pronounce the magic word *Mutabor*. That will make me Caliph, and you Grand Vizier. But for Heaven's sake do not laugh, else we are utterly done for!" ·

And, as he spoke, the Caliph saw the other stork floating slowly above their heads, preparing to alight at the side of the pond close to where they stood. Quickly drawing the little box from his girdle, he took a pinch and offered one to the Grand Vizier. Then, turning eastwards, they each called out *Mutabor*.

In an instant their legs shrunk into long, lean red sticks; the handsome yellow slippers which they wore changed into clumsy storks' feet; wings quickly took the place of arms; their necks shot out ever so far from their shoulders; and soft, downy feathers grew all over their bodies.

"Well, you've got a nice long beak, Grand Vizier," said the Caliph, on recovering from his amazement; "by the beard of the Prophet, in all my life I never saw the like of it!"

"Your Majesty is very gracious," answered the Grand Vizier, bowing low, "but, if I may dare to state it, as a stork you look even more regal, more fascinating than as a Caliph. However, with your will, let us go and listen to what our comrades over there are saying to each other; we must find out if we can really understand the language or not."

By this time the other stork that was flying towards them had alighted. With its beak it kept pluming and arranging its feathers; then it walked towards its companion. The two newly-made storks hurried after it, and came up in time to overhear the following astonishing conversation:

"Good morning to you, Madame Longshanks; you are out early on the meadow this morning!"

"Good morning, dear Mistress Clatterbill; I am just getting myself a little breakfast. Do you think you could fancy a morsel of this lizard? Or perhaps this dainty frog's leg?"

"Thanks very much; but I really have no appetite to-day. Indeed, my visit to this place is for quite another reason. You see, I shall have to dance to-day before my father's guests, so I have just come here for a little quiet practice beforehand."

And as she spoke, the young stork commenced skipping across the turf in the oddest and most extraordinary manner; the Caliph and Mansor looked on in wonder at her movements. At last, when she began to pirouette gracefully upon one toe, with a quaint wriggle of her body and a flutter of her wings, this was more than they could possibly stand; peals of laughter broke from both of them, and it was long before they were able to stop.

"Well, that *was* a joke," gasped the Caliph, "one that gold could never have bought for us. It's a pity, though, that our laughter has driven away those stupid creatures, else I'm sure they would have sung to us next!"

Then the Grand Vizier suddenly remembered about not laughing, and bethought him of the penalty for doing so as long as they were transformed into animals. Horror-struck, he told the Caliph of his fears.

"Potz Mecca and Medina!" cried the latter, "that *would* be a pleasing thing if I should have to remain as I am now — a stork! Just think a minute, what the stupid word was; I can't for the life of me recollect it!"

"We must turn three times towards the east, saying, as we do so, Mu — Mu — what is it? Mu — "

And, with faces looking eastward, they both bent forward until their beaks almost touched the ground. But, alas! the magical word had utterly escaped their memory! Though they bobbed and nodded and called out incessantly, "Mu — Mu — Mu — Mu — "

neither of them could remember it; the poor Caliph and his Vizier were condemned to remain just what they had chosen to be — storks !

Slowly and sadly the two wandered on across the meadows and fields; their mutual grief and dismay quite kept out any thoughts of remedy for their misfortune. They could not put off their storks' skins; neither could they go back to the city and make themselves known; for who would believe a stork, if it said it were a Caliph? And even if the people did, they would scarcely wish to have a stork as their ruler and king.

So for several days they crept about by themselves in various lonely parts of the neighborhood, making what meals they could off the wild fruit and berries growing thereabouts; yet to eat these was rather difficult, owing to their long, ungainly bills. Lizards and frogs failed to tempt their appetite; such delicacies might, as they feared, not impossibly disagree with them. Their only pleasure while in this sad condition was that they had wings and could fly; thus they often soared away to Bagdad, where from the house-tops they could watch all that was going forward.

In the streets there, at first they noticed a great stir and bustle, and heard from all parts a general sound of mourning. But on the fourth day after their enchantment, while sitting on the roof of the Caliph's palace, they saw a splendid procession going by down below. Drums beat, pipes played, and a man dressed in a crimson mantle edged with gold rode past on a richly caparisoned steed, surrounded by numerous attendants in glittering armor. Half the city

followed in his wake; and all the people joined in the
cry: "Hail Mirza! hail Mirza, the ruler of Bagdad!"
As they heard this, the two storks, sitting up there on
the palace-roof, glanced mutually at each other, and
Ghasid the Caliph said: "Can you not guess now,
Grand Vizier, why I have been thus metamorphosed?
This Mirza is none other than the son of my most
deadly enemy, Kàschnur, the magician, he who once,
in an evil hour, swore to wreak his vengeance upon me.
However, I will not yet relinquish hope. Come now,
faithful companion and sharer of my woe, let us together seek the tomb of Mahomed; it may be that in
so holy a place the wizard's spell will lose its power."

So, quitting the roof of the palace, they flew away in
the direction of Medina. But as yet they were not
overskilful in the use of their wings; flying was not all
as pleasant as it looked.

"Oh! my lord," groaned the Vizier, after an hour
was over, "with your permission I really must stop;
I can't hold out any longer. You fly so dreadfully
fast! And besides, evening has now come on, and it
would surely be as well if we looked about for a night's
lodging."

To this Ghasid consented; and, seeing some old ruins
in the valley below them, they flew thither in search of
shelter. The spot in which they had chosen to pass
the night seemed to be the wreck of some old castle.
Many of its halls were as yet unspoiled by time; here
and there stood some splendid pillar that showed how
beautiful the whole building had once been. Ghasid
and his companion went along several passages and
corridors in search of a place that should be both dry

and warm. Suddenly Mansor stopped short, saying in a hurried whisper :

" Oh ! my lord and master, ghosts ! ghosts ! if it were only not absurd for a Grand Vizier, much more for a stork, to be frightened of such things ! But I feel so terrified and uneasy, for close to me I just now heard the most dreadful groans and sighs ! "

The Caliph stopped to listen, and heard distinctly the sound of low weeping ; it was more like the cries of a human being than of an animal. He was about to hasten towards the spot whence the sound came, but the Vizier, seizing him by the wing with his beak, implored him not to expose himself to fresh misery and danger. But it was no use. The Caliph, beneath whose feathers there beat a brave heart, tore himself free, losing not a few feathers in the effort, and hurried down a dark passage to the left. He soon reached a door, which was apparently only half closed ; and now the sound of weeping grew more and more distinct. With his beak he thrust open the door, but remained standing on the threshold, struck dumb with wonder. In the dismal, broken-down room, where daylight only glimmered faintly through a small iron grating, he saw, seated on the ground, a large owl. Tears fell in abundance from its great round eyes, while with hoarse voice it sent forth a wailing from its hooked beak. But on seeing the Caliph and his Grand Vizier, who meanwhile had crept after him, it gave a loud cry of delight. Brushing the tears away with its brown wings, to their mutual surprise it spoke thus to them in perfectly correct Arabic :

" Welcome, welcome, oh storks ! you are to me a

glad sign of my deliverance; for through you, as prophecy once told me, I shall come by great good fortune."

When the Caliph was somewhat recovered from his

surprise, he bent his long neck and spindle legs in the effort to make a very finished bow to the owl, as he said:

"Oh, my dear owl, from what you tell me, we seem to be companions in misery and in misfortune. Yet your hope is surely a vain one that either of us can do aught towards releasing you from the cruel spell that you are under. You will be convinced of our helplessness when you hear the tale of our woes."

The owl begged him to relate his adventures; and this he accordingly did. When he had finished, thanking him, she said:

"And now you shall listen to my sad story; then you will perceive that my misfortunes are no whit less grievous than are yours. My father is an Indian monarch; and I, his only daughter, am named Lusa. Kaschnur — that wicked magician who bewitched you — was also the cause of my misery. One day he came to my father, asking that my hand should be given in marriage to Mirza, his son. My father, being choleric, gave him no other answer than to throw him headlong down the staircase of the palace. But the wretch disguised himself, and met me one afternoon as I sat in

the garden. I had asked for some cooling drink to be
brought, when he, in the dress of a slave, offered me a
potion, which I had no sooner swallowed than I was
instantly changed into my present horrible shape. I
swooned with terror, and he quickly bore me, while
still unconscious, to this dreadful spot, and with awful
voice he cried in my ear: 'Here, here, art thou doomed
to remain, ugly and hideous in form, and despised even
by the beasts themselves. Here, too, thou shalt both
live and die, unless some one of his own free will shall
seek to make you, while still so loathsome an object, his
bride. In this way I am now revenged upon thy arro-
gant father, the king!'

"Since then many months are gone by, and, lonely
and sad, I have led a hermit's life within these barren
walls, shunned by the world, even to beasts detestable.
Nor can the loveliness of nature yield me solace, for
during the daytime I am blind; it is only when the
pale moonlight falls across these gloomy ruins that the
veil is taken from my eyes, and I can see!"

The owl finished speaking, and once again she
brushed away the rising tears with her wing; at the
recital of her grief she had been forced to weep afresh.

The Caliph, who had listened to her story with great
interest, now fell into deep thought.

"If all does not deceive me," said he, "there is some
hidden link between our mutual misfortunes. The
question is, how shall I find the key to this enigma?"

And the owl replied:

"Oh, my lord, such is my belief also. For in early
youth it was once prophesied to me by a wise woman,
that a stork should bring me great joy and good for-

tune. I have thought, too, of a plan by which we might perhaps save ourselves."

This greatly surprised the Caliph. He asked her in what way she hoped to do this.

"The magician," answered she, "who has wrought our mutual misery is wont to visit this ruined castle once in every month. Not far from where we are there is a hall, and in this he holds revel with a number of his boon companions. Many a time have I listened in secret to all that goes on there. It is there that they recount to each other the many villainous deeds that they have done ; perhaps if you play eavesdropper this time you may hear mention of the magic word that you have both forgotten."

"Oh! beloved princess," cried the Caliph, "say only when, at what time this wretch will come; tell me, too, how I may reach the hall that he visits!"

For a moment the owl paused. Then, speaking low, she said : "Do not take it amiss, but it is only upon one condition that I can grant your wish."

"Say on! say on! What is it?" exclaimed Ghasid. "Only command me, and your bidding shall be done!"

"Well, it is that I, too, would gladly be set free ; yet this can only be brought about, if one of you offers me his hand in marriage!"

At this the storks both of them winced somewhat. The Caliph motioned his Vizier to come with him outside in the corridor for a short time.

"Grand Vizier," said he, as they stood before the door, "this is an awkward business, you know; but I think you might manage to marry her all right, eh?"

"Might I indeed!" rejoined the other, "so that

when I got back home my wife would scratch my eyes
out for me? Besides, I am an oldish man; you, again,
are young and unmarried; you are far more in a position to make a beautiful princess your bride."

"That is just the question," sighed the Caliph, as his
wings unconsciously drooped. "Who is to say whether
she *is* young and beautiful, or not? I call it a complete case of buying a pig in a poke!"

They talked long and earnestly upon this point,
until, as the Caliph saw that, rather than marry the
owl, his Vizier preferred to remain a stork, he decided
to do the thing himself. On hearing of his resolve,
the owl was overjoyed. She confessed that they could
not have come at a more seasonable time; in all probability the magicians would reach the castle that very
same night.

Then she led the way along dark and gloomy corridors, until at length a bright light shone upon them
through the
chinks of a half
b r o k e n - d o w n
wall. As they
came up to it,
the owl coun-
selled them to
keep perfectly
still. A gap in
the wall gave
them a full view

of a large hall, beautifully decorated, with pillars at
the sides, and lit up by the blaze of many-colored
lamps. In its centre stood a round table, on which

were spread many choice viands, as though for a great feast. On a long sofa encircling this table eight men were seated. One of these the Caliph instantly recognized as the pedlar of whom he had bought the magic powder. After awhile this man was asked to relate his adventures to the company. Among other things he told them how he had tricked the Caliph and his Vizier.

"What word was it, then, that you gave them?" asked one of the crew.

"'Twas a very hard Latin one — *Mutabor!*"

As the storks, listening breathlessly in their hiding-place, heard this, they were well-nigh crazy with de-

light. Down the corridor they rushed, back to the entrance of the ruins, just as fast as their long legs would carry them; the poor owl could scarcely keep pace with them. Then the Caliph, addressing her, said in moving accents: "Oh, fair one, who has saved both my life and that of my friend, take me now as thy lord and husband, in pledge of our eternal gratitude." With this he turned towards the east. Three times the storks bent their gaunt necks before the sun, just as it rose above the blue hills that edged the horizon; " *Mutabor!*

Mutabor !" was the word that both shouted; in a trice they were transformed; and both master and servant, in the ecstasy of their joy, fell, half laughing, half weeping, into each other's arms. Picture, however, their astonishment as they looked round for their companion! Before them stood a maiden of peerless beauty, clad in the most costly and brilliant apparel, who laughingly gave her hand to the Caliph, as she said, " Methinks you can hardly recognize your friend the owl!"

Yet she it was; and the Caliph was so enchanted with her grace and loveliness that he vehemently declared his transformation into a stork to have been the greatest piece of good fortune that could possibly have been his.

The three then set forth to go to Bagdad. In the pockets of his clothes the Caliph found not only the identical box with the magic powder in it, but his purse of gold as well; so that at the first village they came to he was able to purchase various necessaries for the journey. In due time Bagdad was reached. As they passed through the gates of the city, the Caliph's reappearance caused general wonder among both high and low. He was dead, so every one had believed; and the people were overjoyed at having their beloved monarch back once more in their midst, alive and in health.

In proportion, however, to their delight was now their bitter hatred against Mirza, that infamous liar and impostor. In a body they rushed to the palace, and, seizing the old magician and his son, they took them both prisoners. Kaschnur was condemned, by order of the Caliph, to be hanged in the ruined castle,

in the self-same room where the owl had been impris-
oned.   Mirza, his son, had the choice given to him of
death or of a pinch of the magic powder.   He preferred the latter alternative ; and the Caliph at once
politely offered him the snuff-box.   By this means he
was speedily transformed into a stork, which the Caliph
commanded to be kept in an iron cage and confined in
a part of his palace gardens.

Many and happy were the years that the Caliph
now lived through with his charming bride.   The
pleasantest times were when the Vizier used to pay his
regular afternoon visit.   Then the talk was always of
the days when " they were storks together " ; and sometimes, if the Caliph got sufficiently merry over the
subject, he put dignity aside and gave imitations of the
Grand Vizier as he appeared in the disguise of a stork.
This he did by gravely striding up and down the room,
keeping his legs as straight and as stiff as possible,
chattering, meanwhile, as if with an imaginary beak,
and flapping his arms about as though they were wings.

But it was most delightful to his wife and children
when he went on to mimic the Vizier, turning his face
eastwards and vainly calling out, " Mu — Mu — Mu —
Mu — ! " as he tried to recollect the magic word.   Occasionally, however, when he grew a little too boister-
ous over the matter, the Vizier was wont to threaten
that he would tell her royal highness of the little understanding that had been come to outside the apartment
of Mademoiselle the Owl !

PRINCE PRIGIO

By ANDREW LANG.

CHAPTER I.

HOW THE FAIRIES WERE NOT INVITED TO COURT.

NCE upon a time there reigned in Pantouflia a king and a queen. With almost everything else to make them happy, they wanted one thing: they had no children. This vexed the king even more than the queen, who was very clever and learned, and who had hated dolls when she was a child. However, she, too in spite of all the books she read and all the pictures she painted, would have been glad enough to be the mother of a little prince. The king was anxious to consult the fairies, but the queen would not hear of such a thing. She did not believe in fairies: she said that they had never existed; and that she maintained, though *The History of the Royal Family* was full of chapters about nothing else.

Well, at long and at last they had a little boy, who was generally regarded as the finest baby that had ever been seen. Even her majesty herself remarked that, though she could never believe all the courtiers told her, yet he certainly was a fine child — a very fine child.

Now, the time drew near for the christening party, and the king and queen were sitting at breakfast in their summer parlor talking over it. It was a splendid room, hung with portraits of the royal ancestors. There was Cinderella, the grandmother of the reigning monarch, with her little foot in her glass slipper thrust out before her. There was the Marquis de Carabas, who, as everyone knows, was raised to the throne as prince consort after his marriage with the daughter of the king of the period. On the arm of the throne was seated his celebrated cat, wearing boots. There, too, was a portrait of a beautiful lady, sound asleep: this was Madame La Belle au Bois-dormant, also an ancestress of the royal family. Many other pictures of celebrated persons were hanging on the walls.

"You have asked all the right people, my dear?" said the king.

"Everyone who should be asked," answered the queen.

"People are so touchy on these occasions," said his majesty. "You have not forgotten any of our aunts?"

"No; the old cats!" replied the queen; for the king's aunts were old-fashioned, and did not approve of her, and she knew it.

"They are very kind old ladies in their way," said the king; "and were nice to me when I was a boy."

Then he waited a little, and remarked:

"The fairies, of course, you have invited? It has always been usual, in our family, on an occasion like this; and I think we have neglected them a little of late."

"How *can* you be so *absurd?*" cried the queen. "How often must I tell you that there are *no* fairies? And even if there were — but, no matter; pray let us drop the subject."

"They are very old friends of our family, my dear, that's all," said the king timidly. "Often and often they have been godmothers to us. One, in particular, was most kind and most serviceable to Cinderella I., my own grandmother."

"Your grandmother!" interrupted her majesty. "Fiddle-de-dee! If anyone puts such nonsense into the head of my little Prigio——"

But here the baby was brought in by the nurse, and the queen almost devoured it with kisses. And so the fairies were not invited! It was an extraordinary thing, but none of the nobles could come to the christening party when they learned that the fairies had not been asked. Some were abroad; several were ill; a few were in prison among the Saracens; others were captives in the dens of ogres. The end of it was that the king and queen had to sit down alone, one at each end of a very long table, arrayed with plates and glasses for a hundred guests — for a hundred guests who never came!

"Any soup, my dear?" shouted the king, through a speaking-trumpet; when, suddenly, the air was filled with a sound like the rustling of the wings of birds.

Flitter, flitter, flutter, went the noise; and when the queen looked up, lo and behold! on every seat was a lovely fairy, dressed in green, each with a *most interest-*

ing-looking parcel in her hand. Don't you like opening parcels? The king did, and he was most friendly and polite to the fairies. But the queen, though she saw them distinctly, took no notice of them. You see, she did not believe in fairies, nor in her own eyes, when she saw them. So she talked across the fairies to the king, just as if they had not been there; but the king behaved as politely as if they were *real* — which, of course, they were.

When dinner was over, and when the nurse had brought in the baby, all the fairies gave him the most magnificent presents. One offered a purse which could never be empty; and one a pair of seven-leagued boots; and another a cap of darkness, that nobody might see the prince when he put it on; and another a wishing-cap; and another a carpet, on which, when he sat, he was carried wherever he wished to find himself. Another made him beautiful for ever; and another, brave; and another, lucky: but the last fairy of all, a cross old thing, crept up and said, " My child, you shall be *too* clever! "

This fairy's gift would have pleased the queen, if she had believed in it, more than anything else, because she was so clever herself. But she took no notice at all; and the fairies went each to her own country, and none of them stayed there at the palace, where nobody believed in them, except the king, a little. But the queen tossed all their nice boots and caps, carpets, purses, swords, and all, away into a dark lumber-room; for, of course, she thought that they were *all nonsense*, and merely old rubbish out of books, or pantomime " properties."

CHAPTER II.

PRINCE PRIGIO AND HIS FAMILY.

WELL, the little Prince grew up. I think
I've told you that his name was Prigio —
did I not? Well, that *was* his name.
You cannot think how clever he was. He
argued with his nurse as soon as he could
speak, which was very soon. He argued
that he did not like to be washed, because
the soap got into his eyes. However, when he was told
all about the *pores of the skin,* and how
they could not be healthy if he was not
washed, he at once ceased to
resist, for he was very reasonable. He argued with
his father that he did not
see why there should be
kings who were rich, while
beggars were poor ; and why
the king — who was a little
greedy — should have
poached eggs and plum-
cake at afternoon tea, while

many other persons went without dinner. The king
was so surprised and hurt at these remarks that he
boxed the prince's ears, saying, " I'll teach you to be

too clever, my lad." Then he remembered the awful
curse of the oldest fairy, and was sorry for the rudeness
of the queen. And when the prince, after having his
ears boxed, said that "force was no argument," the
king went away in a rage.

Indeed, I cannot tell you how the prince was hated
by all! He would go down into the kitchen, and show
the cook how to make soup. He would visit the poor
people's cottage, and teach them how to make the beds,
and how to make plum-pudding out of turnip-tops, and
venison cutlets out of rusty bacon. He showed the
fencing-master how to fence, and the professional
cricketer how to bowl, and instructed the rat-catcher
in breeding terriers. He set sums to the Chancellor of
the Exchequer, and assured the Astronomer Royal that
the sun does not go round the earth — which, for my
part, I believe it does. The young ladies of the Court
disliked dancing with him, in spite of his good looks,
because he was always asking, " Have you read this?"
and "Have you read that?"— and when they said they
hadn't, he sneered; and when they said they *had*, he
found them out.

He found out all his tutors and masters in the same
horrid way; correcting the accent of his French teacher,
and trying to get his German tutor not to eat peas with
his knife. He also endeavored to teach the queen-
dowager, his grandmother, an art with which she had
long been perfectly familiar! In fact, he knew everything better than anybody else; and the worst of it was
that he *did*: and he was never in the wrong, and he
always said, "Didn't I tell you so?" And, what was
more, he *had!*

As time went on, Prince Prigio had two younger
brothers, whom everybody liked. They were not a
bit clever, but jolly. Prince Alphonso, the third son,
was round, fat, good-humored, and as brave as a lion.
Prince Enrico, the second, was tall, thin, and a little
sad, but *never* too clever. Both were in love with two
of their own cousins (with the approval of their dear
parents); and all the world said, "What nice, unaffected princes they are!" But Prigio nearly got the
country into several wars by being too clever for the
foreign ambassadors. Now, as Pantouflia was a rich,
lazy country, which hated fighting, this was very
unpleasant, and did not make people love Prince
Prigio any better.

CHAPTER III.

ABOUT THE FIREDRAKE.

F all the people who did not like Prigio, his own dear papa, King Grognio, disliked him most. For the king knew he was not clever, himself. When he was in the counting-house, counting out his money, and when he happened to say, " Sixteen shillings and fourteen and twopence are three pounds, fifteen," it made him wild to hear Prigio whisper, " One pound, ten and twopence " — which, of course, it *is*. And the king was afraid that Prigio would conspire, and get made king himself — which was the last thing Prigio really wanted. He much preferred to idle about, and know everything without seeming to take any trouble.

Well, the king thought and thought. How was he to get Prigio out of the way, and make Enrico or Alphonso his successor? He read in books about it; and all the books showed that, if a king sent his three sons to do anything, it was always the youngest who did it, and got the crown. And he wished he had the chance. Well, it arrived at last.

There was a very hot summer! It began to be hot in March. All the rivers were dried up. The grass did not grow. The corn did not grow. The thermometers exploded with heat. The barometers stood at

SET FAIR. The people were much distressed, and came and broke the palace windows — as they usually do when things go wrong in Pantouflia.

The king consulted the learned men about the Court, who told him that probably a

FIREDRAKE

was in the neighborhood.

Now, the Firedrake is a beast, or bird, about the bigness of an elephant. Its body is made of iron, and it is always red-hot. A more terrible and cruel beast cannot be imagined; for, if you go near it, you are at once broiled by the Firedrake.

But the king was not ill-pleased: "for," thought he, " of course my three sons must go after the brute, the eldest first; and, as usual, it will kill the first two, and be beaten by the youngest. It is a little hard on Enrico, poor boy; but *anything* to get rid of that Prigio!"

Then the king went to Prigio, and said that his country was in danger, and that he was determined to leave the crown to whichever of them would bring him the horns (for it has horns) and tail of the Fire-drake.

"It is an awkward brute to tackle," the king said, "but you are the oldest, my lad; go where glory waits you! Put on your armor, and be off with you!"

This the king said, hoping that either the Firedrake would roast Prince Prigio alive (which he could easily do, as I have said; for he is all over as hot as a red-hot poker), or that, if the prince succeeded, at least his country would be freed from the monster.

But the prince, who was lying on the sofa doing sums in compound division for fun, said in the politest way:

"Thanks to the education your majesty has given me, I have learned that the Firedrake, like the siren, the fairy, and so forth, is a fabulous animal which does not exist. But even granting, for the sake of argument, that there is a Firedrake, your majesty is well aware that there is no kind of use in sending *me*. It is always the eldest son who goes out first and comes to grief on these occasions, and it is always the third son that succeeds. Send Alphonso" (this was the youngest brother), "and *he* will do the trick at once. At least, if he fails, it will be most unusual, and Enrico can try his luck."

Then he went back to his arithmetic and his slate, and the king had to send for Prince Alphonso and Prince Enrico. They both came in very warm; for they had been whipping tops, and the day was unusually hot.

" Look here," said the king, " just you two younger ones look at Prigio! You see how hot it is, and how coolly he takes it, and the country suffering; and all on account of a Firedrake, you know, which has apparently built his nest not far off. Well, I have asked that lout of a brother of yours to kill it, and he says —— "

" That he does not believe in Firedrakes," interrupted Prigio. " The weather's warm enough without going out hunting!"

" Not believe in Firedrakes!" cried Alphonso. " I wonder what you *do* believe in! Just let me get at the creature!" for he was as brave as a lion. " Hi! Page, my chain-armor, helmet, lance, and buckler! *A Molinda! A Molinda!*" which was his *war-cry*.

The page ran to get the armor; but it was *so uncommonly hot* that he dropped it, and put his fingers in his mouth, crying!

" You had better put on flannels, Alphonso, for this kind of work," said Prigio. " And if I were you, I'd take a light garden-engine, full of water, to squirt at the enemy."

" Happy thought!" said Alphonso. " I will!" And off he went, kissed his dear Molinda, bade her keep a lot of dances for him (there was to be a dance when he had killed the Firedrake), and then he rushed to the field!

But he never came back any more!

Everyone wept bitterly — everyone but Prince Prigio; for he thought it was a practical joke, and said that

Alphonso had taken the opportunity to start off on his travels and see the world.

"There is some dreadful mistake, sir," said Prigio to the king. "You know as well as I do that the youngest son has always succeeded, up to now. But I entertain great hopes of Enrico!"

And he grinned; for he fancied it was all *nonsense,* and that there were no Firedrakes.

Enrico was present when Prigio was consoling the king in this unfeeling way.

"Enrico, my boy," said his majesty, "the task awaits you, and the honor. When *you* come back with the horns and tail of the Firedrake, you shall be crown prince; and Prigio shall be made an usher at the Grammar School — it is all he is fit for."

Enrico was not quite so confident as Alphonso had been. He insisted on making his will; and he wrote a poem about the pleasures and advantages of dying young. This is part of it:

> The violet is a blossom sweet,
>   That droops before the day is done —
> Slain by thine overpowering heat,
>   O Sun!
>
> And I, like that sweet purple flower,
>   May roast, or boil, or broil, or bake,
> If burned by thy terrific power,
>   Firedrake!

This poem comforted Enrico more or less, and he showed it to Prigio. But the prince only laughed, and said that the second line of the last verse was not very good; for violets do not "roast, or boil, or broil, or bake."

Enrico tried to improve it, but could not. So he read it to his cousin, Lady Kathleena, just as it was; and she cried over it (though I don't think she understood it); and Enrico cried a little, too.

However, next day he started, with a spear, a patent refrigerator, and a lot of the bottles people throw at fires to put them out.

But *he* never came back again!

After shedding torrents of tears, the king summoned Prince Prigio to his presence.

"Dastard!" he said. "Poltroon! *your* turn, which should have come first, has arrived at last. *You* must fetch me the horns and the tail of the Firedrake. Probably you will be grilled, thank goodness; but who will give me back Enrico and Alphonso?"

"Indeed, your majesty," said Prigio, "you must permit me to correct your policy. Your only reason for despatching your sons in pursuit of this dangerous but I believe *fabulous* animal, was to ascertain which of us would most worthily succeed to your throne, at the date — long may it be deferred!— of your lamented decease. Now, there can be no further question about the matter. I, unworthy as I am, represent the sole hope of the royal family. Therefore to send me after the Firedrake were [1] both dangerous and unnecessary. Dangerous, because, if he treats me as you say he did my brothers — my unhappy brothers, — the throne of Pantouflia will want an heir. But, if I do come back alive — why, I cannot be more the true heir than I am at present; now *can* I? Ask the Lord Chief Justice, if you don't believe *me*."

----

[1] Subjunctive mood! He was a great grammarian!

These arguments were so clearly and undeniably correct that the king, unable to answer them, withdrew into a solitary place where he could express himself with freedom, and give rein to his passions.

CHAPTER IV.

HOW PRINCE PRIGIO WAS DESERTED BY EVERYBODY.

MEANWHILE, Prince Prigio had to suffer many unpleasant things. Though he was the crown prince (and though his arguments were unanswerable), everybody shunned him for a coward. The queen, who did not believe in Firedrakes, alone took his side. He was not only avoided by all, but he had most disagreeable scenes with his own cousins, Lady Molinda and Lady Kathleena. In the garden Lady Molinda met him walking alone, and did not bow to him.

" Dear Molly," said the prince, who liked her, " how have I been so unfortunate as to offend you?"

" My name, sir, is Lady Molinda," she said, very proudly; " and you have sent your own brother to his grave!"

" Oh, excuse me," said the prince, " I am certain he has merely gone off on his travels. He'll come back when he's tired: there *are* no Firedrakes; a French writer says they are 'purement fabuleux,' purely fabulous, you know."

" Prince Alphonso has gone on his travels, and will come back when he is tired! And was he then — tired

—of *me?*" cried poor Molinda, bursting into tears, and forgetting her dignity.

"Oh! I beg your pardon, I never noticed; I'm sure I am very sorry," cried the prince, who, never having been in love himself, never thought of other people. And he tried to take Molinda's hand, but she snatched it from him and ran away through the garden to the palace, leaving Prince Prigio to feel foolish, for once, and ashamed.

As for Lady Kathleena, she swept past him like a queen, without a word. So the prince, for all his cleverness, was not happy.

After several days had gone by, the king returned from the solitary place where he had been speaking his mind. He now felt calmer and better; and so at last he came back to the palace. But on seeing Prince Prigio, who was lolling in a hammock, translating Egyptian hieroglyphs into French poetry for his mother, the king broke out afresh, and made use of the most cruel and impolite expressions.

At last, he gave orders that all the Court should pack up and move to a distant city; and that Prince Prigio should be left alone in the palace by himself. For he was quite unendurable, the king said, and he could not trust his own temper when he thought of him. And he grew so fierce, that even the queen was afraid of him now.

The poor queen cried a good deal; Prigio being her favorite son, on account of his acknowledged ability and talent. But the rest of the courtiers were delighted at leaving Prince Prigio behind. For his part, he, very good-naturedly, showed them the best and shortest road to Falkenstein, the city where they were going; and easily proved that neither the chief secretary for geography, nor the general of the army, knew anything about the matter — which, indeed, they did not.

The ungrateful courtiers left Prigio with hoots and yells, for they disliked him so much that they forgot he would be king one day. He therefore reminded them of this little fact in future history, which made them feel uncomfortable enough, and then lay down in his hammock and went to sleep.

When he wakened, the air was cold and the day was beginning to grow dark. Prince Prigio thought he would go down and dine at a tavern in the town, for no servants had been left with him. But what was his annoyance when he found that his boots, his sword, his cap, his cloak — all his clothes, in fact, except those he wore, — had been taken away by the courtiers, merely to spite him! His wardrobe had been ransacked, and everything that had not been carried off had been cut up, burned, and destroyed. Never was such a spectacle of wicked mischief. It was as if hay had been made of everything he possessed. What was worse, he had not a penny in his pocket to buy new things; and his father had stopped his allowance of fifty thousand pounds a month.

Can you imagine anything more cruel and *unjust* than this conduct? for it was not the prince's fault that he was so clever. The cruel fairy had made him so. But, even if the prince had been born clever (as may have happened to you), was he to be blamed for that? The other people were just as much in fault for being born so stupid; but the world, my dear children, can never be induced to remember this. If you are clever, you will find it best not to let people know it — if you want them to like you.

Well, here was the prince in a pretty plight. Not a pound in his pocket, not a pair of boots to wear, not even a cap to cover his head from the rain ; nothing but cold meat to eat, and never a servant to answer the bell.

CHAPTER V.

WHAT PRINCE PRIGIO FOUND IN THE GARRET.

THE prince walked from room to room of the palace; but, unless he wrapped himself up in a curtain, there was nothing for him to wear when he went out in the rain. At last he climbed up a turret-stair in the very oldest part of the castle, where he had never been before; and at the very top was a little round room, a kind of garret. The prince pushed in the door with some difficulty — not that it was locked, but the handle was rusty, and the wood had swollen with the damp. The room was very dark; only the last gray light of the rainy evening came through a slit of a window, one of those narrow windows that they used to fire arrows out of in old times.

But in the dusk the prince saw a heap of all sorts of things lying on the floor and on the table. There were two caps; he put one on — an old, gray, ugly cap it was, made of felt. There was a pair of boots; and he kicked off his slippers, and got into *them*. They were a good deal worn, but fitted as if they had been made for him. On the table was a purse with just three gold coins — old ones, too — in it; and this, as you may fancy, the prince was very well pleased to put in his pocket. A sword, with a sword-belt, he buckled about his waist; and the rest of the articles, a regular collection of odds and ends, he left just where they were lying.   Then he ran downstairs, and walked out of the hall door.

CHAPTER VI.

WHAT HAPPENED TO PRINCE PRIGIO IN TOWN.

B Y this time the prince was very hungry. The town was just three miles off; but he had such a royal appetite, that he did not like to waste it on bad cookery, and the people of the royal town were bad cooks.

"I wish I were in 'The Bear,' at Gluckstein," said he to himself; for he remembered that there was a very good cook there. But, then, the town was twenty-one leagues away — sixty-three long miles!

No sooner had the prince said this, and taken just three steps, than he found himself at the door of the "Bear Inn" at Gluckstein!

"This is the most extraordinary dream," said he to himself; for he was far too clever, of course, to believe in seven-league boots. Yet he had a pair on at that very moment, and it was they which had carried him in three strides from the palace to Gluckstein!

The truth is, that the prince, in looking about the palace for clothes, had found his way into that very old lumber-room where the magical gifts of the fairies had been thrown by his clever mother, who did not believe in them. But this, of course, the prince did not know.

Now you should be told that seven-league boots only

take those prodigious steps when you say you *want* to go a long distance. Otherwise they would be very inconvenient — when you only want to cross the room, for example. Perhaps this has not been explained to you by your governess?

Well, the prince walked into " The Bear," and it seemed odd to him that nobody took any notice of him. And yet his face was as well known as that of any

man in Pantouflia; for everybody had seen it, at least in pictures. He was so puzzled by not being attended to as usual, that *he quite forgot to take off his cap.* He sat down at a table, however, and shouted " *Kellner !* " at which all the waiters jumped, and looked round in every direction, but nobody came to him. At first he thought they were too busy, but presently another explanation occurred to him.

" The king," he said to himself, " has threatened to execute anybody who speaks to me, or helps me in any way. Well, I don't mean to starve in the midst of plenty, anyhow; here goes! "

The prince rose, and went to the table in the midst of the room, where a huge roast turkey had just been placed. He helped himself to half the breast, some sausages, chestnut stuffing, bread sauce, potatoes, and a bottle of red wine — Burgundy. He then went back to a table in a corner, where he dined very well, nobody taking any notice of him. When he had finished, he sat watching the other people dining, and smoking his cigarette. As he was sitting thus, a very tall man, an officer in the uniform of the Guards, came in, and, walking straight to the prince's table, said: "Kellner, clean this table, and bring in the bill of fare."

With these words, the officer sat down suddenly in the prince's lap, as if he did not see him at all. He was a heavy man, and the prince, enraged at the insult, pushed him away and jumped to his feet. As he did so, *his cap dropped off*. The officer fell on his knees at once, crying:

"Pardon, my prince, pardon! I never saw you!"

This was more than the prince could be expected to believe.

"Nonsense! Count Frederick von Matterhorn," he said; "you must be intoxicated. Sir! you have insulted your prince and your superior officer. Consider yourself under arrest! You shall be sent to a prison to-morrow."

On this, the poor officer appealed piteously to everybody in the tavern. They all declared that they had not seen the prince, nor even had an idea that he was doing them the honor of being in the neighborhood of their town.

More and more offended, and convinced that there was a conspiracy to annoy and insult him, the prince shouted for the landlord, called for his bill, threw down his three pieces of gold without asking for change, and went into the street.

"It is a disgraceful conspiracy," he said. "The king shall answer for this! I shall write to the newspapers at once!"

He was not put in a better temper by the way in which people hustled him in the street. They ran against him exactly as if they did not see him, and then staggered back in the greatest surprise, looking in every direction for the person they had jostled. In one of these encounters, the prince pushed so hard against a poor old beggar woman that she fell down. As he was usually most kind and polite, he pulled off his cap to beg her pardon, when, behold, the beggar woman gave one dreadful scream, and fainted! A crowd was collecting, and the prince, forgetting that he had thrown down all his money in the tavern, pulled out his purse. Then he remembered what he had done, and expected to find it empty; but, lo, there were three pieces of gold in it! Overcome with surprise, he thrust the money into the woman's hand, and put on his cap again. In a moment the crowd, which had been staring at him, rushed away in every direction, with cries of terror, declaring that there was a magician in the town, and a fellow who could appear and disappear at pleasure!

By this time, you or I, or anyone who was not so extremely clever as Prince Prigio, would have understood what was the matter. He had put on, without knowing it, not only the seven-league boots, but the cap of darkness, and had taken Fortunatus's purse, which could never be empty, however often you took all the money out. All those and many other delightful wares the fairies had given him at his christening, and the prince had found them in the dark garret. But the prince was so extremely wise, and learned, and scientific, that he did not believe in fairies, nor in fairy gifts.

"It is indigestion," he said to himself: "those sausages were not of the best; and that Burgundy was extremely strong. Things are not as they appear."

Here, as he was arguing with himself, he was nearly run over by a splendid carriage and six, the driver of which never took the slightest notice of him. Annoyed at this, the prince leaped up behind, threw down the two footmen, who made no resistance, and so was carried to the door of a magnificent palace. He was determined to challenge the gentleman who was in the carriage; but, noticing that he had a very beautiful young lady with him, whom he had never seen before, he followed them into the house, not wishing to alarm the girl, and meaning to speak to the gentleman when he found him alone.

A great ball was going on; but, as usual, nobody took any notice of the prince. He walked among the guests, being careful not to jostle them, and listening to their conversation.

It was all about himself! Everyone had heard of his disgrace, and almost every one cried "Serve him right!" They said that the airs he gave himself were quite unendurable — that nothing was more rude than to be always in the right — that cleverness might be carried far too far — that it was better even to be born stupid ("Like the rest of you," thought the prince); and, in fact, nobody had a good word for him.

Yes, one had! It was the pretty lady of the carriage. I never could tell you how pretty she was. She was tall, with cheeks like white roses blushing: she had dark hair, and very large dark-gray eyes, and her face was the kindest in the world! The prince first thought how nice and good she looked, even before he thought how pretty she looked. *She* stood up for Prince Prigio when her partner would speak ill of him. She had never seen the prince, for she was but newly come to Pantouflia ; but she declared that it was his *misfortune*, not his fault, to be so clever. "And, then, think how hard they made him work at school! Besides," said this kind young lady, " I hear he is extremely handsome, and very brave ; and he has a good heart, for he was kind, I have heard, to a poor boy, and did all his examination papers for him, so that the boy passed first in *everything*. And now he is Minister for Education, though he can't do a line of Greek prose ! "

The prince blushed at this, for he knew his conduct had not been honorable. But he at once fell over head and ears in love with the young lady, a thing he had never done in his life before, because — he said — " Women were so stupid ! " You see he was so clever!

Now, at this very moment — when the prince, all of a sudden, was as deep in love as if he had been the stupidest officer in the room — an extraordinary thing happened ! Something seemed to give a whirr ! in his brain, and in one instant *he knew all about it !* He believed in fairies and fairy gifts, and understood that his cap was the cap of darkness, and his shoes the seven-league boots, and his purse the purse of Fortunatus ! He had read about those things in historical books : but now he believed in them.

CHAPTER VII.

THE PRINCE FALLS IN LOVE.

HE understood all this, and burst out laughing, which nearly frightened an old lady near him out of her wits. Ah! how he wished he was only in evening dress, that he might dance with the charming young lady. But there he was, dressed just as if he were going out to hunt, if any one could have seen him. So, even if he took off his cap of darkness, and became visible, he was no figure for a ball. Once he would not have cared, but now he cared very much indeed.

But the prince was not clever for nothing. He thought for a moment, then went out of the room, and, in three steps of the seven-league boots, was at his empty, dark, cold palace again. He struck a light with a flint and steel, lit a torch, and ran upstairs to the garret. The flaring light of the torch fell on the pile of " rubbish," as the queen would have called it, which he turned over with eager hands. Was there — yes, there *was* another cap! There it lay, a handsome green one with a red feather. The prince pulled off the cap of darkness, put on the other, and said:

"*I wish I were dressed in my best suit of white and gold, with the royal Pantouflia diamonds!*"

In one moment there he was in white and gold, the greatest and most magnificent dandy in the whole world, and the handsomest man!

"How about my boots, I wonder," said the prince; for his seven-league boots were stout riding-boots, not good to dance in, whereas *now* he was in elegant shoes of silk and gold.

He threw down the wishing cap, put on the other — the cap of darkness — and made three strides in the direction of Gluckstein. But he was only three steps nearer it than he had been, and the seven-league boots were standing beside him on the floor!

"No," said the prince; "no man can be in two different pairs of boots at one and the same time! That's mathematics!"

He then hunted about in the lumber-room again till he found a small, shabby, old Persian carpet, the size of a hearthrug. He went to his own room, took a portmanteau in his hand, sat down on the carpet, and said:

"I wish I were in Gluckstein."

In a moment there he found himself; for this was that famous carpet which Prince Hussein bought long ago, in the market at Bisnagar, and which the fairies had brought, with the other presents, to the christening of Prince Prigio.

When he arrived at the house where the ball was going on, he put the magical carpet in the portmanteau, and left it in the cloak-room, receiving a numbered ticket in exchange. Then he marched in all his glory (and, of course, without the cap of darkness) into the room where they were dancing. Everybody made place for him, bowing down to the ground, and the loyal band struck up " The Prince's March!"

> Heaven bless our Prince Prigio!
> What is there he doesn't know?
> Greek, Swiss, German (High and Low),
> And the names of the mountains in Mexico,
> Heaven bless the prince!

He used to be very fond of this march, and the words — some people even said he had made them himself. But now, somehow, he didn't much like it. He went straight to the Duke of Stumpfelbahn, the Hereditary Master of the Ceremonies, and asked to be introduced to the beautiful young lady. She was the daughter of the new English Ambassador, and her name was Lady Rosalind. But she nearly fainted when she heard who it was that wished to dance with her, for she was not at all particularly clever; and the prince had such a bad character for snubbing girls, and asking them difficult questions. However, it was impossible to refuse, and so she danced with the prince, and he danced very well. Then they sat out in the conservatory, among the flowers, where nobody came near them ; and then they danced again, and then the Prince took her down to supper. And all the time he never once said, " Have you read *this?*" or " Have you read *that?*" or, "What! you never heard of Alexander the Great?" or Julius Cæsar, or Michael Angelo, or whoever it might be — horrid, difficult questions he used to ask. That was the way he *used* to go on: but now he only talked to the young lady about *herself;* and she quite left off being shy or frightened, and asked him all about his own country, and about the Firedrake-shooting, and said how fond she was of hunting herself. And the prince said:

" Oh, if *you* wish it, you shall have the horns and tail of a Firedrake to hang up in your hall, to-morrow evening ! "

Then she asked if it was not very dangerous work, Firedrake hunting ; and he said it was nothing, when you knew the trick of it: and he asked her if she would but give him a rose out of her bouquet ; and, in short, he made himself so agreeable and *unaffected*, that she thought him very nice indeed.

For, even a clever person can be nice when he likes — above all, when he is not thinking about himself. And now the prince was thinking of nothing in the world but the daughter of the English ambassador, and how to please her. He got introduced to her father too, and quite won his heart ; and, at last, he was invited to dine next day at the Embassy.

In Pantouflia, it is the custom that a ball must not end while one of the royal family goes on dancing. *This* ball lasted till the light came in, and the birds were singing out of doors, and all the mothers present were sound asleep. Then nothing would satisfy the prince, but that they all should go home singing through the streets; in fact, there never had been so merry a dance in all Pantouflia. The prince had made a point of dancing with almost every girl there: and he had suddenly become the most beloved of the royal family. But everything must end at last; and the prince, putting on the cap of darkness and sitting on the famous carpet, flew back to his lonely castle.

CHAPTER VIII.

PRINCE PRIGIO did not go to bed. It was bright daylight, and he had promised to bring the horns and tail of a Firedrake as a present to a pretty lady. He had said it was easy to do this; but now, as he sat and thought over it, he did not feel so victorious.

"First," he said, "where is the Firedrake?"

He reflected for a little, and then ran upstairs to the garret.

"It *should* be here!" he cried, tossing the fairies' gifts about; "and, by George, here it is!"

Indeed, he had found the spyglass of carved ivory which Prince Ali, in the "Arabian Nights," bought in the bazaar in Schiraz. Now, this glass was made so that, by looking through it, you could see anybody or anything you wished, however far away. Prigio's first idea was to look at his lady. "But she does not expect to be looked at," he thought; "and I *won't!*" On the other hand, he determined to look at the Firedrake; for, of course, he had no delicacy about spying on *him*, the brute.

The prince clapped the glass to his eye, stared out of window, and there, sure enough, he saw the Firedrake. He was floating about in a sea of molten lava, on the top of a volcano. There he was, swimming and diving for pleasure, tossing up the flaming waves, and blowing fountains of fire out of his nostrils, like a whale spouting!

The prince did not like the looks of him.

"With all my cap of darkness, and my shoes of swiftness, and my sword of sharpness, I never could get near that beast," he said; "and if I *did* stalk him, I could not hurt him. Poor little Alphonso! poor Enrico! what plucky fellows they were! I fancied that there was no such thing as a Firedrake: he's not in the Natural History books; and I thought the boys were only making fun, and would be back soon, safe and sound. How horrid being too clever makes one! And now, what *am* I to do?"

What was he to do, indeed? And what would you have done? Bring the horns and tail he must, or perish in the adventure. Otherwise, how could he meet his lady? — why, she would think him a mere braggart!

The prince sat down, and thought and thought; and the day went on, and it was now high noon.

At last he jumped up and rushed into the library, a room where nobody ever went except himself and the queen. There he turned the books upside down, in his haste, till he found an old one, by a French gentleman, Monsieur Cyrano de Bergerac. It was an account of a voyage to the moon, in which there is a great deal of information about matters not generally known; for few travellers have been to the moon. In that book, Prince Prigio fancied he would find something he half remembered, and that would be of use to him. And he *did!* So you see that cleverness, and minding your book, have some advantages, after all. For here the prince learned that there is a very rare beast, called a Remora, which is at least as cold as the Firedrake is hot!

"Now," thought he, "*if I can only make these two fight*, why the Remora may kill the Firedrake, or take the heat out of him, at least, so that I may have a chance."

Then he seized the ivory glass, clapped it to his eye, and looked for the Remora. Just the tip of his nose, as white as snow and as smooth as ice, was sticking out of a chink in a frozen mountain, not far from the burning mountain of the Firedrake.

"Hooray!" said the prince softly to himself; and he jumped like mad into the winged shoes of swiftness, stuck on the cap of darkness, girdled himself with the sword of sharpness, and put a good slice of bread, with some cold tongue, in a wallet, which he slung on his back. Never you fight, if you can help it, except with plenty of food to keep you going and in good heart. Then off he flew, and soon he reached the volcano of the Firedrake.

CHAPTER IX.

THE PRINCE AND THE FIREDRAKE.

IT was dreadfully hot, even high up in the air, where the prince hung invisible. Great burning stones were tossed up by the volcano, and nearly hit him several times. Moreover, the steam and smoke, and the flames which the Firedrake spouted like foam from his nostrils, would have daunted even the bravest man. The sides of the hill, too, were covered with the blackened ashes of his victims, whom he had roasted when they came out to kill him. The garden-engine of poor little Alphonso was lying in the valley, all broken and useless. But the Firedrake, as happy as a wild duck on a lonely loch, was rolling and diving in the liquid flame, all red-hot and full of frolic.

"Hi!" shouted the prince.

The Firedrake rose to the surface, his horns as red as a red crescent-moon, only bigger, and lashing the fire with his hoofs and his blazing tail.

"Who's there?" he said in a hoarse, angry voice. "Just let me get at you!"

"It's me," answered the prince. It was the first time he had forgotten his grammar, but he was terribly excited.

"What do you want?" grunted the beast. "I wish I could see you;" and, horrible to relate, he rose on a pair of wide, flaming wings, and came right at the prince, guided by the sound of his voice.

Now, the prince had never heard that Firedrakes could fly; indeed, he had never believed in them at all, till the night before. For a moment he was numb with terror; then he flew down like a stone to the very bottom of the hill, and shouted:

"Hi!"

"Well," grunted the Firedrake, "what's the matter? Why can't you give a civil answer to a civil question?"

"Will you go back to your hole and swear, on your honor as a Firedrake, to listen quietly?"

"On my sacred word of honor," said the beast, casually scorching an eagle that flew by into ashes. The cinders fell, jingling and crackling, round the prince in a little shower.

Then the Firedrake dived back, with an awful splash of flame, and the mountain roared round him.

The prince now flew high above him, and cried:

"A message from the Remora. He says you are afraid to fight him."

"Don't know him," grunted the Firedrake.

"He sends you his glove," said Prince Prigio, "as a challenge to mortal combat, till death do you part."

Then he dropped his own glove into the fiery lake.

"Does he?" yelled the Firedrake. "Just let me get at him!" and he scrambled out, all redhot as he was.

"I'll go and tell him you're coming," said the prince; and with two strides he was over the frozen mountain of the Remora.

CHAPTER X.

THE PRINCE AND THE REMORA.

IF he had been too warm before, the prince was
too cold now. The hill of the Remora was
one solid mass of frozen steel, and the cold
rushed out of it like the breath of some icy
beast, which indeed it *was*.   All around were
things like marble statues of men in armor: they were
the dead bodies of the knights, horses and all, who had
gone out of old to fight the Remora, and who had been
frosted up by him.   The prince felt his blood stand
still, and he grew faint; but he took heart, for there
was no time to waste.   Yet he could nowhere see the
Remora.

"Hi!" shouted the prince.

Then, from a narrow chink at the bottom of the
smooth, black hill, — a chink no deeper than that
under a door, but a mile wide, — stole out a hideous
head!

It was as flat as the head of a skate-fish, it was
deathly pale, and two chill-blue eyes, dead colored like
stones, looked out of it.

Then there came a whisper, like the breath of the
bitter east wind on a winter day:

"Where are you, and how can I come to you?"

"Here I am!" said the prince from the top of the hill.

Then the flat, white head set itself against the edge of the chink from which it had peeped, and slowly, like the movement of a sheet of ice, it slipped upwards and curled upwards, and up, and up! There seemed no end to it at all; and it moved horribly, without feet, holding on by its own frost to the slippery side of the frozen hill. Now all the lower part of the black hill was covered with the horrid white thing coiled about it in smooth, flat, shiny coils; and still the head was higher than the rest; and still the icy cold came nearer and nearer, like Death.

The prince almost fainted: everything seemed to swim; and in one moment more he would have fallen stiff on the mountain-top, and the white head would have crawled over him, and the cold coils would have slipped over him and turned him to stone. And still the thing slipped up, from the chink under the mountain.

But the prince made a great effort; he moved, and in two steps he was far away, down in the valley where it was not so very cold.

"Hi!" he shouted, as soon as his tongue could move within his chattering teeth.

There came a clear, hissing answer, like frozen words dropping round him:

"Wait till I come down. What do you want?"

Then the white folds began to slide, like melting ice, from the black hill.

Prince Prigio felt the air getting warmer behind him, and colder in front of him.

He looked round, and there were the trees beginning
to blacken in the heat, and the grass looking like a sea
of fire along the plains ; for the Firedrake was coming !

The prince just took time to shout, " The Firedrake
is going to pay you a visit ! " and then he soared to
the top of a neighboring hill, and looked on at what
followed.

CHAPTER XI.

THE BATTLE.

IT was an awful sight to behold! When the Remora heard the name of the Firedrake, his hated enemy, he slipped with wonderful speed from the cleft of the mountain into the valley. On and on and on he poured over rock and tree, as if a frozen river could slide downhill; on and on, till there were miles of him stretching along the valley — miles of the smooth-ribbed, icy creature, crawling and slipping forwards. The green trees dropped their leaves as he advanced; the birds fell down dead from the sky, slain by his frosty breath! But, fast as the Remora stole forward, the Firedrake came quicker yet, flying and clashing his fiery wings. At last they were within striking distance; and the Firedrake, stooping from the air, dashed with his burning horns and flaming feet slap into the body of the Remora.

Then there rose a steam so dreadful, such a white yet fiery vapor of heat, that no one who had not the prince's magic glass could have seen what happened. With horrible grunts and roars the Firedrake tried to burn his way right through the flat body of the Remora, and to chase him to his cleft in the rock. But the Remora, hissing terribly, and visibly melting away in places, yet held his ground; and the prince could see

his cold white folds climbing slowly up the hoofs of the
Firedrake — up and up, till they reached his knees, and
the great burning beast roared like a hundred bulls
with the pain. Then up the Firedrake leaped, and
hovering on his fiery wings, he lighted in the midst
of the Remora's back, and dashed into it with his
horns. But the flat, cruel head writhed backwards, and
slowly bending over on itself, the wounded Remora
slid greedily to fasten again on the limbs of the
Firedrake.

Meanwhile, the prince, safe on his hill, was lunching
on the loaf and the cold tongue he had brought with
him.

"Go it, Remora! Go it, Firedrake! you're gaining. Give it him, Remora!" he shouted in the wildest
excitement.

Nobody had ever seen such a battle; he had it all to
himself, and he never enjoyed anything more. He
hated the Remora so much, that he almost wished the
Firedrake could beat it; for the Firedrake was the more
natural beast of the pair. Still, he was alarmed when
he saw that the vast flat body of the Remora was now
slowly coiling backwards, backwards, into the cleft below
the hill; while a thick wet mist showed how cruelly
it had suffered. But the Firedrake, too, was in an unhappy way; for his legs were now cold and black, his
horns were black also, though his body, especially near
the heart, glowed still like red hot iron.

"Go it Remora!" cried the prince: "his legs are
giving way; he's groggy on his pins! One more effort,
and he won't be able to move!"

Encouraged by this advice, the white, slippery Remora streamed out of his cavern again, more and more of him uncoiling, as if the mountain were quite full of him. He had lost strength, no doubt: for the steam and mist went up from him in clouds, and the hissing of his angry voice grew fainter; but so did the roars of the Firedrake. Presently they sounded more like groans; and at last the Remora slipped up his legs above the knees, and fastened on his very heart of fire. Then the Firedrake stood groaning like a black bull, knee-deep in snow; and still the Remora climbed and climbed.

"Go it now, Firedrake!" shouted the prince; for he knew that if the Remora won, it would be too cold for him to draw near the place, and cut off the Firedrake's head and tail.

"Go it, Drake! he's slackening!" cried the prince again; and the brave Firedrake made one last furious effort, and rising on his wings, dropped just on the spine of his enemy.

The wounded Remora curled back his head again on himself, and again crawled, steaming terribly, towards his enemy. But the struggle was too much for the gallant Remora. The flat, cruel head moved slower; the steam from his thousand wounds grew fiercer; and he gently breathed his last just as the Firedrake, too, fell over and lay exhausted. With one final roar, like the breath of a thousand furnaces, the Firedrake expired.

The prince, watching from the hill-top, could scarcely believe that these two *awful scourges of Nature*, which had so long devastated his country, were actually dead. But when he had looked on for half-an-hour, and only

a river ran where the Remora had been, while the body
of the Firedrake lay stark and cold, he hurried to the
spot.

Drawing the sword of sharpness, he hacked off, at
two blows, the iron head and the tail of the Firedrake.
They were a weary weight to carry; but in a few strides
of the shoes of swiftness he was at his castle, where he
threw down his burden, and nearly fainted with excitement and fatigue.

But the castle clock struck half-past seven; dinner
was at eight, and the poor prince crawled on hands and
knees to the garret.   Here he put on the wishing-cap;
wished for a pint of champagne, a hot bath, and his
best black velvet and diamond suit.   In a moment
these were provided; he bathed, dressed, drank a glass
of wine, packed up the head and tail of the Firedrake,
sat down on the flying carpet, and knocked at the door
of the English ambassador as the clocks were striking
eight in Gluckstein.

Punctuality is the politeness of princes! and a prince
is polite when he is in love!

The prince was received at the door by a stout porter
and led into the hall, where *several* butlers met him,
and he laid the mortal remains of the Firedrake under
the cover of the flying carpet.

Then he was led upstairs; and he made his bow to
the pretty lady, who, of course, made him a magnificent courtesy.   She seemed prettier and kinder than
ever.   The prince was so happy, that he never noticed
how something went wrong about the dinner.   The
ambassador looked about, and seemed to miss someone,
and spoke in a low voice to one of the servants, who

answered also in a low voice, and what he said seemed
to displease the ambassador.   But the prince was so
busy in talking to his lady, and in eating his dinner
too, that he never observed anything unusual.   He had
never been at such a pleasant dinner !

CHAPTER XII.

A TERRIBLE MISFORTUNE.

WHEN the ladies left, and the prince and the other gentlemen were alone, the ambassador appeared more gloomy than ever. At last he took the prince into a corner, on pretence of showing him a rare statue.

"Does your royal highness not know," he asked, "that you are in considerable danger?"

"Still?" said the prince, thinking of the Firedrake.

The ambassador did not know what he meant, for *he* had never heard of the fight, but he answered gravely:

"Never more than now."

Then he showed the prince two proclamations, which had been posted all about the town.

Here is the first:

TO ALL LOYAL SUBJECTS.

Whereas,

Our eldest son, Prince Prigio, hath of late been guilty of several high crimes and misdemeanors.

First: By abandoning the post of danger against the Fire-drake, whereby our beloved sons, Prince Alphonso and Prince Enrico, have perished, and been overdone by that monster.

Secondly : By attending an unseemly revel in the town of Gluckstein, where he brawled in the streets.

Thirdly : By trying to seduce away the hearts of our loyal subjects in that city, and to blow up a party against our crown and our peace.

This is to give warning,

That whoever consorts with, comforts, aids, or abets the said Prince Prigio, is thereby a partner in his treason ; and

That a reward of FIVE THOUSAND PURSES will be given to whomsoever brings the said prince, alive, to our Castle of Falk-enstein.

GROGNIO R.

And here is the second proclamation :

REWARD.

THE FIREDRAKE.

Whereas,

Our dominions have lately been devastated by a Firedrake (the *Salamander Furiosus* of Buffon) ;

This is to advise all,

That whosoever brings the horns and tail of the said Fire-drake to our Castle of Falkenstein, shall receive FIVE THOUSAND PURSES, the position of Crown Prince, with the usual perquisites, and the hand of the king's niece, the Lady Molinda.

GROGNIO R.

"H'm," said the prince ; " I did not think his majesty wrote so well ; " and he would have *liked* to say, " Don't you think we might join the ladies ? "

" But, sir," said the ambassador, "the streets are lined with soldiers ; and I know not how you have escaped them. *Here,* under my roof, you are safe for the moment; but a prolonged stay — excuse my inhospitality — could not but strain the harmonious relations which prevail between the Government of Pantouflia and that which I have the honor to represent."

"We don't want to fight; and no more, I think, do you," said the prince, smiling.

"Then how does your royal highness mean to treat the proclamations?"

"Why, by winning these ten thousand purses. I can tell you £1,000,000 is worth having," said the prince. "I'll deliver up the said prince, alive, at Falkenstein this very night; also the horns and tail of the said Firedrake. But I don't want to marry my Cousin Molly."

"May I remind your royal highness that Falkenstein is three hundred miles away? Moreover, my head butler, Benson, disappeared from the house before dinner, and I fear he went to warn Captain Kopzoffski that you are *here!*"

"That is nothing," said the prince; "but, my dear Lord Kelso, may I not have the pleasure of presenting Lady Rosalind with a little gift, a Philippine which I lost to her last night, merely the head and tail of a Firedrake which I stalked this morning?"

The ambassador was so astonished that he ran straight upstairs, forgetting his manners, and crying:

"Linda! Linda! come down at once; here's a surprise for you!"

Lady Rosalind came sweeping down, with a smile on her kind face. *She* guessed what it was, though the prince had said nothing about it at dinner.

" Lead the way, your royal highness!" cried the ambassador ; and the prince, offering Lady Rosalind his arm, went out into the hall, where he saw neither his carpet nor the horns and tail of the Firedrake!

He turned quite pale, and said :

" Will you kindly ask the servants where the little Persian prayer-rug and the parcel which I brought with me have been placed ? "

Lord Kelso rang the bell, and in came all the servants, with William, the under-butler, at their head.

" William," said his lordship, " where have you put his royal highness's parcel and his carpet ? "

" Please, your lordship," said William, " we think Benson have took them away with him."

" And where is Benson ? "

" We don't know, your lordship.　We think he have been come for."

" Come for — by whom ? "

William stammered, and seemed at a loss for a reply.

" Quick ! answer ! what do you know about it ? "

William said at last, rather as if he were making a speech :

" Your royaliness, and my lords and ladies, it was like this.　His royaliness comed in with a rug over his arm, and summat under it.　And he lays it down on that there seat, and Thomas shows him into the droring-room.　Then Benson says : ' Dinner'll be ready in five minutes ; how tired I do feel!'　Then he takes the libbuty of sitting himself down on his royaliness's rug, and he says, asking your pardon, ' I've had about enough of service here.　I'm about tired, and I thinks of bettering myself.　I wish I was at the king's court, and butler.' But before the words was out of his mouth, off he flies like a shot through the open door, and his royaliness's parcel with him. I run to the door, and there he was, flying right hover the town, in a northerly direction. And that's all I know; for I would not tell a lie, not if it was hever so. And me, and Thomas — as didn't see it, — and cook, we thinks as how Benson was come for. And cook says as she don't wonder at it, neither; for a grumblinger, more ill-conditioneder — "

"Thank you, William," said Lord Kelso; "that will do; you can go, for the present."

CHAPTER XIII.

SURPRISES.

THE prince said nothing, the ambassador said nothing, Lady Rosalind said never a word till they were in the drawing-room. It was a lovely warm evening, and the French windows were wide open on the balcony, which looked over the town and away north to the hills. Below them flowed the clear, green water of the Glutckthal. And still nobody said a word.

At last the prince spoke:

"This is a very strange story, Lord Kelso!"

"Very, sir!" said the ambassador.

"But true," added the prince; "at least, there is no reason in the nature of things why it shouldn't be true."

"I can hardly believe, sir, that the conduct of Benson, whom I always found a most respectable man, deserved—"

"That he should be 'come for,'" said the prince. "Oh, no; it was a mere accident, and might have happened to any of us who chanced to sit down on my carpet."

And then the prince told them, shortly, all about it: how the carpet was one of a number of fairy properties, which had been given him at his christening; and how

so long a time had gone by before he discovered them;
and how, probably, the carpet had carried the butler
where he had said he wanted to go, namely — to the
king's Court at Falkenstein.

"It would not matter so much," added the prince,
"only I had relied on making my peace with his majesty, my father, by aid of those horns and that tail.
He was set on getting them; and if the Lady Rosalind
had not expressed a wish for them, they would to-day
have been in his possession."

"Oh, sir, you honor us too highly," murmured Lady
Rosalind; and the prince blushed and said:

"Not at all! Impossible!"

Then, of course, the ambassador became quite certain
that his daughter was admired by the crown prince,
who was on bad terms with the king of the country;
and a more uncomfortable position for an ambassador
— however, they are used to them.

"What on earth am I to do with the young man?"
he thought. "He can't stay here forever; and without his carpet he can't get away, for the soldiers have
orders to seize him as soon as he appears in the street.
And in the meantime Benson will be pretending that *he*
killed the Firedrake — for he must have got to Falkenstein by now,— and they will be marrying him to the
king's niece, and making my butler crown prince to the
kingdom of Pantouflia! It is dreadful!"

Now all this time the prince was on the balcony,
telling Lady Rosalind all about how he got the Firedrake done for, in the most modest way; for, as he
said: "*I* didn't kill him: and it is really the Remora,
poor fellow, who should marry Molly; but he's dead."

At this very moment there was a *whizz* in the air;
something shot past them, and, through the open window, the king, the queen, Benson, and the mortal
remains of the Firedrake were shot into the ambassador's drawing-room!   *

CHAPTER XIV.

THE KING EXPLAINS.

THE first who recovered his voice and presence of mind was Benson.

"Did your lordship ring for coffee?" he asked, quietly; and when he was told "Yes," he bowed and withdrew, with majestic composure.

When he had gone, the prince threw himself at the king's feet, crying:

"Pardon, pardon, my liege!"

"Don't speak to me, sir!" answered the king, very angrily; and the poor prince threw himself at the feet of the queen.

But she took no notice of him whatever, no more than if he had been a fairy; and the prince heard her murmur, as she pinched her royal arms:

"I shall waken presently; this is nothing out of the way for a dream. Dr. Rumpfino ascribes it to imperfect nutrition."

All this time, the Lady Rosalind, as pale as a marble statue, was leaning against the side of the open window. The prince thought he could do nothing wiser than go and comfort her, so he induced her to sit down on a chair in the balcony, — for he felt that he was not wanted in the drawing-room; — and soon they were talking happily about the stars, which had begun to appear in the summer night.

Meanwhile, the ambassador had induced the king to take a seat; but there was no use in talking to the queen.

"It would be a miracle," she said to herself, "and miracles do not happen; therefore this has not happened. Presently, I shall wake up in my own bed at Falkenstein."

Now, Benson, William, and Thomas brought in the coffee, but the queen took no notice. When they went away, the rest of the company slipped off quietly, and the king was left alone with the ambassador; for the queen could hardly be said to count.

"You want to know all about it, I suppose?" said his majesty, in a sulky voice. "Well, you have a right to, and I shall tell you. We were just sitting down to dinner at Falkenstein, rather late, — hours get later every year, I think — when I heard a row in the premises, and the captain of the guard, Colonel McDougal, came and told us that a man had arrived with the horns and tail of the Firedrake, and was claiming the reward. Her majesty and I rose and went into the outer court, where we found, sitting on that carpet with a glass of beer in his hand, a respectable-looking upper servant, whom I recognized as your butler. He informed us that he had just killed the beast, and showed us the horns and tail, sure enough; there they are! The tail is like the iron handle of a pump, but the horns are genuine. A pair were thrown up by a volcano, in my great-grandfather's time, Giglio I.[1] Excellent coffee this, of yours!"

[1] The History of this Prince may be read in a treatise called "The Rose and the Ring," by M. A. TITMARSH. [W. M. Thackeray. See p. 231.]

The ambassador bowed.

"Well, we asked him *where* he killed the Firedrake, and he said in a garden near Gluckstein. Then he began to speak about the reward, and the 'perkisits,' as he called them, which it seems he had read about in my proclamation. Rather a neat thing; drew it up myself," added his majesty.

"Very much to the point," said the ambassador, wondering what the king was coming to.

"Glad you like it," said the king, much pleased. "Well, where was I? Oh, yes; your man said he had killed the creature in a garden, quite near Gluckstein. I didn't much like the whole affair: he is an alien, you see; and then there was my niece, Molinda — poor girl, *she* was certain to give trouble. Her heart is buried, if I may say so, with poor Alphonso. But the queen is a very remarkable woman — very remarkable —"

"Very!" said the ambassador, with perfect truth.

"'Caitiff!' she cries to your butler," his majesty went on, "'perjured knave, thou liest in thy throat! Gluckstein is a hundred leagues from here, and how sayest thou that thou slewest the monster, and camest hither in a few hours' space?' This had not occurred to me, — I am a plain king, but I at once saw the force of her majesty's argument. 'Yes,' said I; 'how did you manage it?' But he — your man, I mean — was not a bit put out. 'Why, your majesty,' says he, 'I just sat down on that there bit of carpet, wished I was here, and here I *ham*. And I'd be glad, having had the trouble, — and my time not being my own, — to see the color of them perkisits, according to the proclamation.' On this her majesty grew more indignant, if possible. 'Nonsense!' she cried; 'a story out of the "Arabian Nights" is not suited for a modern public, and fails to win æsthetic credence.' These were her very words."

"Her majesty's expressions are ever choice and appropriate," said the ambassador.

"'Sit down there on the carpet, knave,' she went on; 'ourself and consort' — meaning *me* — 'will take our places by thy side, and *I* shall wish us in Gluckstein, at thy master's! When the experiment has failed, thy head shall from thy shoulders be shorn!' So your man merely said, 'Very well, mum, — your majesty, I mean,' and sat down. The queen took her place at the edge of the carpet; I sat between her and the butler, and she said, 'I wish we were in Gluckstein!' Then we rose, flew through the air at an astonishing pace, and here we are! So I suppose the rest of the butler's tale is true, which I regret; but a king's word is sacred, and he shall take the place of that sneak, Prigio. But as we left home before dinner, and as *yours* is over, may I request your lordship to believe that I should be delighted to take something cold?"

The ambassador at once ordered a sumptuous collation, to which the king did full justice; and his majesty was shown to the royal chamber, as he complained of fatigue. The queen accompanied him, remarking that she was sound asleep, but would waken presently. Neither of them said "Good-night" to the prince. Indeed, they did not see him again, for he was on the balcony with Lady Rosalind. They found a great deal to say to each other, and at last the prince asked her to be his wife; and she said that if the king and her

father gave their permission — why, then she would!
After this she went to bed; and the prince, who had
not slept at all the night before, felt very sleepy also.
But he knew that first he had something that must be
done.   So he went into the drawing-room, took his carpet, and wished to be — now, where do you suppose? Beside the dead body of the Firedrake!   There he was in
a moment; and dreadful the body looked, lying stark
and cold in the white moonshine.   Then the prince cut
off its four hoofs, put them in his wallet, and with these
he flew back in a second, and met the ambassador just
as he came from ushering the king to bed.   Then the
prince was shown his own room, where he locked up
the hoofs, the carpet, the cap of darkness, and his other
things in an iron box; and so he went to bed and
dreamed of his Lady Rosalind.

CHAPTER XV.

THE KING'S CHECK.

WHEN they all wakened next morning, their first ideas were confused. It is often confusing to waken in a strange bed, much more so when you have flown through the air, like the king, the queen, and Benson the butler. For her part, the queen was the most perplexed of all; for she did undeniably wake, and yet she was not at home, where she had expected to be. However, she was a determined woman, and stood to it that nothing unusual was occurring. The butler made up his mind to claim the crown princeship and the hand of the Lady Molinda; because, as he justly remarked to William, here was such a chance to better himself as might not soon come in his way again. As for the king, he was only anxious to get back to Falkenstein, and have the whole business settled in a constitutional manner. The ambassador was not sorry to get rid of the royal party; and it was proposed that they should all sit down on the flying carpet, and wish themselves at home again. But the queen would not hear of it: she said it was childish and impossible; so the carriage was got ready for her, and she started without saying a word of good-bye to anyone. The king, Benson, and the prince were not so particular, and they simply flew back to Falkenstein in the usual way, arriving there at 11.35 — a week before her majesty.

The king at once held a Court; the horns and tail of the monster were exhibited amidst general interest, and Benson and the prince were invited to state their claims.

Benson's evidence was taken first. He declined to say exactly where or how he killed the Firedrake. There might be more of them left, he remarked, — young ones, that would take a lot of killing, — and he refused to part with his secret. Only he claimed the reward, which was offered, if you remember, *not* to the man who killed the beast, but to him who brought its horns and tail. This was allowed by the lawyers present to be very sound law; and Benson was cheered by the courtiers, who decidedly preferred him to Prigio, and who, besides, thought he was going to be crown prince. As for Lady Molinda, she was torn by the most painful feelings; for, much as she hated Prigio, she could not bear the idea of marrying Benson. Yet one or the other choice seemed certain.

Unhappy lady! Perhaps no girl was ever more strangely beset by misfortune!

Prince Prigio was now called on to speak. He admitted that the reward was offered for bringing the horns and tail, not for killing the monster. But were the king's *intentions* to go for nothing? When a subject only *meant* well, of course he had to suffer; but when a king said one thing, was he not to be supposed to have meant another? Any fellow with a wagon could *bring* the horns and tail; the difficult thing was to kill the monster. If Benson's claim was allowed, the royal prerogative of saying one thing and meaning something else was in danger.

On hearing this argument, the king so far forgot himself as to cry, "Bravo, well said!" and to clap his hands, whereon all the courtiers shouted and threw up their hats.

The prince then said that whoever had killed the monster could, of course, tell where to find him, and could bring his hoofs. He was ready to do this himself. Was Mr. Benson equally ready? On this being interpreted to him — for he did not speak Pantouflian — Benson grew pale with horror, but fell back on the proclamation. He had brought the horns and tail, and so he must have the perquisites, and the Lady Molinda!

The king's mind was so much confused by this time, that he determined to leave it to the Lady Molinda herself.

"Which of them will you have, my dear?" he asked, in a kind voice.

But poor Molinda merely cried. Then his majesty was almost *driven* to say that he would give the reward to whoever produced the hoofs by that day week. But no sooner had he said this than the prince brought them out of his wallet, and displayed them in open Court. This ended the case; and Benson, after being entertained with sherry and sandwiches in the steward's room, was sent back to his master. And I regret to say that his temper was not at all improved by his failure to better himself. On the contrary, he was unusually cross and disagreeable for several days; but we must, perhaps, make some allowance for his disappointment.

But if Benson was irritated, and suffered from the remarks of his fellow-servants, I do not think we can envy Prince Prigio. Here he was, restored to his position indeed, but by no means to *the royal favor*. For the king disliked him as much as ever, and was as angry as ever about the deaths of Enrico and Alphonso. Nay, he was even *more* angry; and, perhaps, not without reason. He called up Prigio before the whole Court, and thereon the courtiers cheered like anything, but the king cried:

"Silence! McDougal, drag the first man that shouts to the serpent-house in the zoölogical gardens, and lock him up with the rattlesnakes!"

After that the courtiers were very quiet.

"Prince," said the king, as Prigio bowed before the throne, "you are restored to your position, because I cannot break my promise. But your base and malevolent nature is even more conspicuously manifest in your selfish success than in your previous dastardly contempt of duty. Why, confound you!" cried the king, dropping the high style in which he had been speaking, and becoming the *father*, not the *monarch*, — "why, if you *could* kill the Firedrake, did you let your poor little brothers go and be b — b — b — broiled? Eh! what do you say, you sneak? 'You didn't believe there *were* any Firedrakes?' That just comes of your eternal conceit and arrogance! If you were clever enough to kill the creature — and I admit that — you were clever enough to know that what everybody said must be true. 'You have not generally found it so?' Well, you *have* this time, and let it be a lesson to you; not that there is much comfort in that, for it is not likely you will ever have such another chance " — exactly the idea that had occurred to Benson.

Here the king wept, among the tears of the lord chief justice, the poet laureate (who had been awfully frightened when he heard of the rattlesnakes), the maids of honor, the chaplain royal, and everyone but Colonel McDougal, a Scottish soldier of fortune, who maintained a military reserve.

When his majesty had recovered, he said to Prigio (who had not been crying, he was too much absorbed):
" A king's word is his bond.　Bring me a pen, somebody, and my check-book."

The royal check-book, bound in red morocco, was brought in by eight pages, with ink and a pen.　His majesty then filled up and signed the following satisfactory document — (Ah! my children, how I wish my publisher would do as much for *me!*):

No. W. $^{O}_{B}$ 961047.　　　　Falkenstein, July 10, 1768.

The Bank of Pantouflia.

FALKENSTEIN BRANCH.

Pay to *Prince Prigio* ~~~~~~~~~ *or Order,*
Ten Thousand Purses.

£1,000,000.　　　　　　　　*Grognio R.*

" There ! " said his majesty, crossing his check and throwing sand over it, for blotting-paper had not yet been invented ; " there, take *that,* and be off with you ! "

Prince Prigio was respectfully but rapidly obeying
his royal command, for he thought he had better cash
the royal check as soon as possible, when his majesty
yelled:

"Hi! here! come back! I forgot something; you've
got to marry Molinda!"

CHAPTER XVI.

A MELANCHOLY CHAPTER.

THE prince had gone some way, when the king called after him. How he wished he had the seven-league boots on, or that he had the cap of darkness in his pocket! If he had been so lucky, he would now have got back to Gluckstein, and crossed the border with Lady Rosalind. A million of money may not seem much, but a pair of young people who really love each other could live happily on less than the check he had in his pocket. However, the king shouted very loud, as he always did when he meant to be obeyed, and the prince sauntered slowly back again.

"Prigio!" said his majesty, "where were you off to? Don't you remember that this is your wedding-day? My proclamation offered, not only the money (which you have), but the hand of the Lady Molinda, which the Court chaplain will presently make your own. I congratulate you, sir; Molinda is a dear girl."

"I have the highest affection and esteem for my cousin, sir," said the prince, "but —— "

"I'll never marry him!" cried poor Molinda, kneeling at the throne, where her streaming eyes and hair made a pretty and touching picture. "Never! I despise him!"

"I was about to say, sir," the prince went on, "that I cannot possibly have the pleasure of wedding my cousin."

"The family gibbet, I presume, is in good working order?" asked the king of the family executioner, a tall gaunt man in black and scarlet, who was only employed in the case of members of the blood royal.

"Never better, sire," said the man, bowing with more courtliness than his profession indicated.

"Very well," said the king; "Prince Prigio, you have your choice. *There* is the gallows, *here* is Lady Molinda. My duty is painful, but clear. A king's word cannot be broken. Molly, or the gibbet!"

The prince bowed respectfully to Lady Molinda:

"Madam, my cousin," said he, "your clemency will excuse my answer, and you will not misinterpret the apparent discourtesy of my conduct. I am compelled, most unwillingly, to slight your charms, and to select the Extreme Rigor of the Law. Executioner, lead on! Do your duty; for me, *Prigio est prêt;*"—for this was his motto, and meant that he was ready.

Poor lady Molinda could not but be hurt by the

prince's preference for death over marriage to her, little as she liked him.

"Is life, then, so worthless? and is Molinda so terrible a person that you prefer *those* arms," and she pointed to the gibbet, "to *these?*" — here she held out her own, which were very white, round, and pretty: for Molinda was a good-hearted girl, she could not bear to see Prigio put to death; and then, perhaps, she reflected that there are worse positions than the queenship of Pantouflia. For Alphonso was gone — crying would not bring him back.

"Ah, Madam!" said the prince, "you are forgiving —"

"For *you* are brave!" said Molinda, feeling quite a respect for him.

"But neither your heart nor mine is ours to give. Since mine was another's, I understand too well the feeling of *yours!* Do not let us buy life at the price of happiness and honor."

Then, turning to the king, the prince said:

"Sir, is there no way but by death or marriage? You say you cannot keep half only of your promise; and that, if I accept the reward, I must also unite myself with my unwilling cousin. Cannot the whole proclamation be annulled, and will you consider the bargain void if I tear up this flimsy scroll?"

And here the prince fluttered the check for £1,000,-000 in the air.

For a moment the king was tempted; but then he said to himself:

"Never mind, it's only an extra penny on the income-tax." Then, "Keep your dross," he shouted, meaning the million; "but let *me* keep my promise. To chapel at once, or —" and he pointed to the executioner. "The word of a king of Pantouflia is sacred."

"And so is that of a crown prince," answered Prigio; "and *mine* is pledged to a lady."

"She shall be a mourning bride," cried the king savagely, "unless" — here he paused for a moment — "unless you bring me back Alphonso and Enrico, safe and well!"

The prince thought for the space of a flash of lightning.

"I accept the alternative," he said, "if your majesty will grant me my conditions."

"Name them!" said the king.

"Let me be transported to Gluckstein, left there unguarded, and if, in three days, I do not return with my brothers safe and well, your majesty shall be spared a cruel duty. Prigio of Pantouflia will perish by his own hand."

The king, whose mind did not work very quickly, took some minutes to think over it. Then he saw that by granting the prince's conditions, he would either recover his dear sons, or, at least, get rid of Prigio, without the unpleasantness of having him executed. For, though some kings have put their eldest sons to death, and most have wished to do so, they have never been better loved by the people for their Roman virtue.

"Honor bright?" said the king at last.

"Honor bright!" answered the prince, and, for the

first time in many months, the royal father and son shook hands.

"For you, madam," said Prigio in a stately way to Lady Molinda, "in less than a week I trust we shall be taking our vows at the same altar, and that the close of the ceremony which finds us cousins will leave us brother and sister."

Poor Molinda merely stared; for she could not imagine what he meant. In a moment he was gone; and having taken, by the king's permission, the flying carpet, he was back at the ambassador's house in Gluckstein.

CHAPTER XVII.

THE BLACK CAT AND THE BRETHREN.

WHO was glad to see the prince, if it was not Lady Rosalind? The white roses of her cheeks turned to red roses in a moment, and then back to white again, they were so alarmed at the change. So the two went into the gardens together, and talked about a number of things; but at last the prince told her that, before three days were over, all would be well, or all would be over with him. For either he would have brought his brothers back, sound and well, to Falkenstein, or he would not survive his dishonor.

"It is no more than right," he said; "for had I gone first, neither of them would have been sent to meet the monster after I had fallen. And I *should* have fallen, dear Rosalind, if I had faced the Firedrake before I knew *you*."

Then when she asked him why, and what good she had done him, he told her all the story; and how, before he fell in love with her, he didn't believe in fairies, or Firedrakes, or caps of darkness, or anything nice and impossible, but only in horrid useless facts, and chemistry, and geology, and arithmetic, and mathematics, and even political economy. And the **Fire-drake** would have made a mouthful of him, then.

So she was delighted when she heard this, almost as much delighted as she was afraid that he might fail in the most difficult adventure. For it was one thing to egg on a Remora to kill a Firedrake, and quite another to find the princes if they were alive, and restore them if they were dead!

But the prince said he had his plan, and he stayed that night at the ambassador's. Next morning he rose very early, before anyone else was up, that he might not have to say " Good-bye " to Lady Rosalind. Then he flew in a moment to the old lonely castle, where nobody went for fear of ghosts, ever since the Court retired to Falkenstein.

How still it was, how deserted; not a sign of life, and yet the prince was looking everywhere *for some living thing*. He hunted the castle through in vain, and then went out to the stable-yard; but all the dogs, of course, had been taken away, and the farmers had offered homes to the poultry. At last, stretched at full length in a sunny place, the prince found a very old, half-blind, miserable cat. The poor creature was lean and its fur had fallen off in patches; it could no longer catch birds, nor even mice, and there was nobody to give it milk. But cats do not look far into the future; and this old black cat — Frank was his name — had got a breakfast somehow, and was happy in the sun. The prince stood and looked at him pityingly, and he thought that even a sick old cat was, in some ways, happier than most men.

" Well," said the prince at last, " he could not live long anyway, and it must be done. He will feel nothing."

Then he drew the sword of sharpness, and with one turn of his wrist cut the cat's head clean off.

It did not at once change into a beautiful young lady, as perhaps you expect; no, that was improbable, and, as the prince was in love already, would have been vastly inconvenient. The dead cat lay there, like any common cat.

Then the prince built up a heap of straw, with wood on it; and there he laid poor puss, and set fire to the pile. Very soon there was nothing of old black Frank left but ashes!

Then the prince ran upstairs to the fairy cupboard, his heart beating loudly with excitement. The sun was shining through the arrow-shot window; all the yellow motes were dancing in its rays. The light fell on the strange heaps of fairy things — talismans and spells. The prince hunted about here and there, and at last he discovered six ancient water-vessels of black leather, each with a silver plate on it, and on the plate letters engraved. This was what was written on the plates :

AQVA. DE. FONTE. LEONVM.[1]

"Thank heaven!" said the prince. "I thought they were sure to have brought it!"

Then he took one of the old black-leather bottles, and ran downstairs again to the place where he had burned the body of the poor old sick cat.

He opened the bottle, and poured a few drops of the water on the ashes and the dying embers.

Up there sprang a tall, white flame of fire, waving like a tongue of light ; and forth from the heap jumped the most beautiful, strong, funny, black cat that ever was seen!

It was Frank as he had been in the vigor of his youth ; and he knew the prince at once, and rubbed himself against him and purred.

The prince lifted up Frank and kissed his nose for joy; and a bright tear rolled down on Frank's face, and made him rub his nose with his paw in the most comical manner.

Then the prince set him down, and he ran round and round after his tail ; and, lastly, cocked his tail up, and marched proudly after the prince into the castle.

"Oh, Frank!" said Prince Prigio, "no cat since the time of Puss in Boots was ever so well taken care of as you shall be. For, if the fairy water from the Fountain of Lions can bring *you* back to life — why, there is a chance for Alphonso and Enrico!"

[1] Water from the Fountain of Lions.

Then Prigio bustled about, got ready some cold luncheon from the store-room, took all his fairy things that he was likely to need, sat down with them on the flying carpet, and wished himself at the mountain of the Firedrake.

"I have the king now," he said; "for if I can't find the ashes of my brothers, by Jove! I'll! — "

Do you know what he meant to do, if he could not find his brothers? Let every child guess!

Off he flew; and there he was in a second, just beside poor Alphonso's garden-engine. Then Prigio, seeing a little heap of gray ashes beside the engine, watered them with the fairy water; and up jumped Alphonso, as jolly as ever, his sword in his hand.

"Hullo, Prigio!" cried he; "are you come after the monster too? I've been asleep, and I had a kind of dream that he beat me. But the pair of us will tackle him. How is Molinda?"

"Prettier than ever," said Prigio; "but anxious about you. However, the Firedrake's dead and done for; so never mind him. But I left Enrico somewhere about. Just you sit down and wait a minute, till I fetch him."

The prince said this, because he did not wish Alphonso to know that he and Enrico had not had quite the best of it in the affair with the monster.

"All right, old fellow," says Alphonso; "but have you any luncheon with you? Never was so hungry in my life!"

Prince Prigio had thought of this, and he brought out some cold sausage (to which Alphonso was partial) and some bread, with which the younger prince ex-

pressed himself satisfied.   Then Prigio went up the hill
some way, first warning Alphonso *not* to sit on his
carpet for fear of *accidents* like that which happened
to Benson.   In a hollow of the hill, sure enough there
was the sword of Enrico, the diamonds of the hilt
gleaming in the sun.   And there was a little heap of
gray ashes.

The prince poured a few drops of the water from the
Fountain of Lions on them, and up, of course, jumped
Enrico, just as Alphonso had done.

"Sleepy old chap you are, Enrico," said the prince ;
"but come on, Alphonso will have finished the grub
unless we look smart."

So back they came, in time to get their share of
what was going ; and they drank the Remora's very
good health, when Prigio told them about the fight.
But neither of them ever knew that they had been
dead and done for ; because Prigio invented a story
that the mountain was enchanted, and that, as long as
the Firedrake lived, everyone who came there fell
asleep.   He did tell them about the flying carpet, however, which of course did not much surprise them,
because they had read all about it in the "Arabian
Nights " and other historical works.

"And now I'll show you fun ! " said Prigio ; and he
asked them both to take their seats on the carpet, and
wished them to be in the valley of the Remora.

There they were in a moment, among the old knights
whom, if you remember, the Remora had frozen into
stone.   There was quite a troop of them, in all sorts of
armor — Greek and Roman, and Knight Templars like
Front de Bœuf and Brian du Bois Gilbert — all the

brave warriors that had tried to fight the Remora since the world began.

Then Prigio gave each of his brothers some of the water in their caps, and told them to go round pouring a drop or two on each frozen knight.   And as they did it, lo and behold! each knight came alive, with his horse, and lifted his sword and shouted:

" Long live Prince Prigio!"

in Greek, Latin, Egyptian, French, German, and Spanish, — all of which the prince perfectly understood, and spoke like a native.

So he marshalled them in order, and sent them off to ride to Falkenstein and cry:

" Prince Prigio is coming!"

Off they went, the horses' hoofs clattering, banners flying, sunshine glittering on the spear-points. Off they rode to Falkenstein; and when the king saw them come galloping in, I can tell you he had no more notion of hanging Prigio.

CHAPTER XVIII.

THE VERY LAST.

THE princes returned to Gluckstein on the carpet, and went to the best inn, where they dined together and slept. Next morning they, and the ambassador, who had been told all the story, and Lady Rosalind, floated comfortably on the carpet back to Falkenstein, where the king wept like anything on the shoulders of Alphonso and Enrico. They could not make out why he cried so, nor why Lady Molinda and Lady Kathleena cried; but soon they were all laughing and happy again. But then — would you believe he could be so mean? — he refused to keep his royal promise, and restore Prigio to his crown-princeship! Kings are like that.

But Prigio, very quietly asking for the head of the Firedrake, said he'd pour the magic water on *that*, and bring the Firedrake back to life again, unless his majesty behaved rightly. This threat properly frightened King Grognio, and he apologized. Then the king shook hands with Prigio in public, and thanked him, and said he was proud of him. As to Lady Rosalind, the old gentleman quite fell in love with her, and he sent at once to the Chaplain Royal to get into his surplice, and marry all the young people off at once, without waiting for wedding-cakes, and milliners, and all the rest of it.

Now, just as they were forming a procession to march into church, who should appear but the queen! Her majesty had been travelling by post all the time, and, luckily, had heard of none of the doings since Prigio, Benson, and the king left Gluckstein. I say *luckily* because if she *had* heard of them, she would not have believed a word of them. But when she saw Alphonso and Enrico, she was much pleased, and said:

"Naughty boys! Where have you been hiding? The king had some absurd story about your having been killed by a fabulous monster. Bah! don't tell *me*. I always said you would come back after a little trip — didn't I, Prigio?"

"Certainly, madam," said Prigio; "and I said so, too. Didn't I say so?" And all the courtiers cried: "Yes, you did;" but some added, to themselves, "He *always* says, 'Didn't I say so?'"

Then the queen was introduced to Lady Rosalind, and she said it was "rather a short engagement, but she supposed young people understood their own affairs best." And they do! So the three pairs were married, with the utmost rejoicings; and her majesty never, her whole long life, could be got to believe that anything unusual had occurred.

The honeymoon of Prince Prigio and the Crown Princess Rosalind was passed at the castle, where the prince had been deserted by the Court. But now it was delightfully fitted up; and Master Frank marched about the house with his tail in the air, as if the place belonged to him.

Now, on the second day of their honeymoon, the prince and princess were sitting in the garden together, and the prince said, "Are you *quite* happy, my dear?" and Rosalind said, "Yes; *quite.*"

But the prince did not like the tone of her voice, and he said:

"No, there's something; do tell me what it is."

"Well," said Rosalind, putting her head on his shoulder, and speaking very low, "I want everybody to love you as much as I do. No, not quite so very much,—but I want them to like you. Now they *can't,* because they are afraid of you; for you are so awfully clever. Now, couldn't you take the wishing cap, and wish to be no cleverer than other people? Then everybody would like you!"

The prince thought a minute, then he said:

"Your will is law, my dear; anything to please you. Just wait a minute!"

Then he ran upstairs, for the last time, to the fairy garret, and he put on the wishing cap.

"No," thought he to himself, "I won't wish *that.* Every man has one secret from his wife, and this shall be mine."

Then he said aloud: " I WISH TO SEEM NO CLEVERER THAN OTHER PEOPLE."

The prince remained as clever as ever he had been; but, as nobody observed it, he became the most popular prince, and finally the best-beloved king who had ever sat on the throne of Pantouflia.

THE ENCHANTED DOLL

CHAPTER I.

THE story I am about to tell you happened many years ago, long before the railroads had cut up the dancing-grounds of the fairies, or the shrill whistle of the locomotive had frightened the "good people" from the green dells and quiet nooks wherein they are said to have held their merry-makings by the clear moonlight. We never see a fairy nowadays; nevertheless we are glad to talk about them and their doings in the old time. What a pretty sight it must have been to have seen King Oberon's state balls! Let us imagine one of those elfin revels.

There Oberon sits upon his pretty little mushroom throne, under a canopy of feathery fern, while tiny gnats hum merry tunes within the bells of the foxglove and wild convolvulus. See how his courtiers dance round and round until the grass shows a circle of the deepest green! How gracefully their robes of film float in the air, or twine about their fragile limbs! And now, tired with their sport, they throw themselves at the root of some huge field-flower, and drink bright dew from cups gathered from the yellow cowslip.

As I have said, the story I am about to tell you happened years ago, long before the fairies had left us, and begins at that pleasant time of the year when the trees (like good little folk at school) are putting forth the blossoms which give promise of fruit hereafter. The doors and shutters of Jacob Pout's booth (as a shop was called in those days) were thrown open to let in the little breeze that was playing among the lavender in the garden.

Jacob Pout was a doll-maker, and the cleverest craftsman in his trade. He made wooden dolls only — for no one had as yet thought of making dolls out of wax — but they were considered marvels of beauty by all the young ladies who were fortunate enough to possess one. They had such red cheeks, such curly hempen wigs, and legs and arms as good as any wooden doll could wish for. And then they were such dolls to last! You might leave them on the window-sill, in the broad sunshine, without their noses melting away; or you might drop them out of the nursery window without damaging more than a leg or an arm. Ah! Jacob Pout ought to have been a happy man, for his customers were always satisfied with their purchases, and his lathe might have been going every working-day of the week if its owner had not been rather lazy and very envious.

Opposite the doll-maker lived Anthony Stubbs, a clever worker in gold and silver, and an industrious, good-tempered fellow. The shutter of his booth was always the first to be taken down, and there he might be heard whistling and hammering all day, as cheerful as a lark and as busy as a bee. True, he had not many customers, but then his wares were costly in their material, and took a long time to work into cups and salvers and spoons.

Jacob Pout never thought of this as he stood idling his time away at the door of his booth, grumbling that he had been brought up to doll-making, whilst Tony Stubbs never worked upon anything baser than silver. And then, when he saw the alder- men of the ward count down upon Tony's counter twenty pounds for a silver tankard, he nearly choked  with envy at his neighbor's good fortune, never think- ing how many long days it had cost the honest silver- smith to hammer into form the dogs and horsemen which made the cup so valuable. Neither did he think how much time had been spent by Tony Stubbs before he acquired the art of chasing gold and silver; for he had gone over the seas as far as Florence to study in the workshop of the great Cellini, the most renowned craftsman of his time.

Jacob had passed the greater part of a fine summer's afternoon in this discontented spirit, and, having closed his booth, had taken a walk into the country.

London was not the large city that it is now, and its
suburbs were not all brick and mortar as they are at
present, but shady woods and open meadows were to
be found everywhere around it, and thither would the
good citizens resort on high days and holidays. Jacob
Pout, idler that he was, made twice as many holidays
as any of his neighbors, and there was not a pleasant
place in wood or field but Jacob knew of it.

There was no pleasanter spot round London than
Maude's Dingle, in the middle of the small wood which
skirted the boundary wall of the Priory Garden at
Kilbourne (now called Kilburn). When the wind set
that direction you could hear Bow Bells plain enough;
but at other times not a sound of the city could be
heard. Here, on the summer's evening to which our
tale refers, at the foot of an old oak tree, was seated
Jacob Pout. A solitary thrush was singing its hymn
to the evening; no other sound was heard, except the
soft murmurs of the little stream Bourne, which gave
a name to the locality. The song, both of bird and
brook, was lost upon Jacob Pout, for his mind was full
of envious and discontented thoughts, which destroyed
the charm of all things round about him. His eye saw
only visions of the glittering wares of Tony Stubbs.
The twilight came and went, yet there he lay sulky
and miserable. The thrush had long since finished its
hymn, and was at rest; but the little brook could not
be silent until it reached the distant river. Jacob heard
it at last, and, as he listened, the sounds seemed to
become more and more distinct, until he thought he
could define a tune. Yes, it was a march, and played
— so it seemed, at least — by drums, trumpets, and

cymbals. Every moment it became more loud, and evidently proceeded from a hollow beech tree not twenty yards from him.

As he looked in the direction of the sound, he saw — bless me! how he rubbed his eyes! — he saw, coming from a little hole at the foot of the hollow beech, a procession of pigmy people, all gaily dressed, and marching to the music of a full band of elfin players. In the midst, seated in a car not bigger than a walnut shell, was a lady, black as an Ethiopian. She wore armlets and bracelets of gold, and bands of the same precious metal were round her ankles; her dress was of the costliest materials, and made in the picturesque fashion of the East. Jacob felt rather frightened when the procession stopped opposite to him, and his teeth fairly chattered when he saw the Black Fairy descend from her car and advance, with her maids of honor, directly towards the place where he was lying.

The Black Fairy evidently saw that he was afraid, for she smiled, as though to give Jacob courage; but as her smile appeared to have a contrary effect to that which it was intended to produce, she spoke. Oh, what a voice she had! It was sharp and small, and sounded like the noise produced by blowing in the barrel of a watch-key.

"I have often wished to speak to you," said the Black Fairy, "but it would not be considered etiquette in one of my degree to venture abroad, except by moonlight. I have taken a great fancy to you; I have often heard you grumbling in a manner which has done my heart good. I hate people to be contented and grateful; it shows a mean spirit. For my own part,

I have never felt satisfied since I was born, and I am now nearly five thousand years old."

" You look remarkably well for your age," remarked Jacob.

" Not I," said the black lady; " I've seen fairies looking much better who are my senior by a day or two. But I have come to take you under my protection. You are delightfully envious of that miserable milksop, Tony Stubbs. Ha! ha! Depend upon it, Jacob, it's not all gold that glitters in that quarter; half his wares are sham, rely upon it. However, you are a good subject of mine, and deserve to be encouraged."

" Who are you?" thought Jacob.

" I am the Fairy Malice," said the black lady; " and I am only sorry that, as you are a mortal, I cannot make you my Prime Minister; you are well qualified for the post. But, never mind; if you can't serve me in Elf-land, you can do so in your own sphere. Tony Stubbs can't be worth more than three hundred pounds."

" Not that!" shouted Jacob; " not that! If he were sold up to-morrow two hundred pounds would buy him."

" So much the worse for you, then," said the Black Fairy; " you are one hundred pounds the poorer, for I intend to make you just as rich as Tony Stubbs."

" What a fool I've been!" thought Jacob. " This black hag shouldn't have got off so easily had I known that!"

" That's right, abuse me — grumble away," said the fairy. " I can hear your thoughts, and like you the better for having them. Oh, how I love ingratitude!

Now, see what I am going to do for you — look at this." And Jacob saw in the Fairy's hand an ebony doll not bigger than his little finger; it was beautifully carded, and had bracelets and armlets and ankle-bands of silver. Jacob had never seen anything so well done since he had been a doll-maker.

"What do you think that is?" said the Fairy Malice. "That is an Enchanted Doll. Take it home with you; it will sell for just one hundred pounds, and that sum, with what you are worth already, will place you on an equal footing with Tony Stubbs."

Jacob's eyes glistened with delight.

"So long as you are contented the Enchanted Doll will be of no service to you; but should you again deserve my assistance, it will return to you, though her then possessor be living at the Antipodes. Good-night!" And then the procession departed, in the same order in which it arrived.

Jacob went home to bed, and slept soundly until daybreak. When he awoke, he thought he must have been dreaming. No, there was the Enchanted Doll upon the table.

He soon dressed himself and opened the shutter of his booth. He placed the fairy gift upon his board, and sat down to breakfast; but before he had swallowed a mouthful, a strange-looking person entered the shop, and inquired the price of the little black doll.

"One hundred and fifty pounds," answered Jacob.

"Too much," said the stranger; "I am ordered not to exceed one hundred."

There was something in his customer's manner that made Jacob anxious to get rid of him, and therefore he did not chaffer about the matter, but took the stranger's money and gave him the Enchanted Doll.

"What a lucky fellow I am!" said Jacob, as the stranger turned to depart.

"Very," said the doll-buyer — "*at present.*"

CHAPTER II.

WHEN the stranger was out of sight, Jacob put his money into his pouch, and, placing his cap jauntily upon one side of his head, took two or three turns in front of the silversmith's booth, rattling the money in his pouch every time that he passed; but his trick was lost upon Tony Stubbs, who never once looked up from his work. Jacob grew desperate, and entered the silversmith's booth.

"Good morrow, neighbor Stubbs," said the doll-maker.

"Ah!" replied Tony, "is it you, neighbor Pout? I am very glad to see you; for though we live opposite to each other, we seldom exchange more than a nod from week's end to week's end. But that is my fault, I believe; I am always so hard at work that I have no time for a little friendly gossip."

"Just my case too," said Jacob. "I am always at work" (what a fib that was!); "I cannot make dolls fast enough to supply my customers" (that was really true, but he might have done so had he been less idle). "But I have no right to grumble; I make money faster than I can spend it;" and Jacob rattled the coins in his pouch.

"I am rejoiced to hear of your well-doing, neighbor," said Tony, but showing neither by look nor word that he envied Jacob his good fortune. "We have both great reason to be grateful to God, neighbor."

Jacob gave a short cough, and answered, "Yes!" but gratitude had no place in his heart. He was vexed that the silversmith appeared deaf to the jingling of the money in his pouch, and he resolved to try what the sight of the bright coins would produce.

"I have received a large sum — a very large sum — this morning," said Jacob, "and I have some doubt as to the goodness of the coin which has been paid to me. Will you test a few pieces for me, neighbor, and set my mind at rest?"

"With great pleasure," replied Tony; "let me see them."

"There is a small portion of them," said Jacob, throwing down upon the counter a handful of coins, all looking new and bright.

Tony examined them carefully, and tested them by means known in his art. When he had done so, he pronounced them to be of the finest silver, and worth even more than their ratable value. "Unless," said Tony, laughing, "they are made of fairy silver, and if so, neighbor, you have made a bad bargain."

"How?" inquired Jacob.

"Some morning you will find them turned into dirt and stones — at least, so it runs in the legend," answered Tony.

"I have no fear of that," said Jacob, gathering up his money, and pouring it into his pouch with as much display as possible. He then wished the silversmith a good morning, and crossed over to his own booth.

"Fairy silver — ha! ha! dirt and stones!" thought Jacob. "I have made him envious at last." And with this bad thought the wicked doll-maker was contented.

At twelve o'clock the next day Tony Stubbs was seen to close the shutter of his booth, and then hurriedly walk eastward.

"Just like me," thought Jacob; "when I have a fit of the spleen I can never rest at home. I will be bound he is off to the woods for the rest of the day. Just like me."

Jacob was mistaken; in an hour or two the silversmith returned, and his hammer was heard ringing long after the usual hour of work. Again, in the morning, his neighbors were awakened before cockcrow by the sounds which proceeded from Tony's anvil. And so it was, day after day, the noise only ceasing at very long intervals, except about midday, when Tony closed the shutter of his booth and took his hurried walk eastward. All the neighbors remarked that he looked fatigued and unhappy, and the stock of his booth became less and less in spite of his incessant labor. Something was wrong with the silversmith, and everyone pitied him except the doll-maker.

I dare say you would like to know what took him away from home every day, and made him work early and late, and yet grow poorer and poorer? Well, I will tell you.

In the easternmost part of the city was a booth, above which was the sign of the Golden Shears, a sure indication that the owner pursued the ancient and honorable trade of tailor. The place was very clean, but scantily furnished with broadcloth, serge, and taffety, and for some days no one had been seen at work on the tailor's board but little Tom Tit, the apprentice. A good little fellow he was, for though he had no one to keep an eye upon him, he never idled away his time. It was to this shop that the silversmith paid his daily visit, for the tailor was Tony's father.

"Master is better to-day," said Tom Tit, about a week after Tony's first journey, "and the alderman has been here who wanted to put Master in the Fleet prison, and said that, as you had paid some of the money, he need not be frightened any longer about going to prison."

"The alderman has been very kind, Tom," remarked Tony; "he has given me time to pay his debt, and in a month or so I hope to see my father a free man again. You are a good boy, Tom, and I shall not forget your kindness."

Tom tried to say "Thank you, Master Tony," but something in his throat would not let him; he only wiped his eyes with the back of his hand, and then stitched away ten times harder than ever.

While Tom was doing this, Tony had entered a room upstairs, and, kneeling down by the bedside, had asked his father's blessing. The sick man laid his thin hand upon the head of his son, and prayed in silence. When he had finished, the old man's eyes filled with tears, whilst a faint smile lighted up his pale face. "Anthony," said he, "but for your filial love I should now be in a jail."

"I hardly think that, father," replied Tony, gaily, "for I had no sooner told the alderman how cruelly you had been cheated of your goods, than he offered to forego part of the debt; but this I declined, as the money was justly due."

"You did rightly, my dear son, but it grieves me to think that my mis- fortunes should have made you almost a beggar," replied the old man; "but I know that  the good God will bless you, perhaps not with wealth, for that is not always a blessing, but with a happy and contented mind, the sure reward of virtuous actions."

You know now why Tony worked early and late, and why he became poorer and poorer every day, until he had made his father a free man.

Well, it was on May-day that Tony went to the alder- man to make the last payment of his father's debt. May-day was a great holiday in the old time, and the young Londoners used to go to the neighboring woods to bring home the Maypole, which was a straight tree shorn of its branches and dressed out with gay streamers of ribbons and garlands of flowers. They used to dance round the May-pole to the music of a pipe and tabor, and sing merry songs in praise of Maid Marian and Robin Hood; but I question whether the lady or gentleman deserved such honor. Sometimes there were grand pageants of knights in armor and morris-dancers covered with bells and ribbons.

There had never been a grander pageant than the one in Fenchurch Street on the morning when Tony Stubbs paid Alderman Kersey the balance of his father's debt; "all the world and his wife" had come out to see it, and where there was a sight to be seen there Jacob Pout was sure to be. "Yes; he was the foremost in the crowd, shouting more loudly and pushing more rudely than any one else. He had received one or two blows on his crown from the staves of the javelin-men, who were keeping clear the passage to the stand set apart for the Lord Mayor and aldermen, and some of their friends, the richest merchants in the city. As the different aldermen passed along they were cheered and saluted by the bystanders, for in those days it was considered a great honor to be a member of the Corporation of London. Even Jacob Pout took off his cap as Alderman Kersey passed by, and it was not until the worthy magistrate stopped to speak to some one he recognized in the crowd, that Jacob perceived he was hanging on the arm of — Tony Stubbs. On they went, until they came to the Lord Mayor's stand, the steps of which they ascended together. There they stood, in the midst of the grandees of the great City of London, many of whom came to Tony and took him kindly by the hand. Jacob Pout could hardly believe his eyes; but what he saw was the truth, nevertheless. The alderman had told a great number of his friends the story of Tony's conduct, and so pleased were they with his filial love and honesty, that they all resolved to befriend him as much as they could.

Jacob did not remain to see any more of the show, but walked home as fast as he could, and shut himself up in his workshop. His heart was full of envy, and the pleasant sunlight annoyed him. At last twilight came, and then night; the moon shone clear and bright, and sent a light into the room in spite of the curtain. As Jacob sat brooding over what he had seen, the wheel of his lathe turned round, slowly at first, and then revolved with great rapidity. Jacob started up in surprise, and saw a swarm of little fairies engaged in shaping a large block of ebony into the rude form of a doll. The chips of hard wood flew about in all directions, and the wheel whizzed round like a mad thing. At length the lathe stopped; and Jacob saw the pigmies, with chisels and mallets, fashion the head and limbs into the exact resemblance, only a hundred times larger, of the Enchanted Doll he had brought away from Maude's Dingle.

When the fairies had finished their work, they expressed their delight by playing about in the most fantastic manner, now swinging by cobwebs from the ceiling, then climbing up the legs of the table, and turning head over heels from that frightful precipice on to the ground. At length Jacob heard the same music he had heard in the woods, and saw the Fairy Malice and her elfin train come forth from a mouse-hole in the corner of the room.

" Well, Jacob, my dear child," said the black lady, " I am glad you have come to your senses again; I was afraid you would never more be envious enough to release the Enchanted Doll from the power of her last possessor. You see, it gives my people some trouble to restore her — but never mind about that; you are such a dear envious creature that I could do anything for you."

" But what can this lump of wood do for me? Can it introduce me to the Lord Mayor and aldermen, and make me as great a man as Tony Stubbs seems likely to be?" said Jacob, with a sneer. " Besides, who will buy such a lumbering thing as this? The Enchanted Doll was a wonder in doll-making, but this is a clumsy — ugly — "

" Stop, dear, stop!" said the Fairy. " The increased size of the doll is all owing to the increase of your desires; and so it will be, my pretty one, until — but you must excuse me for the present." And, without further ceremony, she and her elfin troop disappeared down the mouse-hole.

In the morning Jacob placed the Enchanted Doll on his board; but though a number of persons stopped to look at it, no one seemed disposed to become a purchaser.

Meanwhile, the shop of the silversmith began to assume a very improved appearance, for the alderman and his friends had given Tony as much work as he could do; and such was Jacob Pout's envy, that I think he would never have sold his Enchanted Doll (for it was only when he was contented that he could part with it), had not Tony fallen dangerously sick, and Jacob envied him no longer.

When reading was a much rarer accomplishment than it is now, and when few of the porters and servants of the citizens knew even the letters of the alphabet, the shopkeepers of London used to hang up in front of their houses pictures and models, which were called signs, to enable persons to distinguish one trader from another. Some of the devices used were very curious, and among those which have come down to us, none seems less suited to the trade which it designates than the Black Doll, which we have all seen hanging over the door of the marine-store dealer.

I have no doubt that our Enchanted Doll was the original of the sign, for it was Tristram Tattersall, dealer in ships' stores, who became the new possessor of Jacob's fairy gift. He had it at a great bargain, for it only cost him a few pounds and, at Jacob's earnest solicitation, a seat at the Lord Mayor's dinner; for even in the old time good eating was a favorite pastime with the citizens of London.

Jacob enjoyed himself greatly during the early part of the banquet; he ate of everything that looked tempting, chuckling all the time at the thought that poor Tony was lying in a sick chamber, taking nothing but physic. As the feast proceeded, Jacob drank so much wine that he became very noisy and troublesome, and before the dinner was over the attendants of the Lord Mayor were compelled to carry the doll-maker out of the Guildhall. It was even said that, for more than an hour, he sat in the stocks, to the great delight of a number of little boys in Cheap (now called Cheapside).

Before we finish this chapter, you will be glad to know that Tony became a great deal better, and that Alderman Kersey called upon him daily; and at length, when Tony was able to sit up, the good alderman took his only daughter, Dorothy, to see him, and there is great reason to believe that the silversmith improved rapidly after the visit.

And Jacob Pout was more envious of his neighbor than ever.

CHAPTER III.

THE money which Jacob had received from Tristram Tattersall was soon expended, for the doll-maker had resolved to make what he called "a figure in the world"; and he did so, to the great amusement of his neighbors, among whom he was no favorite, as his envy and selfishness were well known. He dressed himself in the height of fashion, which was most fantastic and ridiculous. He had a monstrous ruff round his neck, which made his closely cropped head look like a small dumpling in a large platter. He wore stockings of two colors, and bows in his shoes. His breeches were so puffed out about the hips with buckram and wadding that his body seemed to rest upon two drumsticks. How the plain, sober citizens laughed at him as he strutted up and down the street! Then he resolved to favor the Court end of the town with a visit. As he could not walk with any comfort, he made his way to London Bridge stairs, and, hailing a waterman, got into a boat, and desired to be taken to the palace at Westminster. There were no cabs in those days, and persons of all ranks used "the silent highway" (as the River Thames has been called) when they wished to avoid the bustle and noise of the streets. The water-

men were generally quick-witted fellows, and, being
bold and impudent, you can imagine how Jacob fared
in his progress up the river, seated, as he was, in the
stern of the boat, in his large breeches and ruff, and a
little peaked hat with a cocktail feather in it. Some
of the watermen said he looked like a peg-top turned
upside down, whilst others compared him to a Dutch
dram-bottle. When they arrived at Westminster, Jacob
was astonished at the large sum demanded by the waterman for rowing him so short a distance, but when he
was assured that the scullers "never carried noblemen
for less," Jacob pulled out his purse with a grand air,
and paid the money. Poor fool! if he had only known
how he was laughed at the moment his back was
turned, for persons who pretend to be other than they
really are will at all times be exposed to ridicule and
imposition.

"Are you for the bear-baiting to-day?" said a gaily-
dressed young man to Jacob, shortly after he had
landed; "rare sport is expected, I am told, and the
best of the nobility are to be present."

"Why, sir," replied Jacob, "I have never seen a bear
baited. Is the bear-garden easy of access?"

"It is, if you have friends," returned the young man.
"I shall be happy to introduce you; I am of the Duke
of Northumberland's household, and shall be glad to be
of service to so brave a gentleman."

Jacob thanked him for his politeness, and wished
that his city neighbors could see him in such good company. Good company, indeed! The young fellow was
a London thief, who instantly saw that Jacob was a
very likely person to be imposed upon; so, whilst the

conceited doll-maker thought he was in the society of a duke's gentleman, he was but the companion of a rogue and a vagabond.

When they came to the bear-garden, Jacob's friend suddenly discovered that he had no money : of course the doll-maker was too glad to lend a piece of gold to such a desirable acquaintance. None but the best seats would serve the turn of Jacob and his friend, and they were therefore conducted by one of the bear-wards, or attendants, to the gallery set aside for the most distinguished ladies and gentlemen.

"Ladies in a bear-garden?" Yes, in the "good old times," of which we hear so much, the most cruel sports were witnessed by gentlewomen, who from their earliest childhood were accustomed to hear deeds of violence and bloodshed spoken of as praiseworthy actions, and thus they learned to think lightly of physical suffering, and to applaud the endurance and the infliction of pain. Books were rare things in those days, and few had the means of knowing what vast stores of elevating enjoyment were to be found among the stars, among the flowers, and in the earth, and under the waters. It was the ignorance of the past which made cruelty endurable, and it will be the increase of knowledge in the time to come, teaching us that God is everywhere, which will make the meanest creature of value in the eyes of men, and thus preserve from wanton outrage or wicked neglect all things endowed with the consciousness of suffering. Be diligent, therefore, my little friends, to gain and to diffuse knowledge, that you may help on that good time, when kindliness and goodwill shall inhabit the hearts of all the human race.

I will not describe the sufferings of the bear or the dogs, for the victim and its tormentors were alike subject to pain and injury, but proceed with my story. The visitors were leaving their seats, when a loud outcry was raised in that part of the garden where Jacob and his friend had taken their position. "Here's a thief!" cried one, seizing the duke's gentleman.

"Here's his comrade!" shouted another, taking a firm hold of Jacob's ruff.

The bear-wards were not slow in securing the two persons thus denounced, and without much parley they hurled Jacob and his distinguished acquaintance into the arena, where the bear was still chained to the post. The poor brute, smarting from his previous ill-treatment, and fearing, no doubt, that the new-comers were also his enemies, made two or three blows at the doll-maker, who chanced to roll near to him, and rent Jacob's fine clothes into shreds, and with his sharp claws scratched the face of the duke's gentleman. The ridiculous appearance of the suspected thieves roused the mirth of the company, and even the angry bear-wards could not help laughing.

"Let them go now, Robert," said a young nobleman and a great patron of the bear-garden; "they are well served for their knavish practices."

The bear-ward, obedient to his patron's command, conducted the two suspected rogues to the door, and giving each a sound rap with his quarter-staff, bid them

not venture within his walls again, at the peril of their
ears.

The duke's gentleman took to his heels, and Jacob,
ragged, bruised, and disgraced, walked homeward,
accompanied by a troop of the rabble, who are always
inclined to enjoy the misfortunes of any one.

More than a week had passed since this unlucky
occurrence, and Jacob Pout had never crossed the
threshold of his booth, for he thought that the story
was known among his neighbors, and he feared their
jokes and laughter. The good-natured silversmith became greatly concerned for his neighbor, and resolved
to pay him a visit. When Tony got to the doll-
maker's door, he was surprised to see Jacob with a
large axe endeavoring to cut in pieces a beautiful
black doll, dressed like an Eastern princess, but the
hard ebony resisted every effort made to destroy it.
Jacob's old friend had come back to him, but larger
than before, for his envy and hatred of his neighbors
had increased greatly since his own misfortune. During
the week that Jacob had shut himself up he had had
no other companion but the Enchanted Doll, and that
at last became so intolerable to him that he resolved
to cut it in pieces and burn it; but his fairy gift was
not to be so easily disposed of.

"Good morrow, neighbor Pout," said Tony, holding
out his hand. "What a capital piece of workmanship!
I think I never saw anything so exquisitely made.
Surely you were not cutting this up for firewood."

Jacob stammered out something about nobody buying
black dolls, as silly little girls were frightened at black
people.

"What is the price of it?" inquired Tony. "I have been thinking for a long time of a sign for my booth, and the Indian Princess would be a very good one for my craft. What is the price, neighbor?"

Jacob was delighted at the thought of getting rid of what had become to him a horrible thing, and he named a very small sum.

"Agreed!" said Tony. "I will buy it of you, provided you go with me to-night and spend Christmas Eve at the house of a kind friend of mine. I will promise you a hearty welcome. Bring the sign over to my booth, and I will pay you the money."

Tony shook Jacob by the hand, and then took his leave.

"You shall not wait long for your bargain," said the doll-maker, as soon as Tony's back was turned. "An Indian Princess, forsooth! Will nothing suit you for a sign but an Indian Princess? Well, I'll gratify your proud stomach, and rid me of this odious piece of fairy work."

Jacob Pout took the Enchanted Doll in his arms, with the intention of carrying it to the silversmith, but at every step he made towards his own door the doll became heavier and heavier, until he was unable to carry it any farther. The Enchanted Doll could only be parted with when Jacob ceased to be envious and discontented, and at that moment he envied everybody.

The doll did not remain long quiet, but hopped back in the oddest way imaginable to the little room at the back of the shop.

"I'll not endure this!" cried Jacob, in a fury; "I will take it to Tony Stubbs, and he shall keep it!"

But the doll then began to hop about the room, over the chairs, and on to the bed, and the great walnut-tree chest in which Jacob kept his Sunday clothes. The doll-maker pursued it as fast as he was able, but the Enchanted Doll always eluded his grasp, until, heated and exhausted, Jacob threw himself on a chair and fairly cried with vexation.

We will leave him to himself, if you please, and take an imaginary stroll to Holbourne, as it was then, but which is now called Holborn.

There are very few houses to be seen, but all belong to persons of large means. The gardens in front are kept with great care, and, though it is winter time, the broad gravel paths have not a withered leaf upon them. In the parlor windows of one or two of the houses a scarlet geranium is to be seen, in others are ostriches' eggs suspended by silk cords from the ceiling, and here and there are beautiful yellow canary birds, and in one that rare creature, a cockatoo — all presents, no doubt, from sea captains who make the long voyage to the warm countries of the East. That clear, swift stream is the Fleet River (the time will come when it will be a foul ditch), and that large brick house with the bow windows, lighted from within by a blazing fire, is the dwelling of Alderman Kersey. As we are friends of Tony Stubbs, I am sure he will be glad to welcome us. Here we are in the hall. As it is Christmas time, there is a table loaded with good cheer, to which all comers are welcome. This way leads to the principal sitting-room. The floor is strewn with dried rushes and lavender, for the rich Turkey carpet is thought too beautiful to tread upon, and it is therefore thrown over the carved table which stands in the centre of the room. The embroidery on the high backs of the chairs is all the work of Miss Dorothy's fingers, who stands arranging her pretty curls by that mirror of polished steel in a velvet-covered framework, whilst her mother and the maids decorate the buffet with the "white plate," which is only displayed on high-days and holidays. From the bosses and pendants of the ceiling hang bunches of holly and mistletoe, intermingled with bows of gay-colored ribbons. The door opposite leads to the kitchen, which looks like a green bower, so thickly is it covered with ivy and holly. The pewter platters on the shelves shine as brightly as the silver ware in the parlor, and as dinner has been long past (for it is nearly four o'clock), the servants are preparing for the dance, which is to take place in the evening. Here are the fiddlers, and here come the guests. Those are the alderman's apprentices, and the persons just entering the hall are neighbors and old customers of the house, with their wives, sons, and daughters. There are old Mr. Stubbs and good little Tom Tit! Those two who have just entered I hope you know by this time. Tony Stubbs is heartily welcomed by the alderman and Mrs. Kersey, whilst both Dorothy and the silversmith meet each other kindly, but rather sheepishly. What can be the reason? For he has asked her to dance the first dance with him, and Dorothy has answered, "Yes, thank you," although her face is red with blushes. Jacob Pout has been introduced to the alderman and his family by Tony, but the doll-maker seems to be ill at ease with his new friends.

There go the fiddles! The alderman and a buxom

dame of forty lead off, whilst old Mr. Stubbs has the honor of following with Mrs. Kersey; Tony and Dorothy are in the middle of the set and dancing merrily, to the great admiration of the servants, who one and all take part in the dance. What peals of laughter are heard every now and then as some blunder is made in the figure, when Charles, who should have turned to the right, wheels round to the left, and bumps against Mary, who nearly tumbles over Kate, who falls into the arms of Walter, whilst Frank, and Alfred, and Sidney clap their hands and declare that Kate did it on purpose! What a shout of laughter! Huzza! Alderman Kersey has kissed his partner under the mistletoe. All the women are pretending to run away from the kissing-bough, and all the men are dragging them back again — all but Jacob Pout.

Another dance, and another, and blind man's buff and hot cockles have brought us to supper time. All the young men assist in laying out the tables, and placing the benches round them. What a huge Christmas pie is drawn from the oven, where it has been quietly baking unknown to every one but the good-tempered cook and her mistress. There's the baron of beef which was roasted yesterday, and yonder comes John, the alderman's apprentice, bearing the pride of the Christmas feast, the boar's head, decked out with twigs of rosemary. Can you not smell the spiced wine that is steaming in the silver flagon which the alderman bought of Tony, who thought not when he sold it that he should ever drink from it as a guest, and perhaps something more, for pretty Dorothy has nodded to him before she tastes the steaming liquor.

Supper is over, and the kitchen again cleared for dancing; certainly the fiddlers play better than they did before, and everybody dances with twice as much spirit. Everybody seems merrier and happier, except Jacob Pout, who is stealing away from the house and taking the road to the Fields of Finsbury.

You had better remain with the pleasant people at Alderman Kersey's, and join in the carol which will be sung at midnight to usher in the coming Christmas Day. Besides, there will be other games of blind man's buff, hot cockles, and forfeits, and, I have no doubt, snap-dragon and hunt-the-slipper. I will follow Jacob Pout, and tell you all that happened in the next chapter.

CHAPTER IV.

WHEN Jacob went forth from the house of Alderman Kersey, the snow was falling fast ; but, nevertheless, the doll-maker pursued his way to the field, quite regardless of the weather. " It is as plain as the nose on my face," thought Jacob, " the alderman's daughter is to be the wife of Tony Stubbs, and then, of course, the alderman's wealth will all come to Tony, and who knows but some day or other he may become Lord Mayor of London. Just like his luck ! A mean, sneaking fellow as he is, always pretending to be at work ; never taking a day's holiday except upon the regular feasts and festivals. I hate him ! I don't know why, but I can't help it."

I could have told him the reason. Jacob was like many other people in the world who envy and hate every one more successful than themselves.

The moon was shining brightly in the heavens, and the snow (which seems to have been made for moonlight) sparkled like powdered diamonds. The path (which Jacob had tracked with some difficulty) was crossed by a stile, and as he felt wearied by his walk, he resolved to rest there for a time, and then return home. As he drew near to the stile, he saw on the topmost rail some living thing, which moved rapidly from one end to the other. He continued to approach, until he was close enough to discover that it was no other than the Fairy Malice. She was evidently in a very ill humor, in fact she seemed to be in a positive rage, for she walked with her arms folded together, and her little black lips compressed as closely as though they had been glued to each other. Now and then she would stop, stamp her tiny foot, and shake her clenched pigmy hand in the air. Jacob was about to make a hasty retreat, but the fairy was too quick for him.

"Stay where you are!" she screamed: "stay where you are, or I will rack every nerve in your body!"

Jacob felt quite powerless.

"So, you graceless fellow," continued the fairy, "you thought to go unpunished for your cruel treatment of that priceless treasure, the Enchanted Doll. You thought you could hack its beauteous limbs and batter its delicate body with impunity, did you? You thought that precious creature was only hewn out of an insensible log, like your own abominable toys, and could be made into firewood at your will and pleasure? Look here, every blow that you inflicted on that incomparable being was by elfish sympathy endured by me," and the fairy pointed to her bandaged arms and legs, which had hitherto escaped the notice of Jacob.

"But I will be avenged! I am here to-night to punish your ingratitude. It is not often that you find fairies out on a snowy night like this, but my people shall have plenty of work to keep them warm, I warrant you. Advance, archers! and give this ungrateful mortal a proof of your ability."

Jacob heard the old march played, and the surface

of the snow swarmed with black fairies.   Their bright
helmets and breastplates glittered in the moonlight as
they deployed before their potent ruler, until at last
they formed themselves into columns, and marched past
the terror-stricken Jacob, who, in a few minutes, found
himself surrounded by the pigmy army.   The officers
of the different companies conferred together, and, at
a signal from the commander, led their men still closer
to Jacob.   They then halted, and a myriad of arrows,
as fine as hairs, flew from their bows into the body of
the unhappy doll-maker.   Jacob roared with pain.

The Fairy Malice rubbed her hands with delight, and
laughed long and loud at the torture of the unhappy
doll-maker.

" Well done, my gallant archers ! well done ! " cried
the black lady.   " Let our cavalry acquit themselves as
well and they shall be rewarded.   Charge ! "

As she screamed out her command a humming noise
was heard in the air, and a legion of fairies, mounted
upon horned beetles, flew at the head and hands of the
doll-maker ; who, powerless to defend himself, endured
intolerable pain from the lances of his foes.   Malice
was more delighted than before, and laughed so much
that she was obliged to lean upon her attendants.
When she had recovered her breath, she addressed
Jacob as follows: — " Master Doll-maker, you now know
what it is to injure a fairy, and especially the Fairy
Malice.   As I think I have punished you sufficiently
this time, you may go home, Jacob.   We are friends
again."

" Never ! " cried Jacob.   " Never ! I will throw your
horrible gift into the river."

"Don't," said Malice; "if you do it will swim, and come back to you again."

"I will burn it, then!" exclaimed Jacob, almost beside himself with rage.

"Try such a thing at your peril!" screamed the fairy.

"I defy you!—you and your enchantments!" roared Jacob.

"Ha! ha!"—and all the fairies laughed in concert.

"Your own bad heart gives me the power over you, and until *that* changes you are the slave of my servant."

So saying, the fairy waved her wand, and the bright moonlight was instantly changed into darkness. At first Jacob thought a black cloud had passed between him and the moon, but he discovered, to his dismay, that he was surrounded by myriads of bats. He found, however, that the power of motion was restored to him, and began to run homewards, as he thought; but the bats flew with him, and, unable to see his path, he was presently crashing through the thin ice of a pond, from which he emerged dripping with water and shivering with cold. It was not until the church bells of London rang out in concert the advent of the day of promise of "Peace and goodwill to men," and from mansion and cottage a thousand voices were heard carolling a welcome to the blessed Christmas-tide, that his tormentors quitted him. Jacob found he was some distance from home, and it was not without great difficulty, bruised and tired as he was, that he reached the door of his own booth as the sun rose on the Christmas morning. When he entered his bed-chamber, there was the Enchanted Doll, larger and more hideous than ever!

The morning wore on, and Jacob, very miserable, still sat at the window, gazing intently at his neighbor's house. By and by the door opened, and Bridget, Tony's old housekeeper, came out dressed in her best bib and tucker, a sure sign she was going to make holiday. In a few minutes more the silversmith made his appearance, and locking the door, strangely enough walked away leaving the key in the lock. Perhaps he was thinking of pretty Dorothy Kersey — no matter.

Jacob saw all this, but instead of doing the part of a good neighbor by calling Tony back, the wicked doll-maker hoped that the key would attract the attention of some thief who would not hesitate to plunder the silversmith. With this bad feeling Jacob Pout watched all day at the window, but no one passed and saw the key. As the evening set in, Jacob's thoughts grew worse and worse, until at last it occurred to him to carry the doll over to his neighbor's house, and there, by kindling a fire, destroy at once the wealth which he envied and the creature which he dreaded. To his surprise, he found the Enchanted Doll as light as a feather, and, taking it in his arms, he carried it over to his neighbor's house. In a few minutes he returned, and, taking his seat again at the window, prepared to watch the result of the wickedness he had done. Presently smoke issued from the crevices in the shutters of Tony's booth, and then a bright red flame showed that the fire was raging fiercely within. Jacob Pout was rejoicing in the success of his malice and wickedness, when, to his great horror, he saw Tony's door fly open, and from it came the Enchanted Doll, a glowing mass of fire, and make directly for his own booth.

In a minute the room in which he was sitting became filled with smoke, and he heard the wood in his workshop crackling with the flames. At the same moment a great noise at a distance in the street told him that the fires were observed, and Jacob rushed out just as the city watchmen came up with their ladders and firebuckets. By great exertion the fire in Tony's house was put out, but nothing seemed to have power over that which was consuming the booth of the doll-maker.

Jacob stood stupefied for some time; at last it occurred to him that the first money which he had received for the Enchanted Doll was locked up in his old  walnut-tree chest, and, without a moment's pause, he dashed through the flames to secure his treasure, although the room was full of fire and smoke. Jacob contrived to open the chest, but lo! there was nothing but dirt and stones, for the coins he had received were all of fairy silver! His disappointment was so great that he remained kneeling by the side of the chest until the flames gathered all around him, and he would no doubt have perished, had not a young man forced his way through the fire, and dragged the bewildered doll-maker into the street.

Both were nearly suffocated, and it was not until some minutes had elapsed that Jacob could find words to thank his preserver. What must have been his feel-

ings when he found that to Tony Stubbs he was indebted for his preservation!

"This is a sad night for us both, neighbor Pout,"
said the silversmith, "but worse for you than for me.
You have lost all, but my shop has only suffered by the
flames; some of my wares are damaged, but a little
later to bed and a little earlier to rise will put all that
right. But, neighbor," and Tony paused, greatly
moved by the expression of Jacob's face, "you are in
great pain; and, no wonder, for your arm is flayed bare.
Here! some one run for a surgeon, whilst I help him to
bed."

The doll-maker, from shame and suffering, could
make no answer, but allowed the much injured Tony
to lead him to bed. The surgeon came, and pronounced
Jacob's state to be desperate, and desired that he should
be kept perfectly quiet. And so for many days Tony
Stubbs devoted all his time to watching by Jacob's bedside.

Some three weeks had passed since the time of the
fire. One night Tony had retired to rest after talking
very cheerfully, and telling how little damage the fire
had done his wares, and promising Jacob that as soon
as he was well enough to pursue his calling a new lathe
should be bought and a booth furnished for him. One
would have thought that so much kindness from a
person he had wronged so deeply would have awakened
nothing but feelings of gratitude in Jacob Pout, but
envy, hatred, and malice had been too long the cher-
ished passions of his breast to be dismissed without a
struggle.

"So," thought Jacob, "it seems I am to be indebted

for my daily bread to the man I have most hated and envied! Just like my luck! Whilst not one stick of my booth or stock is left unconsumed, this fellow can laugh at his loss, and afford to lend me money to boot. He will be richer shortly, for everybody says he is to marry pretty Dorothy Kersey. What has he done to deserve this?"

"What, indeed!" said a shrill voice close to his ear.

Jacob shook from head to foot, for he knew it was the Black Fairy who had spoken.

"What, indeed!" repeated the fairy. "He envies nobody! He sets fire to no man's dwelling! He thinks not only of his own dear self — fool that he is! But you deserve all you get, and a great deal more into the bargain."

"Leave me!" cried Jacob; "I wish to have done with you forever!"

"How very cruel of you!" sobbed the fairy, "after all I have suffered for you. Why, I have not yet recovered from the effects of the fire; neither has your pretty pet, the Enchanted Doll!"

"Recovered!" gasped Jacob. "Surely it was consumed in the flames!"

"Not so," replied the fairy, with a horrible grin; "I was afraid at one time that this silversmith might have been the death of her, but your love and constancy have quite worked a cure. She is beside you!"

And there it was, sure enough, charred and almost shapeless, but still with enough of form left to distinguish the Enchanted Doll.

The next morning Jacob was much worse. He was in a high state of fever, and wandering and raving in his sleep like one mad. The doctor could not account for the change, and appeared greatly perplexed what to do. Jacob continued in this state for more than three days. When at last his reason returned to him, he heard the sweet voice of a woman earnestly engaged in prayer for his recovery.

Jacob's heart was softened, and the tears rolled down his cheeks as fast as they did down those of Dorothy (for it was she who prayed for him); and when the prayer was finished, Jacob breathed a fervent "Amen!"

As country air was considered to be necessary for Jacob's recovery, Alderman Kersey had him taken in a litter to his house at Holbourne, where — thanks to the careful nursing of Mrs. Kersey and the gentle Dorothy — he was gradually restored to health.

And what became of the Enchanted Doll?

You shall hear.

From the hour that Jacob said "Amen!" to Dorothy's prayer, his cruel tormentor began to diminish in size, until the day before his removal to the house of Alderman Kersey it had dwindled down to the length of a little finger. It would have gone away altogether, but Jacob could not help (from long habit) at times contrasting his conditions with that of Tony Stubbs, and wishing — for a very little while — that he and the silversmith could change places.

One morning, towards the end of May, the bells of Holbourne Church were ringing merrily. All the people at Alderman Kersey's were dressed in their holiday clothes, decked out with large bows of white ribbon, and went smiling about the house, as though some happy event had occurred in the family. And so there

THE MARRIAGE OF TONY STUBBS AND DOROTHY KERSEY.

had! Dorothy Kersey had become the wife of Tony Stubbs. There never was a happier bridal party. Never was? There never could be! And Jacob Pout had been to church to see the marriage ceremony performed; and as he knelt beside them at the altar, he had prayed that God would bless them and reward them for all the good they had done to him, and pardon him all the evil he had done them.

From some strange impulse Jacob (who was now quite strong again) resolved in the afternoon to go to Maude's Dingle. When he arrived there he soon found the knoll on which he had sat when he received his fatal fairy gift, and down he threw himself, rather wearied by his walk. The thrush was singing, and Jacob thought the bird's song seemed full of thankfulness, and that the little brook ran babbling on of a thousand happy things!

He wondered he had never thought so before, until he remembered the evil passions which had hitherto been his companions when he visited the pleasant dingle.

Jacob went back with a light heart to the alderman, and joined heartily in the merry-making. He bade the musicians play their merriest tunes, and was, in fact, the last person left dancing at the end of a jovial reel.

When the guests had left, Jacob went up to his bedchamber and opened a little box, in which he kept his Enchanted Doll, but to his great joy he discovered that it had vanished. For Jacob had ceased to envy—even a little.

The doll-maker was set up in business by his kind friends, Alderman Kersey and Tony Stubbs, and, through the influence of the former, Jacob received a commission from the Lord Mayor to execute two of the largest dolls in the kingdom. I will not vouch for the fact, but it is more than suspected that Gog and Magog, which occupy so prominent a position in the Guildhall of London, are the identical dolls made by Jacob Pout.

THE ROSE AND THE RING

By WILLIAM MAKEPEACE THACKERAY.

CHAPTER I.

Shows How the Royal Family Sate Down to Breakfast.

THIS is Valoroso XXIV., King of Paflagonia, seated with his Queen and only child at their royal breakfast-table, and receiving the letter which announces to his Majesty a proposed visit from Prince Bulbo, heir of Padella, reigning king of Crim Tartary. Remark the delight upon the monarch's royal features. He is so absorbed in the perusal of the King of Crim Tartary's letter, that he allows his eggs to get cold, and leaves his august muffins untasted.

"What! that wicked, brave, delightful Prince Bulbo!" cries Princess Angelica — "so handsome, so accomplished, so witty, — the conqueror of Rimbombamento, where he slew ten thousand giants!"

"Who told you of him, my dear?" asks his Majesty.

"A little bird," says Angelica.

"Poor Giglio!" says mamma, pouring out the tea.

"Bother Giglio!" cries Angelica, tossing up her head, which rustled with a thousand curl papers.

"I wish," growls the King, "I wish Giglio was —"

"Was better? Yes, dear, he is better," says the Queen. "Angelica's little maid, Betsinda, told me so when she came to my room this morning with my early tea."

"You are always drinking tea," said the monarch, with a scowl.

"It is better than drinking port or brandy-and-water," replies her Majesty.

"Well, well, my dear, I only said you were fond of drinking tea," said the King of Paflagonia, with an effort as if to command his temper. "Angelica! I hope you have plenty of new dresses; your milliners' bills are long enough. My dear Queen, you must see and have some parties. I prefer dinners, but of course you will be for balls. Your everlasting blue velvet quite tires me; and, my love, I should like you to have a new necklace. Order one. Not more than a hundred or a hundred and fifty thousand pounds."

"And Giglio, dear," says the Queen.

"GIGLIO MAY GO TO THE —"

"Oh, sir!" screams her Majesty. "Your own nephew! our late King's only son."

"Giglio may go to the tailor's, and order the bills to be sent in to Glumboso to pay. Confound him! I mean bless his dear heart. He need want for nothing; give him a couple of guineas for pocket-money, and you may as well order yourself bracelets, while you are about the necklace, Mrs. V."

Her Majesty, or *Mrs. V.*, as the monarch face-tiously called her (for even royalty will have its sport, and this august family was very much attached), embraced her husband, and, twining her arm around her daughter's waist, they quitted the breakfast-room in order to make all things ready for the princely stranger.

When they were gone, the smile that had lighted up the eyes of the *husband* and *father* fled — the pride of the *King* fled — the MAN was alone. Had I the pen of a G. P. R. James, I would describe Valoroso's torments in the choicest language; in which I would also depict his flashing eye, distended nostril — his dressing-gown, pocket-handkerchief, and boots. But I need not say I have *not* the pen of that novelist; suffice it to say, Valoroso was alone.

He rushed to the cupboard, seizing from the table one of the many egg-cups with which his princely board was served for the matin meal, drew out a bottle of right Nantz or Cognac, filled and emptied the cup several times, and laid it down with a hoarse " Ha, ha, ha! now Valoroso is a man again!"

" But oh!" he went on (still sipping, I am sorry to say), "ere I was a king, I needed not this intoxicating draught; once I detested the hot brandy wine, and quaffed no other fount but nature's rill. It dashes not more quickly o'er the rocks than I did, as, with blunder-buss in hand, I brushed away the early morning dew, and shot the partridge, snipe, or antlered deer! Ah! well may England's dramatist remark, 'Uneasy lies the head that wears a crown!' Why did I steal my nephew's, my young Giglio's — ? Steal! said I; no, no, no, not steal, not steal. Let me withdraw that odious expression. I took, and on my manly head I set, the royal crown of Paflagonia ; I took, and with my royal arm I wield, the sceptral rod of Paflagonia ; I took, and in my outstretched hand I hold, the royal orb of Paflagonia ! Could a poor boy, a snivelling, drivelling boy — was in his nurse's arms but yesterday, and cried for sugar plums and puled for pap — bear up the awful weight of crown, orb, sceptre ? gird on the sword my royal fathers wore, and meet in fight the tough Crimean foe ?"

And then the monarch went on to argue in his own mind (though we need not say that blank verse is not argument) that what he had got it was his duty to keep, and that, if at one time he had entertained ideas of a certain restitution, which shall be nameless, the prospect by a *certain marriage* of uniting two crowns and two nations which had been engaged in bloody and expensive wars, as the Paflagonians and the Crimeans had been, put the idea of Giglio's restoration to the throne out of the question : nay, were his own brother, King Savio, alive, he would certainly will away the crown from his own son in order to bring about such a desirable union.

Thus easily do we deceive ourselves ! Thus do we fancy what we wish is right ! The King took courage, read the papers, finished his muffins and eggs, and rang the bell for his Prime Minister. The Queen, after thinking whether she should go up and see Giglio, who had been sick, thought " Not now. Business first ; pleasure afterwards. I will go and see dear Giglio this afternoon ; and now I will drive to the jeweller's, to look for the necklace and bracelets." The Princess went up into her own room, and made Betsinda, her maid, bring out all her dresses; and as for Giglio, they forgot him as much as I forget what I had for dinner last Tuesday twelvemonth.

CHAPTER II.

How King Valoroso Got the Crown, and Prince Giglio Went
Without.

PAFLAGONIA, ten or twenty thousand years ago, appears to have been one of those kingdoms where the laws of succession were not settled; for when King Savio died, leaving his brother regent of the kingdom, and guardian of Savio's orphan infant, this unfaithful regent took no sort of regard of the late monarch's will; had himself proclaimed sovereign of Paflagonia under the title of King Valoroso XXIV., had a most splendid coronation, and ordered all the nobles of the kingdom to pay him homage. So long as Valoroso gave them plenty of balls at Court, plenty of money, and lucrative places, the Paflagonian nobility did not care who was king; and as for the people, in those early times, they were equally indifferent. The Prince Giglio, by reason of his tender age at his royal father's death, did not feel the loss of his crown and empire. As long as he had plenty of toys and sweetmeats, a holiday five times a week, and a horse and gun to go out shooting when he grew a little older, and, above all, the company of his darling cousin, the King's only child, poor Giglio was perfectly contented; nor did he envy his uncle the royal robes and sceptre, the great hot, uncomfortable throne of state, and the enormous cumbersome crown in which that monarch appeared, from morning till night. King Valoroso's portrait has been left to us; and I think you will agree with me that he must have been sometimes *rather tired* of his velvet, and his diamonds, and his ermine, and his grandeur. I should n't like to sit in that stifling robe with such a thing as that on my head.

No doubt the Queen must have been lovely in her youth; for though she grew rather stout in after life, yet her features, as shown in her portrait, are certainly *pleasing*. If she was fond of flattery, scandal, cards, and fine clothes, let us deal gently with her infirmities, which, after all, may be no greater than our own. She was kind to her nephew; and if she had any scruples of conscience about her husband's taking the young Prince's crown, consoled herself by thinking that the King, though a usurper, was a most respectable man, and that at his death Prince Giglio would be restored to his throne, and share it with his cousin, whom he loved so fondly.

The Prime Minister was Glumboso, an old statesman, who most cheerfully swore fidelity to King Valoroso, and in whose hands the monarch left all the affairs of his kingdom. All Valoroso wanted was plenty of money, plenty of hunting, plenty of flattery, and as little trouble as possible. As long as he had his sport, this monarch cared little how his people paid for it; he engaged in some wars, and of course the Paflagonian newspapers announced that he gained prodigious victories; he had statues erected to himself in every city of the empire; and of course his pictures placed everywhere, and in all the print shops; he was Valoroso the Magnanimous, Valoroso the Victorious, Valoroso the Great, and so forth;—for even in these early times courtiers and people knew how to flatter.

This royal pair had one only child, the Princess Angelica, who, you may be sure, was a paragon in the courtiers' eyes, in her parents', and in her own. It was said she had the longest hair, the largest eyes, the slimmest waist, the smallest foot, and the most lovely complexion of any young lady in the Paflagonian dominions. Her accomplishments were announced to be even superior to her beauty; and governesses used to shame their idle pupils by telling them what Princess Angelica could do. She could play the most difficult pieces of music at sight. She could answer any one of Mangnal's Questions. She knew every date in the history of Paflagonia, and every other country. She knew French, English, Italian, German, Spanish, Hebrew, Greek, Latin, Cappadocian, Samothracian, Ægean, and Crim Tartar. In a word, she was a most accomplished young creature; and her governess and lady-in-waiting was the severe Countess Gruffanuff.

Would you not fancy, from her picture (see p. 239), that Gruffanuff must have been a person of the highest birth? She looks so haughty that I should have thought her a princess at the very least, with a pedigree reaching as far back as the deluge. But this lady was no better born than many other ladies who give themselves airs; and all sensible people laughed at her absurd pretensions; the fact is she had been maid-servant to the

Queen when her Majesty was only Princess, and her husband had been head footman, but after his death or *disappearance*, of which you shall hear presently, this Mrs. Gruffanuff, by flattering, toadying, and wheedling her royal mistress, became a favorite with the Queen (who was rather a weak woman), and her Majesty gave her a title, and made her nursery governess to the Princess.

And now I must tell you about the Princess's learning and accomplishments, for which she had such a wonderful character. Clever Angelica certainly was, but as *idle as possible*. Play at sight, indeed! she could play one or two pieces, and pretend that she had never seen them before; she could answer half a dozen Mangnal's Questions; but then you must take care to ask the *right* ones. As for her languages, she had masters in plenty, but I doubt whether she knew more than a few phrases in each, for all her pretence; and as for her embroidery and her drawing, she showed beautiful specimens, it is true, but *who did them?*

This obliges me to tell the truth, and to do so I must go back ever so far, and tell you about the FAIRY BLACKSTICK.

CHAPTER III.

Tells Who the Fairy Blackstick Was, and Who Were Ever So
Many Grand Personages Besides.

BETWEEN the kingdoms of
Paflagonia and Crim Tartary,
there lived a mysterious personage, who was known in
those countries as the Fairy
Blackstick, from the ebony wand or
crutch which she carried; on which
she rode to the moon sometimes,
or upon other excursions of busi-
ness or pleasure, and with which she performed her
wonders.

When she was young, and had been first taught the
art of conjuring, by the necromancer, her father, she
was always practising her skill, whizzing about from
one kingdom to another upon her black stick, and con-
ferring her fairy favors upon this Prince or that. She
had scores of royal godchildren; turned numberless
wicked people into beasts, birds, millstones, clocks,
pumps, bootjacks, umbrellas, or other absurd shapes;
and in a word was one of the most active and officious
of the whole College of fairies.

But after two or three thousand years of this sport, I

suppose Blackstick grew tired of it. Or perhaps she thought, "What good am I doing by sending this Princess to sleep for a hundred years? by fixing a black pudding on to that booby's nose? by causing diamonds and pearls to drop from one little girl's mouth, and vipers and toads from another's? I begin to think I do as much harm as good by my performances. I might as well shut my incantations up, and allow things to take their natural course.

"There were my two young goddaughters, King Savio's wife, and Duke Padella's wife; I gave them each a present, which was to render them charming in the eyes of their husbands, and secure the affection of those gentlemen as long as they lived. What good did my Rose and my Ring do these two women? None on earth. From having all their whims indulged by their husbands, they became capricious, lazy, ill-humored, absurdly vain, and leered and languished, and fancied themselves irresistibly beautiful, when they were really quite old and hideous, the ridiculous creatures! They used actually to patronize me when I went to pay them a visit: — *me*, the Fairy Blackstick, who knows all the wisdom of the necromancers, and who could have turned them into baboons, and all their diamonds into strings of onions, by a single wave of my rod!" So she locked up her books in her cupboard, declined further magical performances, and scarcely used her wand at all except as a cane to walk about with.

So when Duke Padella's lady had a little son (the Duke was at that time only one of the principal noblemen in Crim Tartary), Blackstick, although invited to

the christening, would not so much as attend; but
merely sent her compliments and a silver papboat for
the baby, which was really not worth a couple of guineas.   About the same time the Queen of Paflagonia
presented his Majesty with a son and heir; and guns
were fired, the capital illuminated, and no end of feasts
ordained to celebrate the young Prince's birth.   It was
thought the fairy, who was asked to be his godmother,
would at least have presented him with an invisible
jacket, a flying horse, a Fortunatus' purse, or some
other valuable token of her favor; but instead, Blackstick went up to the cradle of the child Giglio, when
everybody was admiring him and complimenting his
royal papa and mamma, and said " My poor child, the
best thing I can send you is a *little misfortune*," and
this was all she would utter, to the disgust of Giglio's
parents, who died very soon after, when Giglio's uncle
took the throne, as we read in Chapter I.

In like manner, when CAVOLFIORE, King of Crim
Tartary, had a christening of his only child, ROSALBA,
the Fairy Blackstick, who had been invited, was not
more gracious than in Prince Giglio's case.   Whilst
everybody was expatiating over the beauty of the darling child, and congratulating its parents, the Fairy
Blackstick looked very sadly at the baby and its
mother, and said : " My good woman (for the Fairy
was very familiar, and no more minded a Queen
than a washerwoman) — my good woman, these people
who are following you will be the first to turn
against you; and, as for this little lady, the best
thing I can wish her is a *little misfortune*."   So she
touched Rosalba with her black wand, looked severely

at the courtiers, motioned the Queen an adieu with her hand, and sailed slowly up into the air out of the window.

When she was gone, the Court people, who had been awed and silent in her presence, began to speak. "What an odious Fairy she is [they said] — a pretty Fairy, indeed! Why, she went to the King of Paflagonia's christening, and pretended to do all sorts of things for that family; and what has happened — the Prince, her godson, has been turned off his throne by his uncle. Would we allow our sweet Princess to be deprived of her rights by an enemy? Never, never, never, never!"

And they all shouted in a chorus, "Never, never, never, never!"

Now, I should like to know, and how did these fine courtiers show their fidelity? One of King Cavolfiore's vassals, the Duke Padella just mentioned, rebelled against the King, who went out to chastise his rebellious subject. "Any one rebel against our beloved and august monarch!" cried the courtiers; "any one resist *him*? He is invincible, irresistible. He will bring home Padella a prisoner; and tie him to a donkey's tail, and drive him round the town, saying: 'This is the way the great Cavolfiore treats rebels.'"

The King went forth to vanquish Padella; and the poor Queen, who was a very timid, anxious creature, grew so frightened and ill, that I am sorry to say she died, leaving injunctions with her ladies to take care of the dear little Rosalba. Of course they said they would. Of course they vowed they would die rather

than any harm should happen to the Princess. At
first the *Crim Tartar Court Journal* stated that the
King was obtaining great victories over the audacious
rebel; then it was announced that the troops of the
infamous Padella were in flight; then it was said that
the royal army would soon come up with the enemy;
and then — then the news came that King Cavolfiore
was vanquished and slain by His Majesty, King Padella
the First!

At this news, half the courtiers ran off to pay their
duty to the conquering chief, and the other half ran
away, laying hands on all the best articles in the
palace, and poor little Rosalba was left there quite
alone — quite alone; and she toddled from one room
to another, crying: "Countess! Duchess! [only she
said 'Tountess, Duttess,' not being able to speak plain]
bring me my mutton sop; my Royal Highness hungry!
Tountess, Duttess!" And she went from the private
apartments into the throne-room and nobody was there;
and thence into the ball-room, and nobody was there;
and thence into the pages' room, and nobody was
there; and she toddled down the great staircase into
the hall, and nobody was there; and the door was
open, and she went into the court, and into the garden,
and thence into the wilderness, and thence into the
forest where the wild beasts live, and was never heard
of any more!

A piece of her torn mantle and one of her shoes
were found in the wood in the mouths of two lioness's
cubs, whom KING PADELLA and a royal hunting party
shot — for he was King now, and reigned over Crim
Tartary. "So the poor little Princess is done for,"

said he; "well, what's done can't be helped. Gentlemen, let us go to luncheon!" And one of the courtiers
took up the shoe and put it in his pocket. And there
was an end of Rosalba!

CHAPTER IV.

How Blackstick was not Asked to the Princess Angelica's Christening.

WHEN the Princess Angelica was born, her parents not only did not ask the Fairy Blackstick to the christening party, but gave orders to their porter absolutely to refuse her if she called. This porter's name was Gruffanuff, and he had been selected for the post by their Royal Highnesses because he was a very tall, fierce man, who could say "Not at home" to a tradesman or an unwelcome visitor with a rudeness which frightened most such persons away. He was the husband of that Countess whose picture we have just seen, and as long as they were together they quarrelled from morning till night. Now this fellow tried his rudeness once too often, as you shall hear. For the Fairy Blackstick coming to call upon the Prince and Princess, who were actually sitting at the open drawing-room window, Gruffanuff not only denied them, but made the most *odious vulgar sign* as he was going to slam the door in the Fairy's face! "Git away, hold Blackstick!" said he. "I tell you, Master and Missis ain't at home to you;" and he was, as we have said, *going* to slam the door.

But the Fairy, with her wand, prevented the door being shut; and Gruffanuff came out again in a fury, swearing in the most abominable way, and asking the Fairy "whether she thought he was a-going to stay at that there door hall day?"

"You *are* going to stay at that door all day and all night, and for many a long year," the Fairy said, very majestically; and Gruffanuff, coming out of the door, straddling before it with his great calves, burst out laughing, and cried: "Ha, ha, ha! this *is* a good un! Ha—ah—what's this? Let me down—O—o—H'm!" and then he was dumb!

For, as the Fairy waved her wand over him, he felt himself rising off the ground, and fluttering up against the door, and then, as if a screw ran into his stomach, he felt a dreadful pain there, and was pinned to the door; and then his arms flew up over his head; and his legs, after writhing about wildly, twisted under his body; and he felt cold, cold, growing over him, as if he was turning into metal, and he said: "O—o—H'm!" and could say no more, because he was dumb.

He *was* turned into metal! He was from being *brazen, brass!* He was neither more nor less than a knocker! And there he was, nailed to the door in the blazing summer day, till he burned almost red-hot; and there he was, nailed to the door all the bitter winter nights, till his brass nose was dropping with icicles. And the postman came and rapped at him, and the vulgarest boy with a letter came and hit him up against the door. And the King and Queen (Prince and Princess they were then), coming home from a walk that evening, the King said: "Hullo, my dear! you have had a new knocker put on the door. Why, it's rather like our porter in the face! What has become of that boozy vagabond?" And the housemaid came and scrubbed his nose with sandpaper. And once, when the Princess Angelica's little sister was born, he was tied up in an old kid glove; and, another night, some *larking* young men tried to wrench him off, and put him to the most excruciating agony with a turnscrew. And then the Queen had a fancy to have the color of the door altered; and the painters dabbed him over the mouth and eyes, and nearly choked him, as they painted him pea-green. I warrant he had leisure to repent of having been rude to the Fairy Blackstick!

As for his wife, she did not miss him; and as he was always guzzling beer at the public-house, and notoriously quarrelling with his wife, and in debt to the tradesmen, it was supposed he had run away from all these evils and emigrated to Australia or America. And when the Prince and Princess chose to become King and Queen, they left their old house, and nobody thought of the porter any more.

CHAPTER V.

How Princess Angelica Took a Little Maid.

ONE day, when the Princess Angelica was quite a little girl, she was walking in the garden of the palace, with Mrs. Gruffanuff, the governess, holding a parasol over her head to keep her sweet complexion from the freckles, and Angelica was carrying a bun to feed the swans and ducks in the royal pond.

They had not reached the duck-pond, when there came toddling up to them such a funny little girl! She had a great quantity of hair blowing about her chubby little cheeks, and looked as if she had not been washed or combed for ever so long. She wore a ragged bit of a cloak, and had only one shoe on.

"You little wretch, who let you in here?" asked Gruffanuff.

"Dive me dat bun," said the little girl, "me vely hungry."

"Hungry! what is that?" asked Princess Angelica, and gave the child the bun.

"Oh, Princess!" said Gruffanuff, "how good, how kind, how truly angelical you are! See, your Majesties, she said to the King and Queen, who now came up, along with their nephew, Prince Giglio, "how kind the Princess is! She met this little dirty wretch in the garden — I can't tell how she came in here, or why the guards did not shoot her dead at the gate! — and the dear darling of a Princess has given her the whole of her bun!"

"I didn't want it," said Angelica.

"But you are a darling little angel all the same," says the governess.

"Yes; I know I am," said Angelica. "Dirty little girl, don't you think I am very pretty?" Indeed, she had on the finest of little dresses and hats, and, as her hair was carefully curled, she really looked very well.

"Oh, pooty, pooty!" says the little girl, capering about, laughing, and dancing, and munching her bun; and as she ate it she began to sing, "Oh what fun to have a plum bun! how I wis it never was done!" At which, and her funny accent, Angelica, Giglio, and the King and Queen began to laugh very merrily.

"I can dance as well as sing," says the little girl. "I can dance, and I can sing, and I can do all sorts of ting." And she ran to a flower-bed, and pulling a few polyanthuses, rhododendrons, and other flowers, made herself a little wreath, and danced before the King and Queen so drolly and prettily that everybody was delighted.

"Who was your mother — who were your relations, little girl?" said the Queen.

The little girl said: "Little lion was my brudder; great big lioness my mudder; neber heard of any udder." And she capered away on her one shoe, and everybody was exceedingly diverted.

So Angelica said to the Queen: "Mamma, my parrot

flew away yesterday out of its cage, and I don't care any more for any of my toys, and I think this funny little dirty child will amuse me. I will take her home and give her some of my old frocks."

"Oh, the generous darling!" says Gruffanuff.

"Which I have worn ever so many times, and am quite tired of," Angelica went on; "and she shall be my little maid. Will you go home with me, little dirty girl?"

The child clapped her hands, and said: "Go home with you — yes! You pooty Princess! — Have a nice dinner and wear a new dress!"

And they all laughed again, and took home the child to the palace, where, when she was washed and combed, and had one of the Princess's frocks given to her, she looked as handsome as Angelica, almost. Not that she ever thought so; for this little lady never imagined that anybody in the world could be as pretty, as good, or as clever as herself. In order that the little girl should not become too proud and conceited, Mrs. Gruffanuff took her old ragged mantle and one shoe, and put them into a glass box, with a card laid upon them, upon which was written: "These were the old clothes in which little BETSINDA was found when the great goodness and admirable kindness of her Royal Highness, the Princess Angelica, received this little outcast." And the date was added, and the box locked up.

For a while little Betsinda was a great favorite with the Princess, and she danced, and sang, and made her little rhymes, to amuse her mistress. But then the Princess got a monkey, and afterwards a little dog, and afterwards a doll, and did not care for Betsinda any more, who became very melancholy and quiet, and sang no more funny songs, because nobody cared to hear her. And then, as she grew older, she was made a little lady's-maid to the Princess; and though she had no wages, she worked and mended, and put Angelica's hair in papers, and was never cross when scolded, and was always eager to please her mistress, and was always up early and to bed late, and at hand when wanted, and in fact became a perfect little maid. So the two girls grew up, and when the Princess came out, Betsinda was never tired of waiting on her; and made her dresses better than the best milliner, and was useful in a hundred ways. Whilst the Princess was having her masters, Betsinda would sit and watch them; and in this way she picked up a great deal of learning; for she was always awake, though her mistress was not, and listened to the wise professors when Angelica was yawning, or thinking of the next ball. And when the dancing-master came, Betsinda learned along with Angelica; and when the music-master came, she watched him, and practised the Princess's pieces when Angelica was away at balls and parties; and when the drawing-master came, she took note of all he said and did; and the same with French, Italian, and all other languages — she learned them from the teacher who came to Angelica. When the Princess was going out of an evening she would say: " My good Betsinda, you may as well finish what I have begun." "Yes, Miss," Betsinda would say, and sit down very cheerful, not to *finish* what Angelica begun, but to *do* it.

For instance, the Princess would begin a head of a warrior, let us say, and when it was begun it was something like this.

But when it was done, the warrior was like this, only handsomer still if possible), and the Princess put her name to the drawing; and the Court and King and Queen, and above all poor Giglio, admired the picture of all things, and said: "Was there ever a genius like Angelica?" So, I am sorry to say, was it with the Princess's embroidery and other accomplishments; and Angelica actually believed that she did these things herself, and received all the flattery of the Court as if every word of it was true. Thus she began to think that there was no young woman in all the world equal to herself, and that there was no young man good enough for her. As for Betsinda, as she heard none of these phrases, she was not puffed up by them, and being a most grateful, good-natured girl, she was only too anxious to do everything which might give her mistress pleasure. Now you begin to perceive that Angelica had faults of her own, and was by no means such a wonder of wonders as people represented her Royal Highness to be.

CHAPTER VI.

How Prince Giglio Behaved Himself.

AND now let us speak about Prince Giglio, the nephew of the reigning monarch of Paflagonia. It has already been stated, in page 236, that as long as he had a smart coat to wear, a good horse to ride, and money in his pocket, or rather to take out of his pocket, for he was very good-natured, my young Prince did not care for the loss of his crown and sceptre, being a thoughtless youth, not much inclined to politics or any kind of learning. So his tutor had a sinecure. Giglio would not learn classics or mathematics, and the Lord Chancellor of Paflagonia, SQUARETOSO, pulled a very long face because the Prince could not be got to study the Paflagonian laws and constitution; but on the other hand, the King's gamekeepers and huntsmen found the Prince an apt pupil; the dancing-master pronounced that he was a most elegant and assiduous scholar; the First Lord of the Billiard Table gave the most flattering reports of the Prince's skill; so did the Groom of the Tennis Court; and as for the Captain of the Guard and Fencing Master, the *valiant* and *veteran* Count KUTASOFF HEDZ-

OFF, he avowed that since he ran the General of Crim Tartary, the dreadful Grumbuskin, through the body, he never had encountered so expert a swordsman as Prince Giglio.

I hope you do not imagine that there was any impropriety in the Prince and Princess walking together in the palace garden, and because Giglio kissed Angelica's hand in a polite manner. In the first place they are cousins; next, the Queen is walking in the garden too (you cannot see her for she happens to be behind that tree), and her majesty always wished that Angelica and Giglio should marry: so did Giglio: so did Angelica sometimes, for she thought her cousin very handsome, brave, and good-natured; but then you know she was so clever and knew so many things, and poor Giglio knew nothing, and had no conversation. When they looked at the stars, what did Giglio know of the heavenly bodies? Once, when on a sweet night in a balcony where they were standing, Angelica said: "There is the Bear." "Where?" says Giglio; "don't be afraid, Angelica! if a dozen bears come, I will kill them rather than they shall hurt you." "Oh, you silly creature!" says she, "you are very good, but you are not very wise." When they looked at the flowers, Giglio was utterly unacquainted with botany, and had never heard of Linnæus. When the butterflies passed, Giglio knew nothing about them, being as ignorant of entomology as I am of algebra. So you see, Angelica, though she liked Giglio pretty well, despised him on account of his ignorance. I think she probably valued *her own learning* rather too much; but to think too well of one's self is the fault of people of all ages and both sexes. Finally, when nobody else was there, Angelica liked her cousin well enough.

King Valoroso was very delicate in health, and withal so fond of good dinners (which were prepared for him by his French cook, Marmitonio), that it was supposed he could not live long. Now the idea of anything happening to the King struck the artful Prime-Minister and the designing old lady-in-waiting with terror. For, thought Glumboso and the Countess, "when Prince Giglio marries his cousin and comes to the throne, what a pretty position we shall be in, whom he dislikes, and who have always been unkind to him. We shall lose our places in a trice; Gruffanuff will have to give up all the jewels, laces, snuff-boxes, rings, and watches which belonged to the Queen, Giglio's mother; and Glumboso will be forced to refund two hundred and seventeen thousand millions nine hundred and eighty-seven thousand four hundred and thirty-nine pounds, thirteen shillings, and sixpence halfpenny, money left to Prince Giglio by his poor dead father." So the Lady of Honor and the Prime Minister hated Giglio because they had done him a wrong; and these unprincipled people invented a hundred cruel stories about poor Giglio, in order to influence the King, Queen, and Princess against him: how he was so ignorant that he could not spell the commonest words, and actually wrote Valoroso Valloroso, and spelt Angelica with two l's; how he drank a great deal too much wine at dinner, and was always idling in the stables with the grooms; how he owed ever so much money at the pastry-cook's and the haberdasher's; how he used to go to sleep at church; how he was fond of playing cards with the pages. So did the Queen like playing cards; so did the King go to sleep at church, and eat and drink too much; and if Giglio owed a trifle for tarts, who owed him two hundred and seventeen thousand millions nine hundred and eighty-seven thousand four hundred and thirty-nine pounds, thirteen shillings, and sixpence halfpenny, I should like to know? Detractors and tale-bearers (in my humble opinion) had better look at *home*. All this back-biting and slandering had effect upon Princess Angelica, who began to look coldly on her cousin, then to laugh at him and scorn him for being so stupid, then to sneer at him for having vulgar associates; and at court balls, dinners, and so forth, to treat him so unkindly that poor Giglio became quite ill, took to his bed, and sent for the doctor.

His Majesty King Valoroso, as we have seen, had his own reasons for disliking his nephew; and as for those innocent readers who ask why? I beg (with the permission of their dear parents) to refer them to Shakespeare's pages, where they will read why King John disliked Prince Arthur. With the Queen, his royal but weak-minded aunt, when Giglio was out of sight he was out of mind. While she had her whist and her evening parties, she cared for little else.

I dare say *two villains*, who shall be nameless, wished Doctor Pildrafto, the Court Physician, had killed Giglio right out, but he only bled and physicked him so severely that the Prince was kept to his room for several months and grew as thin as a post.

Whilst he was lying sick in this way, there came to the Court of Paflagonia a famous painter, whose name was Tomaso Lorenzo, and who was Painter in Ordinary to the King of Crim Tartary, Paflagonia's neighbor. Tomaso Lorenzo painted all the Court, who were delighted with his work; for even Countess Gruffanuff looked young and Glumboso good-humored in his pictures. "He flatters very much," some people said. "Nay!" says Princess Angelica, "I am above flattery, and I think he did not make my picture handsome enough. I can't bear to hear a man of genius unjustly cried down, and I hope my dear papa will make Lorenzo a knight of his Order of the Cucumber."

The Princess Angelica, although the courtiers vowed Her Royal Highness could draw so *beautifully* that the idea of her taking lessons was absurd, yet chose to have Lorenzo for a teacher, and it was wonderful, *as long as she painted in his studio*, what beautiful pictures she made! Some of the performances were engraved for the Book of Beauty; others were sold for enormous sums at Charity Bazaars. She wrote the *signatures* under the drawings, no doubt, but I think I know who did the pictures — this artful painter, who had come with other designs on Angelica than merely to teach her to draw.

One day, Lorenzo showed the Princess a portrait of a young man in armor, with fair hair and the loveliest blue eyes, and an expression at once melancholy and interesting.

"Dear Signor Lorenzo, who is this?" asked the Princess. "I never saw any one so handsome," says Countess Gruffanuff (the old humbug).

"That," said the painter, "that, madam, is the portrait of my august young master, His Royal Highness Bulbo, Crown Prince of Crim Tartary, Duke of Acroceraunia, Marquis of Poluphloisboio, and Knight Grand

Cross of the Order of the Pumpkin. That is the Order of the Pumpkin glittering on his manly breast, and received by his Royal Highness from his august father, his Majesty King PADELLA I., for his gallantry at the battle of Rimbombamento, when he slew with his own princely hand the King of Ograria and two hundred and eleven giants of the two hundred and eighteen who formed the King's body-guard. The remainder were destroyed by the brave Crim Tartar army after an obstinate combat, in which the Crim Tartars suffered severely."

What a Prince! thought Angelica: so brave — so calm-looking — so young — what a hero!

"He is as accomplished as he is brave," continued the Court Painter. "He knows all languages perfectly, sings deliciously, plays every instrument, composes operas which have been acted a thousand nights running at the Imperial Theatre of Crim Tartary, and danced in a ballet there before the King and Queen, in which he looked so beautiful, that his cousin, the lovely daughter of the King of Circassia, died for love of him."

"Why did he not marry the poor Princess?" asked Angelica, with a sigh.

"Because they were *first cousins*, Madam, and the clergy forbid these unions," said the painter. "And, besides, the young Prince had given his royal heart *elsewhere*."

"And to whom?" asked Her Royal Highness.

"I am not at liberty to mention the Princess's name," answered the Painter.

"But you may tell me the first letter of it," gasped out the Princess.

"That your Royal Highness is at liberty to guess," says Lorenzo.

"Does it begin with a Z?" asked Angelica.

The Painter said it wasn't a Z; then she tried a Y; then an X; then a W, and went so backwards through almost the whole alphabet.

When she came to D, and it wasn't D, she grew very much excited; when she came to C, and it wasn't C, she was still more nervous; when she came to B, *and it wasn't B,* "O dearest Gruffanuff," she said, "lend me your smelling bottle!" and, hiding her head in the Countess's shoulder, she faintly whispered: "Ah, Signor, can it be A?"

"It was A; and though I may not, by my Royal Master's orders, tell your Royal Highness the Princess's name, whom he fondly, madly, devotedly, rapturously loves, I may show you her portrait," says this slyboots: and leading the Princess up to a gilt frame he drew a curtain which was before it.

O goodness, the frame contained a LOOKING-GLASS! and Angelica saw her own face!

CHAPTER VII.

How Giglio and Angelica Had a Quarrel.

THE Court Painter of His Majesty the King of Crim Tartary returned to that monarch's dominions, carrying away a number of sketches which he had made in the Paflagonian capital (you know, of course, my dears, that the name of that capital is Blombodinga); but the most charming of all his pieces was a portrait of the Princess Angelica, which all the Crim Tartar nobles came to see. With this work the King was so delighted, that he decorated the Painter with his Order of the Pumpkin (sixth class), and the artist became Sir Tomaso Lorenzo, K.P., thenceforth.

King Valoroso also sent Sir Tomaso his Order of the Cucumber, besides a handsome order for money, for he painted the King, Queen, and principal nobility while at Blombodinga, and became all the fashion, to the perfect rage of all the artists in Paflagonia, where the King used to point to the portrait of Prince Bulbo, which Sir Tomaso had left behind him, and say: "Which among you can paint a picture like that?"

It hung in the royal parlor over the royal sideboard, and Princess Angelica could always look at it as she sat making the tea. Each day it seemed to grow handsomer and handsomer, and the Princess grew so fond of looking at it, that she would often spill the tea over the cloth, at which her father and mother would wink and wag their heads, and say to each other: "Aha! we see how things are going."

In the meanwhile poor Giglio lay up-stairs very sick in his chamber, though he took all the doctor's horrible medicines like a good young lad; as I hope *you* do, my dears, when you are ill and mamma sends for the medical man. And the only person who visited Giglio (besides his friend, the captain of the guard, who was almost always busy or on parade) was little Betsinda, the housemaid, who used to do his bedroom and sitting-room out, bring him his gruel, and warm his bed.

When the little housemaid came to him in the morning and evening, Prince Giglio used to say: "Betsinda! Betsinda! how is the Princess Angelica?"

And Betsinda used to answer: "The Princess is very well, thank you, my Lord." And Giglio would heave a sigh, and think: if Angelica were sick I am sure *I* should not be very well.

Then Giglio would say: "Betsinda, has the Princess Angelica asked for me to-day?" And Betsinda would answer: "No, my Lord, not to-day"; or, "She was very busy practising the piano when I saw her"; or, "She was writing invitations for an evening party, and did not speak to me"; or make some excuse or other not strictly consonant with truth; for Betsinda was such a good-natured creature, that she strove to do everything to prevent annoyance to Prince Giglio, and even brought him up roast chicken and jellies from the kitchen (when the doctor allowed them, and Giglio was getting better), saying " that the Princess had made the jelly, or the bread-sauce, with her own hands, on purpose for Giglio."

When Giglio heard this he took heart and began to mend immediately ; and gobbled up all the jelly, and picked the last bone of the chicken — drumsticks, merry-thought, sides'-bones, back, pope's-nose, and all — thanking his dear Angelica ; and he felt so much better the next day, that he dressed and went downstairs, where, whom should he meet but Angelica going into the drawing-room. All the covers were off the chairs, the chandeliers taken out of the bags, the damask curtains uncovered, the work and things carried away, and the handsomest albums on the tables. Angelica had her hair in papers ; in a word, it was evident there was going to be a party.

" Heavens, Giglio ! " cries Angelica ; " *you* here in such a dress ! What a figure you are ! "

" Yes, dear Angelica, I am come down-stairs, and feel so well to-day, thanks to the *fowl* and the *jelly*."

" What do I know about fowls and jellies, that you allude to them in that rude way ? " says Angelica.

" Why, didn't — didn't you send them, Angelica dear ? " says Giglio.

" I send them indeed ! Angelica dear ! No, Giglio dear," says she, mocking him, " *I* was engaged in getting the rooms ready for His Royal Highness the Prince of Crim Tartary, who is coming to pay my papa's Court a visit."

" The — Prince — of — Crim — Tartary ! " Giglio said, aghast.

"Yes, the Prince of Crim Tartary," says Angelica, mocking him. "I dare say you never heard of such a country. What *did* you ever hear of? You don't know whether Crim Tartary is on the Red Sea or on the Black Sea, I dare say."

"Yes, I do; it's on the Red Sea," says Giglio; at which the Princess burst out laughing at him, and said: "Oh, you ninny! You are so ignorant, you are really not fit for society! You know nothing but about horses and dogs; and are only fit to dine with my Royal Father's heaviest dragoons. Don't look so surprised at me, sir; go and put your best clothes on to receive the Prince, and let me get the drawing-room ready."

Giglio said: "O Angelica, Angelica, I didn't think this of you. *This* wasn't your language to me when you gave me this ring, and I gave you mine in the garden, and you gave me that k——"

But what k was we never shall know, for Angelica, in a rage, cried: "Get out, you saucy, rude creature! How dare you remind me of your rudeness? As for your little trumpery twopenny ring, there, sir, there!" And she flung it out of the window.

"It was my mother's marriage ring," cried Giglio.

"*I* don't care whose marriage ring it was," cries Angelica. "Marry the person who picks it up if she's a woman; you sha'n't marry *me*. And give me back *my* ring. I've no patience with people who boast about the things they give away! *I* know who'll give me much finer things than you ever gave me. A beggarly ring indeed, not worth five shillings!"

Now Angelica little knew that the ring which Giglio had given her was a fairy ring: if a man wore it, it made all the women in love with him; if a woman, all the gentlemen. The Queen, Giglio's mother, quite an ordinary looking person, was admired immensely while she wore this ring, and her husband was frantic when she was ill. But when she called her little Giglio to her, and put the ring on his finger, King Savio did not seem to care for his wife so much any more, but transferred all his love to little Giglio. So did everybody love him as long as he had the ring, but when, as quite a child, he gave it to Angelica, people began to love and admire *her;* and Giglio, as the saying is, played only second fiddle.

"Yes," says Angelica, going on in her foolish, ungrateful way, "*I* know who'll give me much finer things than your beggarly little pearl nonsense."

"Very good, Miss! You may take back your ring, too!" says Giglio, his eyes flashing fire at her, and then, as if his eyes had been suddenly opened, he cried out: "Ha, what does this mean? Is *this* the woman I have been in love with all my life? Have I been such a ninny as to throw away my regard upon you? Why — actually — yes — you are a little crooked!"

"Oh, you wretch!" cries Angelica.

"And, upon my conscience, you — you squint a little."

"E!" cries Angelica.

"And your hair is red — and you are marked with the small-pox — and what? you have three false teeth — and one leg shorter than the other!"

"You brute, you brute, you!" Angelica screamed out; and as she seized the ring with one hand, she dealt Giglio one, two, three, smacks on the face, and

would have pulled the hair off his head had he not
started laughing, and crying:

"O dear me, Angelica, don't pull out *my* hair, it
hurts! You might remove a great deal of *your own*,
as I perceive, without scissors or pulling at all. O, ho,
ho! ha, ha, ha! he, he, he!"

And he nearly choked himself with laughing, and
she with rage, when, with a low bow, and dressed in
his Court habit, Count Gambabella, the first lord-in-
waiting, entered and said: "Royal Highnesses! Their
Majesties expect you in the Pink Throne-room, where
they await the arrival of the Prince of CRIM TARTARY."

CHAPTER VIII.

How Gruffanuff Picked the Fairy Ring Up, and Prince Bulbo
Came to Court.

PRINCE BULBO'S arrival had set all the Court in a flutter: everybody was ordered to put his or her best clothes on: the footmen had their gala-liveries; the Lord Chancellor his new wig; the Guards their last new tunics; and Countess Gruffanuff you may be sure was glad of an opportunity of decorating *her* old person with her finest things. She was walking through the court of the Palace on her way to wait upon their Majesties, when she spied something glittering on the pavement, and bade the boy in buttons who was holding up her train, to go and pick up the article shining yonder. He was an ugly little wretch, in some of the late groom-porter's old clothes cut down, and much too tight for him; and yet, when he had taken up the ring (as it turned out to be), and was carrying it to his mistress, she thought he looked like a little cupid. He gave the ring to her; it was a trumpery little thing enough, but too small for any of her old knuckles, so she put it into her pocket.

"O mum!" says the boy, looking at her, "how, how beyoutiful you do look, mum, to-day, mum!"

"And you, too, Jacky," she was going to say;
but, looking down at him — no, he was no longer
good-looking at all — but only the carroty-haired little
Jacky of the morning. However, praise is welcome
from the ugliest of men or boys, and Gruffanuff, bidding the boy hold up her train, walked on in high
good humor. The Guards saluted her with peculiar
respect. Captain Hedzoff, in the ante-room, said:
"My dear madam, you look like an angel to-day."
And so, bowing and smirking, Gruffanuff went in and
took her place behind her Royal Master and Mistress,
who were in the throne-room, awaiting the Prince of
Crim Tartary. Princess Angelica sat at their feet, and
behind the King's chair stood Prince Giglio, looking
very savage.

The Prince of Crim Tartary made his appearance,
attended by Baron Sleibootz, his chamberlain, and
followed by a black page, carrying the most beautiful
crown you ever saw! He was dressed in his travelling
costume, and his hair, as you see, was a little in dis-
order. "I have ridden three hundred miles since
breakfast," said he, "so eager was I to behold the
Prin — the Court, and august family of Paflagonia,
and I could not wait one minute before appearing in
your Majesties' presences."

Giglio, from behind the throne, burst out into a roar
of contemptuous laughter; but all the Royal party, in
fact, were so flurried, that they did not hear this little
outbreak. "Your R. H. is welcome in any dress," says
the King. "Glumboso, a chair for his Royal Highness."

"Any dress his Royal Highness wears *is* a Court
dress," says Princess Angelica, smiling graciously.

"Ah! but you should see my other clothes," said the Prince. "I should have had them on, but that stupid carrier has not brought them. Who's that laughing?"

It was Giglio laughing. "I was laughing," he said, "because you said just now that you were in such a hurry to see the Princess, that you could not wait to change your dress; and now you say you come in those clothes because you have no others."

"And who are you?" says Prince Bulbo, very fiercely.

"My father was King of this country, and I am his only son, Prince!" replies Giglio, with equal haughtiness.

"Ha!" said the King and Glumboso, looking very flurried; but the former, collecting himself, said: "Dear Prince Bulbo, I forgot to introduce to your Royal Highness my dear nephew, his Royal Highness Prince Giglio! Know each other! Embrace each other! Giglio, give his Royal Highness your hand!" and Giglio, giving his hand, squeezed poor Bulbo's until the tears ran out of his eyes. Glumboso now brought a chair for the royal visitor, and placed it on the platform on which the King, Queen, and Prince were seated; but the chair was on the edge of the platform, and as Bulbo sat down, it toppled over, and he with it, rolling over and over, and bellowing like a bull. Giglio roared still louder at this disaster, but it was with laughter: so did all the court when Prince Bulbo got up, for though when he entered the room he appeared not very ridiculous, as he stood up from his fall for a moment, he looked so exceedingly plain and foolish, that nobody could help laughing at him. When he had entered the room, he was observed to carry a rose in his hand, which fell out as he tumbled.

" My rose ! my rose ! " cried Bulbo, and his chamberlain dashed forwards and picked it up, and gave it to the Prince, who put it in his waistcoat. Then people wondered why they had laughed, there was nothing particularly ridiculous in him. He was rather short, rather stout, rather red-haired, but in fine for a Prince not so bad.

So they sat and talked, the royal personages together, the Crim Tartar officers with those of Paflagonia — Giglio very comfortable with Gruffanuff behind the throne. He looked at her with such tender eyes, that her heart was all in a flutter. " Oh, dear Prince, she said, " how could you speak so haughtily in presence of their majesties? I protest I thought I should have fainted."

" I should have caught you in my arms," said Giglio, looking raptures.

" Why were you so cruel to Prince Bulbo, dear Prince ? " says Gruff.

" Because I hate him," says Gil.

" You are jealous of him, and still love poor Angelica," cries Gruffanuff, putting her handkerchief to her eyes.

" I did, but I love her no more ! " Giglio cried. " I despise her ! Were she heiress to twenty thousand thrones, I would despise her and scorn her. But why speak of thrones ? I have lost mine. I am too weak to recover it — I am alone, and have no friend."

" Oh, say not so, dear Prince ! " says Gruffanuff.

" Besides," says he, " I am so happy here *behind the*

throne that I would not change my place, no, not for the throne of the world!"

"What are you two people chattering about there?" says the Queen, who was rather good-natured, though not overburthened with wisdom. "It is time to dress for dinner. Giglio, show Prince Bulbo to his room. Prince, if your clothes have not come we shall be very happy to see you as you are." But when Prince Bulbo got to his bedroom, his luggage was there and unpacked; and the hairdresser coming in, cut and curled him entirely to his own satisfaction; and when the dinner-bell rang, the royal company had not to wait above five-and-twenty minutes until Bulbo appeared, during which time the King, who could not bear to wait, grew as sulky as possible. As for Giglio, he never left Madam Gruffanuff all this time, but stood with her in the embrasure of a window paying her compliments. At length the Groom of the Chambers announced his Royal Highness the Prince of Crim Tartary! and the noble company went into the royal dining-room. It was quite a small party: only the King and Queen, the Princess, whom Bulbo took out, the two Princes, Countess Gruffanuff, Glumboso the Prime Minister, and Prince Bulbo's chamberlain. You may be sure they had a very good dinner — let every boy and girl think of what he or she likes best, and fancy it on the table.[1]

The Princess talked incessantly all dinner-time to the Prince of Crimea, who ate an immense deal too much, and never took his eyes off his plate, except when

---

[1] Here a very pretty game may be played by all the children saying what they like best for dinner.

Giglio, who was carving a goose, sent a quantity of stuffing and onion sauce into one of them. Giglio only burst out a-laughing as the Crimean Prince wiped his shirt-front and face with his scented pocket-handkerchief. He did not make Prince Bulbo any apology. When the Prince looked at him, Giglio would not look that way. When Prince Bulbo said: "Prince Giglio, may I have the honor of taking a glass of wine with you?" Giglio *wouldn't* answer. All his talk and his eyes were for Countess Gruffanuff, who you may be sure was pleased with Giglio's attentions, the vain old creature! When he was not complimenting her, he was making fun of Prince Bulbo, so loud that Gruffanuff was always tapping him with her fan, and saying: "O you satirical Prince! O fie, the Prince will hear!" "Well, I don't mind," says Giglio, louder still. The King and Queen luckily did not hear; for her Majesty was a little deaf, and the King thought so much about his own dinner, and, besides, made such a dreadful noise, hobgobbling in eating it, that he heard nothing else. After dinner his Majesty and the Queen went to sleep in their arm-chairs.

This was the time when Giglio began his tricks with Prince Bulbo, plying that young gentleman with port, sherry, madeira, champagne, marsala, cherry-brandy, and pale ale, of all of which Master Bulbo drank without stint. But in plying his guest, Giglio was obliged to drink himself, and, I am sorry to say, took more than was good for him, so that the young men were very noisy, rude, and foolish when they joined the ladies after dinner; and dearly did they pay for that imprudence, as now, my darlings, you shall hear!

Bulbo went and sat by the piano, where Angelica was playing and singing, and he sang out of tune, and he upset the coffee when the footman brought it, and he laughed out of place, and talked absurdly, and fell asleep and snored horridly. Booh, the nasty pig! But as he lay there stretched on the pink satin sofa, Angelica still persisted in thinking him the most beautiful of human beings. No doubt the magic rose which Bulbo wore caused this infatuation on Angelica's part: but is she the first young woman who has thought a silly fellow charming?

Giglio must go and sit by Gruffanuff, whose old face he too every moment began to find more lovely. He paid the most outrageous compliments to her: There never was such a darling — Older than he was? — Fiddle-de-de! He would marry her — he would have nothing but her!

To marry the heir to the throne! Here was a chance! The artful hussy actually got a sheet of paper and wrote upon it: "This is to give notice that I, Giglio, only son of Savio, King of Paflagonia, hereby promise to marry the charming and virtuous Barbara Griselda, Countess Gruffanuff, and widow of the late Jenkins Gruffanuff, Esq."

"What is it you are writing? you charming Gruffy!" says Giglio, who was lolling on the sofa by the writing-table.

"Only an order for you to sign, dear Prince, for giving coals and blankets to the poor this cold weather. Look! the King and Queen are both asleep, and your Royal Highness's order will do."

So Giglio, who was very good-natured, as Gruffy well

knew, signed the order immediately; and when she had it in her pocket you may fancy what airs she gave herself. She was ready to flounce out of the room before the Queen herself, as now she was the wife of the *rightful* King of Paflagonia! She would not speak to Glumboso, whom she thought a brute for depriving her *dear husband* of the crown! And when candles came, and she had helped to undress the Queen and Princess, she went into her own room, and actually practised on a sheet of paper, "Griselda Paflagonia," "Barbara Regina," "Grizelda Barbara Paf. Reg.," and I don't know what signatures besides, against the day when she should be Queen, forsooth!

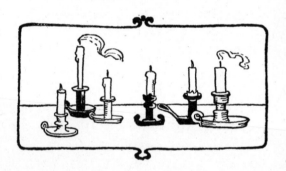

CHAPTER IX.

How Betsinda Got the Warming-Pan.

LITTLE Betsinda came in to put Gruffanuff's hair in paper; and the Countess was so pleased, that, for a wonder, she complimented Betsinda. "Betsinda!" she said, "you dressed my hair very nicely to-day; I promised you a little present. Here are five sh — no, here is a pretty little ring, that I picked — that I have had some time." And she gave Betsinda the ring she had picked up in the Court. It fitted Betsinda exactly.

"It's like the ring the Princess used to wear," says the maid.

"No such thing," says Gruffanuff, "I have had it ever so long. There — tuck me up quite comfortable; and now, as it's a very cold night (the snow is beating in at the window), you may go and warm dear Prince Giglio's bed, like a good girl, and then you may unrip my green silk, and then you can just do me up a little cap for the morning, and then you can mend that hole in my silk stocking, and then you can go to bed, Betsinda. Mind, I shall want my cup of tea at five o'clock in the morning."

"I suppose I had best warm both the young gentlemen's beds, ma'am," says Betsinda.

Gruffanuff, for reply, said, " Hau-au-ho ! — Grau-haw-hoo ! — Hong-hrho ! " In fact, she was snoring sound asleep.

Her room, you know, is next to the King and Queen, and the Princess is next to them. So pretty Betsinda went away for the coals to the kitchen, and filled the royal warming-pan.

Now, she was a very kind, merry, civil, pretty girl; but there must have been something very captivating about her this evening, for all the women in the servants' hall began to scold and abuse her. The housekeeper said she was a pert, stuck-up thing; the upper-housemaid asked, how dare she wear such ringlets and ribbons, it was quite improper! The cook (for there was a woman-cook as well as a man cook) said to the kitchen-maid that *she* never could see any thing in that creetur ; but as for the men, every one of them, coachman John, Buttons the page, and Monsieur, the Prince of Crim Tartary's valet, started up, and said —

" My eyes !
" O mussy !
" O jemmany !
" O ciel !
} What a pretty girl Betsinda is ! "

" Hands off; none of your impertinence, you vulgar, low people ! " says Betsinda, walking off with her pan of coals. She heard the young gentlemen playing at billiards as she went up-stairs: first to Prince Giglio's bed, which she warmed, and then to Prince Bulbo's room.

He came in just as she had done; and as soon as he saw her, " O! O! O! O! O! O! what a beyou — oo — ootiful creature you are. You angel — you peri — you rosebud, let me be thy bulbul — thy Bulbo, too! Fly to the desert, fly with me! I never saw a young gazelle to glad me with its dark blue eye that had eyes like thine. Thou nymph of beauty, take, take this young heart. A truer never did itself sustain within a soldier's waistcoat. Be mine! Be mine! Be Princess of Crim Tartary! My Royal father will approve our union; and, as for that little carroty-haired Angelica, I do not care a fig for her any more."

"Go away, your Royal Highness, and go to bed, please," said Betsinda, with the warming-pan.

But Bulbo said: "No, never, till thou swearest to be mine, thou lovely, blushing, chambermaid divine! Here, at thy feet, the Royal Bulbo lies, the trembling captive of Betsinda's eyes."

And he went on, making himself so *absurd and ridiculous*, that Betsinda, who was full of fun, gave him a touch with the warming-pan, which, I promise you, made him cry "O-o-o-o!" in a very different manner.

Prince Bulbo made such a noise that Prince Giglio, who heard him from the next room, came in to see what was the matter. As soon as he saw what was taking place, Giglio, in a fury, rushed on Bulbo, kicked him in the rudest manner up to the ceiling, and went on kicking him till his hair was quite out of curl.

Poor Betsinda did not know whether to laugh or to cry; the kicking certainly must hurt the Prince, but then he looked so droll! When Giglio had done knocking him up and down to the ground, and whilst he went into a corner rubbing himself, what do you think Giglio does? He goes down on his knees to Betsinda, takes her hand, begs her to accept his heart, and offers to marry her that moment. Fancy Betsinda's condition, who had been in love with the Prince ever since she first saw him in the palace garden, when she was quite a little child.

"Oh, divine Betsinda!" says the Prince, "how have I lived fifteen years in thy company without seeing thy perfections? What woman in all Europe, Asia, Africa, and America, nay, in Australia, only it is not yet discovered, can presume to be thy equal? Angelica? Pish! Gruffanuff? Phoo! The Queen? Ha, ha! Thou art my Queen. Thou art the real Angelica, because thou art really angelic."

"Oh, Prince! I am but a poor chambermaid," says Betsinda, looking, however, very much pleased.

"Didst thou not tend me in my sickness, when all forsook me?" continues Giglio. "Did not thy gentle hand smooth my pillow, and bring me jelly and roast chicken?"

"Yes, dear Prince, I did," says Betsinda, "and I sewed your Royal Highness's shirt-buttons on too, if you please, your Royal Highness," cries this artless maiden.

When poor Prince Bulbo, who was now madly in love with Betsinda, heard this declaration, when he saw the unmistakable glances which she flung upon Giglio, Bulbo began to cry bitterly, and tore quantities of hair out of his head, till it all covered the room like so much tow.

Betsinda had left the warming-pan on the floor while the Princes were going on with their conversation, and as they began now to quarrel and be very fierce with one another, she thought proper to run away.

" You great big blubbering booby, tearing your hair in the corner there; of course you will give me satisfaction for insulting Betsinda. *You* dare to kneel down at Princess Giglio's knees and kiss her hand!"

" She's not Princess Giglio!" roars out Bulbo. " She shall be Princess Bulbo, no other shall be Princess Bulbo."

" You are engaged to my cousin!" bellows out Giglio.

" I hate your cousin," says Bulbo.

" You shall give me satisfaction for insulting her!" cries Giglio in a fury.

" I'll have your life."

" I'll run you through."

" I'll cut your throat."

" I'll blow your brains out."

" I'll knock your head off."

" I'll send a friend to you in the morning."

" I'll send a bullet into you in the afternoon."

" We'll meet again," says Giglio, shaking his fist in Bulbo's face; and seizing up the warming-pan, he kissed it because, forsooth, Betsinda had carried it, and rushed down-stairs. What should he see on the landing but his Majesty talking to Betsinda, whom he called all sorts of fond names. His Majesty had heard a row in the building, so he stated, and smelling something burning had come out to see what the matter was.

" It's the young gentlemen smoking, perhaps, sir," says Betsinda.

" Charming chambermaid," says the King (like all the rest of them), " never mind the young men! Turn thy eyes on a middle-aged autocrat, who has been considered not ill-looking in his time."

"Oh, sir! what will her Majesty say?" cries Betsinda.

"Her Majesty!" laughs the monarch. "Her Majesty be hanged. Am I not Autocrat of Paflagonia? Have I not blocks, ropes, axes, hangmen — ha? Runs not a river by my palace wall? Have I not sacks to sew up wives withal? Say but the word, that thou wilt be mine own, — your mistress straightway in a sack is sewn, and thou the sharer of my heart and throne."

When Giglio heard these atrocious sentiments, he forgot the respect usually paid to Royalty, lifted up the warming-pan and knocked down the King as flat as a pancake; after which, Master Giglio took to his heels and ran away, and Betsinda went off screaming, and the Queen, the Princess, and Gruffanuff all came out of their rooms. Fancy their feelings on beholding their husband, father, sovereign, in this posture!

CHAPTER X.

How King Valoroso was in a Dreadful Passion.

S the coals began to burn him, the
King came to himself and stood up.
"Ho! my captain of the guards!" his
majesty exclaimed, stamping his royal
feet with rage. O piteous spectacle!
The King's nose was bent quite crooked
by the blow of Prince Giglio! His Majesty
ground his teeth with rage. "Hedzoff," he
said, taking a death warrant out of his
dressing-gown pocket, "Hedzoff, good Hedzoff, seize
upon the Prince. Thou'lt find him in his chamber
two pair up. But now he dared, with sacrilegious
hand, to strike the sacred night-cap of a king — Hedzoff, and floor me with a warming-pan! Away, no
more demur, the villain dies! See it be done, or
else, — h'm! — ha! — h'm! mind thine own eyes!"
and followed by the ladies, and lifting up the tails of
his dressing-gown, the King entered his own apartment.

Captain Hedzoff was very much affected, having a
sincere love for Giglio. "Poor, poor Giglio!" he said,
the tears rolling over his manly face, and dripping
down his moustachios; "my noble young prince, is it
my hand must lead thee to death?"

"Lead him to fiddlestick, Hedzoff," said a female voice. It was Gruffanuff, who had come out in her dressing-gown when she heard the noise. "The King said you were to hang the Prince. Well, hang the Prince."

"I don't understand you," says Hedzoff, who was not a very clever man.

"You Gaby! he didn't say *which* Prince," says Gruffanuff.

"No; he didn't say which, certainly," said Hedzoff.

"Well, then, take Bulbo, and hang *him!*"

When Captain Hedzoff heard this he began to dance about for joy. "Obedience is a soldier's honor," says he. "Prince Bulbo's head will do capitally," and he went to arrest the Prince the very first thing next morning.

He knocked at the door. "Who's there?" says Bulbo. "Captain Hedzoff? Step in, pray, my good Captain. I'm delighted to see you. I have been expecting you."

"Have you?" says Hedzoff.

"Sleibootz, my Chamberlain, will act for me," says the Prince.

"I beg your Royal Highness's pardon, but you will have to act for yourself, and it's a pity to wake Baron Sleibootz."

The Prince Bulbo still seemed to take the matter very coolly. "Of course, Captain," says he, "you are come about that affair with Prince Giglio."

"Precisely," says Hedzoff, "that affair of Prince Giglio."

"Is it to be pistols or swords, Captain?" asks Bulbo.

"I'm a pretty good hand with both, and I'll do for Prince Giglio as sure as my name is my Royal Highness Prince Bulbo."

"There's some mistake, my lord," says the Captain. "The business is done with *axes* among us."

"Axes? That's sharp work," says Bulbo. "Call my Chamberlain; he'll be my second, and in ten minutes I flatter myself you'll see Master Giglio's head off his impertinent shoulders. I'm hungry for his blood! Hoo-oo, aw!" and he looked as savage as an ogre.

"I beg your pardon, sir, but by this warrant I am to take you prisoner, and hand you over to — to the executioner."

"Pooh, pooh, my good man! — Stop, I say — ho! — hulloa!" was all that this luckless prince was enabled to say, for Hedzoff's Guards seizing him, tied a handkerchief over his mouth and face, and carried him to the place of execution.

The King, who happened to be talking to Glumboso, saw him pass, and took a pinch of snuff, and said: "So much for Giglio. Now let's go to breakfast."

The Captain of the Guard handed over his prisoner to the Sheriff, with the fatal order:

"AT SIGHT CUT OFF THE BEARER'S HEAD.
VALOROSO XXIV."

"It's a mistake," said Bulbo, who did not seem to understand the business in the least.

"Poo — poo — pooh," says the Sheriff. "Fetch Jack Ketch instantly. Jack Ketch!"

And poor Bulbo was led to the scaffold, where an executioner with a block and a tremendous axe was always ready in case he should be wanted.

But we must now revert to Giglio and Betsinda.

CHAPTER XI.

What Gruffanuff Did to Giglio and Betsinda.

GRUFFANUFF, who had seen what had happened with the King, and knew that Giglio must come to grief, got up very early the next morning, and went to devise some plans for rescuing her darling husband, as the silly old thing insisted on calling him. She found him walking up and down the garden, thinking of a rhyme for Betsinda (*tinder* and *winda* were all he could find), and indeed having forgotten all about the past evening, except that Betsinda was the most lovely of beings.

"Well, dear Giglio," says Gruff.

"Well, dear Gruffy," says Giglio, only *he* was quite satirical.

"I have been thinking, darling, what you must do in this scrape. You must fly the country for a while."

"What scrape? — fly the country? Never without her I love, Countess," says Giglio.

"No, she will accompany you, dear Prince," she says, in her most coaxing accents. "First we must get the jewels belonging to our royal parents, and those of her and his present Majesty. Here is the key, duck; they are all yours you know by right, for you are the rightful King of Paflagonia, and your wife will be the rightful Queen."

" Will she ? " says Giglio.

" Yes; and having got the jewels, go to Glumboso's apartment, where, under his bed, you will find sacks containing money to the amount of £217,000,000,987,-439 13s. 6½d., all belonging to you, for he took it out of your royal father's room on the day of his death. With this we will fly."

" *We* will fly ? " says Giglio.

" Yes, you and your bride — your affianced love — your Gruffy ! " says the Countess, with a languishing leer.

" *You*, my bride ! " says Giglio.   " You, you hideous old woman ! "

" O you, you wretch ! didn't you give me this paper promising marriage ? " cries Gruff.

" Get away, you old goose ! I love Betsinda and Betsinda only ! "   And in a fit of terror he ran from her as quickly as he could.

" He ! he ! he ! " shrieks out Gruff, " a promise is a promise, if there are laws in Paflagonia !   And as for that monster, that wretch, that fiend, that ugly little vixen — as for that upstart, that ingrate, that beast, Betsinda, Master Giglio will have no little difficulty in discovering her whereabouts.   He may look very long before finding *her*, I warrant.   He little knows that Miss Betsinda is —— "

Is — what ?   Now, you shall hear.   Poor Betsinda got up at five in winter's morning to bring her cruel mistress her tea; and instead of finding her in a good humor, found Gruffy as cross as two sticks. The Countess boxed Betsinda's ears half a dozen times whilst she was dressing; but as poor little Betsinda was used to this kind of treatment, she did not feel any special alarm. "And now," says she, "when her Majesty rings her bell twice, I'll trouble you, miss, to attend."

So when the Queen's bell rang twice, Betsinda came to her Majesty and made a pretty little curtsey. The Queen, the Princess, and Gruffanuff were all three in the room. As soon as they saw her they began,

"You wretch!" says the Queen.

"You little vulgar thing!" says the Princess.

"You beast!" says Gruffanuff.

"Get out of my sight!" says the Queen.

"Go away with you, do!" says the Princess.

"Quit the premises!" says Gruffanuff.

Alas! and woe is me! very lamentable events had occurred to Betsinda that morning, and all in consequence of that fatal warming-pan business of the previous night. The King had offered to marry her; of course her Majesty the Queen was jealous: Bulbo had fallen in love with her; of course Angelica was furious: Giglio was in love with her, and O what a fury Gruffy was in!

"Take off that $\begin{Bmatrix} \text{cap} \\ \text{petticoat} \\ \text{gown} \end{Bmatrix}$ I gave you," they said, all at once,

and began tearing the clothes off poor Betsinda.

"How dare you flirt with $\begin{Bmatrix} \text{the King?"} \\ \text{Prince Bulbo?"} \\ \text{Prince Giglio?"} \end{Bmatrix}$ cried the Queen, the Princess, and Countess.

"Give her the rags she wore when she came into the house, and turn her out of it!" cries the Queen.

"Mind she does not go with *my* shoes on, which I lent her so kindly," says the Princess; and indeed the Princess's shoes were a great deal too big for Betsinda.

"Come with me, you filthy hussy!" and taking up the Queen's poker, the cruel Gruffanuff drove Betsinda into her room.

The Countess went to the glass box in which she had kept Betsinda's old cloak and shoe this ever so long, and said: "Take those rags, you little beggar creature, and strip off every thing belonging to honest people, and go about your business"; and she actually tore off the poor little delicate thing's back almost all her things, and told her to be off out of the house.

Poor Betsinda huddled the cloak round her back, on which were embroidered the letters PRIN . . . ROSAL . . . and then came a great rent.

As for the shoe, what was she to do with one poor little tootsey sandal? the string was still to it, so she hung it round her neck.

"Won't you give me a pair of shoes to go out in the snow, mum, if you please, mum!" cried the poor child.

"No, you wicked beast!" says Gruffanuff, driving her along with the poker — driving her down the cold stairs — driving her through the cold hall — flinging her out into the cold street, so that the knocker itself shed tears to see her!

But a kind fairy made the soft snow warm for her little feet, and she wrapped herself up in the ermine of her mantle and was gone.

"And now let us think about breakfast," says the greedy Queen.

"What dress shall I put on, mamma? the pink or the pea-green," says Angelica. "Which do you think the dear Prince will like best?"

"Mrs. V.!" sings out the King from his dressing-room. "Let us have sausages for breakfast! Remember we have Prince Bulbo staying with us!"

And they all went to get ready.

Nine o'clock came, and they were all in the breakfast-room, and no Prince Bulbo as yet. The urn was hissing and humming; the muffins were smoking—such a heap of muffins! the eggs were done, there was a pot of raspberry jam, and coffee, and a beautiful chicken and tongue on the side table. Marmitonio the cook brought in the sausages. O how nice they smelt!

"Where is Bulbo?" said the King. "John, where is His Royal Highness?"

John said he had a took hup His Roilighnessesses shaving-water, and his clothes and things, and he wasn't in his room, which he sposed His Royliness was just stepped hout.

"Stepped out before breakfast in the snow! Impossible!" says the King, sticking his fork into a sausage. "My dear, take one. Angelica won't you have a saveloy?" The Princess took one, being very fond of them; and at this moment Glumboso entered with Captain Hedzoff, both looking very much disturbed. "I am afraid your Majesty—" cries Glumboso. "No business before breakfast, Glum!" says the King. "Breakfast first, business next. Mrs. V., some more sugar!"

" Sire, I am afraid if we wait till after breakfast it will be too late," says Glumboso. " He — he — he'll be hanged at half-past nine."

"Don't talk about hanging and spoil my breakfast, you unkind, vulgar man you!" cries the Princess. "John, some mustard. Pray who is to be hanged?"

" Sire, it is the Prince," whispers Glumboso to the King.

" Talk about business after breakfast, I tell you!" says his Majesty, quite sulky.

" We shall have a war, Sire, depend on it," says the Minister. "His father, King Padella —— "

" His father, King *who* ?" says the King. "King Padella is not Giglio's father. My brother, King Savio, was Giglio's father."

" It's Prince Bulbo they are hanging, Sire, not Prince Giglio," says the Prime Minister.

" You told me to hang the Prince, and I took the ugly one," says Hedzoff. " I didn't, of course, think your Majesty intended to murder your own flesh and blood!"

The King for all reply flung the plate of sausages at Hedzoff's head. The Princess cried out Hee-karee-karee! and fell down in a fainting fit.

" Turn the cock of the urn upon her Royal Highness," said the King, and the boiling water gradually revived her. His Majesty looked at his watch, compared it by the clock in the parlor, and by that of the church in the square opposite; then he wound it up; then he looked at it again. " The great question is," says he, " am I fast or am I slow? If I'm slow, we may as well go on with breakfast. If I'm fast, why there is just the possibility of saving Prince Bulbo. It's a doosid awkward mistake and upon my word, Hedzoff, I have the greatest mind to have you hanged too."

" Sire, I did but my duty; a soldier has but his orders. I didn't expect after forty-seven years of faithful service that my sovereign would think of putting me to a felon's death!"

"A hundred thousand plagues upon you! Can't you see that while you are talking my Bulbo is being hung!" screamed the Princess.

" By Jove! she's always right, that girl, and I'm so absent," says the King, looking at his watch again. " Ha! there go the drums! What a doosid awkward thing though!"

" O papa, you goose! Write the reprieve, and let me run with it," cries the Princess — and she got a sheet of paper, and pen and ink, and laid them before the King.

" Confound it! Where are my spectacles!" the monarch exclaimed. "Angelica! Go up into my bedroom, look under my pillow, not your mamma's; there you'll see my keys. Bring them down to me, and — Well, well! what impetuous things these girls are!" Angelica was gone, and had run up panting to the bedroom, and found the keys, and was back again before the King had finished a muffin. " Now love," says he, " you must go all the way back for my desk, in which my spectacles are. If you *would* but have heard me out. . . . Be hanged to her! There she is off again! Angelica! ANGELICA!" When his Majesty called in his *loud* voice, she knew she must obey, and came back.

"My dear, when you go out of a room how often have I told you, *shut the door*. That's a darling. That's all." At last the keys and the desk and the spectacles were got, and the King mended his pen, and signed his name to a reprieve, and Angelica ran with it as swift as the wind. "You'd better stay, my love, and finish the muffins. There's no use going. Be sure it's too late. Hand me over that raspberry jam, please," said the monarch. "Bong! Bawong! There goes the half hour. I knew it was."

Angelica ran, and ran, and ran, and ran. She ran up Fore Street, and down High Street, and through the Market-place, and down to the left, and over the bridge, and up the blind alley, and back again, and round by the Castle, and so along by the Haberdasher's on the right, opposite the lamp-post, and round the square, and she came — she came to the *Execution place*, where she saw Bulbo laying his head on the block!!! The executioner raised his axe, but at that moment the Princess came panting up and cried Reprieve. "Reprieve!" screamed the Princess. "Reprieve!" shouted all the people. Up the scaffold stairs she sprang, with the agility of a lighter of lamps; and flinging herself in Bulbo's arms, regardless of all ceremony, she cried out: "O my prince! my lord! my love! my Bulbo! Thine Angelica has been in time to save thy precious existence, sweet rosebud; to prevent thy being nipped in thy young bloom! Had aught befallen thee, Angelica too had died, and welcomed death that joined her to her Bulbo."

"H'm! there's no accounting for tastes," said Bulbo, looking so very much puzzled and uncomfortable that

"THINE ANGELICA HAS BEEN IN TIME TO SAVE THY
PRECIOUS EXISTENCE."

the Princess, in tones of tenderest strain, asked the cause of his disquiet.

"I tell you what it is, Angelica," said he, "since I came here yesterday there has been such a row, and disturbance, and quarrelling, and fighting, and chopping of heads off, and the deuce to pay, that I am inclined to go back to Crim Tartary."

"But with me as thy bride, my Bulbo! Though wherever thou art is Crim Tartary to me, my bold, my beautiful, my Bulbo!"

"Well, well, I suppose we must be married," says Bulbo. "Doctor, you came to read the funeral service — read the marriage service, will you? What must be, must. That will satisfy Angelica, and then, in the name of peace and quietness, do let us go back to breakfast."

Bulbo had carried a rose in his mouth all the time of the dismal ceremony. It was a fairy rose, and he was told by his mother that he ought never to part with it. So he had kept it between his teeth, even when he laid his poor head upon the block, hoping vaguely that some chance would turn up in his favor. As he began to speak to Angelica, he forgot about the rose, and of course it dropped out of his mouth. The romantic Princess instantly stooped and seized it. "Sweet rose!" she exclaimed, "that bloomed upon my Bulbo's lip, never, never will I part from thee!" and she placed it in her bosom. And you know Bulbo *couldn't* ask her to give the rose back again. And they went to breakfast; and as they walked, it appeared to Bulbo that Angelica become more exquisitely lovely every moment.

He was frantic until they were married; and now, strange to say, it was Angelica who didn't care about him! He knelt down, he kissed her hand, he prayed and begged; he cried with admiration, while she for her part said she really thought they might wait; it seemed to her he was not handsome any more — no, not at all, quite the reverse, and not clever, no, very stupid, and not well-bred, like Giglio; no, on the contrary, dreadfully vul —

What, I cannot say, for King Valoroso roared out "*Pooh*, stuff!" in a terrible voice. "We will have no more of this shilly-shallying! Call the Archbishop, and let the Prince and Princess be married off-hand!"

So, married they were, and I am sure for my part I trust they will be happy.

CHAPTER XII.

How Betsinda Fled, and What Became of Her.

BETSINDA wandered on and on, till she passed through the town gates, and so on the great Crim Tartary road, the very way on which Giglio, too, was going. "Ah!" thought she, as the diligence passed her, of which the conductor was blowing a delightful tune on his horn, "how I should like to be on that coach!" But the coach and the jingling horses were very soon gone. She little knew who was in it, though very likely she was thinking of him all the time.

Then came an empty cart, returning from market; and the driver being a kind man, and seeing such a very pretty girl trudging along the road with bare feet, most good-naturedly gave her a seat. He said he lived on the confines of the forest, where his old father was a woodman, and, if she liked, he would take her so far on her road. All roads were the same to little Betsinda, so she very thankfully took this one.

And the carter put a cloth round her bare feet, and gave her some bread and cold bacon, and was very kind to her. For all that she was very cold and melancholy. When after travelling on and on, evening came, and all the black pines were bending with snow, and there, at last, was the comfortable light beaming in the woodman's windows, and so they arrived, and went into his cottage. He was an old man, and had a number of children, who were just at supper, with nice hot bread-and-milk, when their elder brother arrived with the cart. And they jumped and clapped their hands; for they were good children, and he had brought them toys from the town. And when they saw the pretty stranger they ran to her, and brought her to the fire, and rubbed her poor little feet, and brought her bread-and-milk.

"Look, Father!" they said to the old woodman, "look at this poor girl, and see what pretty cold feet she has. They are as white as our milk! And look and see what an odd cloak she has, just like the bit of velvet that hangs up in our cupboard, and which you found that day the little cubs were killed by King Padella in the forest! And look, why bless us all! she has got round her neck just such another little shoe as that you brought home, and have shown us so often — a little blue velvet shoe!"

"What," said the old woodman, "what is all this about a shoe and a cloak?"

And Betsinda explained that she had been left, when quite a little child, at the town with this cloak and this shoe. And the persons who had taken care of her had — had been angry with her for no fault, she hoped, of her own. And they had sent her away with her old clothes — and here, in fact, she was. She remembered having been in a forest — and perhaps it was a dream — it was so very odd and strange — having lived in a cave with lions there; and, before that, having lived in a very, very fine house, as fine as a king's, in a town.

When the woodman heard this, he was so astonished, it was quite curious to see how astonished he was. He went to his cupboard, and took out of a stocking a five-shilling piece of King Cavolfiore, and vowed it was exactly like the young woman. And then he produced the shoe and piece of velvet which he had kept so long, and compared them with the things which Betsinda wore. In Betsinda's little shoe was written, "Hopkins, maker to the Royal Family;" so in the other shoe was written, "Hopkins, maker to the Royal Family." In the inside of Betsinda's piece of cloak was embroidered, " PRIN ROSAL "; in the other piece of cloak was embroidered, " CESS BA. No. 246." So that when put together you read, " PRINCESS ROSALBA. No. 246."

On seeing this, the dear old woodman fell down on his knee, saying: " O my Princess, O my gracious royal lady, O my rightful Queen of Crim Tartary, — I hail thee — I acknowledge thee — I do thee homage!" And in token of his fealty, he rubbed his venerable nose three times on the ground, and put the Princess's foot on his head.

" Why," said she, " my good woodman, you must be a nobleman of my royal father's court!" For in her lowly retreat, and under the name of Betsinda, HER MAJESTY, ROSALBA, Queen of Crim Tartary, had read of the customs of all foreign courts and nations.

" Marry, indeed, am I, my gracious liege — the poor

Lord Spinachi, once — the humble woodman these fifteen years syne. Ever since the tyrant, Padella (may ruin overtake the treacherous knave!), dismissed me from my post of First Lord."

"First Lord of the Toothpick and Joint Keeper of the Snuff-box? I mind me! Thou heldest these posts under our royal sire. They are restored to thee, Lord Spinachi! I make thee knight of the second class of our Order of the Pumpkin (the first class being reserved for crowned heads alone). Rise Marquis of Spinachi!" And with indescribable majesty, the Queen, who had no sword handy, waved the pewter spoon with which she had been taking her bread-and-milk, over the bald head of the old nobleman, whose tears absolutely made a puddle on the ground, and whose dear children went to bed that night Lords and Ladies Bartolomeo, Ubaldo, Catarina, and Ottavia degli Spinachi!

The acquaintance HER MAJESTY showed with the history, and *noble families* of her empire, was wonderful. "The House of Broccoli should remain faithful to us," she said; "they were ever welcome at our Court. Have the Articocchi, as was their wont, turned to the Rising Sun? The family of Sauerkraut must sure be with us — they were ever welcome in the halls of King Cavolfiore." And so she went on enumerating quite a list of the nobility and gentry of Crim Tartary, so admirably had her Majesty profited by her studies while in exile.

The old Marquis of Spinachi said he could answer for them all; that the whole country groaned under Padella's tyranny, and longed to return to its rightful sovereign; and late as it was, he sent his children who knew the forest well, to summon this nobleman and that; and when his eldest son, who had been rubbing the horse down and giving him his supper, came into the house for his own, the Marquis told him to put his boots on, and a saddle on the mare, and ride hither and thither to such and such people.

When the young man heard who his companion in the cart had been, he too knelt down and put her royal foot on his head; he too bedewed the ground with his tears; he was frantically in love with her as everybody now was who saw her; so were the young Lords Bartolomeo and Ubaldo, who punched each other's little heads out of jealousy: and so when they came from the east and west, at the summons of the Marquis degli Spinachi, were the Crim Tartar Lords who still remained faithful to the House of Cavolfiore. They were such very old gentlemen for the most part, that her Majesty never suspected their absurd passion, and went among them quite unaware of the havoc her beauty was causing, until an old blind Lord who had joined her party, told her what the truth was; after which, for fear of making the people too much in love with her, she always wore a veil. She went about, privately, from one nobleman's castle to another; and they visited amongst themselves again, and had meetings, and composed proclamations and counter-proclamations, and distributed all the best places of the kingdom amongst one another, and selected who of the opposition party should be executed when the Queen came to her own. And so in about a year they were ready to move.

The party of Fidelity was in truth composed of very feeble old fogies for the most part; they went about

the country waving their old swords and flags, **and**
calling " God save the Queen ! " and King Padella happening to be absent upon an invasion, they had their
own way for a little, and to be sure the people were
very enthusiastic whenever they saw the Queen ; otherwise the vulgar took matters very quietly, for they
said, as far as they could recollect, they were pretty
well as much taxed in Cavolfiore's time, as now in
Padella's.

CHAPTER XIII.

How Queen Rosalba Came to the Castle of the Bold Count Hogginarmo.

HER Majesty, having indeed nothing else to give, made all her followers Knights of the Pumpkin, and marquises, earls, and baronets, and they had a little court for her, and made her a little crown of gilt paper, and a robe of cotton velvet, and they quarrelled about the places to be given away in her court, and about rank and precedence and dignities; — you can't think how they quarrelled! The poor Queen was very tired of her honors before she had them a month, and I dare say sighed sometimes even to be a lady's maid again. But we must all do our duty in our respective stations, so the Queen resigned herself to perform hers.

We have said how it happened that none of the Usurper's troops came out to oppose this Army of Fidelity: it pottered along as nimbly as the gout of the principal commanders allowed; it consisted of twice as many officers as soldiers; and at length passed near the estates of one of the most powerful noblemen of the country, who had not declared for the Queen, but of whom her party had hope, as he was always quarrelling with King Padella.

When they came close to his park gates, this noble-man sent to say he would wait upon her Majesty ; he was a most powerful warrior, and his name was Count Hogginarmo, whose helmet it took two strong negroes to carry. He knelt down before her and said : " Madam and liege lady ! it becomes the great nobles of the Cri-mean realm to show every outward sign of respect to the wearer of the crown, whoever that may be. We testify to our own nobility in acknowledging yours. The bold Hogginarmo bends the knee to the first of the aristocracy of his country."

Rosalba said, " The bold Count of Hogginarmo was uncommonly kind." But she felt afraid of him, even while he was kneeling, and his eyes scowled at her from between his whiskers, which grew up to them.

" The first Count of the Empire, madam," he went on, " salutes the Sovereign. The Prince addresses him-self to the not more noble lady ! Madam ! my hand is free, and I offer it, and my heart and my sword to your service ! My three wives lie buried in my ances-tral vaults. The third perished but a year since, and this heart pines for a consort ! Deign to be mine, and I swear to bring to your bridal table the head of King Padella, the eyes and nose of his son, Prince Bulbo, the right hand and ears of the usurping sovereign of Pafla-gonia, which country shall thenceforth be an appanage to your — to *our* Crown ! Say yes ; Hogginarmo is not accustomed to be denied. Indeed, I cannot con-template the possibility of a refusal : for frightful would be the result, dreadful the murders, furious the devastations, horrible the tyranny, tremendous the tor-tures, misery, taxation, which the people of this realm

will endure if Hogginarmo's wrath be aroused! I see
consent in your Majesty's lovely eyes — their glances
fill my soul with rapture!"

"O sir," Rosalba said, withdrawing her hand in great
fright, "your Lordship is exceedingly kind, but I am
sorry to tell you that I have a prior attachment to a
young gentleman by the name of — Prince — Giglio —
and never — never can marry any one but him."

Who can describe Hogginarmo's wrath at this remark? Rising up from the ground, he ground his
teeth, so that fire flashed out of his mouth, from which
at the same time issued remarks and language so *loud,
violent, and improper*, that this pen shall never repeat
them! "R-r-r-r-r — Rejected! Fiends and perdition!
The bold Hogginarmo rejected! All the world shall
hear of my rage; and you, Madam, you above all
shall rue it!" And kicking the two negroes before
him, he rushed away, his whiskers streaming in the
wind.

Her Majesty's Privy Council was in a dreadful panic
when they saw Hogginarmo issue from the royal presence in such a towering rage, making footballs of the
poor negroes, — a panic which the events justified.
They marched off from Hogginarmo's park very crest-
fallen, and in another half-hour they were met by that
rapacious chieftain with a few of his followers, who
cut, slashed, charged, whacked, banged, and pommelled
amongst them, took the Queen prisoner, and drove the
Army of Fidelity to I don't know where.

Poor Queen! Hogginarmo, her conqueror, would
not condescend to see her. "Get a horse-van!" he
said to his grooms, "Clap the hussy into it, and send

her, with my compliments, to his Majesty King Padella."

Along with his lovely prisoner, Hogginarmo sent a letter full of servile compliments and loathsome flatteries to King Padella, for whose life and that of his royal family the *hypocritical humbug* pretended to offer the most fulsome prayers. And Hogginarmo promised speedily to pay his humble homage at his august master's throne, of which he begged leave to be counted the most loyal and constant defender. Such a *wary* old *bird* as King Padella was not to be caught by Master Hogginarmo's *chaff*, and we shall hear presently how the tyrant treated his upstart vassal. No, no; depend on't two such rogues do not trust one another.

So this poor Queen was laid in the straw like Margery Daw, and driven along in the dark ever so many miles to the Court, where King Padella had now arrived, having vanquished all his enemies, murdered most of them, and brought some of the richest into captivity with him for the purpose of torturing them and finding out where they had hidden their money.

Rosalba heard their shrieks and groans in the dungeon in which she was thrust ; a most awful black hole, full of bats, rats, mice, toads, frogs, mosquitoes, bugs, fleas, serpents, and every kind of horror. No light was let into it, otherwise the gaolers might have seen her and fallen in love with her, as an owl that lived up in the roof of the tower did, and a cat you know, who can see in the dark, and having set its green eyes on Rosalba never would be got to go back to the turnkey's wife to whom it belonged. And the toads in the dungeon came and kissed her feet, and the vipers wound round her neck and arms, and never hurt her, so charming was this poor Princess in the midst of her misfortunes.

At last, after she had been kept in this place *ever so long*, the door of the dungeon opened and the terrible KING PADELLA came in.

But what he said and did must be reserved for another chapter, as we must now go back to Prince Giglio.

CHAPTER XIV.

What became of Giglio.

THE idea of marrying such an old crea-ture as Gruffanuff frightened Prince Giglio so that he ran up to his room, packed his trunks, fetched in a couple of porters, and was off to the diligence-office in a twinkling.

It was well that he was so quick in his operations, did not dawdle over his luggage, and took the early coach, for as soon as the mistake about Prince Bulbo was found out, that cruel Glumboso sent up a couple of policemen to Prince Giglio's room, with orders that he should be carried to Newgate, and his head taken off before twelve o'clock. But the coach was out of the Paflagonian dominions before two o'clock; and I dare say the express that was sent after Prince Giglio did not ride very quick, for many people in Paflagonia had a regard for Giglio, as the son of their old sovereign; a Prince who, with all his weaknesses, was very much better than his brother — the usurping, lazy, careless, passionate, tyrannical, reigning monarch. That prince busied himself with the balls, fêtes, masquerades, hunting parties, and so forth, which he thought proper to give, on occasion of his daughter's marriage, to Prince

Bulbo; and let us trust was not sorry in his own heart that his brother's son had escaped the scaffold.

It was very cold weather, and the snow was on the ground, and Giglio, who gave his name as simple Mr. Giles, was very glad to get a comfortable place in the coupé of the diligence, where he sat with the conductor and another gentleman. At the first stage from Blombodinga, as they stopped to change horses, there came up to the diligence a very ordinary, vulgar-looking woman, with a bag under her arm, who asked for a place. All the inside places were taken, and the young woman was informed that if she wished to travel, she must go upon the roof; and the passenger inside with Giglio (a rude person, I should think) put his head out of the window, and said : " Nice weather for travelling outside! I wish you a pleasant journey, my dear." The poor woman coughed very much, and Giglio pitied her. "I will give up my place to her," says he, rather than she should travel in the cold air with that horrid cough." On which the vulgar traveller said : " *You'd* keep her warm, I am sure, if it's a *muff* she wants." On which Giglio pulled his nose, boxed his ears, hit him in the eye, and gave this vulgar person a warning never to call him *muff* again.

Then he sprang up gaily on to the roof of the diligence, and made himself very comfortable in the straw. The vulgar traveller got down only at the next station, and Giglio took his place again, and talked to the person next to him. She appeared to be a most agreeable, well-informed, and entertaining female. They travelled together till night, and she gave Giglio all sorts of things out of the bag which she carried, and which indeed seemed to contain the most wonderful collection of articles. He was thirsty — out there came a pint bottle of Bass's pale ale, and a silver mug! Hungry — she took out a cold fowl, some slices of ham, bread, salt, and a most delicious piece of cold plum-pudding, and a little glass of brandy afterwards.

As they travelled, this plain-looking, queer woman talked to Giglio on a variety of subjects, in which the poor Prince showed his ignorance as much as she did her capacity. He owned, with many blushes, how ignorant he was ; on which the lady said : " My dear Gigl — my good Mr. Giles, you are a young man, and have plenty of time before you. You have nothing to do but to improve yourself. Who knows but that you may find use for your knowledge some day ? When — when you may be wanted at home, as some people may be."

" Good Heavens, madam ! " says he, " do you know me ? "

" I know a number of funny things," says the lady. " I have been at some people's christenings, and turned away from other folk's doors. I have seen some people spoilt by good fortune, and others, as I hope, improved by hardship. I advise you to stay at the town where the coach stops for the night. Stay there and study, and remember your old friend to whom you were kind."

" And who is my old friend ? " asked Giglio.

" When you want any thing," says the lady, " look in this bag, which I leave to you as a present, and be grateful to — "

" To whom, madam ? " says he.

"To the Fairy Blackstick," says the lady, flying out of the window. And when Giglio asked the conductor if he knew where the lady was, "What lady?" says the man; "there has been no lady in this coach, except the old woman, who got out at the last stage." And Giglio thought he had been dreaming. But there was the bag which Blackstick had given him lying on his lap; and when he came to the town he took it in his hand and went into the inn.

They gave him a very bad bedroom, and Giglio, when he woke in the morning, fancying himself in the Royal Palace at home, called, "John, Charles, Thomas! My chocolate — my dressing-gown — my slippers"; but nobody came. There was no bell, so he went and bawled out for waiter on the top of the stairs.

The landlady came up.

"What are you a hollaring and a bellaring for here, young man?" says she.

"There's no warm water — no servants; my boots are not even cleaned."

"He, he! Clean 'em yourself," says the landlady. "You young students give yourselves pretty airs. I never heard such impudence."

"I'll quit the house this instant," says Giglio.

"The sooner the better, young man. Pay your bill and be off. All my rooms is wanted for gentlefolks, and not for such as you."

"You may well keep the Bear Inn," said Giglio. "You should have yourself painted as the sign."

The landlady of the Bear went away *growling*. And Giglio returned to his room, where the first thing he saw was the fairy bag lying on the table, which seemed to give a little hop as he came in. " I hope it has some breakfast in it," says Giglio, " for I have only a very little money left." And on opening the bag, what do you think was there; a blacking-brush and a pot of Warren's jet, and on the pot was written:

> " Poor young men their boots must black,
> Use me and cork me and put me back."

So Giglio laughed and blacked his boots, and put back the brush and the bottle into the bag.

When he had done dressing himself, the bag gave another little hop, and he went to it and took out —

1. A table-cloth and a napkin.

2. A sugar-basin full of the best loaf-sugar.

4, 6, 8, 10. Two forks, two teaspoons, two knives, and a pair of sugar-tongs, and a butter-knife, all marked G.

11, 12, 13. A tea-cup, saucer, and slop-basin.

14. A jug full of delicious cream.

15. A canister with black tea and green.

16. A large tea-urn and boiling water.

17. A sauce-pan, containing three eggs nicely done.

18. A quarter of a pound of best Epping butter.

19. A brown loaf.

And if he hadn't enough now for a good breakfast, I should like to know who ever had one !

Giglio, having had his breakfast, popped all the things back into the bag, and went out looking for lodgings. I forgot to say that this celebrated university town was called Bosforo.

He took a modest lodging opposite the Schools, paid his bill at the inn, and went to his apartment with his trunk, carpet-bag, and not forgetting, we may be sure, his *other* bag.

When he opened his trunk, which the day before he had filled with his best clothes, he found it contained only books. And in the first of them which he opened there was written —

> " Clothes for the back, books for the head :
> Read, and remember them when they are read."

And in his bag, when Giglio looked in it, he found a student's cap and gown, a writing-book full of paper, an inkstand, pens, and a Johnson's dictionary, which was very useful to him, as his spelling had been sadly neglected.

So he sat down and worked away, very, very hard for a whole year, during which " Mr. Giles " was quite an example to all the students in the University of Bosforo. He never got into any riots or disturbances. The professors all spoke well of him, and the students liked him, too ; so that, when at examination, he took all the prizes, viz. : —

The Spelling Prize	The French Prize
The Writing Prize	The Arithmetic Prize
The History Prize	The Latin Prize
The Catechism Prize	The Good Conduct Prize,

all his fellow students said, " Hurray ! Hurray for Giles ! Giles is the boy — the students' joy ! Hurray for Giles ! " And he brought quite a quantity of medals, crowns, books, and tokens of distinction home to his lodgings.

One day after the examinations, as he was diverting himself at a coffee-house with two friends (did I tell you that in his bag, every Saturday night, he found just enough to pay his bills, with a guinea over, for pocket money? Didn't I tell you? Well, he did, as sure as twice twenty makes forty-five), he chanced to look in the "Bosforo Chronicle," and read off, quite easily (for he could spell, read, and write the longest words now) the following —

"ROMANTIC CIRCUMSTANCE. — One of the most extraordinary adventures that we have ever heard has set the neighboring country of Crim Tartary in a state of great excitement.

"It will be remembered that when the present revered sovereign of Crim Tartary, his Majesty King *Padella*, took possession of the throne, after having vanquished, in the terrific battle of Blunderbusco, the late King *Cavolfiore*, that Prince's only child, the Princess Rosalba, was not found in the royal palace, of which King Padella took possession, and, it was said, had strayed into the forest (being abandoned by all her attendants), where she had been eaten up by those ferocious lions, the last pair of which were captured some time since, and brought to the Tower, after killing several hundred persons.

"His Majesty King Padella, who has the kindest heart in the world, was grieved at the accident which had occurred to the harmless little Princess, for whom his Majesty's known benevolence would certainly have provided a fitting establishment. But her death seemed to be certain. The mangled remains of a cloak, and a little shoe, were found in the forest, during a hunting party, in which the intrepid sovereign of Crim Tartary slew two of the lions' cubs with his own spear. And these interesting relics of an innocent little creature

were carried home and kept by their finder, the Baron
Spinachi, formerly an officer in Cavolfiore's household.
The Baron was disgraced in consequence of his known
legitimist opinions, and has lived for some time in the
humble capacity of a wood-cutter, in a forest, on the
outskirts of the Kingdom of Crim Tartary.

"Last Tuesday week Baron Spinachi and a number
of gentlemen, attached to the former dynasty, appeared
in arms, crying 'God save Rosalba, the First Queen of
Crim Tartary!' and surrounding a lady whom report
describes as '*beautiful exceedingly.*' Her history *may* be
authentic, *is* certainly most romantic.

"The personage calling herself Rosalba states that
she was brought out of the forest, fifteen years since, by
a lady in a car, drawn by dragons (this account is certainly *improbable*), that she was left in the Palace Garden of Blombodinga, where her Royal Highness the
Princess Angelica, now married to his Royal Highness
Bulbo, Crown Prince of Crim Tartary, found the child,
and, with *that elegant benevolence* which has always distinguished the heiress of the throne of Paflagonia, gave
the little outcast a *shelter and a home!* Her parents not
being known, and her garb very humble, the foundling
was educated in the Palace in a menial capacity, under
the name of *Betsinda.*

"She did not give satisfaction, and was dismissed,
carrying with her, certainly, part of a mantle and a
shoe, which she had on when first found. According
to her statement she quitted Blombodinga about a year
ago, since which time she has been with the Spinachi
family. On the very same morning the Prince Giglio,
nephew to the King of Paflagonia, a young Prince

whose character for *talent* and *order* were, to say truth, *none of the highest*, also quitted Blombodinga, and has not been since heard of!"

"What an extraordinary story!" said Smith and Jones, two young students, Giglio's especial friends.

· "Ha! what is this?" Giglio went on reading—

"SECOND EDITION, EXPRESS.—We hear that the troop under Baron Spinachi has been surrounded, and utterly routed, by General Count Hogginarmo, and the *soi-disant* Princess is sent a prisoner to the capital.

"UNIVERSITY NEWS.—Yesterday, at the Schools, the distinguished young student, Mr. Giles, read a Latin oration, and was complimented by the Chancellor of Bosforo, Dr. Prugnaro, with the highest University honor—the wooden spoon."

"Never mind that stuff," says *Giles*, greatly disturbed. "Come home with me, my friends—partakers of my academic toils—I have that to tell shall astonish your honest minds."

"Go it, old boy!" cried the impetuous Smith.

"Talk away, my buck!" says Jones, a lively fellow.

With an air of indescribable dignity, Giglio, checked their natural, but no more seemly familiarity. "Jones, Smith, my good friends," said the PRINCE, "disguise is henceforth useless, I am no more the humble student Giles, I am the descendant of a royal line."

"*Atavis edite regibus*, I know, old co——," cried Jones, he was going to say old cock, but a flash from THE ROYAL EYE again awed him.

"Friends," continued the Prince, "I am that Giglio, I am, in fact, Paflagonia. Rise, Smith, and kneel not in the public street. Jones, thou true heart! My faithless uncle, when I was a baby, filched from me that brave crown my father left me, bred me all young and careless of my rights, like unto hapless Hamlet, Prince of Denmark ; and had I any thoughts about my wrongs, soothed me with promises of near redress. I should espouse his daughter, young Angelica ; we two indeed should reign in Paflagonia. His words were false — false as Angelica's heart! — false as Angelica's hair, color, front teeth! She looked with her skew eyes upon young Bulbo, Crim Tartary's stupid heir, and she preferred him. 'Twas then I turned my eyes upon Betsinda — Rosalba, as she now is. And I saw in her the blushing sum of all perfection ; the pink of maiden modesty ; the nymph that my fond heart had ever woo'd in dreams," etc., etc.

(I don't give this speech, which was very fine, but very long ; and though Smith and Jones knew nothing about the circumstances, my dear reader does, so I go on.)

The Prince and his young friends hastened home to his apartment, highly excited by the intelligence, as no doubt by the *royal narrator's* admirable manner of recounting it, and they ran up to his room where he had worked so hard at his books.

On his writing-table was his bag, grown so long that the Prince could not help remarking it. He went to it, opened it, and what do you think he found in it ?

A splendid long, gold-handled, red-velvet-scabbard, cut-and-thrust sword, and on the sheath was embroidered, " ROSALBA FOR EVER ! "

He drew out the sword, which flashed and illuminated the whole room, and called out " Rosalba for ever!" Smith and Jones following him, but quite respectfully this time, and taking the time from his Royal Highness.

And now his trunk opened with a sudden pong, and out there came three ostrich feathers in a gold crown, surrounding a beautiful shining steel helmet, a cuirass, a pair of spurs, finally a complete suit of armor.

The books on Giglio's shelves were all gone. Where there had been some great dictionaries, Giglio's friends found two pairs of Jack-boots, labelled "Lieutenant Smith," "—— Jones, Esq." which fitted them to a nicety. Besides, there were helmets, back and breast plates, swords, etc., just like in Mr. G. P. R. James's novels, and that evening three cavaliers might have been seen issuing from the gates of Bosforo, in whom the porters, proctors, etc., never thought of recognizing the young Prince and his friends.

They got horses at a livery stable-keeper's, and never drew bridle until they reached the last town on the frontier, before you come to Crim Tartary. Here, as their animals were tired, and the cavaliers hungry, they stopped and refreshed at a hostel. I could make a chapter of this if I were like some writers, but I like to cram my measure tight down, you see, and give you a great deal for your money, and in a word, they had some bread and cheese and ale up-stairs on the balcony of the inn. As they were drinking, drums and trumpets sounded nearer and nearer, the market-place was filled with soldiers, and his Royal Highness looking forth, recognized the Paflagonian banners, and the Paflagonian national air which the bands were playing.

The troops all made for the tavern at once, and as

"GIVE UP MY SWORD! GIGLIO GIVE UP HIS SWORD!"

they came up Giglio exclaimed, on beholding their leader: "Whom do I see? Yes! No! It is, it is! Phoo! No, it can't be! Yes! It is my friend, my gallant, faithful veteran, Captain Hedzoff! Ho! Hedzoff! Knowest thou not thy Prince, thy Giglio? Good Corporal, methinks we once were friends. Ha, Sergeant, an' my memory serves me right, we have had many a bout at single stick."

"I' faith, we have a many, good my Lord," says the Sergeant.

"Tell me, what means this mighty armament," continued his Royal Highness from the balcony, "and whither march my Paflagonians?"

Hedzoff's head fell. "My Lord," he said, "we march as the allies of great Padella, Crim Tartary's monarch."

"Crim Tartary's usurper, gallant Hedzoff! Crim Tartary's grim tyrant, honest Hedzoff!" said the Prince, on the balcony, quite sarcastically.

"A soldier, Prince, must needs obey his orders: mine are to help his Majesty Padella. And also (though alack that I should say it!) to seize wherever I should light upon him —"

"First catch your hare! ha, Hedzoff!" exclaimed his Royal Highness.

"— On the body of *Giglio*, whilome Prince of Paflagonia," Hedzoff went on, with indescribable emotion. "My Prince, give up your sword without ado. Look! we are thirty thousand men to one!"

"Give up my sword! Giglio give up his sword!" cried the Prince; and stepping well forward on to the balcony, the royal youth, *without preparation*, delivered a speech so magnificent, that no report can do justice to it. It was all in blank verse (in which, from this time, he invariably spoke, as more becoming his majestic station). It lasted for three days and three nights, during which not a single person who heard him was tired, or remarked the difference between daylight and dark. The soldiers only cheering tremendously, when occasionally, once in nine hours, the Prince paused to suck an orange, which Jones took out of the bag. He explained in terms which we say we shall not attempt to convey, the whole history of the previous transaction: and his determination not only not to give up his sword, but to assume his rightful crown: and at the end of this extraordinary, this truly *gigantic* effort, Captain Hedzoff flung up his helmet, and cried: "Hurray! Hurray! Long live King Giglio!"

Such were the consequences of having employed his time well at College!

When the excitement had ceased, beer was ordered out for the army, and their Sovereign himself did not disdain a little! And now it was with some alarm that Captain Hedzoff told him his division was only the advanced guard of the Paflagonian contingent, hastening to King Padella's aid. The main force being a day's march in the rear under his Royal Highness Prince Bulbo.

"We will wait here, good friend, to beat the Prince," his Majesty said, "and *then* will make his royal Father wince."

CHAPTER XV.

We Return to Rosalba.

KING PADELLA made very similar proposals to Rosalba to those which she had received from the various princes who, as we have seen, had fallen in love with her. His Majesty was a widower, and offered to marry his fair captive that instant, but she declined his invitation in her usual polite, gentle manner, stating that Prince Giglio was her love, and that any other union was out of the question. Having tried tears and supplications in vain, this violent-tempered monster menaced her with threats and tortures; but she declared she would rather suffer all these than accept the hand of her father's murderer, who left her finally, uttering the most awful imprecations, and bidding her prepare for death on the following morning.

All night long the King spent in advising how he should get rid of this obdurate young creature. Cutting off her head was much too easy a death for her; hanging was so common in his Majesty's dominions that it no longer afforded him any sport: finally, he bethought himself of a pair of lions which had lately been sent to him as presents, and he determined, with these ferocious brutes, to hunt poor Rosalba down.

Adjoining his castle was an amphitheatre where the Prince indulged in bull-baiting, rat-hunting, and other ferocious sports. The two lions were kept in a cage under this place ; their roaring might be heard over the whole city, the inhabitants of which, I am sorry to say, thronged in numbers to see a poor young lady gobbled up by two wild beasts.

The King took his place in the royal box, having the officers of his court around and the Count Hogginarmo by his side, upon whom his Majesty was observed to look very fiercely ; the fact is royal spies had told the monarch of Hogginarmo's behavior, his proposals to Rosalba, and his offer to fight for the crown. Black as thunder looked King Padella at this proud noble, as they sat in the front seats of the theatre waiting to see the tragedy whereof poor Rosalba was to be the heroine.

At length that princess was brought out in her night-gown, with all her beautiful hair falling down her back, and looking so pretty that even the beef-eaters and keepers of the wild animals wept plentifully at seeing her. And she walked with her poor little feet (only luckily the arena was covered with sawdust) and went and leaned up against a great stone in the centre of the amphitheatre, round which the court and the people were seated in boxes with bars before them, for fear of the great, fierce, red-maned, black-throated, long-tailed, roaring, bellowing, rushing lions. And now the gates were opened, and with a wurrawar-rurawarar two great lean, hungry, roaring lions rushed out of their den where they had been kept for three weeks on nothing but a little toast-and-water, and dashed straight up to the stone where poor Rosalba was waiting. Commend her to your patron saints, all you kind people, for she is in a dreadful state.

There was a hum and a buzz all through the circus, and the fierce King Padella even felt a little compassion. But Count Hogginarmo, seated by his Majesty, roared out, " Hurray ! Now for it ! Soo-soo-ooo ! " that noble-man being uncommonly angry still at Rosalba's refusal of him.

But O strange event ! O remarkable circumstance ! O extraordinary coincidence, which I am sure none of you could *by any possibility* have divined ! When the lions came to Rosalba, instead of devouring her with their great teeth, it was with kisses they gobbled her up ! They licked her pretty feet, they nuzzled their noses in her lap, they moo'd ; they seemed to say : " Dear, dear sister, don't you recollect your brothers in the forest ? " And she put her pretty white arms round their tawny necks, and kissed them.

King Padella was much astonished. The Count Hogginarmo was extremely disgusted. " Pooh ! " the Count cried. " Gammon ! " exclaimed his Lordship. " These lions are tame beasts come from Wombwell's or Astley's. It is a shame to put people off in this way. I believe they are little boys dressed up in door-mats. They are no lions at all."

" Ha ! " said the King, " you dare to say ' gammon ' to your sovereign, do you ? These lions are no lions at all, aren't they ? Ho ! my beef-eaters ! Ho ! my body-guard ! Take this Count Hogginarmo and fling him into the circus ! Give him a sword and buckler ; let him keep his armor on, and his weather-eye out, and fight these lions."

The haughty Hogginarmo laid down his opera-glass, and looked scowling round at the King and his attendants. "Touch me not, dogs!" he said, "or by St. Nicholas the Elder I will gore you! Your majesty thinks Hogginarmo is afraid? No, not of a hundred thousand lions! Follow me down into the circus, King Padella, and match thyself against one of yon brutes. Thou darest not. Let them both come on, then!" And opening a grating of the box, he jumped lightly down into the circus.

Wurra wurra wurra wur-aw-aw-aw ! ! !
In about two minutes
The Count Hogginarmo was
GOBBLED UP
by
those lions,
bones, boots, and all,
and
There was an
End of him.

At this the King said: "Serve him right, the rebellious ruffian! And now, as those lions won't eat that young woman ——"

"Let her off!—let her off!" cried the crowd.

"NO!" roared the King. "Let the beef-eaters go down and chop her into small pieces. If the lions defend her, let the archers shoot them to death. That hussy shall die in tortures!"

"A-a-ah!" cried the crowd. "Shame! shame!"

"Who dares cry out shame?" cried the furious potentate (so little can tyrants command their passions). "Fling any scoundrel who says a word down among the lions!" I warrant you there was a dead silence then, which was broken by a pang arang pang pang-karangpang, and a knight and a herald rode in at the farther end of the circus. The knight, in full armor, with his visor up, and bearing a letter on the point of his lance.

"Ha!" exclaimed the King, "by my fay, 'tis Elephant and Castle, pursuivant of my brother of Paflagonia, and the Knight, as my memory serves me, is the gallant Captain Hedzoff! What news from Paflagonia, gallant Hedzoff? Elephant and Castle, beshrew me, thy trumpeting must have made thee thirsty. What will my trusty herald like to drink?"

"Bespeaking first safe conduct from your Lordship," said Captain Hedzoff, "before we take a drink of any thing, permit us to deliver our king's message."

"My Lordship, ha?" said Crim Tartary, frowning terrifically. "That title soundeth strange in the anointed ears of a crowned king. Straightway speak out your message, knight and herald!"

Reining up his charger in a most elegant manner close under the King's balcony, Hedzoff turned to the herald and bade him begin.

Elephant and Castle, dropping his trumpet over his shoulder, took a large sheet of paper out of his hat, and began to read:

"O yes! O yes! O yes! Know all men by these presents, that we, Giglio, King of Paflagonia, Grand Duke of Cappadocia, Sovereign Prince of Turkey and the Sausage Islands, having assumed our rightful throne and title, long time falsely borne by our usurping uncle, styling himself King of Paflagonia —"

"Ha!" growled Padella.

"— Hereby summon the false traitor, Padella, calling himself King of Crim Tartary —"

The King's curses were dreadful. "Go on, Elephant and Castle!" said the intrepid Hedzoff.

"To release from cowardly imprisonment his liege lady and rightful sovereign, ROSALBA, Queen of Crim Tartary, and restore her to her royal throne, in default of which, I, Giglio, proclaim the said Padella sneak, traitor, humbug, usurper, and coward. I challenge him to meet me, with fists or with pistols, with battle-axe or sword, with blunderbuss or single-stick, alone or at the head of his army, on foot or on horseback, and will prove my words upon his wicked, ugly body!"

"God save the King!" said Captain Hedzoff, executing a demivolte, two semilunes, and three caracols.

"Is that all?" said Padella, with the terrific calm of concentrated fury.

"That, sir, is all my Royal Master's message. Here is his Majesty's letter in autograph, and here is his glove, and if any gentleman of Crim Tartary chooses to find fault with his Majesty's expressions, I, Tuffskin Hedzoff, Captain of the Guard, am very much at his service," and he waved his lance and looked at the assembly all round.

"And what says my good brother of Paflagonia, my dear son's father-in-law to this rubbish?" asked the King.

"The King's uncle hath been deprived of the crown he unjustly wore," said Hedzoff gravely. "He and his ex-minister, Glumboso, are now in prison waiting the sentence of my royal Master. After the battle of Bombardaro —"

"Of what?" asked the surprised Padella.

"Of Bombardaro, where my liege, his present Majesty, would have performed prodigies of valor, but that the whole of his uncle's army came over to our side, with the exception of Prince Bulbo."

"Ah! my boy, my boy, my Bulbo was no traitor!" cried Padella.

"Prince Bulbo, far from coming over to us, ran away, sir; but I caught him. The Prince is a prisoner in our army, and the most terrific tortures await him if a hair of the Princess Rosalba's head is injured."

"Do they?" exclaimed the furious Padella, who was now perfectly *livid* with rage. "Do they, indeed. So much the worse for Bulbo. I've twenty sons as lovely each as Bulbo. Not one but is as fit to reign as Bulbo. Whip, whack, flog, starve, rack, punish, torture Bulbo — break all his bones — roast him or flay him alive — pull all his pretty teeth out one by one. But justly dear as Bulbo is to me, — joy of my eyes, fond treasure of my soul! ha, ha, ha, ha! revenge is dearer still. Ho! torturers, rack-men, executioners — light up the fires and make the pincers hot! get lots of boiling lead! — Bring out ROSALBA!"

CHAPTER XVI.

How Hedzoff Rode Back Again to King Giglio.

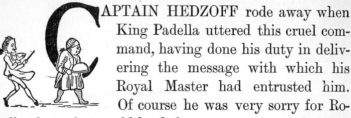

APTAIN HEDZOFF rode away when King Padella uttered this cruel command, having done his duty in delivering the message with which his Royal Master had entrusted him. Of course he was very sorry for Rosalba, but what could he do?

So he returned to King Giglio's camp and found the young monarch in a disturbed state of mind, smoking cigars in the royal tent. His Majesty's agitation was not appeased by the news that was brought by his ambassador. "The brutal ruthless ruffian royal wretch!" Giglio exclaimed. "As England's poesy has well remarked, 'The man that lays his hand upon a woman, save in the way of kindness, is a villain.' Ha, Hedzoff?"

"That he is, your Majesty," said the attendant.

"And didst thou see her flung into oil? and didn't the soothing oil — the emollient oil, refuse to boil, good Hedzoff — and to spoil the fairest lady ever eyes did look on?"

"Faith, good, my liege, I had no heart to look and see a beauteous lady boiling down; I took your royal message to Padella, and bore it back to you. I told him you would hold Prince Bulbo answerable. He only said that he had twenty sons as good as Bulbo, and forthwith he bade the ruthless executioners proceed."

" O cruel father — O unhappy son ! " cried the King. " Go, some of you, and bring Prince Bulbo hither."

Bulbo was brought in chains, looking very uncomfortable. Though a prisoner, he had been tolerably happy, perhaps because his mind was at rest, and all the fighting was over, and he was playing at marbles with his guards, when the King sent for him.

" O my poor Bulbo," said his Majesty, with looks of infinite compassion, " hast thou heard the news [for you see Giglio wanted to break the thing gently to the Prince], thy brutal father has condemned Rosalba — p-p-p-ut her to death, P-p-p-prince Bulbo ! "

" What, killed Betsinda, Boo-hoo-hoo," cried out Bulbo. " Betsinda ! pretty Betsinda ! dear Betsinda ! She was the dearest little girl in the world. I love her better twenty thousand times even than Angelica," and he went on expressing his grief in so hearty and unaffected a manner that the King was quite touched by it, and said, shaking Bulbo's hand, that he wished he had known Bulbo sooner.

Bulbo, quite unconsciously, and meaning for the best, offered to come and sit with his Majesty, and smoke a cigar with him, and console him. The *royal kindness* supplied Bulbo with a cigar ; he had not had one, he said, since he was taken prisoner.

And now think what must have been the feelings of the most *merciful of monarchs*, when he informed his prisoner, that in consequence of King Padella's *cruel and dastardly behavior* to Rosalba, Prince Bulbo must instantly be executed ! The noble Giglio could not

restrain his tears, nor could the Grenadiers, nor the
officers, nor could Bulbo himself, when the matter was
explained to him, and he was brought to understand
that his Majesty's promise, of course, was *above everything*, and Bulbo must submit.   So poor Bulbo was led
out, Hedzoff trying to console him, by pointing out
that if he had won the battle of Bombardaro he might
have hanged Prince Giglio.   " Yes!   But that is no
comfort to me now ! " said poor Bulbo ; nor indeed was
it, poor fellow.

He was told the business would be done the next
morning at eight, and was taken back to his dungeon,
where every attention was paid to him.   The gaoler's
wife sent him tea, and the turnkey's daughter begged
him to write his name in her album, where a many
gentlemen had wrote it on like occasions !   " Bother
your album ! " says Bulbo.   The undertaker came and
measured him for the handsomest coffin which money
could buy — even this didn't console Bulbo.   The cook
brought him dishes which he once used to like ; but he
wouldn't touch them ; he sat down and began writing
an adieu to Angelica, as the clock kept always ticking,
and the hands drawing nearer to next morning.   The
barber came in at night, and offered to shave him for
the next day.   Prince Bulbo kicked him away, and
went on writing a few words to Princess Angelica, as
the clock kept always ticking, and the hands hopping
nearer and nearer to next morning.   He got up on the
top of a hat-box, on the top of a chair, on the top of
his bed, on the top of his table, and looked out to see
whether he might escape, as the clock kept always ticking and the hands drawing nearer, and nearer, and
nearer.

But looking out of the window was one thing, and jumping another; and the town-clock struck seven. So he got into bed for a little sleep, but the gaoler came and woke him, and said: "Git up, your Royal Ighness, if you please, it's *ten minutes to eight!*"

So poor Bulbo got up; he had gone to bed in his clothes (the lazy boy), and he shook himself, and said he didn't mind about dressing, or having any breakfast, thank you; and he saw the soldiers who had come for him. "Lead on!" he said; and they led the way, deeply affected; and they came into the court-yard, and out into the square, and there was King Giglio come to take leave of him, and his Majesty most kindly shook hands with him, and the *gloomy procession* marched on — when hark!

Haw — wurraw — wurraw — aworr!

A roar of wild beasts was heard. And who should come riding into the town, frightening away the boys, and even the beadle and policeman, but ROSALBA!

The fact is, that when Captain Hedzoff entered into the Court of Snapdragon Castle, and was discoursing with King Padella, the lions made a dash at the open gate, gobbled up the six beef-eaters in a jiffy, and away they went with Rosalba on the back of one of them, and they carried her, turn and turn about, till they came to the city where Prince Giglio's army was encamped.

When the KING heard of the QUEEN's arrival you may think how he rushed out of his breakfast-room to hand Her Majesty off her lion! . The lions were grown as fat as pigs now, having had Hogginarmo and all those beef-eaters, and were so tame any body might pat them.

While Giglio knelt (most gracefully) and helped the

Princess, Bulbo, for his part, rushed up and kissed the lion. He flung his arms round the forest monarch; he hugged him, and laughed and cried for joy. "Oh, you darling old beast, Oh, how glad I am to see you, and the dear, dear Bets — that is, Rosalba."

"What, is it you? poor Bulbo," said the Queen, "Oh, how glad I am to see you;" and she gave him her hand to kiss. King Giglio slapped him most kindly on the back, and said, "Bulbo, my boy, I am delighted, for your sake, that her Majesty has arrived."

"So am I," said Bulbo; "and *you know why.*" Captain Hedzoff here came up. "Sire, it is half-past eight; shall we proceed with the execution?"

"Execution, what for?" asked Bulbo.

"An officer only knows his orders," replied Captain Hedzoff, showing his warrant, on which His Majesty King Giglio smilingly said, Prince Bulbo was reprieved this time, and most graciously invited him to breakfast.

CHAPTER XVII.

How a Tremendous Battle Took Place, and Who Won It.

AS soon as King Padella heard, what we know already, that his victim, the lovely Rosalba, had escaped him, his Majesty's fury knew no bounds, and he pitched the Lord Chancellor, Lord Chamberlain, and every officer of the crown whom he could set eyes on, into the caldron of boiling oil prepared for the Princess. Then he ordered out his whole army, horse, foot, and artillery; and set forth at the head of an innumerable host, and I should think twenty thousand drummers, trumpeters, and fifers.

King Giglio's advanced guard, you may be sure, kept that monarch acquainted with the enemy's dealings, and he was in no wise disconcerted. He was much too polite to alarm the Princess, his lovely guest, with any unnecessary rumors of battles impending; on the contrary, he did every thing to amuse and divert her; gave her a most elegant breakfast, dinner, lunch, and got up a ball for her that evening, when he danced with her every single dance.

Poor Bulbo was taken into favor again, and allowed to go quite free now. He had new clothes given him, was called "My good cousin" by his Majesty, and was treated with the greatest distinction by everybody. But it was easy to see he was very melancholy. The fact is, the sight of Betsinda, who looked perfectly lovely in an elegant new dress, set poor Bulbo frantic in love with her again. And he never thought about Angelica, now Princess Bulbo, whom he had left at home, and who, as we know, did not care much about him.

The King, dancing the twenty-fifth polka with Rosalba, remarked with wonder the ring she wore; and then Rosalba told him how she had got it from Gruffanuff, who no doubt had picked it up when Angelica flung it away.

"Yes," says the Fairy Blackstick, who had come to see the young people, and who had very likely certain plans regarding them. "That ring I gave the Queen, Giglio's mother, who was not, saving your presence, a very wise woman; it is enchanted, and whoever wears it looks beautiful in the eyes of the world. I made poor Prince Bulbo, when he was christened, the present of a rose which made him look handsome while he had it; but he gave it to Angelica, who instantly looked beautiful again, whilst Bulbo relapsed into his natural plainness."

"Rosalba needs no ring, I am sure," says Giglio, with a low bow. "She is beautiful enough, in my eyes, without any enchanted aid."

"O sir," said Rosalba.

"Take off the ring and try," said the King, and

resolutely drew the ring off her finger. In *his* eyes she looked just as handsome as before!

The King was thinking of throwing the ring away, as it was so dangerous and made all the people so mad about Rosalba, but being a prince of great humor, and good humor too, he cast his eyes upon a poor youth who happened to be looking on very disconsolately, and said:

"Bulbo, my poor lad! come and try on this ring. The Princess Rosalba makes it a present to you." The magic properties of this ring were uncommonly strong, for no sooner had Bulbo put it on, but lo and behold! he appeared a personable, agreeable young prince enough, — with a fine complexion, fair hair, rather stout, and with bandy legs; but these were encased in such a beautiful pair of yellow morocco boots that nobody remarked them. And Bulbo's spirits rose up almost immediately after he had looked in the glass, and he talked to their Majesties in the most lively, agreeable manner, and danced opposite the Queen with one of the prettiest maids of honor, and after looking at her Majesty, could not help saying: "How very odd; she is very pretty, but not so *extraordinarily* handsome." "Oh no, by no means!" says the Maid of Honor.

"But what care I, dear sir," says the Queen, who overheard them, "if *you* think I am good-looking enough?"

His Majesty's glance in reply to this affectionate speech was such that no painter could draw it. And the Fairy Blackstick said: "Bless you, my darling children! Now you are united and happy; and now you see what I said from the first, that a little misfortune has done you both good. *You*, Giglio, had you been bred in prosperity, would scarcely have learned to read or write, — you would have been idle and extravagant, and could not have been a good king as now you will be. You, Rosalba, would have been so flattered that your little head might have been turned like Angelica's who thought herself too good for Giglio."

"As if anybody could be good enough for *him*," cried Rosalba.

"O you, you darling!" says Giglio. And so she was; and he was just holding out his arms in order to give her a hug before the whole company, when a messenger came rushing in, and said: "My Lord, the enemy!"

"To arms!" cries Giglio.

"Oh, mercy!" says Rosalba, and fainted of course. He snatched one kiss from her lips, and rushed *forth to the field* of battle!

The fairy had provided King Giglio with a suit of armor, which was not only embroidered all over with jewels, and blinding to your eyes to look at, but was water-proof, gun-proof, and sword-proof; so that in the midst of the very hottest battles his Majesty rode about as calmly as if he had been a British grenadier at Alma. Were I engaged in fighting for my country, *I* should like such a suit of armor as Prince Giglio wore; but you know he was a prince of a fairy tale, and they always have these wonderful things.

Besides the fairy armor, the Prince had a fairy horse, which would gallop at any pace you please; and a fairy sword, which would lengthen, and run through a whole regiment of enemies at once. With such a weapon at command, I wonder, for my part, he thought of ordering his army out; but forth they all came in magnificent new uniforms, Hedzoff and the Prince's two college friends each commanding a division, and his Majesty prancing in person at the head of them all.

Ah! if I had the pen of a Sir Archibald Alison, my dear friends, would I not now entertain you with the account of a most tremendous shindy? Should not fine blows be struck? dreadful wounds be delivered? arrows darken the air? cannon balls crash through the battalions? cavalry charge infantry? infantry pitch into cavalry? bugles blow; drums beat; horses neigh; fifes sing; soldiers roar, swear, hurray; officers shout out: "Forward, my men!" "This way, lads!" "Give it 'em, boys. Fight for King Giglio, and the cause of right!" "King Padella forever!" Would I not describe all this, I say, and in the very finest language, too? But this humble pen does not possess the skill necessary for the description of combats. In a word, the overthrow of King Padella's army was so complete, that if they had been Russians you could not have wished them to be more utterly smashed and confounded.

As for that usurping monarch, having performed acts of valor much more considerable than could be expected of a royal ruffian and usurper, who had such a bad cause, and who was so cruel to women, — as for King Padella, I say, when his army ran away the King ran away too, kicking his first general, Prince Punchikoff, from his saddle, and galloping away on the Prince's horse, having indeed had twenty-five or twenty-six of his own shot under him. Hedzoff coming up, and finding Punchikoff down, as you may imagine very speedily disposed of *him*. Meanwhile King Padella was scampering off as hard as his horse could lay legs to ground. Fast as he scampered, I promise you somebody else galloped faster; and that individual, as no doubt you are aware, was the Royal Giglio, who kept bawling out: "Stay, traitor! Turn, miscreant, and defend thyself! Stand, tyrant, coward, ruffian, royal wretch, till I cut thy ugly head from thy usurping shoulders!" And with his fairy sword, which elongated itself at will, his Majesty kept poking and prodding Padella in the back, until that wicked monarch roared with anguish.

When he was fairly brought to bay, Padella turned and dealt Prince Giglio a prodigious crack over the sconce with his battle-axe, a most enormous weapon, which had cut down I don't know how many regiments in the course of the afternoon. But, Law bless you! though the blow fell right down on his Majesty's helmet, it made no more impression than if Padella had struck him with a pat of butter; his battle-axe crumpled up in Padella's hand, and the Royal Giglio laughed for very scorn at the impotent efforts of that atrocious usurper.

At the ill success of his blow the Crim Tartar monarch was justly irritated. "If," says he to Giglio, "you ride a fairy horse, and wear fairy armor, what on earth is the use of my hitting you? I may as well give myself up a prisoner at once. Your Majesty won't, I suppose, be so mean as to strike a poor fellow who can't strike again?"

The justice of Padella's remark struck the magnanimous Giglio. "Do you yield yourself a prisoner, Padella?" says he.

"Of course I do," says Padella.

"Do you acknowledge Rosalba as your rightful Queen, and give up the crown and all your treasures to your rightful mistress?"

"If I must I must," says Padella, who was naturally very sulky.

By this time King Giglio's aides-de-camp had come up, whom his Majesty ordered to bind the prisoner. And they tied his hands behind him, and bound his legs tight under his horse, having set him with his face to the tail; and in this fashion he was led back to King Giglio's quarters, and thrust into the very dungeon where young Bulbo had been confined.

Padella (who was a very different person in the depth of his distress to Padella the proud wearer of the Crim Tartar crown) now most affectionately and earnestly asked to see his son — his dear eldest boy — his darling Bulbo; and that good-natured young man never once reproached his haughty parent for his unkind conduct the day before, when he would have left Bulbo to be shot without any pity, but came to see his father, and spoke to him through the grating of the door, beyond which he was not allowed to go, and brought him some sandwiches from the grand supper which his Majesty was giving above stairs, in honor of the brilliant victory which had just been achieved.

"I cannot stay with you long, sir," says Bulbo, who

was in his best ball dress, as he handed his father in the prog, " I am engaged to dance the next quadrille with her Majesty Queen Rosalba, and I hear the fiddles playing at this very moment."

So Bulbo went back to the ball-room, and the wretched Padella ate his solitary supper in silence and tears.

All was now joy in King Giglio's circle. Dancing, feasting, fun, illuminations, and jollifications of all sorts ensued. The people through whose villages they passed were ordered to illuminate their cottages at night, and scatter flowers on the roads during the day. They were requested, and I promise you they did not like to refuse, to serve the troops liberally with eatables and wine ; besides, the army was enriched by the immense quantity of plunder which was found in King Padella's camp, and taken from his soldiers, who (after they had given up every thing) were allowed to fraternize with the conquerors, and the united forces marched back by easy stages towards King Giglio's capital, his royal banner and that of Queen Rosalba being carried in front of the troops. Hedzoff was made a Duke and a Field Marshal, Smith and Jones were promoted to be Earls, the Crim Tartar Order of the Pumpkin and the Paflagonian decoration of the Cucumber were freely distributed by their Majesties to the army. Queen Rosalba wore the Paflagonian Ribbon of the Cucumber across her riding habit, whilst King Giglio never appeared without the grand Cordon of the Pumpkin. How the people cheered them as they rode along side by side ! They were pronounced to be the handsomest couple ever seen : that was a matter of course ; but they really *were* very handsome, and, had they been otherwise, would have looked so, they were so happy ! Their Majesties were never separated during the whole day, but breakfasted, dined, and supped together always, and rode side by side, interchanging elegant compliments, and indulging in the most delightful conversation. At night, her Majesty's ladies of honor (who had all rallied round her the day after King Padella's defeat) came and conducted her to the apartments prepared for her ; whilst King Giglio, surrounded by his gentlemen, withdrew to his own royal quarters. It was agreed they should be married as soon as they reached the capital, and orders were despatched to the Archbishop of Blombodinga, to hold himself in readiness to perform the interesting ceremony. Duke Hedzoff carried the message, and gave instructions to have the Royal Castle splendidly refurnished and painted afresh. The Duke seized Glumboso, the Ex-Prime Minister, and made him refund that considerable sum of money which the old scoundrel had secreted out of the late King's treasure. He also clapped Valoroso into prison (who, by the way, had been dethroned for some considerable period past), and when the ex-monarch weakly remonstrated, Hedzoff said : " A soldier, sir, knows but his duty ; my orders are to lock you up along with the Ex-King Padella, whom I have brought hither a prisoner under guard." So these two ex-royal personages were sent for a year to the House of Correction, and thereafter were obliged to become monks, of the severest Order of Flagellants, in which state, by fasting, by vigils, by flogging (which they administered to one another, humbly but resolutely), no doubt they exhibited a repentance for their past misdeeds, usurpations, and private and public crimes.

As for Glumboso, that rogue was sent to the galleys, and never had an opportunity to steal any more.

CHAPTER XVIII.

How They All Journeyed Back to the Capital.

THE Fairy Blackstick, by whose means this young King and Queen had certainly won their respective crowns back, would come not unfrequently to pay them a little visit — as they were riding in their triumphal progress towards Giglio's capital — change her wand into a pony, and travel by their Majesties' side, giving them the very best advice. I am not sure that King Giglio did not think the Fairy and her advice rather a bore, fancying it was his own valor and merits which had put him on his throne and conquered Padella; and, in fine, I fear he rather gave himself airs towards his best friend and patroness. She exhorted him to deal justly by his subjects, to draw mildly on the taxes, never to break his promise when he had once given it, — and in all respects to be a good king.

"A good king, my dear Fairy!" cries Rosalba. "Of course he will. Break his promise! Can you fancy my Giglio would ever do any thing so improper, so unlike him? No! never!" And she looked fondly towards Giglio, whom she thought a pattern of perfection.

"Why is Fairy Blackstick always advising me, and

telling me how to manage my government, and warning me to keep my word? Does she suppose that I am not a man of sense and a man of honor?" asks Giglio testily. "Methinks she rather presumes upon her position."

"Hush! dear Giglio," says Rosalba. "You know Blackstick has been very kind to us, and we must not offend her." But the Fairy was not listening to Giglio's testy observations; she had fallen back, and was trotting on her pony by Bulbo's side, who rode a donkey, and made himself generally beloved in the army by his cheerfulness, kindness, and good humor to everybody. He was eager to see his darling Angelica. He thought there never was such a charming being. Blackstick did not tell him it was the possession of the magic rose that made Angelica so lovely in his eyes. She brought him the very best accounts of his little wife, whose misfortunes and humiliations had indeed very greatly improved her; and you see she could whisk off on her wand a hundred miles in a minute, and be back in no time, and so carry polite messages from Bulbo to Angelica, and from Angelica to Bulbo, and comfort that young man upon his journey.

When the Royal party arrived at the last stage before you reach Blombodinga, who should be in waiting, in her carriage there with her lady of honor by her side, but the Princess Angelica. She rushed into her husband's arms, scarcely stopping to make a passing courtesy to the King and Queen. She had no eyes but for Bulbo, who appeared perfectly lovely to her on account of the fairy ring which he wore, whilst she herself, wearing the magic rose in her bonnet, seemed entirely beautiful to the enraptured Bulbo.

A splendid luncheon was served to the Royal party, of which the Archbishop, the Chancellor, Duke Hedzoff, Countess Gruffanuff, and all our friends partook; the Fairy Blackstick being seated on the left of King Giglio, with Bulbo and Angelica beside her. You could hear the joy-bells ringing in the capital, and the guns which the citizens were firing off in honor of their Majesties.

"What can have induced that hideous old Gruffanuff to dress herself up in such an absurd way? Did you ask her to be your bridesmaid, my dear?" says Giglio to Rosalba. "What a figure of fun Gruffy is!"

Gruffy was seated opposite their Majesties, between the Archbishop and the Lord Chancellor, and a figure of fun she certainly was, for she was dressed in a low white silk dress, with lace over, a wreath of white roses on her wig, a splendid lace veil, and her yellow old neck was covered with diamonds. She ogled the King in such a manner that His Majesty burst out laughing.

"Eleven o'clock!" cries Giglio, as the great Cathedral bell of Blombodinga tolled that hour. "Gentlemen and ladies, we must be starting. Archbishop, you must be at church I think before twelve?"

"We must be at church before twelve," sighs out Gruffanuff in a languishing voice, hiding her old face behind her fan.

"And then I shall be the happiest man in my dominions," cries Giglio, with an elegant bow to the blushing Rosalba.

"O my Giglio! O my dear Majesty!" exclaims

Gruffanuff; "and can it be that this happy moment at length has arrived —"

"Of course it has arrived," says the King.

"— And that I am about to become the enraptured bride of my adored Giglio!" continues Gruffanuff. "Lend me a smelling-bottle, somebody. I certainly shall faint with joy."

"*You* my bride?" roars out Giglio.

"*You* marry my Prince?" cries poor little Rosalba.

"Pooh! Nonsense! The woman's mad!" exclaims the King. And all the courtiers exhibited by their countenances and expressions, marks of surprise, or ridicule, or incredulity, or wonder.

"I should like to know who else is going to be married, if I am not?" shrieks out Gruffanuff. "I should like to know if King Giglio is a gentleman, and if there is such a thing as justice in Paflagonia? Lord Chancellor! my Lord Archbishop! will your lordships sit by and see a poor, fond, confiding, tender creature put upon? Has not Prince Giglio promised to marry his Barbara? Is not this Giglio's signature? Does not this paper declare that he is mine, and only mine?" And she handed to his Grace the Archbishop the document which the Prince signed that evening when she wore the magic ring, and Giglio drank so much champagne. And the old Archbishop, taking out his eye-glasses, read: "'This is to give notice that I, Giglio, only son of Savio, King of Paflagonia, hereby promise to marry the charming Barbara Griselda Countess Gruffanuff and widow of the late Jenkins Gruffanuff, Esq.'"

"H'm," says the Archbishop, "the document is certainly a — a document."

"Phoo," says the Lord Chancellor, "the signature is not in his Majesty's handwriting." Indeed, since his studies at Bosforo, Giglio had made an immense improvement in caligraphy.

"Is it your handwriting, Giglio?" cries the Fairy Blackstick, with an awful severity of countenance.

"Y — y — y — es," poor Giglio gasps out. "I had quite forgotten the confounded paper; she can't mean to hold me by it. You old wretch, what will you take to let me off? Help the Queen, some one, — Her Majesty has fainted."

"Chop her head off!"
"Smother the old witch!"
"Pitch her into the river!"

Exclaimed the impetuous Hedzoff, the ardent Smith, and the faithful Jones.

But Gruffanuff flung her arms round the Archbishop's neck, and bellowed out, "Justice, justice my Lord Chancellor!" so loudly, that her piercing shrieks caused everybody to pause. As for Rosalba, she was borne away lifeless by her ladies; and you may imagine the look of agony which Giglio cast towards that lovely being, as his hope, his joy, his darling, his all in all, was thus removed, and in her place the horrid old Gruffanuff rushed up to his side, and once more shrieked out, "Justice! justice!"

"Won't you take that sum of money which Glumboso hid?" says Giglio, "two hundred and eighteen thousand millions, or thereabouts. It's a handsome sum."

"I will have that and you too!" says Gruffanuff.

" Let us throw the crown jewels into the bargain," gasps out Giglio.

" I will wear them by my Giglio's side ! " says Gruff-anuff.

" Will half, three-quarters, five-sixths, nineteen-twentieths, of my kingdom do, Countess ? " asks the trembling monarch.

" What were all Europe to me without *you*, my Giglio ? " cries Gruff, kissing his hand.

" I won't, I can't, I sha'n't, —I'll resign the crown first," shouts Giglio, tearing away his hand ; but Gruff clung to it.

" I have a competency, my love," she says, " and with thee and a cottage thy Barbara will be happy."

Giglio was half mad with rage by this time. " I will not marry her," says he. " O Fairy, Fairy, give me counsel ! " And as he spoke he looked wildly round at the severe face of the Fairy Blackstick.

" ' Why is Fairy Blackstick always advising me, and warning me to keep my word ? Does she suppose that I am not a man of honor ? ' " said the Fairy, quoting Giglio's own haughty words. He quailed under the brightness of her eyes ; he felt that there was no escape for him from that awful inquisition.

" Well, Archbishop," said he, in a dreadful voice, that made his Grace start, " since this Fairy has led me to the height of happiness but to dash me down into the depths of despair, since I am to lose Rosalba, let me at least keep my honor. Get up, Countess, and let us be married ; I can keep my word, but I can die afterwards."

" O dear Giglio," cries Gruffanuff, skipping up, " I

knew, I knew I could trust thee — I knew that my Prince was the soul of honor. Jump into your carriages, ladies and gentlemen, and let us go to church at once; and as for dying, dear Giglio, no, no : — thou wilt forget that insignificant little chambermaid of a Queen — thou wilt live to be consoled by thy Barbara! She wishes to be a Queen, and not a Queen Dowager, my gracious Lord!" and hanging upon poor Giglio's arm, and leering and grinning in his face in the most disgusting manner, this old wretch tripped off in her white satin shoes, and jumped into the very carriage which had been got ready to convey Giglio and Rosalba to church. The cannons roared again, the bells pealed triple bobmajors, the people came out flinging flowers upon the path of the royal bride and bridegroom, and Gruff looked out of the gilt coach window and bowed and grinned to them. Phoo! the horrid old wretch!

CHAPTER XIX.

And Now We Come to the Last Scene in the Pantomime.

THE many ups and downs of her life had given the Princess Rosalba prodigious strength of mind, and that highly principled young woman presently recovered from her fainting-fit out of which Fairy Blackstick, by a precious essence which the Fairy always carried in her pocket, awakened her. Instead of tearing her hair, crying and bemoaning herself, and fainting again, as many young women would have done, Rosalba remembered that she owed an example of firmness to her subjects, and though she loved Giglio more than her life, was determined, as she told the Fairy, not to interfere between him and justice, or to cause him to break his royal word.

"I cannot marry him, but I shall love him always," says she to Blackstick; "I will go and be present at his marriage with the countess, and sign the book, and wish them happy with all my heart. I will see, when I get home, whether I cannot make the new Queen some handsome presents. The Crim Tartary crown diamonds are uncommonly fine, and I shall never have any use for them. I will live and die unmarried like Queen Elizabeth, and, of course, I shall leave my crown to Giglio when I quit this world. Let us go and see them married, my dear Fairy, let me say my one last farewell to him; and then, if you please, I will return to my own dominions."

So the Fairy kissed Rosalba with peculiar tenderness, and at once changed her wand into a very comfortable coach-and-four, with a steady coachman, and two respectable footmen behind; and the Fairy and Rosalba got into the coach, which Angelica and Bulbo entered after them. As for honest Bulbo, he was blubbering in the most pathetic manner, quite overcome by Rosalba's misfortune. She was touched by the honest fellow's sympathy, promised to restore to him the confiscated estates of Duke Padella his father, and created him, as he sat there in the coach, Prince, Highness, and First Grandee of the Crim Tartar Empire. The coach moved on, and, being a fairy coach, soon came up with the bridal procession.

Before the ceremony at the church it was the custom in Paflagonia, as it is in other countries, for the bride and bridegroom to sign the Contract of Marriage, which was to be witnessed by the Chancellor, Minister, Lord Mayor, and principal officers of state. Now, as the Royal Palace was being painted and furnished anew, it was not ready for the reception of the King and his bride, who proposed at first to take up their residence at the Prince's palace, that one which Valoroso occupied when Angelica was born, and before he usurped the throne.

So the marriage party drove up to the palace: the dignitaries got out of their carriages and stood aside;

poor Rosalba stepped out of her coach, supported by Bulbo, and stood almost fainting up against the railings, so as to have a last look of her dear Giglio. As for Blackstick, she, according to her custom, had flown out of the coach window in some inscrutable manner, and was now standing at the palace door.

Giglio came up the steps with his horrible bride on his arm, looking as pale as if he were going to execution. He only frowned at the Fairy Blackstick — he was angry with her, and thought she came to insult his misery.

"Get out of the way, pray," says Gruffanuff, haughtily. "I wonder why you are always poking your nose into other people's affairs?"

"Are you determined to make this poor young man unhappy?" says Blackstick.

"To marry him, yes! What business is it of yours? Pray, madam, don't say 'you' to a Queen," cries Gruffanuff.

"You won't take the money he offered you?"

"No."

"You won't let him off his bargain, though you know you cheated him when you made him sign the paper?"

"Impudence! Policemen, remove this woman!" cries Gruffanuff. And the policemen were rushing forward, but with a wave of her wand the Fairy struck them all like so many statues in their places.

"You won't take anything in exchange for your bond, Mrs. Gruffanuff," cries the Fairy, with awful severity. "I speak for the last time."

"No," shrieks Gruffanuff, stamping with her foot.

"I'll have my husband, my husband, my husband!"

"You SHALL HAVE YOUR HUSBAND!" the Fairy Blackstick cried; and advancing a step laid her hand upon the nose of the KNOCKER.

As she touched it, the brass nose seemed to elongate, the open mouth opened still wider, and uttered a roar which made everybody start. The eyes rolled wildly; the arms and legs uncurled themselves, writhed about, and seemed to lengthen with each twist; the knocker expanded into a figure in yellow livery, six feet high; the screws by which it was fixed to the door unloosed themselves, and JENKINS GRUFFANUFF once more trod the threshold off which he had been lifted more than twenty years ago!

"Master's not at home," says Jenkins, just in his old voice; and Mrs. Jenkins, giving a dreadful *youp*, fell down in a fit, in which nobody minded her.

For everybody was shouting: "Huzzay! huzzay!" "Hip, hip, hurray!" "Long live the King and Queen!" "Were such things ever seen?" "No, never, never, never!" "The Fairy Blackstick for-ever!"

The bells were ringing double peals, the guns roaring and banging most prodigiously. Bulbo was embracing everybody; the Lord Chancellor was flinging up his wig and shouting like a madman; Hedzoff had got the Archbishop round the waist, and they were dancing a jig for joy; and as for Giglio, I leave you to imagine what *he* was doing, and if he kissed Rosalba once, twice, — twenty thousand times, I'm sure I don't think he was wrong.

So Gruffanuff opened the hall door with a low bow, just as he had been accustomed to do, and they all went in and signed the book, and then they went to church and were married, and the Fairy Blackstick sailed away on her cane, and was never more heard of in Paflagonia.

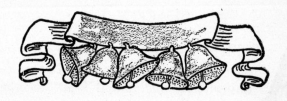

PETER SCHLEMIHL, THE SHADOWLESS MAN

By ADELBERT VON CHAMISSO.

CHAPTER I.

AFTER a prosperous, but to me a very wearisome, voyage, we came at last into port. Immediately on landing I got together my few effects; and, squeezing myself through the crowd, went into the nearest and humblest inn which first met my gaze. On asking for a room the waiter looked at me from head to foot, and conducted me to one. I asked for some cold water, and for the correct address of Mr. Thomas Jones, which was described as being "by the north gate, the first country-house to the right, a large new house of red and white marble, with many pillars." This was enough. As the day was not yet far advanced, I untied my bundle, took out my newly-turned black coat, dressed myself in my best clothes, and, with my letter of recommendation, set out for the man who was to assist me in the attainment of my moderate wishes.

After proceeding up the north street, I reached the gate, and saw the marble columns glittering through

the trees.   Having wiped the dust from my shoes with
my pocket-handkerchief, and readjusted my cravat, I
rang the bell — offering up at the same time a silent
prayer.   The door flew open, and the porter sent in my
name.   I had soon the honor to be invited into the
park, where Mr. Jones was walking with a few friends.
I recognized him at once by his corpulency and self-
complacent air.   He received me very well — just as
a rich man receives a poor devil; and, turning to me,
took my letter.   " Oh, from my brother ! it is a long
time since I heard from him : is he well ? — Yonder,"
he went on, — turning to the company, and pointing to
a distant hill — " yonder is the site of the new building."   He broke the seal without discontinuing the
conversation, which turned upon riches.   " The man,"
he said, " who does not possess at least a million is a
poor wretch."   " Oh, how true ! " I exclaimed, in the
fulness of my heart.   He seemed pleased at this, and
replied with a smile, " Stop here, my dear friend;
afterwards I shal , perhaps, have time to tell you what
I think of this," pointing to the letter, which he then
put into his pocket, and turned round to the company,
offering his arm to a young lady.   His example was
followed by the other gentlemen, each politely escort-
ing a lady ; and the whole party proceeded towards
a little hill thickly planted with blooming roses.

I followed without troubling any one, for none took
the least further notice of me.   The party was in high
spirits — lounging about and jesting — speaking sometimes of trifling matters very seriously, and of serious
matters as triflingly — and exercising their wit in particular to great advantage on their absent friends and

their affairs. I was too ignorant of what they were talking about to understand much of it, and too anxious and absorbed in my own reflections to occupy myself with the solution of such enigmas as their conversation presented.

By this time we had reached the thicket of roses. The lovely Fanny, who seemed to be the queen of the day, was obstinately bent on plucking a rose-branch for herself, and in the attempt pricked her finger with a thorn. The crimson stream, as if flowing from the dark-tinted rose, tinged her fair hand with the purple current. This circumstance set the whole company in commotion; and court-plaster was called for. A quiet, elderly man, tall and meagre-looking, who was one of the company, but whom I had not before observed, immediately put his hand into the tight breast-pocket of his old-fashioned coat of gray sarsnet, pulled out a small letter-case, opened it, and, with a most respectful bow, presented the lady with the wished-for article. She received it without noticing the giver, or thanking him. The wound was bound up, and the party proceeded along the hill towards the back part, from which they enjoyed an extensive view across the green labyrinth of the park to the wide-spreading ocean. The view was truly a magnificent one. A slight speck was observed on the horizon, between the dark flood and the azure sky. " A telescope ! " called out Mr. Jones ; but before any of the servants could answer the summons the gray man, with a modest bow, drew his hand from his pocket, and presented a beautiful Dollond's telescope to Mr. Jones, who, on looking through it, informed the company that the speck in the distance was the ship which had sailed yesterday, and which was detained within sight of the haven by contrary winds. The telescope passed from hand to hand, but was not returned to the owner, whom I gazed at with astonishment, and could not conceive how so large an instrument could have proceeded from so small a pocket. This, however, seemed to excite surprise in no one; and the gray man appeared to create as little interest as myself.

Refreshments were now brought forward, consisting of the rarest fruits from all parts of the world, served up in the most costly dishes. Mr. Jones did the honors with unaffected grace, and addressed me for the second time, saying, "You had better eat; you did not get such things at sea." I acknowledged his politeness with a bow, which, however, he did not perceive, having turned round to speak with some one else.

The party would willingly have stopped some time here on the declivity of the hill to enjoy the extensive prospect before them, had they not been apprehensive of the dampness of the grass. "How delightful it would be," exclaimed some one, "if we had a Turkey carpet to lay down here!" The wish was scarcely expressed when the man in the gray coat put his hand in his pocket, and, with a modest and even humble air, pulled out a rich Turkish carpet, embroidered in gold. The servant received it as a matter of course, and spread it out on the desired spot; and, without any ceremony, the company seated themselves on it. Confounded by what I saw, I gazed again at the man, his pocket, and the carpet, which was more than twenty feet in length and ten in breadth, and rubbed my eyes, not knowing what to think, particularly as no one saw anything extraordinary in the matter.

I would gladly have made some inquiries respecting the man, and asked who he was, but knew not to whom to address myself, for I felt almost more afraid of the servants than of their master.   At length I took courage, and stepping up to a young man who seemed of less consequence than the others, and who was more frequently standing by himself, I begged of him, in a low tone, to tell me who the obliging gentleman was in the gray cloak.   " That man who looks like a piece of thread just escaped from a tailor's needle? "   " Yes; he who is standing alone yonder."   " I do not know," was the reply; and to avoid, as it seemed, any further conversation with me, he turned away, and spoke of some commonplace matters with a neighbor.

The sun's rays now being stronger, the ladies complained of feeling oppressed by the heat; and the lovely Fanny, turning carelessly to the gray man, to whom I had not yet observed that any one had addressed the most trifling question, asked him if, perhaps, he had not a tent about him. He replied with a low bow, as if some unmerited honor had been conferred upon him; and, putting his hand in his pocket, drew from it canvas, poles, cord, iron — in short, everything belonging to the most splendid tent for a party of pleasure.   The young gentlemen assisted in pitching it, and it covered the whole carpet, but no one seemed to think that there was anything extraordinary in it.

I had long secretly felt uneasy — indeed, almost horrified; but how was this feeling increased when, at the next wish expressed, I saw him take from his pocket

three horses! Yes, Adelbert, three large beautiful
steeds, with saddles and bridles, out of the very pocket
whence had already issued a letter-case, a telescope, a
carpet twenty feet long and ten in breadth, and a pavil-
ion of the same extent, with all its appurtenances!
Did I not assure you that my own eyes had seen all
this, you would certainly disbelieve it.

This man, although he appeared so humble and embarrassed in his air and manners, and passed so un-
heeded, had inspired me with such a feeling of horror
by the unearthly paleness of his countenance, from
which I could not avert my eyes, that I was unable
longer to endure it.

I determined, therefore, to steal away from the
company, which appeared no difficult matter from the
undistinguished part I acted in it. I resolved to return
to the town, and pay another visit to Mr. Jones the
following morning, and, at the same time, make some
inquiries of him relative to the extraordinary man in
gray, provided I could command sufficient courage.
Would to Heaven that such good fortune had awaited
me.

I had stolen safely down the hill, through the
thicket of roses, and now found myself on an open
plain; but fearing lest I should be met out of the
proper path, crossing the grass I cast an inquisitive
glance around, and started as I beheld the man in the
gray cloak advancing towards me. He took off his
hat, and made me a lower bow than mortal had ever
yet favored me with. It was evident that he wished
to address me, and I could not avoid encountering him
without seeming rude. I returned his salutation,

therefore, and stood bareheaded in the sunshine, as if rooted to the ground. I gazed at him with the utmost horror, and felt like a bird fascinated by a serpent.

He affected himself to have an air of embarrassment. With his eyes on the ground he bowed several times, drew nearer, and at last, without looking up, addressed me in a low and hesitating voice, almost in the tone of a suppliant, " Will you, sir, excuse my importunity in venturing to intrude upon you in so unusual a manner ? I have a request to make — would you most graciously be pleased to allow me — ? " " Hold ! for Heaven's sake ! " I exclaimed ; " what can I do for a man who " — I stopped in some confusion, which he seemed to share. After a moment's pause he resumed, " During the short time I have had the pleasure to be in your company, I have — permit me, sir, to say — beheld with unspeakable admiration your most beautiful shadow, and remarked the air of noble indifference with which you, at the same time, turn from the glorious picture at your feet, as if disdaining to vouch-safe a glance at it. Excuse the boldness of my pro-posal, but perhaps you would have no objection to sell me your shadow ? " He stopped, while my head turned round like a mill-wheel. What was I to think of so extraordinary a proposal ? To sell my shadow ! " He must be mad," thought I ; and assuming a tone more in character with the submissiveness of his own, I replied, " My good friend, are you not content with your own shadow ? This would be a bargain of a strange nature indeed ! "

" I have in my pocket," he said, " many things which may possess some value in your eyes ; for that inestimable shadow I should deem the highest price too little."

A cold shuddering came over me as I recollected the pocket; and I could not conceive what had induced me to style him " *good friend*," which I took care not to repeat, endeavoring to make up for it by a studied politeness.

I now resumed the conversation: " But, sir, — excuse your humble servant — I am at a loss to comprehend your meaning, — my shadow? — how can I? "

"Permit me," he exclaimed, interrupting me, " to gather up the noble image as it lies on the ground, and to take it into my possession. As to the manner of accomplishing it, leave that to me. In return, and as an evidence of my gratitude, I shall leave you to choose among all the treasures I have in my pocket, among which are a variety of enchanting articles, not exactly adapted for you, who, I am sure, would like better to have the wishing-cap of Fortunatus, all made new and sound again, and a lucky purse which also belonged to him."

"Fortunatus's purse! " cried I; and, great as was my mental anguish, with that one word he had penetrated the deepest recesses of my soul. A feeling of giddiness came over me, and double ducats glittered before my eyes.

" Be pleased, gracious sir, to examine this purse, and make a trial of its contents." He put his hand in his pocket, and drew forth a large, strongly stitched bag of stout Cordovan leather, with a couple of strings to match, and presented it to me. I seized it, took out ten gold pieces, then ten more, and this I repeated again and again. Instantly I held out my hand to him. "Done," said I; "the bargain is made; my shadow for the purse." "Agreed," he answered; and immediately kneeling down, I beheld him, with extraordinary dexterity, gently loosen my shadow from the grass, lift it up, fold it together, and at last put it in his pocket. He then rose, bowed once more to me, and directed his steps towards the rose-bushes. I fancied I heard him quietly laughing to himself. However, I held the purse fast by the two strings. The earth was basking beneath the brightness of the sun; but I presently lost all consciousness.

On recovering my senses, I hastened to quit a place where I hoped there was nothing further to detain me. I first filled my pockets with gold, then fastened the strings of the purse round my neck, and concealed it in my bosom. I passed unnoticed out of the park, gained the high-road, and took the way to town. As I was thoughtfully approaching the gate, I heard some one behind me exclaiming, "Young man! young man! you have lost your shadow!" I turned, and perceived an old woman calling after me. "Thank you, my good woman," said I; and throwing her a piece of gold for her well-intended information, I stepped under the trees. At the gate, again, it was my fate to hear the sentry inquiring where the gentleman had left his shadow; and immediately I heard a couple of women exclaiming, "Just look! the poor man has no shadow." All this began to depress me, and I carefully avoided walking in the sun; but this could not everywhere be the case; for in the next broad street I had to cross, and, unfortunately for me, at the very hour in which the boys were coming out of school, a humpbacked lout of a fellow — I see him yet —soon made the discovery that I was without a shadow, and communicated the news, with loud outcries, to a knot of young urchins. The whole swarm proceeded immediately to reconnoitre me, and to pelt me with mud. " People," cried they, " are generally accustomed to take their shadows with them when they walk in the sunshine."

In order to drive them away I threw gold by hand-fuls among them, and sprang into a hackney-coach which some compassionate spectators sent to my rescue.

As soon as I found myself alone in the rolling vehicle I began to weep bitterly. I had by this time a mis-giving that, in the same degree in which gold in this world prevails over merit and virtue, by so much one's shadow excels gold; and now that I had sacrificed my conscience for riches, and given my shadow in exchange for mere gold, what on earth would become of me?

As the coach stopped at the door of my late inn, I felt much perplexed, and not at all disposed to enter so wretched an abode. I called for my things, and received them with an air of contempt, threw down a few gold pieces, and desired to be conducted to a first-rate hotel. This house had a northern aspect, so that I had nothing to fear from the sun. I dismissed the coachman with gold, asked to be conducted to the best apartment, and locked myself up in it as soon as possible.

Imagine, my friend, what I then set about ! O my dear Chamisso! even to you I blush to mention what follows.

I drew the ill-fated purse from my bosom; and, in a sort of frenzy that raged like a self-fed fire within me, I took out gold — gold — gold — more and more, till I strewed it on the floor, trampled upon it, and feasting on its very sound and brilliancy, added coins to coins, rolling and revelling on the gorgeous bed, until I sank exhausted.

Thus passed away that day and evening; and as my door remained locked, night found me still lying on the gold, where, at last, sleep overpowered me.

Then I dreamed of you, and fancied I stood behind the glass door of your little room, and saw you seated at your table between a skeleton and a bunch of dried plants; before you lay open the works of Haller, Humboldt, and Linnæus; on your sofa a volume of Goethe, and the enchanted Ring. I stood a long time contemplating you, and everything in your apartment; and again turning my gaze upon you, I perceived that you were motionless — you did not breathe — you were dead.

I awoke — it seemed yet early — my watch had stopped. I felt thirsty, faint, and worn out, for since the preceding morning I had not tasted food. I now cast from me, with loathing and disgust, the very gold with which but a short time before I had satiated my foolish heart. Now I knew not where to put it — I dared not leave it lying there. I examined my purse to see if it would hold it, — impossible! Neither of my windows opened on the sea. I had no other resource but, with toil and great fatigue, to drag it to a huge chest which stood in a closet in my room, where I placed it all, with the exception of a handful or two.

Then I threw myself, exhausted, into an armchair, till the people of the house should be up and stirring. As soon as possible I sent for some refreshment, and desired to see the landlord.

I entered into some conversation with this man respecting the arrangement of my future establishment. He recommended for my personal attendant one Bendel, whose honest and intelligent countenance immediately prepossessed me in his favor. It is this individual whose persevering attachment has consoled me in all the miseries of my life, and enabled me to bear up under my wretched lot. I was occupied the whole day in my room with servants in want of a situation and tradesmen of every description. I decided on my future plans, and purchased various articles of *vertù* and splendid jewels, in order to get rid of some of my gold; but nothing seemed to diminish the inexhaustible heap.

I now reflected on my situation with the utmost uneasiness. I dared not take a single step beyond my own door; and in the evening I had forty wax tapers lighted before I ventured to leave the shade. I reflected with horror on the frightful encounter with the schoolboys; yet I resolved, if I could command sufficient courage, to put the public opinion to a second trial. The nights were now moonlight. Late in the evening I wrapped myself in a large cloak, pulled my hat over my eyes, and, trembling like a criminal, stole out of the house.

I did not venture to leave the friendly shadow of the houses until I had reached a distant part of the town; and then I emerged into the broad moonlight, fully prepared to hear my fate from the lips of the passers-by.

Spare me, my beloved friend, the painful recital of all that I was doomed to endure. The women often expressed the deepest sympathy for me — a sympathy not less piercing to my soul than the scoffs of the young people, and the proud contempt of the men, particularly of the more corpulent, who threw an ample shadow before them. A fair and beauteous maiden, apparently accompanied by her parents, who gravely kept looking straight before them, chanced to cast a beaming glance on me, but was evidently startled at perceiving that I was without a shadow; and hiding her lovely face in her veil, and holding down her head, passed silently on.

This was past all endurance. Tears streamed from my eyes; and with a heart pierced through and through, I once more took refuge in the shade. I leant on the houses for support, and reached home at a late hour, worn-out with fatigue.

I passed a sleepless night. My first care the following morning was, to devise some means of discovering the man in the gray cloak. Perhaps I may succeed in finding him; and how fortunate it were if he should be as ill satisfied with his bargain as I am with mine!

I desired Bendel to be sent for, who seemed to possess some tact and ability. I minutely described to him the individual who possessed a treasure without which life itself was rendered a burden to me. I mentioned the time and place at which I had seen him, named all the persons who were present, and concluded with the following directions : — He was to inquire for a Dollond's telescope, a Turkey carpet interwoven with gold, a marquee, and, finally, for some black steeds — the history, without entering into particulars, of all these being singularly connected with the mysterious character who seemed to pass unnoticed by every one, but whose appearance had destroyed the peace and happiness of my life.

As I spoke I produced as much gold as I could hold in my two hands, and added jewels and precious stones of still greater value. " Bendel," said I, " this smooths many a path, and renders that easy which seems almost impossible. Be not sparing of it, for I am not so; but go, and rejoice your master with intelligence on which depend all his hopes."

He departed, and returned late and melancholy. None of Mr. Jones' servants, none of his guests (and Bendel had spoken to them all) had the slightest recollection of the man in the gray cloak. The new telescope was still there, but no one knew how it had come; and the tent and Turkey carpet were still stretched out on the hill. The servants boasted of their master's wealth; but no one seemed to know by what means he had become possessed of these newly-acquired luxuries. He was gratified; and it gave him no concern to be ignorant how they had come to him. The black coursers which had been mounted on that day were in the stables of the young gentlemen of the party, who admired them as the munificent present of Mr. Jones.

Such was the information I gained from Bendel's detailed account; but in spite of this unsatisfactory result, his zeal and prudence deserved and received my commendation.   In a gloomy mood, I made him a sign to withdraw.

"I have, sir," he continued, "laid before you all the information in my power relative to the subject of the most importance to you. I have now a message to deliver which I received early this morning from a person at the gate, as I was proceeding to execute the commission in which I have so unfortunately failed. The man's words were precisely these: 'Tell your master, Peter Schlemihl, he will not see me here again. I am going to cross the sea; a favorable wind now calls all the passengers on board; but in a year and a day I shall have the honor of paying him a visit; when, in all probability, I shall have a proposal to make to him of a very agreeable nature. Commend me to him most respectfully, with many thanks.' I inquired his name, but he said you would remember him."

"What sort of person was he?" cried I, in great emotion; and Bendel described the man in the gray coat feature by feature, word for word; in short, the very individual in search of whom he had been sent. "How unfortunate!" cried I bitterly; "it was himself." Scales, as it were, fell from Bendel's eyes. "Yes, it was he," cried he; "undoubtedly it was he; and fool, madman that I was, I did not recognize him —I did not, and have betrayed my master!" He then broke out into a torrent of self-reproach; and his distress really excited my compassion. I endeavored to console him, repeatedly assuring him that I entertained no doubt of his fidelity; and despatched him immediately to the wharf, to discover, if possible, some trace of the extraordinary being. But on that very morning

many vessels which had been detained in port by contrary winds had set sail, all bound to different parts of
the globe; and the gray man had disappeared like
a shadow.

.   .   .   .

Of what use were wings to a man fast bound in
chains of iron? They would but increase the horror
of his despair. Like the dragon guarding his treasure,
I remained cut off from all human intercourse, and
starving amidst my very gold, for it gave me no
pleasure: I anathematized it as the source of all my
wretchedness.

Sole depository of my fearful secret, I trembled
before the meanest of my attendants, whom, at the
same time, I envied: for he possessed a shadow, and
could venture to go out in the daytime; while I shut
myself up in my room day and night, and indulged in
all the bitterness of grief.

One individual, however, was daily pining away
before my eyes — my faithful Bendel, who was the
victim of silent self-reproach, tormenting himself with
the idea that he had betrayed the confidence reposed
in him by a good master, in failing to recognize the
individual in quest of whom he had been sent, and
with whom he had been led to believe that my melancholy fate was closely connected. Still, I had nothing
to accuse him with, as I recognized in the occurrence
the mysterious character of the unknown.

In order to leave no means untried, I one day despatched Bendel with a costly ring to the most cele-

brated artist in the town, desiring him to wait upon me. He came; and, dismissing the attendants, I secured the door, placing myself opposite to him, and, after extolling his art, with a heavy heart came to the point, first enjoining the strictest secrecy.

"For a person," said I, "who most unfortunately has lost his shadow, could you paint a false one?"

"Do you speak of the natural shadow?"

"Precisely so."

"But," he asked, "by what awkward negligence can a man have lost his shadow?"

"How it occurred," I answered, "is of no consequence: but it was in this manner"—(and here I uttered an unblushing falsehood)—"he was travelling in Russia last winter, and one bitterly cold day it froze so intensely, that his shadow remained so fixed to the ground, that it was found impossible to remove it."

"The false shadow that I might paint," said the artist, "would be liable to be lost on the slightest movement, particularly in a person who, from your account, cares so little about his shadow. A person without a shadow should keep out of the sun; that is the only safe and rational plan."

He rose and took his leave, casting so penetrating a look at me that I shrank from it. I sank back in my chair, and hid my face in my hands.

In this attitude Bendel found me, and was about to withdraw silently and respectfully on seeing me in such a state of grief. Looking up, overwhelmed with my sorrows, I felt that I must communicate them to him. "Bendel," I exclaimed—"Bendel, you, the only being who sees and respects my grief too much to inquire into its cause — you, who seem silently and sincerely to sympathize with me — come and share my confidence. The extent of my wealth I have not with-held from you, neither will I conceal from you the extent of my grief. Bendel! forsake me not. Bendel, you see me rich, free, beneficent; you fancy all the world in my power; yet you must have observed that I shun it, and avoid all human intercourse. You think, Bendel, that the world and I are at variance; and you yourself, perhaps, will abandon me when I acquaint you with this fearful secret. Bendel, I am rich, free, generous; but, O God, I have *no shadow!*"

"No shadow!" exclaimed the faithful young man, tears starting from his eyes. "Alas! that I am born to serve a master without a shadow!" He was silent, and again I hid my face in my hands.

"Bendel," at last I tremblingly resumed, "you have now my confidence; you may betray me — go — bear witness against me!"

He seemed to be agitated with conflicting feelings; at last he threw himself at my feet and seized my hand, which he bathed with his tears. "No," he exclaimed; "whatever the world may say, I neither can nor will forsake my excellent master because he has lost his shadow. I will rather do what is right than what may seem prudent. I will remain with you — I will shade you with my own shadow — I will assist you when I can — and when I cannot, I will weep with you."

I fell upon his neck, astonished at sentiments so unusual; for it was very evident that he was not prompted by the love of money.

My mode of life and my fate now became somewhat different. It is incredible with what provident foresight Bendel contrived to conceal my deficiency. Everywhere he was before me and with me, providing against every contingency, and in cases of unlooked-for danger flying to shield me with his own shadow, for he was taller and stouter than myself. Thus I once more ventured among mankind, and began to take a part in worldly affairs. I was compelled, indeed, to affect certain peculiarities and whims; but in a rich man they seem only appropriate; and so long as the truth was kept concealed I enjoyed all the honor and respect which gold could procure.

I now looked forward with more composure to the promised visit of the mysterious unknown at the expiration of the year and a day.

I was very sensible that I could not venture to remain long in a place where I had once been seen without a shadow, and where I might easily be betrayed; and perhaps, too, I recollected my first introduction to Mr. Jones, and this was by no means a pleasing reminiscence. However, I wished just to make a trial here, that I might with greater ease and security visit some other place. But my vanity for some time withheld me, for it is in this quality of our race that the anchor takes the firmest hold.

Even the lovely Fanny, whom I again met in several places, without her seeming to recollect that she had ever seen me before, bestowed some notice on me; for wit and understanding were mine in abundance now. When I spoke, I was listened to; and I was at a loss to know how I had so easily acquired the art of commanding attention, and giving the tone to the conversation.

The impression which I perceived I had made upon this fair one completely turned my brain; and this was just what she wished. After that, I pursued her with infinite pains through every obstacle. My vanity was only intent on exciting hers to make a conquest of me; but although the intoxication disturbed my head, it failed to make the least impression on my heart.

But why detail to you the oft-repeated story which I have so often heard from yourself?

However, in the old and well-known drama in which I played so worn-out a part a catastrophe occurred of quite a peculiar nature, in a manner equally unexpected to her, to me, and to everybody.

One beautiful evening, I had, according to my usual custom, assembled a party in a garden, and was walking arm-in-arm with Fanny at a little distance from the rest of the company, and pouring into her ear the

usual well-turned phrases, while she was demurely
gazing on vacancy, and now and then gently returning
the pressure of my hand. The moon suddenly emerged
from behind a cloud at her back. Fanny perceived only
her own shadow before us. She started, looked at me
with terror, and then again on the ground in search of
my shadow. All that was passing in her mind was so
strangely depicted in her countenance, that I should
have burst into a loud fit of laughter had I not suddenly felt my blood run cold within me. I suffered
her to fall from my arm in a fainting-fit, shot with the
rapidity of an arrow through the astonished guests,
reached the gate, threw myself into the first conveyance
I met with, and returned to the town, where this time,
unfortunately, I had left the wary Bendel. He was
alarmed on seeing me: one word explained all. Post-
horses were immediately procured. I took with me
none of my servants, one cunning knave only excepted,
called Rascal, who had by his adroitness become very
serviceable to me, and who at present knew nothing
of what had occurred. I travelled thirty leagues that
night; having left Bendel behind to discharge my
servants, pay my debts, and bring me all that was
necessary.

When he came up with me next day I threw myself
into his arms, vowing to avoid such follies and to be
more careful for the future. . . . .

CHAPTER II.

IT was yet early when I was suddenly awoke by voices in hot dispute in my antechamber. I listened. Bendel was forbidding Rascal to enter my room, who swore he would receive no orders from his equals, and insisted on forcing his way. The faithful Bendel reminded him that if such words reached his master's ears, he would turn him out of an excellent place. Rascal threatened to strike him if he persisted in refusing his entrance.

By this time, having half dressed myself, I angrily threw open the door, and addressing myself to Rascal, inquired what he meant by such disgraceful conduct. He drew back a couple of steps, and coolly answered, "Count Peter, may I beg most respectfully that you will favor me with a sight of your shadow? The sun is now shining brightly in the court below."

I stood as if struck by a thunderbolt, and for some time was unable to speak. At last I asked him how a servant could dare to behave so towards his master. He interrupted me by saying, quite coolly "A servant may be a very honorable man, and unwilling to serve a shadowless master — I request my dismissal."

I felt that I must adopt a softer tone, and replied, "But, Rascal, my good fellow, who can have put such strange ideas into your head? How can you imagine — "

He again interrupted me in the same tone — " People say you have no shadow. In short, let me see your shadow, or give me my dismissal."

Bendel, pale and trembling, but more collected than myself, made a sign to me. I had recourse to the all-powerful influence of gold. But even gold had lost its power — Rascal threw it at my feet : " From a shadow-less man," he said, " I will take nothing."

Turning his back upon me, and putting on his hat, he then slowly left the room, whistling a tune. I stood, with Bendel, as if petrified, gazing after him.

With a deep sigh and a heavy heart I now prepared to keep my engagement, and to appear in the forester's garden like a criminal before his judge. I entered by the shady arbor, which had received the name of Count Peter's arbor, where we had appointed to meet. The mother advanced with a cheerful air ; Minna sat fair and beautiful as the early snow of autumn reposing on the departing flowers, soon to be dissolved and lost in the cold stream.

The ranger, with a written paper in his hand, was walking up and down in an agitated manner, and struggling to suppress his feelings — his usually un-moved countenance being one moment flushed, and the next perfectly pale. He came forward as I entered, and, in a faltering voice, requested a private conversa-tion with me. The path by which he requested me to follow him led to an open spot in the garden, where the sun was shining. I sat down. A long silence ensued, which even the good woman herself did not venture to break. The ranger, in an agitated manner, paced up and down with unequal steps. At last he stood still ;

and glancing over the paper he held in his hand, he said, addressing me with a penetrating look, " Count Peter, do you know one Peter Schlemihl?" I was silent.

"A man," he continued, " of excellent character and extraordinary endowments."

He paused for an answer. — "And supposing I myself were that very man?"

" You!" he exclaimed passionately; " he has lost his shadow!"

" Oh, my suspicion is true!" cried Minna; "I have long known it — he has no shadow!" And she threw herself into her mother's arms, who, convulsively clasping her to her bosom, reproached her for having so long, to her hurt, kept such a secret. But, like the fabled Arethusa, her tears, as from a fountain, flowed more abundantly, and her sobs increased at my approach.

"And so," said the ranger fiercely, " you have not scrupled, with unparalleled shamelessness, to deceive both her and me; and you pretended to love her, forsooth! — her whom you have reduced to the state in which you now see her. See how she weeps! — Oh, shocking, shocking!"

By this time I had lost all presence of mind, and I answered confusedly, "After all, it is but a shadow, a mere shadow, which a man can do very well without; and really it is not worth the while to make all this noise about such a trifle." Feeling the groundlessness of what I was saying, I ceased, and no one condescended to reply. At last I added, " What is lost to-day may be found to-morrow."

" Be pleased, sir," continued the ranger, in great

wrath — "be pleased to explain how you have lost your shadow."

Here again an excuse was ready: "A boor of a fellow," said I, "one day trod so rudely on my shadow that he tore a large hole in it. I sent it to be repaired — for gold can do wonders — and yesterday I expected it home again."

"Very well," answered the ranger. "You are a suitor for my daughter's hand, and so are others. As a father I am bound to provide for her. I will give you three days to seek your shadow. Return to me in the course of that time with a well fitted shadow, and you shall receive a hearty welcome; otherwise, on the fourth day — remember, on the fourth day — my daughter becomes the wife of another."

I now attempted to say one word to Minna; but, sobbing more violently, she clung still closer to her mother, who made a sign for me to withdraw. I obeyed; and now the world seemed shut out from me forever.

Having escaped from the affectionate care of Bendel, I now wandered wildly through the neighboring woods and meadows. Drops of anguish fell from my brow, deep groans burst from my bosom — frenzied despair raged within me.

I knew not how long this had lasted, when I felt myself seized by the sleeve on a sunny heath. I stopped, and looking up, beheld the gray-coated man, who appeared to have run himself out of breath in pursuing me. He immediately began: "I had," said he, "appointed this day; but your impatience anticipated it. All, however, may yet be right. Take my advice — redeem your shadow, which is at your command, and return immediately to the ranger's garden, where you will be well received, and all the past will seem a mere joke. As for Rascal — who has betrayed you in order to pay his addresses to Minna — leave him to me; he is just a fit subject for me."

I stood like one in a dream. "This day?" I considered again. He was right — I had made a mistake of a day. I felt in my bosom for the purse. He perceived my intention, and drew back.

"No, Count Peter; the purse is in good hands — pray keep it." I gazed at him with looks of astonishment and inquiry. "I only beg a trifle as a token of remembrance. Be so good as to sign this memorandum." On the parchment, which he held out to me, were these words: "By virtue of this present, to which I have appended my signature, I hereby bequeath my soul to the holder, after its natural separation from my body."

I gazed in mute astonishment alternately at the paper and the gray unknown. In the meantime he had dipped a new pen in a drop of blood which was issuing from a scratch in my hand just made by a thorn. He presented it to me. "Who are you?" at last I exclaimed. "What can it signify?" he answered; "do you not perceive who I am? A poor devil — a sort of scholar and philosopher, who obtains but poor thanks from his friends for his admirable arts, and whose only amusement on earth consists in his small experiments. But just sign this; to the right, exactly underneath — Peter Schlemihl."

I shook my head, and replied, "Excuse me, sir; I cannot sign that."

"Cannot!" he exclaimed; "and why not?"

"Because it appears to me a hazardous thing to exchange my soul for my shadow."

"Hazardous!" he exclaimed, bursting into a loud laugh. "And pray, may I be allowed to inquire what sort of a thing your soul is?—have you ever seen it?—and what do you mean to do with it after your death? You ought to think yourself fortunate in meeting with a customer who, during your life, in exchange for this infinitely minute quantity, this galvanic principle, this polarized agency, or whatever other foolish name you may give it, is willing to bestow on you something substantial—in a word, your own identical shadow—by virtue of which you will obtain your beloved Minna, and arrive at the accomplishment of all your wishes; or do you prefer giving up the poor young girl to the power of that contemptible scoundrel Rascal? Nay, you shall behold her with your own eyes. Come here; I will lend you an invisible cap (he drew something out of his pocket), and we will enter the ranger's garden unseen."

I must confess that I felt excessively ashamed to be thus laughed at by the gray stranger. I detested him from the very bottom of my soul; and I really believe this personal antipathy, more than principle or previously-formed opinion, restrained me from purchasing my shadow, much as I stood in need of it, at such an expense. Besides, the thought was insupportable of making this proposed visit in his society. To behold this hateful sneak, this mocking fiend, place himself between me and my beloved, between our torn and bleeding hearts, was too revolting an idea to be enter-

tained for a moment. I considered the past as irrevo-
cable, my own misery as inevitable; and turning to the
gray man, I said, "I have exchanged my shadow for
this very extraordinary purse, and I have sufficiently
repented it. For heaven's sake let the transaction be
declared null and void!" He shook his head, and his
countenance assumed an expression of the most sinister
cast. I continued, "I will make no exchange whatever, even for the sake of my shadow, nor will I sign
the paper. It follows, also, that the incognito visit
you propose to me would afford you far more en-
tertainment than it could possibly give me. Accept
my excuses, there-
fore; and, since it
must be so, let us
part."

"I am sorry,
Mr. Schle-
mihl, that
you   thus
obstinately
persist in
rejecting
my friend-
ly offer.
Perhaps
another
time I may
be more fortunate. Farewell! May we shortly meet
again! But, à *propos*, allow me to show you that I do
not undervalue my purchase, but preserve it carefully."
So saying, he drew my shadow out of his pocket; and

shaking it cleverly out of its folds, he stretched it out at his feet in the sun — so that he stood between two obedient shadows, his own and mine, which was compelled to follow and comply with his every movement.

On again beholding my poor shadow after so long a separation, and seeing it degraded to so vile a bondage at the very time that I was so unspeakably in want of it, my heart was ready to burst, and I wept bitterly. The detested wretch stood exulting over his prey, and unblushingly renewed his proposal. " One stroke of your pen, and the unhappy Minna is rescued from the clutches of the villain Rascal, and transferred to the arms of the high-born Count Peter — merely a stroke of your pen ! "

My tears broke out with renewed violence ; but I turned away from him, and made a sign for him to be gone.

Bendel, whose deep solicitude had induced him to come in search of me, arrived at this very moment. The good and faithful creature, on seeing me weeping, and that a shadow (evidently mine) was in the power of the mysterious unknown, determined to rescue it by force, should that be necessary ; and disdaining to use any finesse, he desired him directly, and without any disputing, to restore my property. Instead of a reply, the gray man turned his back on the worthy fellow and was making off. But Bendel raised his buckthorn stick ; and following close upon him, after repeated commands, but in vain, to restore the shadow, he made him feel the whole force of his powerful arm. The gray man, as if accustomed to such treatment, held down his head, slouched his shoulders, and, with short and noiseless steps, pursued his way over the heath, carrying with him my shadow, and also my faithful servant. For a long time I heard hollow sounds ringing through the waste, until at last they died away in the distance, and I was again left to solitude and misery.

Alone on the wild heath, I disburdened my heart of an insupportable load by giving free vent to my tears. But I saw no bounds, no relief, to my surpassing wretchedness; and I drank in the fresh poison which the mysterious stranger had poured into my wounds with a furious avidity. As I retraced in my mind the loved image of my Minna, and depicted her sweet countenance all pale and in tears, such as I had beheld her in my late disgrace, the bold and sarcastic visage of Rascal would ever and anon thrust itself between us. I hid my face, and fled rapidly over the plains; but the horrible vision unrelentingly pursued me, till at last I sank breathless on the ground, and bedewed it with a fresh torrent of tears — and all this for a shadow — a shadow which one stroke of the pen would repurchase. I pondered on the singular proposal, and on my hesitation to comply with it. My mind was confused — I had lost the power of judging or comprehending. The day was waning apace. I satisfied the cravings of hunger with a few wild fruits, and quenched my thirst at a neighboring stream. Night came on; I threw myself down under a tree, and was awoke by the damp morning air from an uneasy sleep, in which I had fancied myself struggling in the agonies of death. Bendel had certainly lost all trace of me, and I was glad of it. I did not wish to return among my fellow-creatures —

I shunned them as the hunted deer flies before its pursuers.   Thus I passed three melancholy days.

I found myself on the morning of the fourth on a sandy plain, basking in the rays of the sun, and sitting on a fragment of rock; for it was sweet to enjoy the genial warmth of which I had so long been deprived. Despair still preyed on my heart.   Suddenly a slight sound startled me; I looked round, prepared to fly, but saw no one.   On the sunlit sand before me flitted the shadow of a man not unlike my own; and wandering about alone, it seemed to have lost its master.   This sight powerfully excited me.   " Shadow! " thought I, " art thou in search of thy master? in me thou shalt find him."   And I sprang forward to seize it, fancying that could I succeed in treading so exactly in its traces as to step in its footmarks, it would attach itself to me, and in time become accustomed to me, and follow all my movements.

The shadow, as I moved, took to flight, and I commenced a hot chase after the airy fugitive, solely excited by the hope of being delivered from my present dreadful situation;   the bare idea inspired me with fresh strength and vigor.

The shadow now fled towards a distant wood, among whose shades I must necessarily have lost it.   Seeing this, my heart beat wild with fright, my ardor increased and lent wings to my speed.   I was evidently gaining on the shadow — I came nearer and nearer — I was within reach of it, when it suddenly stopped and turned towards me.   Like a lion darting on its prey I made a powerful spring and fell unexpectedly upon a hard substance.   Then followed, from an invisible

hand, the most terrible blows in the ribs that any one
ever received. The effect of my terror made me endeavor convulsively to strike and grasp at the unseen
object before me. The rapidity of my motions brought
me to the ground, where I lay stretched out with a
man under me, whom I held tight, and who now
became visible.

The whole affair was now explained. The man had
undoubtedly possessed the bird's nest which communi-
cates its charm of invisibility to its possessor, though
not equally so to his shadow; and this nest he had
now thrown away. I looked all round, and soon discovered the shadow of this invisible nest. I sprang
towards it, and was fortunate enough to seize the
precious booty, and immediately became invisible and
shadowless.

The moment the man regained his feet he looked all
round over the wide sunny plain to discover his fortunate vanquisher, but could see neither him nor his
shadow, the latter seeming particularly to be the object
of his search; for previous to our encounter he had
not had leisure to observe that I was shadowless, and
he could not be aware of it. Becoming convinced that
all traces of me were lost, he began to tear his hair,
and give himself up to all the frenzy of despair. In
the meantime, this newly acquired treasure communicated to me both the ability and the desire to mix
again among mankind.

I was at no loss for a pretext to vindicate this unjust
robbery — or, rather, so deadened had I become, I felt
no need of a pretext; and in order to dissipate every
idea of the kind, I hastened on, regardless of the un-

happy man, whose fearful lamentations long resounded in my ears.   Such, at the time, were my impressions of all the circumstances of this affair.

I now ardently desired to return to the ranger's garden, in order to ascertain in person the truth of the information communicated by the odious unknown ; but I knew not where I was, until, ascending an eminence to take a survey of the surrounding country, I perceived, from its summit, the little town and the gardens almost at my feet.   My heart beat violently, and tears of a nature very different from those I had lately shed filled my eyes.   I should, then, once more behold her !

Anxiety now hastened my steps.   Unseen I met some peasants coming from the town ; they were talking of me, of Rascal, and of the ranger.   I would not stay to listen to their conversation, but proceeded on.   My bosom thrilled with expectation as I entered the garden.   At this moment I heard something like a hollow laugh, which caused me involuntarily to shudder. I cast a rapid glance around, but could see no one.   I passed on ; presently I fancied I heard the sound of footsteps close to me, but no one was within sight. My ears must have deceived me.

It was early ; no one was in Count Peter's bower — the gardens were deserted.   I traversed all the well-known paths, and penetrated even to the dwelling-house itself.   The same rustling sound became now more and more audible.   With anguished feelings I sat down on a seat placed in the sunny space before the door, and actually felt some invisible fiend take a place by me, and heard him utter a sarcastic laugh.   The key was turned in the door, which was opened.   The forest-master appeared with a paper in his hand. Suddenly my head was, as it were, enveloped in a mist. I looked up, and, oh horror! the gray-coated man was at my side, peering in my face with a satanic grin. He had extended the mist-cap he wore over my head. His shadow and my own were lying together at his feet in perfect amity. He kept twirling in his hand the well-known parchment with an air of indifference; and while the ranger, absorbed in thought, and intent upon his paper, paced up and down the arbor, my tormentor confidentially leaned towards me, and whispered, "So, Mr. Schlemihl, you have at length accepted my invitation, and here we sit, two heads under one hood, as the saying is. Well, well, all in good time. But now you can return me my bird's nest — you have no further occasion for it; and I am sure you are too honorable a man to withhold it from me. No need of thanks, I assure you; I had infinite pleasure in lending it to you." He took it out of my unresisting hand, put it into his pocket, and then broke into so loud a laugh at my expense, that the forest-master turned round, startled at the sound. I was petrified. "You must acknowledge," he continued, "that in our position a hood is much more convenient. It serves to conceal not only a man, but his shadow, or as many shadows as he chooses to carry. I, for instance, to-day bring two, you perceive." He laughed again. "Take notice, Schlemihl, that what a man refuses to do with a good grace in the first instance, he is always in the end compelled to do. I am still of opinion that you ought to redeem your shadow and claim your bride (for it is yet time); and as to Rascal, he shall dangle at a rope's end — no difficult matter, so long as we can find a bit. As a mark of friendship I will give you my cap into the bargain."

The mother now came out, and the following conversation took place : "What is Minna doing?" "She is weeping." "Silly child! what good can that do?" "None, certainly; but it is so soon to bestow her hand on another. O husband, you are too harsh to your poor child." "No, wife; you view things in a wrong light. When she finds herself the wife of a wealthy and honorable man, her tears will soon cease; she will waken out of a dream, as it were, happy and grateful to Heaven and to her parents, as you will see." "Heaven grant it may be so!" replied the wife. "She has, indeed, now considerable property; but after the noise occasioned by her unlucky affair with that adventurer, do you imagine that she is likely soon to meet with so advantageous a match as Mr. Rascal? Do you know the extent of Mr. Rascal's influence and wealth? Why, he has purchased with ready money, in this country, six millions of landed property, free from all encumbrances. I have had all the documents in my hands. It was he who outbid me everywhere when I was about to make a desirable purchase; and, besides, he has bills on Mr. Thomas Jones' house to the amount of three millions and a half." "He must have been a prodigious thief!" "How foolishly you talk! he wisely saved where others squandered their property." "A mere livery-servant!" "Nonsense! he has at all events an unexceptionable shadow." "True, but . . ."

While this conversation was passing, the gray-coated man looked at me with a satirical smile.

The door opened, and Minna entered, leaning on the arm of her female attendant, silent tears flowing down her fair but pallid face. She seated herself in the chair which had been placed for her under the lime-trees, and her father took a stool by her side. He gently raised her hand; and as her tears flowed afresh, he addressed her in the most affectionate manner: —

"My own dear, good child — my Minna — will act reasonably, and not afflict her poor old father, who only wishes to make her happy. My dearest child, this blow has shaken you — dreadfully, I know it; but you have been saved, as by a miracle, from a miserable fate, my Minna. You loved the unworthy villain most tenderly before his treachery was discovered: I feel all this, Minna; and far be it from me to reproach you for it — in fact, I myself loved him so long as I considered him to be a person of rank: you now see yourself how differently it has turned out. Every dog has a shadow; and the idea of my child having been on the eve of uniting herself to a man who . . . but I am sure you will think no more of him. A suitor has just appeared for you in the person of a man who does not fear the sun — an honorable man — no prince indeed, but a man worth ten millions of golden ducats sterling — a sum nearly ten times larger than your fortune consists of — a man, too, who will make my dear child happy — nay, do not oppose me — be my own good, dutiful child — allow your loving father to provide for you, and to dry up these tears. Promise to bestow your hand on Mr. Rascal. Speak, my child: will you not?"

Minna could scarcely summon strength to reply that

she had now no longer any hopes or desires on earth, and that she was entirely at her father's disposal. Rascal was therefore immediately sent for, and entered the room with his usual forwardness ; but Minna in the meantime had swooned away.

My detested companion looked at me indignantly, and whispered, " Can you endure this? . Have you no blood in your veins ? " He instantly pricked my finger, which bled. " Yes, positively," he exclaimed, " you have some blood left! — come, sign." The parchment and pen were in my hand ! . . .

CHAPTER III.

. . . .

KNOW not whether to ascribe it to excitement of mind, exhaustion of physical strength (for during the last few days I had scarcely tasted anything), or the antipathy I felt to the society of my fiendish companion; but just as I was about to sign the fatal paper, I fell into a deep swoon, and remained for a long time as if dead. The first sounds which greeted my ear on recovering my consciousness were those of cursing and imprecation; I opened my eyes — it was dusk; my hateful companion was overwhelming me with reproaches. "Is not this behaving like an old woman? Come, rise up, and finish quickly what you were going to do; or perhaps you have changed your determination, and prefer to lie groaning there?"

I raised myself with difficulty from the ground, and gazed around me without speaking a word. It was late in the evening, and I heard strains of festive music proceeding from the ranger's brilliantly illuminated house; groups of company were lounging about the gardens; two persons approached, and seating themselves on the bench I had lately occupied, began to converse on the subject of the marriage which had taken place that morning between the wealthy Mr. Rascal and Minna. All was then over.

I tore off the cap which rendered me invisible; and my companion having disappeared, I plunged in silence into the thickest gloom of the grove, rapidly passed Count Peter's bower towards the entrance-gate; but my tormentor still haunted me, and loaded me with reproaches. "And is this all the gratitude I am to expect from you, Mr. Schlemihl — you, whom I have been watching all the weary day, until you should recover from your nervous attack? What a fool's part I have been enacting! It is of no use flying from me, Mr. Perverse — we are inseparable — you have my gold, I have your shadow; this exchange deprives us both of peace. Did you ever hear of a man's shadow leaving him? — yours follows me until you receive it again into favor, and thus free me from it. Disgust and weariness sooner or later will compel you to do what you should have done gladly at first. In vain you strive with fate!"

He continued unceasingly in the same tone, uttering constant sarcasms about the gold and the shadow, till I was completely bewildered. To fly from him was impossible. I had pursued my way through the empty streets towards my own house, which I could scarcely recognize — the windows were broken to pieces, no light was visible, the doors were shut, and the bustle of domestics had ceased. My companion burst into a loud laugh. "Yes, yes," said he, "you see the state of things: however, you will find your friend Bendel at home; he was sent back the other day so fatigued, that I assure you he has never left the house since. He will have a fine story to tell! So I wish you a very good night — may we shortly meet again!"

I had repeatedly rung the bell: at last a light appeared; and Bendel inquired from within who was there. The poor fellow could scarcely contain himself at the sound of my voice. The door flew open, and we were locked in each other's arms. I found him sadly changed; he was looking ill and feeble. I, too, was altered; my hair had become quite gray. He conducted me through the desolate apartments to an inner room, which had escaped the general wreck. After partaking of some refreshment, we seated ourselves; and, with fresh lamentations, he began to tell me that the gray withered old man whom he had met with my shadow had insensibly led him such a zigzag race, that he had lost all traces of me, and at last sank down exhausted with fatigue; that, unable to find me, he had returned home, when, shortly after, the mob, at Rascal's instigation, assembled violently before the house, broke the windows, and by all sorts of excesses completely satiated their fury. Thus had they treated their benefactor. My servants had fled in all directions. The police had banished me from the town as a suspicious character, and granted me an interval of twenty-four hours to leave the territory. Bendel added many particulars as to the information I had already obtained respecting Rascal's wealth and marriage. This villain, it seems — who was the author of all the measures taken against me — became possessed of my secret nearly from the beginning, and, tempted by the love of money, had supplied himself with a key to my chest, and from that time had been laying the foundation of his present wealth. Bendel related all this with many tears, and wept for joy that I was once more safely restored to him, after all his fears and anxieties for me. In me, however, such a state of things only awoke despair.

My dreadful fate now stared me in the face in all its gigantic and unchangeable horror. The source of tears was exhausted within me; no groans escaped my breast; but with cool indifference I bared my unprotected head to the blast. "Bendel," said I, "You know my fate; this heavy visitation is a punishment for my early sins: but as for you, my innocent friend, I can no longer permit you to share my destiny. I will depart this very night — saddle me a horse — I will set out alone. Remain here, Bendel — I insist upon it: there must be some chests of gold still left in the house — take them, they are yours. I shall be a restless and solitary wanderer on the face of the earth; but should better days arise, and fortune once more smile propitiously on me, then I will not forget your steady fidelity; for in hours of deep distress your faithful bosom has been the depository of my sorrows." With a bursting heart, the worthy Bendel prepared to obey this last command of his master; for I was deaf to all his arguments, and blind to his tears. My horse was brought — I pressed my weeping friend to my bosom — threw myself into the saddle, and, under the friendly shades of night, quitted this sepulchre of my existence, indifferent which road my horse should take; for now on this side the grave I had neither wishes, hopes, nor fears.

NOTES

THOMAS BAILEY ALDRICH, the author of the poem of "Baby Bell," "The Story of a Bad Boy," and "Marjorie Daw," was born in Portsmouth, N.H., Nov. 11, 1836. A part of his boyhood was passed in Louisiana, his father being a merchant in New Orleans. In 1850 he returned to Portsmouth, and at the period of his father's death in 1852 was preparing to enter Harvard College, but the offer of a desk in the banking house of an uncle in New York caused him to change his purpose. At the end of three years, having meanwhile become known as a contributor to journals and magazines, he retired from commercial pursuits. During the next ten years he occupied editorial positions on the *New York Evening Mirror*, N. P. Willis's *Home Journal*, and *The Illustrated News*, and was literary reader for a large publishing firm in New York. In the early part of the Civil War he was for a time attached to Blenker's division, Army of the Potomac, as newspaper correspondent. In 1865 he married and removed to Boston to take charge of *Every Saturday*, a weekly journal established by Ticknor & Fields, which he conducted until 1874. In 1881 he succeeded Mr. W. D. Howells, as editor of *The Atlantic Monthly*, and nine years later resigned the chair in order to devote himself to personal literary work and foreign travel. The degree of A. M. was conferred upon him by Yale in 1883, and by Harvard in 1896. A series of his short stories has appeared in the *Revue des Deux Mondes*, and many of his books have been translated into French, Danish, German, Spanish, and Dutch. In 1893 his tragedy of "Mercedes" was successfully produced at Palmer's Theater, New York. Mr. Aldrich's principal publications are in book form: "The Ballad of Baby Bell, and Other Poems," 1858; "Poems," 1865; "The Story of a Bad Boy," 1869; "Cloth of Gold," 1873; "Flower and Thorn," 1876; "Mercedes, and Later Lyrics," 1883; "Marjorie Daw and Other People," 1873; "Prudence Palfrey," 1874; "The Queen of Sheba," 1877; "The Stillwater Tragedy," 1880; "From Ponkapog to Pesth," 1883; "Wyndham Towers, a Poem," 1889; "The Sisters' Tragedy," 1890; "An Old Town by the Sea," 1893; "Two Bites of a Cherry, and Other Tales," 1893; "Unguarded Gates," 1895; "Judith and Holofernes, a Poem," 1896. A complete edition of his writings was issued in eight volumes in 1897.

THE ARABIAN NIGHTS. The origin of "The Arabian Nights" is lost in the mists of antiquity. The authorities agree that the book probably took its present form in Cairo more than five hundred years ago; but that the recollection was based on an older volume gathered from Persian and other Oriental sources, while the individual stories have been orally circulated for thousands of years.

"The Arabian Nights" was introduced into Europe by A. Galland's French version in 1704. The best English version for scholars are those of Lane and Burton.

CHAMISSO, ADELBERT VON, a German lyric poet, born, 1781; died, 1838; went with a Russian exploring expedition around the world; afterwards custodian of the Botanical Garden of Berlin. He wrote many ballads and romances. "Peter Schemihl," the man who lost his shadow, has been translated into almost all languages of Europe.

FOUQUÉ, DE LA MOTTE, born in Germany, 1777; died, 1843; served in the army in 1794 and 1813. He wrote besides, "Undine," "Sigurd," "Sintram and His Companions," "The Magic Ring," "Aslaugas Knight," "The Two Captains," etc.

LANG, A., born in Scotland, 1844, one of the most prolific writers of his time. Translated "Aucassin and Nicolette," "Perrault's Popular Tales," wrote many volumes of verse, "Ballades in Blue Chinas," "Ballades of Books," "Rhymes à la Mode." Among his heavier works are "Custom and Myth," "Myth, Ritual, and Religion," and his translation with Professor Butcher of the "Odyssey."

Notes

LEMON, MARK, born in London, 1809 ; died, 1870. One of the founders of the London paper *Punch,* which he edited until his death. He wrote farces, melodramas, operettas, and children's stories, and was a successful lecturer and public reader.

SWIFT, JONATHAN, Dean of St. Patrick's, Dublin, Ireland. Born, 1667 ; died, 1745. He wrote much on matters literary and political. His most famous work is " Gulliver's Travels." Only part of it is here given.

THACKERAY, W. M., one of England's most famous novelists, born, 1811 ; died, 1862. He wrote " Vanity Fair," " Pendennis," " The Newcomes," among others, and was the first editor of the *Cornhill Magazine.* " The Rose and the Ring " was the only book he wrote specially for children.

TALES OF FANTASY

SUGGESTIONS FOR SUPPLEMENTARY READING